OUT OF THE MIRY CLAY

BLANDFORDIA NOBILIS – THE CHRISTMAS BELL

"He lifted me out of the pit of despair,
out of the mud and the mire.
He set my feet on solid ground
and steadied me as I walked along."

Psalms 40:2 NLT

Navi Za Parr

Ark House Press
arkhousepress.com

Cataloguing in Publication Data:
Title: Out of the Miry Clay
ISBN: 978-1-7643820-1-4 (pbk)
Subjects: [FIC042030] FICTION / Christian / Historical; [FIC026000] FICTION / Religious; [FIC145000] FICTION / Places / Australia & Oceania.

Design by initiateagency.com

TABLE OF CONTENTS

ACKNOWLEDGEMENT

Although Mrs Caroline Chisholm is a true-life heroine, the depiction in this novel is purely fictitious. I have aimed to portray her character without writing any true-life events. Caroline Chisholm had a profound impact on Australian society and contributed greatly to the foundation of a family centred culture.

All other characters in this book are entirely fictitious. Including the Aboriginal peoples in the story. The story being set in the 1850s means that all characters would be long deceased if they had represented real historical individuals by happenstance.

I dedicate this work to the triune God who created me, redeemed me, and sustains me through all.

Veni Sancte Spiritus

Come Holy Spirit

I give my life and my work to you as a living sacrifice.

LEGEND

I Isabelle

G Gareth

X Father Xavier

N Narrator [Sorcha]

"There once was a man named Job
Who lived in the land of Uz.
He was blameless—
A man of complete integrity.
He feared God and stayed away from evil."

Job 1:1 NLT

CHAPTER 1

Isabelle

Even in the dark of night, I am not afraid, because
he is always there beside me.

Psalms 23:4

June 1849, Ellesmere Port, England

It was in the summer of my eighteenth year that it all began. Before that time, I lived a contented, happy life, much loved by my family and neighbours alike.

Then…

The fragrance of the summer meadow increased my euphoria as I skipped and twirled every other step on my way home. My meeting with Angus and the minister had progressed our cause. The banns would be read at the next meeting and then again, the following two Sundays after that. Our nuptials were to be celebrated in only nine months. It was to be a spring wedding. I had waited since I was fourteen for the day we could commit our lives to be joined. I would soon be turned seventeen, the age my mother and my father insisted I reach before I could wed. Mother's mother was a midwife and warned the family often of a confinement at too young an age. Even though my granda was an apothecary and knew the potions needed to reduce the risk. He was known to say it did not always work.

"Would it hurt to wait? It will only prove your love for each other. If not, it may save you from being wed to the wrong husband." He said it to me many more times than I needed to hear it. Angus and I patiently waited. Neither of us willing to risk an early death for me.

My Granda and I spent many hours together as he taught me the herbs and medicines he prepared. My grandma and mother taught me the trade of dressmaking. A suitable trade for a woman. The mixing of medicines accommodated communities to accuse women of witchcraft. More so if the woman was also beautiful. The family had seen it happen in their past. My great-grandmother was a healer. When another woman took a fancy to her husband, she cooked up a tale and accused my great-grandmother of witchcraft.

She was burned at the stake!

No females in our family have been allowed to practice the art of mixing medicines since. We can be midwives, but we leave the art of potions to the men. I thought that in the age of enlightenment, we could leave those superstitious belief systems behind.

But apparently not!

Every day, I witnessed an example of the mob reducing the intelligence of the individual.

There in the meadow, as I walked by, I heard the young urchins encouraging each other in foolishness. Alone, they were all sensible boys. Together, they planned mischief.

"Hello, young masters." The boys rushed enthusiastically to my side. They had learnt from experience that I often carried boiled lollies in a pouch.

"Hello, Miss Isabelle."

"Are you well today?"

"Is your pouch weighing you down at all?"

"We seed you skippin' and wanted to hold you up, but we have no pistol."

"Would we make good highwaymen?"

They all spoke at once. Not waiting for answers. At the last suggestion, they started prancing around, pretending to have pistols, and pantomiming a holdup. Their theatrics gave me the opportunity to speak. Their amusing antics begot a broad smile on my lips. My heart was happy, and I had no desire to quell the happiness of others.

"No highwayman is a good man, boys. Would it not be better to ask me politely to share what I have in my pouch?"

"What if you say NO?"

With that question, their motion ceased, and they wore a concerned look on their faces as they waited for my reply.

"Well then, you would need to accept my decision, as you would want me to accept your decision if you choose not to share one day. There is no joy in receiving a gift that is not a gift."

"Oh! Yes, Miss Isabelle."

"It's nice to see you today."

"You look happy."

"What's planning?" Frederick's eyes were big with curiosity and enthusiasm, which I knew his mother found hard to contain.

"Do not look so sad, boys. I am in a mood to share. Today, I have peppermints. Two each. And Jimmy, please take one home for Becca. I heard that she has been unwell."

I was nearly knocked over by the mob's enthusiasm as they reached in to collect their gifts. My heart soared again with the joy of meeting joy in others. It was my favourite pastime. Mam told me often, *"You are destined to be poor, Isabelle; you give so much away. But you will also be rich in friends because more people take joy in receiving than do in giving."*

I heard the chatter of the shop as I entered through the back door. I stopped to clean the dirt from my hemline and polish the dust from my boots before assisting customers. My mother could be pedantic, but the business thrived, so it seemed that her rules brought success.

"Hello, Mama, Hello, Grandma, Hello, Mrs Wilson, are you well today?"

"Yes, young Isabelle. I am very well. I saw young Angus Howe returning to the shipyard on my way across town. How is it that that young man did not see you home before attending to himself?"

"I was so elated that I wanted to take time in the meadow, Mrs Wilson. Angus has orders to fill so that a home can be purchased in the new year." With difficulty containing my emotions, I added, "We are to be wed in the spring." The smile I wore was so large, the muscles in my face hurt.

"Well, now, it's about time the two of you made it official. I know of a few lasses who will have their noses out of joint, though. Some hoping that Mr Howe would notice them before the banns could be read."

"I have felt very secure in his affections. I have never seen his eye wander. It is a wonder that they could be hopeful. It will all be put to surety soon. Then they can settle their affection on another man. They will be much happier when they give away the false hope."

"You are very sure of yourself, lass." Mrs Wilson gave me an appraising look. "I can see why, though. You are a rare beauty with a sweet disposition to go with it. Why would Mr Howe look aside?"

I was stunned by her unsolicited praise. I understood my value but had never thought of myself as being in any way more attractive than most of the girls in my Sunday school class. We each had our own unique beauty.

The rest of the day floated by with me in a swing suspended from the clouds. My mother dismissed me early from the shop saying, *"You are ineffective in your current frame of mind."* I was instructed to go home via my granda's apothecary shop, pick up a package, and then head straight home to prepare the evening meal.

When I arrived at Granda's shop, there was a crowd forming in the front. A crowd that looked like a mob! I was curious and apprehensive at the same time. The mob felt angry! The mob felt volatile! I felt fear as I moved toward the front of the crowd and heard snippets of the accusations that were being voiced.

"'Twas the peppermints."

"Found in young Jimmy's pocket."

"Vomiting the poison."

"Cold sweats."

"Convulsing like the demons had control."

"Blue in the fingers."

"Lilith saw 'tall. I heard her testimony meself."

"There she be!"

I just reached the safety of the front door and barrelled through as the mob recognised me to be the one they sought. I cannot say why they did not first go to the dressmaking shop. Perhaps because the lollies were made at Granda's shop. One thing I was sure of: there was nothing wrong with the peppermints. I had been eating them sporadically all day and had given some to the rector, with no ill effect. Angus did not like peppermint, so he did not partake. It took some effort to close the door that was being pushed by the mob. Granda slid the bar across the wooden door. We turned to look at each other with puzzled looks. Neither of us understood what events had roused the mob.

I threw myself into Granda's arms and buried my face in his chest. He always smelled of strength and spice. I could still hear some of the rumblings of the mob that gathered outside Granda's shop.

"I am afraid, Granda. They are calling me a witch. What could have happened?"

My voice was muffled by Granda's woollen vest as he sought to soothe my fear. Fear in the face of a mob that was growing increasingly hostile. Neither of us knew how to overcome the siege.

"Quiet yourself, Isabelle. Your fear will not improve the outcome. Let us pray and ask our Heavenly Father to intervene." Granda immediately began to pray. "Heavenly Father, we surrender ourselves to you now in our hour of need and ask that you show us the way forward. The way forward which will keep all souls safe. Those within and those without. Please help the mob outside our door to hear reason, and to disperse, so that whatever event has transpired to fill them all with fear may be managed. Please help all those gathered outside this shop understand that their fear does not need to be translated into anger. That their fear and anger are better resolved by forgiveness rather than finding a target to punish. Also, I ask that your Holy Spirit fill us now with a pervading peace, so that we are more able to act with love and kindness toward our neighbours who behave like our enemies."

I was filled suddenly with an intense calm. I knew that God would prevail and that I would be saved from the mob. In the next moment, we heard the commotion of someone trying to push themselves through to the front of the crowd at the same instant a rock flew through the front window. The energy of the mob was compounding. Feeding off each other. Encouraging each other to greater extremes of hysteria. The pressure needing release.

As I watched the crowd out front, a brave man fought his way to the front. He fought his way forward against opposition from those desperate to be in the thick of action. I watched the event unfold with an unnatural calm. It was two men who finally stepped up onto the raised flagstones at the front of the shop. Dr Wilson and a '*Watchman*' from the dockyard police force, by the name of Robert Wright.

"Quiet yourselves! Calm your behaviour before another tragedy is visited upon the first. We have had enough bad tidings for today. Listen to me and listen to this watchman's witness."

At those words, the mob settled. They wanted all the tales they could be told. The story did not unfold as expected, though. Robert, being a first cousin of Lilith, was expected to tell more of the same tale that they had already heard.

The mob rumbled and throbbed like a seething cauldron of oil about to spit and spill.

They listened and bubbled with intensely felt comments.

The Doctor was perceptive. No novice of human behaviour.

He saw that it would be a momentous task to alter the direction of the mob that had formed.

Changing their opinion would be like changing the direction of the tide contrary to the moon's orbit.

"Listen up! You have been told that a peppermint found in the pocket of young Jimmy was a sample of the lollies given to the boys by Isabelle. This was reportedly witnessed by Lilith Wright. I tell you that after examining the boys, I am convinced that those lollies were harmless and not the cause of their deaths."

Loud rumblings of conjecture followed the doctor's statement until a spokesman interjected. The Doctor needed to be quick in his tale before he became collateral damage as the mob pushed through to take me.

"Lilith, that there Robert's cousin, told us she saw the witch give poisoned lollies to the children. We need to stop her before she can harm others with her potions."

The mob gave a "**Here! Here**!"

Robert Wright, the local watchman, took the stage next. He held both hands up in front to indicate he needed quiet.

"Dr Wilson was assured that the lollies were harmless peppermints and, after noting the berry stains on the boy's hands, asked me to investigate the field in which the boys played. I found these!"

Robert held up a sample of berries, which were well known to cause death. The crowd simmered, then went off the boil. Enraptured with the tale unfolding before them. The Doctor then announced.

"To be certain and so that you can all be sure of our lovely Isabelle, I then took the peppermint found in the pocket of young Jimmy and ate it. It has now been three hours, and no illness has followed."

Some in the crowd mumbled and looked at me through the window. The message clear: *'We will never trust you again'.* The stories that had circulated for hours had left a stain on my reputation.

The watchmen dispersed the crowd, telling them all to attend to their families as night approached with speed.

When the crowd had dispersed, Granda unbolted the shop door and allowed the Doctor to enter.

"I think you have gathered that I have some grave news. This was not a good way for you to find out that the five boys you spoke to in the field today have all died this afternoon. It will take some time for the community to recover. I hope, Isabelle, that you will be able to forgive them, looking for a cause of the tragedy in the form of someone they can punish. Their grief and their fear caused them to be angry. They sought someone to focus that anger on. I am deeply sorry they supposed a loving young woman like yourself capable of such an evil. In their defence, they were out of their minds with grief and not sensible. It is no excuse, but people are as they are. And when a mob forms, they carry each other along in foolishness. I will encourage all, and I will hope that they come back to the knowledge that you are a precious and gracious young woman who deserves to be treated with value."

Dr Wilson then turned to my grandfather and asked that he also forgive the mob for their foolishness.

"It was a dangerous situation. We have had many conversations in the past about the dangers of superstition ruling behaviour rather than science."

"The divergence is that faith in God is in a different class to '*superstition*'. The scientist does not always see the difference."

"I will admit that I do not."

"Having faith in something unseen is not necessarily superstition. Superstition is believing in a construct of human thought. Truth or falsehood! The belief often changes to suit what you want or feel. Believing that truth can be anything you want it to be.

Faith is believing in an absolute truth told to humanity by the Creator. I do not always **want** to believe what God tells me is the truth. Sometimes, I learn the truth in what I have been told, by doing what I have been told not to do and then living through the consequences. Faith is believing in something that is the unseen truth. Faith is a gift given to us from God. Faith in God gives us direction for behaviour that is absolute, unchangeable, and beneficial to all people."[1] I saw the willingness to hear switch off in the Doctor's demeanour.

"Good evening then. I will see you tomorrow. I have some medications that I need made up. I will send over a list in the morning and pick them up in the afternoon." The Doctor's abruptness was a common response to an opinion he did not like.

Mam insisted that I spend the next day recuperating from the trauma of the previous day. I insisted that I would accompany her to the dressmaking shop rather than be alone. I felt the need to stay in company. I felt panic rise at the thought of being left alone. I was much afraid of the mob forming again whilst I was alone. I was sure that I would not cope with another encounter like that of the previous evening. God had protected us, but the look I saw in the people's eyes left me convinced that they might turn on me at the smallest provocation.

The truth and my good intentions had not prevented our community from wanting to burn me for witchcraft. I was convinced it would not matter how well behaved I was; at any moment, I could

---

1 Hebrews 11

be accused. Once the thought had been implanted, it would not be easily removed. The law may have been on my side, but a mob is hard to convict for a crime. Rumours saying that I claimed to have magical powers could have had me sentenced to a term of imprisonment. No matter that they were not true. If two people collaborated, they could cause me harm.

From then forward, anyone who wanted to do me harm could easily do me harm. All they needed to do was throw accusations until a conviction was established. Mam suggested that I was being paranoid. But Mam had not seen the distrust and hatred emanating from some of those in the crowd. Some were relatives of the five young boys, some were not. Even though the evidence showed my innocence, those who wanted someone to blame judged me and found me guilty. The Doctor and the Watchman presented a sound argument, but those who did not want to be convinced were of the same opinion still.

Dr Wilson stepped through the door of my mother's shop as I pondered my future.

"Good morning to you, Mrs Lindsay. I come to fetch the package for Mrs Wilson. Sorry to say, she is afraid of public opinion and is reluctant to step into the shop before the tide of opinion turns another way. As it no doubt will before long. There will be a new scandal soon enough. I expect you have sufficient strength to weather the storm."

"Why, Dr Wilson, surely it has all been put to rest by your brave oratory yesterday evening."

"I fear not! The first thing out of every patient's mouth so far this morning has been on the topic of young Miss Isabelle. I have had several patients afraid that they are being poisoned slowly by the lollies she so generously passes out. I have assured them that no such thing was happening."

"But how can that be? There is no sense in the fear."

"As you know, fear has no sense. I am as surprised as you are that these superstitious imaginings are still so evident in our community. The witch hunts stopped over a century ago. The uneducated are so easily swayed in their opinions. I suspect that there may be a campaign afoot."

"Surely Isabelle could not have an enemy that is perpetrating lies on purpose. I believe that Isabelle is well loved by everyone she meets. She has a rare charm. Isabelle is gifted at loving people."

"I would not say that too loudly, nor too often, Mrs Lindsay. Lest they start to accuse, that Isabelle claims to have power over people."

As Dr Wilson left the shop, my father walked through the entrance. A circumstance so unusual that my mother and grandmother dropped their work onto the bench. They were speechless! Papa closed and locked the shop front; turned to us and announced.

"I have called a family meeting. I believe it is imperative that we act in unity and that we act swiftly. I have come from the yard where I have heard many comments about Issy. The whole community seems to be afire with negative talk about our Issy. It is claimed that she contrives to manipulate the young boys, and even men, to do her will. It is said that she puts potions into her sweets that cause them to be compliant. It is also said that Lilith and Gertrude have heard Isabelle claim she can ask them to do anything, and they will comply. I have not yet heard where Angus stands on the matter. As I passed him in the yard, I asked him to accompany me. I regret to say that he was at that time being engaged by the talk of several other workers. He did not appear to be disclaiming their accusations. I hope that he will slip away and join us soon. I suspect that the lad has not the bravery to be seen making his way here."

My mother sat heavily. Her face danced through disbelief, then realisation, and finally horror.

"What are we to do?"

My grandmother brandished a look of long suffering and resignation.

"So! It happens again. The mob rises and cares little for the individual caught in its trap. There is usually a sinister individual behind the gossip. I suppose there is no need to find out the motive for this malicious talk. It is most likely too late to undo the damage." And on the outward sigh. "Isabelle is so young."

We heard a knock at the back door. Papa made his way into the back room, mumbling.

"This says a lot about what is to come."

"Hello, Angus, please come in."

"I'm sorry, sir, I think it best that I do not enter. You understand, I have sisters and Mother to support. I just wanted to let you know that I will be speaking to the rector this day. I will not be able to go ahead with the nuptials, you see. I cannot have it said that I am too weak to stand against the charms of Isabelle."

"I think it be weak that you do not stand for the integrity of one you claimed to have loved these past three years. Is Isabelle different today than she was yesterday?"

"Sir, perhaps I was only deceived of her character as Lilith and her brother suggest. There is much in what they say. Isabelle does hand out sweets and talks many young'uns into being her friend."

"I can see that you have been swayed. I would not attempt to sway you back, as I would not want my Isabelle wed to a spineless cur such as you are. It is only good that we have found out your true nature before the banns were read."

We heard from the shop room all that was said at the back door. I was devastated. I could not comprehend that what had happened was real.

The man I had thought to be my hero and my lover was gone from me.

At his own choosing!

It was surreal.

I felt confused and deceived.

It could not be true.

We had been committed to each other for three years.

I wanted to talk to him. Help him to see reason.

But then I thought, '*No, wait!*'

He had just said he could not trust himself to talk to me because he would be supernaturally influenced.

I questioned if it could be true. Was I unnatural?

And again, *'But no wait!'*

That was not sensible. I only wanted to be nice so that others might feel the same joy I had previously felt.

Devastation took hold. My future spread before me as a bleak and lonely place. For sure enough, I knew, when Angus shunned me, I would never find another man to be husband. Because of his actions, I became a social outcast. The realisation hit me with force, and I began to crumble. My face contorted as the tears of travail escaped. My mother sought to comfort me with an embrace. We all knew there was nothing to say. The significance and impact of the events that had unfolded could not be undone. I had been set on a path that was unknown and unexpected. My life was taken up in a storm funnel to be tossed out at random, in a shape not yet determined.

My father walked over to me after my sobbing abated and put his hand on my shoulder.

"You are blessed, Isabelle, to have escaped marriage to a coward unable to think for himself. You will see. God has a plan for you. Put your trust in him, and he will cause you to prosper. He has promised this in his word:

> 'Trust in the Lord with all thine heart; and lean not unto thine own understanding. In all thy ways acknowledge him, and he shall direct thy paths.'[2]

"Now, when it seems hardest, is the best time to seek him out."

"I cannot see his blessing, Papa! I am wondering if the evil I see in the people around me is all that there is. That we are tossed here and there with no grand plan, and no hope but to become evil so that we may combat evil."

"We will seek the plan that God has in mind and plan for your future. I know that you are hurting now, and that life seems bleak. The grief will pass. For now, I suggest you retire and soak up some solitude. Let us give up business for today and walk home together."

We shut the shop and walked the block to our home as a group, with me in the centre. My family wanted to protect me from the watchful, distrusting stares that people I had called friends sent my way. As soon as we had closed the door behind us, the family headed in to make a cup of tea and settle around the kitchen table. Papa placed his hands on my shoulders and simply said,

---

2 Proverbs 3:5-6 KJV

"We will call you when dinner is served."

My family discussed what could be done without my input.

As I looked forlorn, I was left to participate in normal life without the requirement that my activity achieve much. I knew plans were being made, but I had no idea what those plans were. I was not interested in much at all. Just as I started to emerge from the clouds, I heard that Angus had wed Lilith, quickly, *'so that Isabelle's influence over him would be broken.'* I spent another week in the drearies before the family came together for a conference.

It had been decided and arranged that I would leave for London the following week. My cousins were working on a ship that would carry families, meaning to emigrate to the colonies. I looked on as if they were all talking about someone else.

"Alfred and Jenifer will be here in four days. There is still much to do. I am very grateful that they have taken time out to come and fetch Isabelle. I do not want to leave the family during this current climate. Anything could happen. I feel a burden for Isabelle to find safety in another place, and at the same time, I know that I need to stay here."

This was said by my father. He was wearing one of the most worried looks I had ever seen him wear. My grandmother nearly spat her next comment. I had never seen Grandma with such distaste written in her features.

"The harm one jealous young girl can cause. It is that Lilith Wright who needs to be charged with exerting unlawful influence."

"True Mother, but what she has done cannot be undone. Unless the whole family emigrates, we will have to continue living in this community. We will need to put our effort into forgiveness and pray that the tide does not turn against every female in the family. We have not the funds for us all to travel. We need to do what we can to protect May and young Alison from malicious gossip and unfounded accusations."

"As you say. We have not the funds for us all to travel, elsewise we would. I would start packing this day."

May was not so ready to move continents.

"I would miss Marcus' family if we moved with you all. I am not yet ready to believe that everyone in our community believes what is being said. Marcus' family have been supportive. It will all blow away on the wind that carries Isabelle away." May then turned to me and said, "I'm sorry, Issy, I do not want you to leave. I will miss your cheerful self every day. Little Alison will miss knowing her aunty, and I am very grieved about that. But I have resigned myself to the truth. Too much damage has been done to your reputation for you to have a life with proper community interaction in this place. As unfair as it is. I hope you can see that we do not want to lose you. And we do not seek to make our own lives easier. We are trying to make a way for you to have a good life in another place; away from the stain that Lilith has marked you with."

May's face took on a look of distaste as she added. "And all for the attentions of a coward like Angus. I still believe that if he had stood by you and wed you as he had planned, the gossiping would have died away, and the gossips been left for God to judge." Everyone looked downcast after May's mini speech.

It was my turn to talk. It had been three weeks coming. "I also am resigned to the truth. There can be no happy future for me here. Lilith and her brother have seen to that. It is my suspicion that Lilith needed to marry in haste. She has been retiring from games, looking pale and refusing the peppermints which she always loved so much."

"I think you may be right in that." Perhaps Grandma, who is the local midwife, had noticed things also.

"It is no good reason to destroy my life. I do not understand why God would allow it. Now I hear I am to travel to the other side of the world.

"Alone!

"With no family to go through life with.

"No family to watch out for me.

"No family to care for me.

"And no family for which to care!

"I am very much afraid. And the grief at losing Angus, even though he was not what I thought him to be, will be exacerbated with the grief of leaving all of you behind."

Tears rolled down my face. My heart was heavy and sore. I had not experienced loss since my little brother Gregory died following a fall into the canal, and afterward developed the morbid throat. We all helped each other through that time. But I was to be alone. And so very far away. I sobbed uncontrollably, so May prepared some tea while Mam hugged me.

The conference would continue, and I would have to stay. I needed the information my family was trying to give me. Granda went to the kitchen, I think to add something to my tea. He was always taking care of us. I would miss him more than anyone.

When I regained my composure, Papa once again attempted to give me the information I needed despite my sniffles and glazed eyes.

"We have combined funds and purchased for you a ticket on a ship, sailing out of London, in September of next year. Alfred and William have told me of a righteous woman, even though she is a papist.

"She has been campaigning for the emigration of free settlers in family groups. She has commissioned the building of ships for travel to the colonies in the southern hemisphere. And she has worked diligently toward the formation of the Family Colonisation Loan Society. We will all provide you with half of your fare and some funds for you to establish yourself in a living when you arrive.

"This Mrs Chisholm is currently looking for an upstairs maid. It is not a great position, but it is a living. We have arranged for you to take this position until the ship sails. It has also been arranged that you will travel with a family of farmers during the voyage. Your uncle and aunt have been to meet this family and assured me that you will be safe. They have three young sons aged fifteen, thirteen, and twelve. Their daughter died from the morbid throat but four years ago. The mother would like to have a female companion for the journey. When you arrive, you will be billeted with a childless couple who have petitioned for a daughter. The husband is a tailor, and the wife is a dressmaker. I think that you could not ask for a better position.

"I believe that our Heavenly Father goes before you to prepare the way. I regret that he wants to take you from us in this way, but he has saved you from marrying Angus. And for that, we are all truly grateful. I hope that it will not take long for you to perceive his hand at work in all this."

There was so much to take in that most of the details went straight through without finding purchase. When I looked up from my lap, my father saw my dilemma.

"I will write it all down for you, Issy." His tone, sympathetic and subdued. I could see that all my family felt a little guilty. Not that they were at fault. In truth, they had done the best that could be done.

CHAPTER 2

Gareth

"Blessed are those who mourn, for they shall be comforted."

Matthew 5:4 ESV

"He has sent me to tell those who mourn that the time of the LORD's favour has come, and with it, the day of God's anger against their enemies. To all who mourn in Israel, he will give a crown of beauty for ashes, a joyous blessing instead of mourning, festive praise instead of despair. In their righteousness, they will be like great oaks that the LORD has planted for his own glory."

Isaiah 61:2-3 NLT

March 1849, Clinterty, Scotland

Gareth's tale began in the spring he celebrated his success of surviving twenty-one years of life in a country fraught with turmoil, famine, and pestilence. He told me that he was a *'wee bit wild'* during those twenty-one years, distressing his Ma and Da, *'making hay'* with his peers; running free and often barefoot, with little food to nourish the body but plenty of joy in community life.

"Gareth! Gareth! Come quickly! 'Tis Molly! She has been taken down wit' d same sickness as d others. She be fad'n fast. She's ask'n tae see ye."

"Is there really need for such haste, Mary? I saw her only yesterdee; she seemed in fine health, though tired out from caring for the rest."

"Aye! I fear she's passin' as we speak."

I picked up my heels and ran the three miles tae the Robertson farm. Red-faced and panting from the exertion in frosty temperatures, I cleaned off me shoes before entering the large farmhouse.

"Hullo Doug, are ye the only one about? Ye look much improved since last week. Have ye had some nourishment? Ye be needing more than milk. Is there nae any corn or oats tae have with the drink? Potatoes, maybe?"

"Nae, there isnae. We can talk later. Ye must be in a hurry. Molly is calling for ye; though I can barely make out a word."

"I've never been tae her room, Doug. I'm nae sure which door tae enter. I'm hesitant tae be opening each door in turn."

"Up one level, second door tae the left. Mrs Barclay is tending her. I'm sorry, Gareth. We all thought Molly would recover, so we didnae send for ye sooner. It has been so quick."

I made me way to the first floor and didnae hesitate at the door. I knocked and let meself in. Mrs Barclay was offended, but I couldne care less.

Me vision was only for Molly, lying pale and yellowed on the bed. I could see that she was gravely ill. There was a puffiness tae her face that wasnae usually there. Her eyes, glazed and yellow, looked at me with a vagueness I hadnae seen before in Molly.

I took her clammy hand and kissed her palm. I couldne kiss her blue lips when she was struggling for every breath. I heard the tightness in her throat and crackling in her chest.

The shock at seeing her like that caused me to freeze from fright.

It was minutes before I could speak.

"Molly, me love." I broke, then restrained a sob. "Can ye see yer way tae staying with me? I dinnae know how I can survive without yer. Doug will be lost. Already yer the only two surviving. I beg ye please, nae tae follow yer Ma, Da and brother Fergus into the next life. Can you please remain with us here? We need ye!"

I was thinking mostly of meself, but when Molly recovered, she would want tae be alive. The famine couldne last forever.

Molly gurgled and croaked a reply of sorts. I tried to make out what she said. I only understood a few words. I caught their meaning.

"I cannae fight on." The wheezed intake of breath drowned me afeart heart. "Ye must stay close tae Doug. He will need….."

I understood Molly's meaning.

Me Molly had given up the fight.

She was always kinder than she was strong.

Molly was blessed with a cooperative nature, more sweet kindness and instant smiles than endurance.

In that moment, I understood that we were to be separated until I also passed over tae the next life.

With nourishing food, the family would have survived. But with the second season of potato blight and the Laird's taxes so high, all the cash crops had been sold tae keep the farm. Why did God let nasty things happen tae good Christian folk?

I sat by her bed as the priest arrived.

I participated in the last rites in a trance.

I prayed and asked God to accept Molly into his presence. I knew Molly would be with him soon. I saw the spirit of death hovering over her face. An ugly, skeletal-like mask that glimmered and then was gone. With Doug next tae me, we prayed.

"Into yer hands we commit our beloved sister."

Then we walked away, each to be alone in our grief. Leaving the aunties tae prepare the body for burial.

I meandered back toward town where me family waited for news. I spoke to them, still in a trance. I closed the shop and went tae hibernate in me room. I had oft been referred to as a bear of a man. I thought it time tae act on the image. I refused all food. I drank water and nothing else for a week. Slowly, I began tae emerge from me stupor. I wrestled with God. I questioned God. I accused God. I found God wanting. I didnae hear God speak.

Each one in me family came tae speak reason tae me. Each one had counsel for me tae hear. Each one claimed that God knew what he was doing. Some claimed that the Robertsons must have been out of favour with God. I knew that couldne be the explanation which I sought. Molly was as close to an angel as one could be. And the other Robertsons were God fearing, attending the confessional and mass every week. Nooo! 'Twas nae the truth. I grew angry 'cause I could find nae answer. I spoke me mind tae the God who had betrayed me, and eventually He spoke to me. When finally, I quieted down. I heard what He had been trying tae say. First, a few words with an audible voice.

"I love you and Molly both!"

Then, when He had me attention, with impression and years of hearing the word of God from the bible readings in the Kirk. I had the understanding.

God didnae cause Lord Ashley tae take the cash crops. Lord Ashley's own selfish free will did that. God willnae take our free will from us. He loves us! He counsels us tae be generous rather than greedy. Bad things happen when people are careless with the lives of others. Storing up treasures whilst watching others go hungry. Our illness and lack of prosperity are more a consequence of choice. Our choices and the choices of others. Choices that are sometimes imposed upon us by the greedy and selfish. My God loves me! And He wants me tae surrender me life tae Him so that He can direct the steps of me life.

I laid meself prostrate on the ground.

Me arms before me, and forehead tae the ground.

I asked me Heavenly Father tae forgive me thinking that he would cause Molly harm as a matter of his design.

I asked that He forgive me blaming him for the bad things that happen.

I asked Him tae forgive me, me carelessness in how me behaviour frightened me family.

I asked Him tae forgive me carelessness regarding other people's concerns.

I asked that He help me tae become a better person. Tae look for the way He wants me tae step.

I also asked me Heavenly Father tae forgive the people who lined their own pockets at the expense of me family.

And I asked that me saviour in heaven forgive me for hating those people.

I spent an hour prostrate before I stood and began me life afresh. I shifted me thinking. From then on, each moment was a new opportunity.

G "Oh! Thank the Lord. The bear has left his cave."

"Okay, Ma! There's nae need to be smart. There has been more food for all while I was in retreat. Now, however, I am famished. I will be needing a double portion if it can be spared. 'Tis a new man you see before ye."

"Well, ye have but half hour tae ready yerself for the funeral. And it's fortunate ye didnae disgrace us by staying abed any longer. The funeral was delayed by the weather. The ground being so hard, and so many to bury. Ye can be eating leftovers then, on yer way."

I moved with speed and purpose on hearing that proclamation. I had been more closed off than I realised, not even knowing that the funeral would be that day. I needed tae check on Doug. I had given me word tae Molly.

N Gareth set a brisk pace for his hike to the Kirk. Slowing only as he drew close. Gareth entered via the rear entrance and genuflected. Crossing himself with the holy water as he bowed his spirit to God.

"Please fill me with peace and help me tae help Doug."

Gareth stood and scanned the inside of the sanctuary, looking for Doug, who was seated in the front pew. Gareth walked slowly toward the front pew and took a seat next tae his best friend. Doug looked up slowly. A stoic expression fixed on his face.

"Ye made it then. I was nae sure ye would rise before the burial. Me Aunty has helped organise all. I was next tae useless."

There were four coffins lined up at the front of the Kirk. Most of the small community of Clinterty were present. The Robertson family were well respected, and Molly much loved. Molly spent much of her time visiting and helping neighbours. Maybe it would have been better if she had cared for herself more. But then she would not have been Molly.

The priest chanted the Mass.

Incense filled the sanctuary.

An ethereal quietness pervaded the sanctuary, with Father Xavier the only one speaking. The only other sound was the occasional, uncontrolled sniffle or sob that reverberated off the stone walls.

Doug and I were too shocked tae give vent tae our emotions. That came later over a dram or two.

It took many relatives tae carry the four coffins tae the grave site. I assisted with Molly, Doug with his mother.

Aunty Meaghan and her sole surviving daughter, Adeline, organised everything needed for the wake. How they did such a thorough job, such a short time after losing most of their own family, I didnae know. But I was grateful that Doug was spared the chore. In truth, looking at him, I knew he would not have been capable.

There was plenty of talk. Plenty tae reminisce. Plenty tae drink. The community donated a plate each, so there was plenty tae eat for that day. The next day we needed tae talk reality and create possibilities for our futures.

I turned from thanking Molly's aunty for the fine wake and found Father Xavier hovering, waiting tae talk with me. Expecting tae be given a lecture on shirking responsibilities, I braced meself. Tae me surprise, Father Xavier was sympathetic in offering his condolences. The next statement left me fluctuating between curious and suspicious.

"I'm glad to see you exited your cave in time for the Requiem, Gareth. Your Mam has been concerned about you." 'Tis never good when Mam starts talking tae the priest.

"I'm aware, Father. Mam has said her piece tae me about it."

"I would like you to come see me at the rectory tomorrow. There is someone I would like you to meet. I believe he has a story, which God would like you to hear. Shall we say eleven in the am? That should give you time to open your shop and set things in order."

A summons from the priest is nae negotiable. Even when delivered as an invitation.

"For certain, Father, I'll be there."

"Bring Doug along with you," Father Xavier said quietly, as he smiled sagely and walked away.

I did as Father Xavier instructed and opened me shop for business for the first time since Molly passed. The customers poured in, and it was 10am before I had time to breathe. There were caskets for others tae be built and furnishings tae be mended. Apparently, life would go on! And I would be needed tae participate in the community. Me heart was not present, and I had a hard time offering up a smile. But the community needed their cabinet maker to fulfil his function. At ten, I closed the door and hung the 'out tae lunch' plaque. I made me way to the Robertson Farm to convince Doug tae share with me the joy of visiting the rectory.

"Nae! Why would I want tae be visiting the priest? Can he be bringing me family back from the dead? I'm done with the Church. Can see no point in pretending otherwise."

"Father Xavier was very mysterious, and he specifically told me tae bring ye. What harm can this one visit do?"

"It can set me tae hurting more, is what it can do. I have enough hurt tae deal with for now. I dinnae want more."

"I had a visitation with the Almighty, Doug. He has helped me tae cope with the hurting. He will help ye also if ye allow. Are ye nae curious at all? Father Xavier has never before invited us tae the rectory. It may distract from the hurt. Please come with me. I dinnae want tae go alone."

"What will the get-out code be? For if I need tae leave?"

"Draw a circle as always."

N The fog of grief made it difficult for them to stay present in the moment. So distracted were they that other people passed and said their greeting without the men being aware. Their vision of the present was blurred. They could not have told you what the weather was. Their overwhelmed senses had no room to acknowledge wet, cold, wind, or sunshine. Touch, smell, hearing, even vision were impaired. There was no room for input into their fugue state.

The entrance to the rectory was before them, but they had no recollection of the journey. When Gareth raised his hand to knock the ring on the door, the door opened before his grasp held. Their approach had been scrutinised by the people within. Their state of mind, observed.

The priest was sympathetic. He was a man who cared for his parish and was often misunderstood. As the person who offered correction as often as encouragement, he was viewed as one to be avoided when the conscience stung.

Father Xavier had genuine concern for the families who were decimated by the 'Blight' and pestilence. It was unfair that the poor paid the price for the sins of the wealthy. But there was little he could do. He supervised a soup kitchen, but the English lords insisted that the locals anglicise their names to receive the soup. Many resisted adopting the customs of their conquerors. The highland clans helped many to emigrate as a solution to a population that could not be fed. If they emigrated, then there were fewer mouths to feed. Father Xavier could see the benefit of the scheme. Benefit to those who left and to those who stayed. He took advice from his bishops and invited Mr Foster from the Family Colonisation Loan Society to visit and talk to families that might benefit from sponsorship.

Before Gareth and Doug could be shown into the parlour, Father Xavier addressed Mr Foster regarding the prospective recruits.

"They are good lads. Consumed with grief today, as they have recently lost many of their family members. You can see by the way they approached the building without once looking up to see their surroundings that they are not themselves yet. It's a wonder they were not run down by the Laird's horse as he left."

"It was good of the Laird to offer twenty-five per cent of their passage. If the lads can come up with the next twenty-five per cent, then the Loan Society can help them with the rest. Are there any women who would travel with them, though? The colony certainly needs marriageable young women. We have so few good women. Mistress Chisholm is of the opinion that marriageable young women would bring stability to the colony. And good Christian principles."

"Aye, they have family in a similar situation."

Gareth and Doug entered the room with curiosity and a small measure of trepidation. Both wondering about what the good Father wanted to speak with them? And who was the man with a swarthy complexion? The strangeness of the invitation settled on Gareth. What had he been expecting after all?

The two men chorused with matching nods of the head.

"Good morning tae ye Father." Then waited. They had no expectations. They barely had plans for their next steps.

"Good day to you. Mr Forbes, Mr Robertson, I would like you to meet Mr Foster. Mr Foster is an agent for the Family Colonisation Loan Scheme. We will discuss what that is over lunch if that is alright with you both."

Gareth and Doug made not a move; then compelled themselves to acknowledge the introduction. Their thinking homogeneous. *'What could Father Xavier be up to now?'* He was known to have interfering ways.

"Come, join us for lunch. We have a lot to discuss."

"Thank ye, Father, we were nae expecting lunch."

"Let's move to the dining room now. I'm for an early lunch, and we will be able to think better with nourishment."

"The circle has come early, but I see nothing for it; let's be movin' to the table, Gareth. Small mercies I'll grant."

"A good feed can do nae harm. Thank ye, Father, for the kind invitation tae yer table, but me Ma will be wondering where I am if I dinnae show for lunch."

"I've spoken to Mrs Forbes. She will be expecting you to eat at my table this day."

"Yes, Father!"

What else could be said? Gareth and Doug followed Father Xavier to the dining room, where a hearty rather than sumptuous meal was laid out. Father Xavier was a man who ate well but chose to keep his diet simple so that more could be given to his starving parishioners.

"This looks very good, Father, where would ye like us tae be seated?"

The long dining table was set with four settings in the centre. Each end left bare.

"Take any setting, it will be of no consequence."

Gareth and Doug took the side of the table closest to the door, leaving the other for Mr Foster and Father Xavier.

The décor in the room was not what Gareth would have expected. With light breezy tones of green and Birch wood rather than the fashionable mahogany, burgundy and dark forest greens. There were watercolours of tropical birds adorning the pale straw-coloured walls. Father Xavier noticed Gareth taking in the room and commented.

"I spent time in New Caledonia and loved my time there."

Chapter 3

FCLS

The Family Colonisation Loan Society was developed by Caroline Chisholm with the hope of changing the 'wildness' of the Australian penal colony into a family centred society. Caroline Chisholm saw the need to instil some moral standing into a community built on punishment, banishment, and greed. The influx of Gold Miners into a society that was already compromised in societal mores did not improve the balance. Mrs Chisholm formulated a solution and canvassed her cause. "Voluntary immigration of families with farming skills" was expected to balance the society and improve moral standards in the colony.

April 1849. Clinterty, Scotland

N Mr Foster understood the restless look in the eyes of Gareth and Doug. The young men in front of him looked like they had not been properly nourished in years. A common story amongst the Celtic peoples. So, as the men ate, Mr Foster spoke. He started the talk about the Family Colonisation Loan Society as soon as the meal was served.

"We have a scheme which I believe would be ideally suited to your situation, Mr Forbes and Mr Robertson."

The boys acknowledged the monologue with polite nods as they ate the meal with a gusto derived from not having had a full stomach for a year.

"We are looking for families to fill the ships that we are currently chartering for the express purpose of carrying free settlers to the colony of New South Wales, on the great southland. We require families who are twelve strong with a desire to build a new life. It is not an easy trip, and it will require lots of hard work in a place that is so different that all the natural laws of agriculture are challenged. The families need to be comprised of men and women of good moral standing, preferably from the same family. Uncles, aunties, brothers, and sisters. It is advised that only those with strong health undertake the adventure, as the physical demands will be rigorous. The very young and the very old could possibly join you later.

"It is a requirement that you pay passage; however, the Family Colonisation Loan Society will loan you half the passage fare and half what it will require to set you up in the colony, with the trade in which you are skilled. It is expected that you will have repaid the loan two years following your arrival. Hard work and application will be required of you. This is not an adventure for the faint of heart.

"I am told, Mr Forbes, that you are a cabinet maker, and you, Mr Robertson, are a farmer. The colony needs both. Skilled workers are in short supply. Farmers with knowledge are also few and far between. There have been many failures where would-be farmers have taken a selection and been unable to bring in a harvest. Partly due to a lack of agricultural expertise and partly due to the land they are attempting to tame. I am not saying the task will be easy. Best you research the literature as much as you can before leaving Scotland. We will have some meetings for educational purposes before you sail if you choose to take up the offer.

"Do you think you could manage to gather sufficient family members who might want to try their hand at emigration? It is a bold move, but those who prepare and work hard succeed, in my opinion."

Mr Foster paused and displayed indecision before continuing.

"You are in a fortunate situation, you have a benefactor who is willing to provide half of your half of passage. This would make it easier for your family group to gather the funds for the undertaking."

The crease between the eyes of both Gareth and Doug deepened as Mr Foster spoke. Not seeing how they could fulfil the criteria.

Which question to ask first?

With tight lips, Doug managed to speak first. It was altogether suspicious that a 'benefactor' offered such a large sum of money, with no reason given.

"Who might our benefactor be then? I'm fiercely curious who would want tae see me travellin' tae the other side of the world. About as far as I could get from me ancestral lands. I may only have a small holding, but it is me family's land and free of any encumbrance."

"Lord Ashley. I grant that I can see ulterior motives. But it still might be a good offer. If you can see your way to humbling your pride, you may be able to make the most of the situation. Lord Ashley asked that his name not be mentioned. But I see how his motives may not be altruistic and would not want you to be taken advantage of in your time of mourning."

"The bastard! He squeezes me family till they're so weak they die from influenza. Then he pretends tae be generous."

Doug spat his comment with emotion exacerbated by grief and anger. His fists, still holding knife and fork, came down with such force the plates jumped, and a glass tipped. Gareth felt the resentment toward Lord Ashley in his core. The pure evil it took to behave that way was beyond his understanding.

"True, it is that it is all yours, Doug. But yer family are starving tae keep it that way. What's left of them, that is. With all yer closest gone, are ye still keen tae hold onto it? Might be better tae sell for a good price, tae the pretentious benefactor, and take his grant as well. I know there is little holding me tae this country now. The English have taken what they can and push harder every day tae take the rest. 'Tis no right, and 'tis no fair. But it is what it is. Perhaps we could get the best price we can and move tae start afresh. Accept what others have done in greed, but move away, so that they dinnae conquer our whole lives."

Doug drew a circle on the tablecloth with his finger dipped in spilt wine. He then stood and walked out without saying another word. Gareth felt torn. He felt the Holy Spirit quicken his spirit, encouraging him to stay and hear the rest of the offer. He hungered to give in to pride and follow his friend out the door. It was a bitter pill to swallow, to accept the offer from the English Lord who was doing all he could to destroy the Scottish rebels. The English lord who manipulated and schemed. Who did what he could to destroy the morale and spirit, as well as take their property. The lord who made a spectacle of bringing in English peasants and paying them a better living than the locals.

Gareth chose to stay and hear Mr Foster's exposition but was subdued in his manner by a battle within. Gareth averted his eyes from the speaker as often as he connected. He had no ill will toward Father Xavier nor Mr Foster. It was the reality of submitting to the remorseless machinations of an evil man that rubbed. Gareth stayed to listen and to evaluate. He listened to the Holy Ghost and knew in his heart that, for some reason he could not understand, it was the choice which God would have him make.

"Sometimes, Gareth, God leads us through the valley of the shadow of death and into a promised land. Trust that wherever God leads you, he is always there taking care of you."

"Thankee Father, 'tis as you say. I aim tae trust in him as our Saint Francis did the same. If he can look after the birds in the field, then he can be looking after me also[3]. I will chase after Doug now and see if he can be talked around. I think it would be the best thing for him. I'll talk tae Ma and Da. And I'll see who else feels displaced enough tae undertake such an adventure."

"I will call on you in a week, then, to discuss things further."

"I'll let Ma know tae expect ye, Father. I'll have an answer for ye then. Good day."

Gareth walked away from the meeting determined to pray heavily. He needed direction. He also needed help convincing Doug and the rest of his family. He could not see that many would be willing to

---

[3] Matthew 6[26]

risk all by travelling to the other side of the world. To never see again, the family left behind.

'Do ye hear me, Lord? Is this what ye want? And who do ye have in mind to go with me?'

Gareth made his way directly back to the workshop. He spent the afternoon making plans to call a gathering so that the scheme could be put to the whole family. If twelve volunteered to go, then he would step up to lead them.

"A daunting task, but a task that could be managed. If 'tis yer will, Lord."

Gareth did not work alone. His cousin overheard him talking to God aloud.

"And what task would that be, Gareth? Yer've been distracted all afternoon, and I for one, would like tae know with what."

Gareth, ready to talk, decided that then was a good time to start the calling to gather. He straightened away from his work and brought his focus to his cousin.

"We will be needing tae gather tae discuss that very thing. Can I rely on ye tae start spreading the word, Ryan? Two days hence at the Craigieburn Tavern. Sunset, I think."

"Can I have a little more information tae spread, Gareth? Tae encourage attendance."

"Tell all, 'tis a gathering at the Tavern. That should be enough. Drinking and talking around the fire."

"As ye say, but I'm mighty curious."

"Then ye'll be wanting tae join us!"

Gareth knew that telling Ryan to spread the word would take care of his side of the family. One word to his ma, and Edinburgh would know the next day. Aunty Fiona could talk up a fierce storm.

After closing the shop, Gareth asked Ryan to stop at his mother's place on his way home and let her know that '*Gareth would be visiting Aunty Meaghan. He could be expected tae return but two hours late.*' With a three-quarter hour walk each way, and time spent over a cup of watered whiskey with a short chat. Gareth hoped to be home for the evening meal.

Gareth planned a lengthy chat with his immediate family that evening. Hoping to convince his mother that it was a good opportunity.

Not an easy task.

He knew he would travel regardless but preferred his mother to be happy.

Gareth had an almost imperceptible spring in his step as he made his way over familiar trails. The hope of a future brought some healing from the sadness of loss. Molly still occupied his thoughts most of his waking hours and haunted his sleep as well. The walk to Aunty Meaghan's home was like a walk down memory lane. He and Molly had spent many a day exploring the country with Aunty Meaghan's children before they passed so suddenly. Days of jolly mischief and fanciful thinking. The overwhelming sadness gripped Gareth with a suddenness as his thoughts became lost in memory. It was the squeak of unoiled hinges that brought him back to the present.

"Well now, and what is bringing ye tae darken me doorstep this lovely spring evenin'?"

Gareth looked around and noticed the weather for the first time. The gentle mist had been falling unnoticed, long enough for a sheen to develop on his coat. Gareth heaved a sigh as he tried to lift his spirits before he spoke. Wanting to encourage Aunty Meaghan with hope for a future, he took a silent minute to look around and take his fill of the moment before proselytising the scheme. The sun shining through the mist displayed a rainbow of promise.

"Well, will ye look at that. God's promise to protect us and all. We sure need a bit more of that around here."

"Aye! It does make me heart sore tae see such a sight. I believe that God is about tae give us an opportunity, Aunty. Would ye join us for a gathering at the Craigieburn, sunset, two days hence? I have a proposal tae put tae anyone with ears tae hear."

"Come on in, Gareth, and have a drink with me. Ye've had a long walk. There may be a biscuit or two if Adeline has nae finished them off by now."

Adeline, Meaghan's widowed daughter, joined them in the parlour with warm watered whisky in glasses and the last of the biscuits. Adeline heard the end of her mother's comment and sniffed.

"Don't be telling stories that make me appear the glutton, Ma. Even if 'tis only Gareth."

Gareth stopped to socialise over a drink for a short while but refused to enlighten his aunt and cousin about the details he would share with everyone at once. Gareth had no desire tae speak the same information over and over.

"Aunty, can you please share the call tae gathering? I would like tae put the plan tae all the family if I can."

"Sure, and we can all spend time speculatin', and thinking up fanciful stories. Are ye sure ye're ready for the effort it will take tae put out the wildest of those speculations? Ye can be sure they will be many and varied."

"'Tis sure I am. Good eve, Aunty."

With that, Gareth placed his hat on his head to protect against the chill rolling in as twilight descended into night. Gareth lengthened his stride and picked up his speed to make it home for supper.

CHAPTER 4

Into Service

"It is the LORD who goes before you. He will be with you; he will not leave you or forsake you. Do not fear or be dismayed."

Deuteronomy 31:8 ESV

July 1849, Islington, London

The carriage slowed at the doorstep of an elegant, but not large, townhouse on a crescent, near a green, about two miles from the Thames River. A walking distance of about three-quarters of an hour. All lawns were closely clipped, and the trees pruned to unnatural shapes.

Two servants waited by the front door, and a footman waited near the curb as my carriage rolled past. It appeared they were expecting the arrival of a family member or important guest.

My carriage rolled into the rear courtyard near the entrance to the kitchen. The groom sent to escort me from the barge dock on the Thames descended and opened the carriage door. This was not like the fancy carriages that were then pulling up to the front entrance, but it had kept me safe. And spared me a confusing walk carrying luggage through unfamiliar streets. I was grateful for the courtesy paid to me by the housekeeper. It was unusual to treat a maid with such consideration. And I knew it well.

The kitchen was large and well ventilated. The smell of breakfast mingled with the smells of preparation for the noon-time meal. Two kitchen maids worked on an abandoned table, set with a morning meal for staff. The staff appeared to have quickly left the table to attend the arrival at the front door. Perhaps the arrival was not planned. Not being familiar with the ways of grand houses, I was unsure.

Managing to fulfil the role of upstairs maid would be a challenge. It was bewildering that I could have been offered the position. I only hoped that I could keep my mistress happy, as I was in very great need of keeping the position. What I did not then know was that the housekeeper had the power to make my life peaceful. More so than the mistress. The housekeeper may not have had a choice over who was hired, but she had the power to control my life for the year in which I was preparing to undertake the journey ahead.

"Hi then. And you must be the starling the mistress has employed instead of our dear Rose. Well, that shock of 'air will be a chore to 'ide. You've missed the upstairs maids sitting for brunch. You'll 'ave to wait for nunch. Take a seat, I s'pose I can give you a drink of tea from the footmen's fare while you're waiting for Mrs Gretsch, the 'ousekeeper. My name is Mrs Shaw to you. What would your name be then?"

Mrs Shaw pulled a chair out from a small table in the corner near a window. The table seemed to be Mrs Shaw's personal workspace. There were some recipes scattered on the table, and a quill with a small pot of ink. Seemingly, Mrs Shaw could read and write. Not common for household help. Even with the less than friendly welcome, Mrs Shaw had the look of a heartily friendly person. She gave off an aura of love and joy.

I could not help but read the recipe closest to me, and a small smile crossed my features.

"Do you like fruit puddings then?" Mrs Shaw had noticed me perusing the recipe.

"My name is Isabelle. Yes, I think I like anything containing cinnamon. It has healing properties to go with the wonderful taste. We could not afford to use the spice often at home."

Mrs Shaw gave me a look that suggested I had revealed too much about myself. But I was not accustomed to being reserved.

"Well, Isabelle. Apparently, you know your letters. You 'ad best keep that information to yourself, and don't be caught reading any of the mistress's writings or mail. The family like to keep their privacy."

"Yes, of course I will respect the family's privacy."

"It is not as simple as you think. You 'ave to tidy without reading. Put your mind to it."

"Yes, Ma'am."

"I'm not the 'ma'am'. It's 'yes, Cook'. Or 'yes, Mrs Shaw'. You 'ave a lot to learn, lass. For your sake, I 'ope you learn quickly."

I had no reason to expect benevolence from the other staff. They possibly had no idea why I was hired rather than Rose. And I had no desire to inform them of the treatment I had received from my community at home. It would only have sown seeds of doubt. I planned to speak only of my family. Of my family, I could tell true stories of joy and fun.

I was grateful for the position secured for me by my aunt. I was not sure how it was managed. Who knew whom? However, I aimed to do the best I could and make the lives of the people around me a little better in small ways.

I had regained some of my friendly nature but would never again be able to trust without question. I feared my reserve would make me appear aloof.

Regrettable!

It could not be helped.

Despite my situation, I looked forward to meeting a new community.

Leaving behind everyone I knew left me feeling adrift. Adrift, waiting to write my future. A future filled with new people and new ways of doing things. I prayed I would adapt quickly to my changing circumstances.

It scared me but also promised hope.

I needed to find others who would be undertaking the adventure into the unknown with me. People who could be friends. Friends who would journey with me and join with me in preparing for a new and possibly strange land.

I was not to meet my Aunt Alison and Uncle Alfred until my first half-day off. A note was delivered in the early afternoon, telling me where to meet them on Sunday morning, but I was not given the half-day off in my first week. When my situation was secured, my aunt organised for me to have Sunday mornings free to attend church with her, and Monday evenings to attend meetings of the Family Colonisation Loan Society. They had meetings for the purpose of education on Monday evenings. My opinion of the venture was not considered. It was the only option presented to me. One of the footmen who was also planning to take passage on the FCLS ships kindly offered to walk me to the meeting when they were not held at the house.

From our first meeting, it was obvious to me, and everyone else, that the Housekeeper, Mrs Gretsch, did not share her Mistress' benevolent frame of mind. Following her meeting with Mrs Chisholm on her arrival home, Mrs Gretsch made her way to the kitchen to make sure the newbie knew her place. I was asked to stand when Mrs Gretsch entered the room.

I gained my feet in record time and placed the chair under the table. I turned to face the woman who approached me. Dressed all in black, but with an elegant cut to her dress. Her clothing gave no clue to her background. Her speaking voice was polite and friendly, but there was an artifice in her eyes that others may not have recognised. I felt the coercion as she came close to stand over me and intimidate. My intuition suggested a woman of fallen family circumstances. Perhaps her husband had fallen in one of the many battles in which our countrymen fought. I did my best to gain her approval, but my efforts failed.

I made a small curtsy at her approach.

"Good morning to you, Ma'am," I said as she penetrated my person with a look. I feared she could see through to my undergarments. And maybe saw what I had eaten for breakfast.

"You may call me Mrs Gretsch."

"Yes, Mrs Gretsch."

"And not speak before you have been asked a question."

I said nothing following that instruction and persevered through her malevolent perusal. The pause in dialogue lengthened into an atmosphere of dread that permeated the kitchen in which we all stood. Finally, in a voice dripping with condescension, Mrs Gretch deigned to address me.

"We will call you Isa. Isabelle is far too flamboyant for a maid. Have you ever been in service girl?"

As her question did not seem rhetorical, I answered. I concluded that I would need to be very careful. Although the demeanour did not portray the housekeeper's intent, I could feel the malevolence that oozed from her spirit. My voice faltered.

"No, Mrs Gretsch. This will be the first time. I have been trained as a dressmaker by my mother."

"I do not recall asking you that question, Isa. Remember your instructions the first time they are given."

"Yes, Mrs Gretsch."

Tears welled at the back of my eyes, and I found it difficult to be attentive to the instructions that followed. That became a part of my daily routine. Mrs Gretsch found a reason to criticise before giving instructions. I am convinced it was by design. The result was a constant reservoir of criticisms at her disposal because I found it difficult to function when deliberately wounded.

"Molly will take you in hand to teach you the basics. Rachel's sister Rose was being trained to take the position you now hold before your Aunt Alison spoke to Mrs Chisholm about *your* need to relocate immediately. We have not been told the reasons behind your need.

We have been left to conjecture and have come up with some fanciful tales of woe. Mind that you do nothing to lend credence to those tales."

I gasped a little before I caught myself. My eyes grew large, and the room sniggered. How was I to avoid doing the unknown thing that reinforced a wrong belief, if I did not know what that belief was?

"We could hardly ask Rachel to be nice to you. That would be beyond reasonable."

Molly had a kind face and a sweet smile. Her appearance inspired immediate trust. I believed in that moment that she was a kind and reasonable girl. I knew that I could not live suspicious of all and maintain a sweet manner myself. I felt the need to trust in the goodness of others and hoped that I would be treated fairly.

"Come this way, will you then. We 'ave little time to waste settling you in. We must be to work promptly if we are to 'ave the lady's luggage unpacked when she is ready to change her clothes. I'll show you where to put your bag. You can settle in later. You're to share quarters with me also."

Molly led me through a labyrinth of hallways and stairs as we made our way to the top levels of the townhouse. I thought it would take weeks to learn how to navigate inside the house. I concluded that I would need to be Molly's shadow that first week, or I would become lost and be sure to make a wrong turn.

No sooner had the thought occurred to me than Molly disappeared. She had left me as soon as I stepped into the small room that we were to share. I put my small carpet bag down and made haste to follow after her. To my dismay, I looked to the left, the way we had approached, and I looked to my right, the only other choice, but Molly was nowhere to be seen. I was bewildered and disorientated.

Unsure how I could have lost Molly and consequently myself. I decided to make haste and attempted to retrace my steps. I did not hear the whispers in the darkened room down the hall.

"Shhh!"

"She's gone t' other way, Molly, 'tis safe to be whisperin'. T'anks for turnin' 'er about. Maybe she'll be leaving within a week."

"She didn't even notice that we traversed the same corridors more than once. We may not see 'er again till nightfall, when the candles will be like beacons."

"C'mon, we better get our work done."

Molly and Rachel scuttled in the opposite direction from me. I wandered! And tried to retrace the steps I had taken with Molly but soon realised that we had turned in circles more than once. My understanding grew. I had been set up.

'I will now appear tardy. It is hard to see sweet Molly as an enemy, but it seems that I will need to be careful of everyone.'

With cool logic, I eliminated corridors and slowly made my way to the lower levels, but I could hardly start opening doors in the hope of locating Molly at work. Desperate though I was to find her.

While I stood in the middle of a large hallway looking perplexed and indecisive, a footman entered the hallway from a concealed stairway at the end of the corridor. When he spotted me, he approached, and I expected to be reprimanded or taken to Mrs Gretsch. Instead, I found a kindred spirit.

"Morning … eh...Isa. Best use the name our Mrs Gretsch has given you. I'll introduce myself, given that Mrs Gretsch decided to keep you in the dark about all our names. I suspect, to embarrass you each time you need to address one of us. I'm Phillip. It's a pleasure to meet you."

"Good day to you, Phillip. It seems that lovely Molly, with such a sweet demeanour, has played a prank on me. I am now lost with no way of knowing where I should be. Would you please show me where it is that I should be?"

I was unsure who I could trust. Phillip seemed nice, but then, so had Molly. By his next statement, I saw that Phillip was both observant and discerning.

"You can trust me, Isa. I will be a fellow traveller. Mrs Chisholm has entrusted me with escorting you to the FCLS meetings when they are not in this very house. It's not safe to walk the streets alone after dark."

"It seems that I have made some enemies before I arrived. I did not know that I would be taking another's place in the household."

"There will always be another waiting in the wings to take up service in a house with such a generous employer."

We walked as we talked, and I soon found myself outside a door where voices could be heard from within. They were jolly as they discussed the trouble in which they expected I would find myself.

"I will leave you before you open the door. I would not want others to know I helped you. Beware, young Isa, people are not always as they seem."

Phillip walked away briskly, with obvious purpose and direction. I was privileged to hear, before I entered, the truth about Molly and Rachel's friendship.

The start of my new role as an upstairs maid left me feeling unsettled about my future. I wondered if anything would work out for me ever again. Phillip seemed to be on my side, but I had doubts. I sighed to myself. I had sunk to the level of sides.

'Oh, happy life, where have you gone? It would be good if even one person could be true.'

I opened the door and entered. Both maids stopped their work and their laughter when they spotted me. Molly regained her smile and her pretence in a heartbeat. It was hard not to be drawn in by the sweetness of her nature. I needed to work hard at putting no trust in her. I paid close attention to work and stuck like glue to her side for the rest of that day. I even followed her out to the privy, crossed my legs, and took no drink, so they could not give me the slip again. I slowly learnt how to navigate the corridors and the stairways of the house. I made it difficult for them to catch me with the same prank twice.

The house and the ways of the house were not complex to learn. I paid close attention. It was not possible to show me the wrong way to do something and still satisfy the demands of the Mistress. The diabolical duo tried at every turn to confuse my education and lead me astray. But I paid close attention to the way things in a room were left when the door was closed. It was a challenging way to learn. Being asked to complete a task in a certain way, then watching to see my teachers put my efforts to right when they thought I was not looking.

I began to live in a state of hyper alertness. It became a part of my nature, and I found that I was very fatigued at the end of the day. I also needed to sleep lightly. I awakened more than once with my hand in a basin of warm water or the like. Molly and Rachel wasted no opportunity to make my life difficult. In their endeavours, they had Mrs Gretsch's approval. The sadder I looked, the more they received praise. I never thought to become a person who rarely smiled.

Three days following my arrival, I was summoned to the library where I found Mrs Chisholm seated behind her desk and Mrs Gretsch standing beside. I had quickly tidied my hair and ensured that my hands were clean. I bobbed a curtsy as I had seen Molly do on occasion when addressed by the mistress. I stood and waited. Mrs Gretsch had made the expectation clear on the first day, and many times since, with curt rebukes and the back of her hand across my face as a response to any unsolicited communication. I had learnt to believe that diminutive communication was what Mrs Chisholm also expected from me.

"I must say, from your aunt's communication, I expected a sanguine and witty character. I was led to expect a young lady with a quick smile and forthright manners. Instead, I discover a scarred rabbit. Are you unwell, Isabelle?"

To her credit, Mrs Chisholm looked genuinely concerned about my welfare. I could not tell her, however, about the treatment I had been receiving since my arrival in her household.

"I am well, Mrs Chisholm."

Mrs Chisholm waited for me to say more. Mrs Gretsch looked at me gloatingly. I was unsure if I should continue. As the silence lengthened, I considered the possibility that Mrs Gretsch behaved in a way contrary to her mistress's approval. Perhaps I was meant to say more. I was unfamiliar with the new side to my personality. An attitude of fear had grown quickly.

"How do you find your new position, Isabelle?"

"Thank you, Mrs Chisholm, for the opportunity that you have given me to work out a living."

"That is not really an answer, Isabelle. I would like you to speak your mind. I need to know that you have the resilience for the trip ahead."

I looked up fleetingly to see the kind eyes of a benevolent lady. I took a deep breath and did my best to give the kind of answer I would have given before my torment had begun.

"I enjoy the work, Mrs Chisholm. I observe that there is much joy in your household, Ma'am. It is a pleasure to be working for you. It is a position which is new to me as I was formerly training with my mother to be a dressmaker." I smiled at this remembrance.

"Perhaps we could put those skills to use making garments for some of the sponsored immigrants. Would you be willing to sew in your spare time, Isabelle? I would provide the makings. It would bless some of the poorer families and set them in a good position before their journeys begin. There are also plenty of poor who visit the parish. They also could benefit from well-made garments."

"Yes, Ma'am. It would be my pleasure to help others in need."

Mrs Gretsch pinched in her mouth and turned so that Mrs Chisholm could not see her face.

Mrs Gretsch struggled to maintain her practised artifice.

Mrs Chisholm had a kind heart. My hope for the future was restored. Mrs Gretsch, I still needed to deal with on a daily basis, but her power over me was destined to end. I purposed in myself then, to create a calendar and mark off the days.

That was day three out of four hundred and twenty-seven, plus a few in the following September. We were due to sail in a little over a year. I decided that I could survive the situation. My mother always told me that I was as resilient as I was charming. The trick was to retain my charm whilst succeeding in resilience.

"I am pleased to hear that, Isabelle. And thank you for sharing some of who you are as a person."

At that moment, Phillip entered the room, made an elegant bow and waited.

"Thank you, Phillip, for making haste with the packages and returning promptly. Have you met Isabelle yet?"

To my surprise, Phillip replied in the negative.

"No, Ma'am. I have not had the pleasure."

From Phillip's address to Mrs Chisholm, I gathered that Mrs Gretsch was the only one who demanded diminutive communication. Or perhaps I was the only one Mrs Gretsch demanded minimal communication from. A method of torture reserved for me.

"It is not such a large household, Phillip. How have you not met Isabelle yet?"

Mrs Chisholm noticed small details about her household without appearing to manage the lives of her servants.

"I believe that Isabelle may be engaged in duties away from the kitchen when the footmen take their breaks."

It was not accidental. It was by design. Mrs Gretsch minimised the opportunity for me to develop friendships. Phillip, as a member of the FCLS, was a potential ally. Mrs Chisholm looked thoughtful and glanced in the direction of Mrs Gretsch without directly looking at her.

"Very well, Phillip. I have a plan for you to accompany Isabelle to the education meetings at the FCLS. I am afraid that it is not safe for young ladies to be walking alone at night." Mrs Chisholm turned then to the housekeeper. "Mrs Gretsch, I would like you to arrange for Isabelle and Phillip to be free of household duties every Monday from five in the evening so they may prepare for the adventure that lays ahead."

"Yes, Mrs Chisholm. I will rearrange the work roster immediately."

Mrs Gretsch had obvious recoil at the idea but made an appearance of supporting the benevolence of her employer. I sensed that a 'pound of flesh' would be extracted later. I glanced at her eyes to see a cold malevolence. I glanced at Phillip to see fear emanating. Something I did not expect.

As it was Monday, Mrs Gretsch sent Phillip to find me at five o'clock. I only had time to drink a glass of water and don my walking boots. As we walked, Phillip passed me a small calico wrap. Inside I found a portion of bread, dried apple pieces and a cube of cheese.

"Mrs Shaw likes me as a match for her daughter, Bridget. She would not see me go hungry on an errand for the Mistress."

"Thank you for sharing. It is good to see that there is still some kindness in the world. Did you devour enough for yourself?" I offered with a smile. "I know my brothers can eat twenty times this amount and not feel the food touching the sides of their stomach."

"I will admit that I ate more than half. It is not an equal share, Isa. I hope you will forgive my gluttony. It was hard to stop and leave you any."

The comment was delivered with a lightness that suggested Phillip felt neither guilt nor regret. Evidently, Phillip felt confident that I would not resent him, the larger portion of a meal not meant for two.

We arrived at the building which housed the FCLS, as many others were also arriving. To my surprise, my Aunt Alison was waiting to greet me just inside the door.

"Oh, Isabelle!" Aunt Alison let out with a sigh. "Let me take a good look at you. What an awful experience."

Phillip's interest was ignited by my aunt's greeting, so I quickly tried to put out the flame. Truly, it was a losing battle. Mrs Gretsch had lit a taper and sent all the staff looking for chaff.

"I am well, Aunt Alison. I have put it behind me and plan to focus on making my future in a foreign land a good future."

"I am glad to hear that you sound enthusiastic, Isabelle. It is not what I expected. Your mother asked me to make sure you are faring well, as you were very grieved shortly before you left Ellesmere. I am glad that you will have an attitude to learn before you set sail. I missed you at church, so I had a chat with Caroline, and she assured me she would clear your tasks so that you would be free in the future."

What could I do, other than try to turn my situation to good? The option of staying in the employ of Mrs Chisholm long term was unthinkable with the atmosphere in the house. Counting down the days made it bearable.

"Tell me, Isabelle, have you met Mrs Chisholm yet?"

"Yes, Aunt, she seems like a sensible and generous Lady."

"Caroline has asked me to bring you to her for a conversation over supper. I hope that you agree it was the right thing for me to do when I accepted her invitation for you. I hope it will not be awkward, given that Mrs Chisholm is your employer. I know that you are smart enough to compartmentalise your life, Isabelle."

"I will do as you say, Aunt. Thinking of my life in two compartments will help me to manage what promises to be precarious circumstances. And I look forward to learning what I can from Mrs Chisholm before sailing. I liked her very much during our brief encounter."

Aunt Alison's concern was piqued by my mention of precarious circumstances. She did not let the matter drop.

"How do the circumstances seem precarious Isabelle? You have stated yourself that you believe Caroline to be reasonable and generous. You have made me curious. Please tell me if you have any concerns. Your mother has charged me with your care whilst you are in London, and I mean to take care of you as best I can."

"Oh, Aunt, Mrs Chisholm is a kind and generous lady, but it seems that I have taken a position that a favourite of the housekeeper was destined for. Mrs Gretsch is not happy to have me there. No matter how good Mrs Chisholm is, I fear that my life in her home will be difficult. I will persevere and do my best to fit in and not make waves. I cannot give up the position, though. I need to live somehow. The favoured Rose will only need to wait until we set sail."

"I'm sorry to hear that there are some difficulties. Perseverance is a good strength, and it seems this is your opportunity to grow in perseverance. Let me know if you think you are unsafe. I will step in and protect you. I am glad that you seem to be very mature about the difficulties in life. Sometimes we need to keep strong in the face of attack. Not fighting back and let our Heavenly Father fight the battle for us."

My only qualm, which I chose not to voice, was: How do you define unsafe? If the change in my personality was anything to go by, then the situation was unsafe. I did not believe myself in any danger of physical harm, so I concluded that my situation must be deemed safe.

"I'm not confident in my beliefs at this time, Aunt. I know that God saved me from the crowd on that horrible day. But how can his people behave so badly? Praising Angus and Lilith yet condemning me and treating me with continued suspicion."

"Remember that God loves his people despite their faults. We are all learning to be more like him. I think some people have the intelligence to learn more quickly than others. Be gentle with the slow learners, Isabelle. God is eternally merciful with us."

We walked toward the meeting room in silence for a few steps, each consumed in our own thoughts.

"I have arranged for you to have Sunday mornings off to attend church with me, Isabelle. It is a short walk from where you are, but I will pick you up and show you the way on the first Sunday. We will leave your home at seven in the morning. Come, let us find a seat where we can see the speaker."

Phillip had left me to converse with my aunt shortly after arriving. I saw him then on the other side of the room, talking to a young lady whose eyes glowed with admiration. However, he did not seem to be aware of the young lady's charm. His attention was not engaged. He continuously scanned the room for someone or something.

The speaker was entertaining. He told many stories about his time in the colony of New South Wales. It all sounded so alien that I was both apprehensive and excited at the same time. He inspired in me a desire for adventure, of which I had been previously unaware. I looked around the room to see fanciful sketches of creatures that could not possibly be true renderings. And a hue of green that was ancient in appearance.

I began to see my future as an adventure rather than an exile.

CHAPTER 5

Life in the FCLS

"Darkness cannot drive out darkness; only light can do that. Hate cannot drive out hate; only love can do that."

Martin Luther King, Jr[4]

August 1849, London

I With a heart lifted above the daily concerns that had beset me since my arrival in London, I made my way toward the refreshment table. Aunt Alison had excused herself and promised to return quickly. I was aware of the many strangers milling about. Some deep in conversation, some like me, making their way to the tea table. I

4 Galatians 5:16-26

could feel a buzz of enthusiasm and found that it lifted my soul. The happy excitement of the crowd, contagious.

As I reached to take a cup of tea from the pretty young lady serving, a stranger spoke from behind my left shoulder.

"Excuse me, Miss, I have seen you here a few times before and hope to offer a hand of friendship. My name is Chloe. Do you mind? I know it is a little bold of me, but I would like to meet as many of my fellow travellers as possible. I hope you do not mind?"

I turned to see the Botticelli Madonna, whom I had seen talking to Phillip the first time I attended a meeting. She looked at me with such enthusiasm in her offered friendship, I wondered if I had misread the interaction I had seen earlier. Was it possible she looked on all her acquaintances with an air of kind regard? After what happened to me; after the community turned on me; it was hard to trust that anyone could be genuinely kind.

Chloe had extraordinarily curly platinum blonde hair; a face oval and luminescent like a pearl; a button nose; and eyes of a most vibrant hazel with a hint of orange, a colour I had never before seen. No one could have resisted feeling affection for her. She had the plump face of a child that inspires protection and a roundness of figure that every man would return his gaze to, over and over. I was drawn to her. Her personality and her features. I felt fear bubble up inside and worked hard to remain polite.

"I do not mind." I sounded stiff to my own ears. "My name is Isabelle." I decided to echo Chloe's informal introduction and paste a smile on my face. I did need to make friends for my journey, regardless of my fears. "I saw you talking to Phillip earlier. Do you know him well?"

"I have been seeing Phillip at these meetings for the past three months. I hope we are growing a friendship that will last in the new colony."

I was surprised by Chloe's freedom in sharing information about herself. Another sign that I had become unwilling to trust in the goodness of others.

"And you, Isabelle, have you known Philip long? I have seen you arriving together."

"I have known Phillip for only a short while. I have taken up a position with Mrs Chisholm until my ship sails." I saw tension leave Chloe's shoulders and guessed that she was inspecting her competition.

"I'll admit, I am rather fond of Phillip. I hope we can become friends no matter which way the wind turns."

The young lady continued to shock me with her forthrightness. Did she not know that people cannot always be trusted - to be fair, nor to be merciful? Only a few months previous, I had been the same.

Vulnerable!

I felt a protectiveness rise in me. I did not want to see Chloe hurt in the way I had been hurt.

My aunt returned as we finished the introduction, and before we could become more acquainted.

"I am sorry, Isabelle; I was stopped to talk no less than three times on my way through the crowd. I told them all that I needed to retrieve my niece before starting a conversation. I am pleased to see that you have met Chloe."

"How are you, dear? Is your aunt well?"

"Yes, Mrs Lindsay, Aunt Gertrude is well today. She promised to be present at the meeting next week. My aunt wanted one more week to recover before venturing into the cold air."

"Isabelle, Mrs Chisholm is waiting to talk to us, so we will make our way to the north reading room before mingling."

My aunt turned to Chloe.

"It was so good of you to introduce yourself to Isabelle. Would you consider coming to tea one afternoon if I can arrange for Isabelle to visit?"

"I would be delighted, Mrs Lindsay." Chloe turned to me and gave me a radiant smile. "I look forward to us meeting again."

Chloe glided to another couple and began a conversation as I followed my aunt through the hall. My aunt and I made our way through the mingling people, toward a doorway with double doors made from Oak. The interior of the room was lined with shelves of books. There were twin lounges close to the window and a large, round Oak desk in the centre with five chairs placed around. The desk with ink wells in the centre gave off a scent of exotic ink made from port wine, and the beeswax polish used on the woodwork. The room was observably meant for communal study.

Mrs Chisholm was seated on one side of the desk, deep in discussion with a young lady. The conversation was intense. The voices were not raised, but their features were very animated. At first, I thought them to be disagreeing, but then I saw Mrs Chisholm nodding in approval and concluded that the young lady had been challenged in her knowledge and given a passionate reply. When Mrs Chisholm looked up and saw my aunt and me, she called a greeting and asked us to sit at the lounges. Mrs Chisholm then moved and settled on the lounges with us.

"I am so glad that you made it to today's meeting, Isabelle. I could see during the lecture that you became enthused." At the look of alarm on my face Mrs Chisholm nodded benevolently. "Yes, Isabelle, I did take a peek at your reaction a couple of times. I want to make sure that the people who undertake this journey are well prepared. Your Aunt Alison has explained the traumatic circumstances that led you to consider this adventure, so I was a little concerned that you were complying without any real interest."

That had certainly been the case before the evening's meeting. It was a good thing that the man speaking that night was dynamic.

"But I could see from your involvement with the speaker that you have been inspired. Your face became more radiant as the lecture progressed. I am so happy for you. This must be the future that God had in mind for you all along."

"Thank you, Mrs Chisholm, for your attention. Mr Foster was inspiring. What an interesting life he has had. I am now curious to see some of the things which he has described."

We sat and chatted for another ten minutes before the milling of people close by indicated to me that others wished to speak with Mrs Chisholm. Her conversation was much sought after. Aunt Alison had noticed also.

"Thank you very much, Caroline, for taking my niece into your home and being so generous with your attention. I see we are being a little greedy with the same tonight. May I call to see you during the week? I would very much like to have a longer catch-up."

"That would be lovely, Alison. I am hungry for some fellowship with an evangelical. I will be at home on Friday. Do you think you will be out calling on Friday?"

"I think Friday will be a good day for calling. I will see you then."

My aunt glided from the lounge, and I followed. We mingled for another hour before Phillip came to find me. I felt very weary and had considered hunting for him. We both had an extremely early start in the morning. Mrs Gretsch had complied with Mrs Chisholm's instructions about giving us time to attend the meeting. But Mrs Gretsch did not make it easy for us. We had both been assigned extra tasks '*to make up for our indolence*' on the Monday evening. Apparently, Tuesday before dawn was the only time those tasks could be fulfilled.

"Shall we be walking home now, Isa?"

My aunt looked at me quizzically, following the manner of Phillip's address. I shrugged my shoulders at her and suggested with my movements that we would talk about that later. I introduced Phillip to my aunt before we retreated, but we did not converse longer. We both wanted to be home asleep.

"You're an evangelical, then. I could not help but overhear your aunt talking to the curate Brown. It seems that we will not be attending the same church. I am given the Saturday evening to attend Mass. I'm told that someone needs to serve on Sunday morning, and I am one of the chosen."

"Yes, I have grown up in a non-conformist family. I was confirmed in my faith when I was twelve. But of late, I have been questioning many things."

"I would be thankful for the company if you ever choose to join me one Saturday for the Vigil. If you want to talk at any time, leave a linen plait tied to the bench under the almond tree, and I will find you. I know that Mrs Gretsch has made a decision to cause you grief. I cannot be seen as your friend, or I risk joining you in that place of pariah. I can see no advantage to either of us if that be the case. I hope you accept my offer of secret friendship."

I was desperate for friendship, yet I felt that something in his offer was amiss. Doesn't a true '*friend*' stand up for their friend? I could not fault Phillip, though. I longed for an ally, but his thinking was not flawed. There was no advantage to both of us being targets. I needed to be satisfied with a '*secret*' friendship. I was saddened, but I understood.

I was alone!

The days drifted together. Each one the same as the one before. I had to maintain an attitude of alertness to prevent falling into one of the many traps laid for me. The vindictive staff who continued to resent my intrusion into their plans did not give up. They knew that it was only for a time, as I would be departing on the *Slains Castle* in only twelve months.

But that made no difference.

They intended to torture me until the very end, regardless. I was always given many tasks on a Saturday so that others could visit family. A circumstance that left me no space to attend the Vigil Mass with Phillip. Maybe that was for the best. I knew my family would not understand me attending a papist service. Even so, I was curious to see the difference between our methods of devotion.

Sunday mornings and Monday evenings were a welcome release from the house, which felt so oppressive. The friendships I developed gave me the space to breathe. My aunt protected me from idle gossip at the FCLS meetings and in the small congregation of Evangelicals who attended the parish close to Mrs Chisholm's home. I overheard my aunt on many occasions claiming that my naturally curious spirit had led me to seek the adventure of travelling to the colonies. A curiosity enriched when I heard the FCLS advertised in Liverpool. She claimed that I had written and asked her to make the needed introductions. A small deviation from the absolute truth, and a slightly larger omission, for which I hoped she would be forgiven. I knew that her deception benefited me. God knew that I was innocent of the charges laid against me in my hometown. But I had learnt the hard way; mobs are guided by gossip and do not allow the truth to get in the way of a good story.

I jumped out of my skin when Mrs Chisholm tapped my shoulder one day.

"Isabelle, did you not hear me?"

In honesty, I had not. I was lost in reliving the day the mob had confronted me. I had a few silent tears slowly descending the crevices of my face. I did not lift my eyes to Mrs Chisholm because I hoped my tears would remain unseen.

"No, Mrs Chisholm, I did not. I missed what you said to me. What can I do to serve you?"

After a long pause in which I felt Mrs Chisholm study me quizzically, she gave me an instruction. That time I heard what was said, and how it was said. I feared that I would need to give an explanation.

"I would like you to bring me a pot of tea and two cups, please, Isabelle. And would you please ask Cook to include two slices of her cinnamon cake; it is a favourite of mine."

I cleared the tears off my face before I entered the kitchen. I could not allow the other staff to see my weakness. The ridicule would have destroyed my peace even further. I made haste to prepare the tray, but Mrs Gretsch pushed me away.

"Molly will take the tray in, Isa. You go back to cleaning the statues in the hall."

"Yes, Mrs Gretsch."

I kept my eyes down, backed away from the tray, and returned to the hall where Mrs Chisholm had found me. I could see from where I was that Mrs Chisholm was seated on a double lounge in the library. I feared that Mrs Chisholm's intent had been for me to serve the tea. I felt torn. I could not argue with Mrs Gretsch, nor could I boldly announce to Mrs Chisholm that the task had been taken from my care. I simply waited for the situation to unfold.

Molly made her way down the hall and entered the library with the tray. I heard her announce to Mrs Chisholm when she placed the tray on the functional table in front of the lounge.

"Please forgive the delay, Mrs Chisholm. Isa spoke that we needed to bring you a tray and then left quickly without telling of your exact location." After looking at the tray, Mrs Chisholm asked,

"Did Isabelle mention that I requested cinnamon cake with my tea?"

"Oh no, that she didn't, Mistress."

"Would you please find Isabelle and ask her to attend me, Molly. And bring me two slices of cake."

Molly left the room with a smirk on her face and approached me with joy.

"The Mrs wants to see ya, Isa." With a broad smile, Molly added, "Good luck." It was the malice behind the actions that hurt the most.

I approached the library with uncertainty. My fear had me expecting the irrational. Molly arrived with the cake as I stepped through the doorway with my head hanging. Her step more enthusiastic than mine, she arrived at Mrs Chisolm's side before me. Mrs Chisholm, however, showed no sign of irritation as I approached the table. She calmly asked me to serve. Molly shot me a resentful look as she passed to exit the room.

"Please pour two cups, Isabelle, close the door, and take a seat next to me." Her tone was gentle.

I did as I was asked, and wondered as I progressed through the actions: What could be coming next?

"As you are a special appointee to the position you hold, I have purposed not to interfere in Mrs Gretsch's management of your work, Isabelle. Are you upset by anything in the household?"

"No, Mrs Chisholm." I ventured as I looked up into her kind eyes for the first time that day. There was little to gain from informing Mrs Chisholm about the details regarding what transpired during my days of service.

"I am pleased to hear that, Isabelle. I know this is unorthodox, but I could easily see that you were upset. I know that you experienced a rough time in Ellesmere, and I wish to make sure you are adjusting well to your new circumstances. It is hard to go from being a skilled tradeswoman to a household servant. It is a season, remember, and will be different in the colony.

"Your aunt and I have received a request from a couple in Sydney Town to find for them a young lady who might consider being their apprentice. The Master is a tailor, and the Mistress is a dressmaker. They have been unable to have children and have asked me to help them. I met them in Sydney Town before I left and remember them to be God fearing and generous people. I was going to speak to you about this Monday next, but when I saw you so upset, I hoped to encourage you."

I remembered that my father had mentioned something like what Mrs Chisholm was saying, but that time was blurry in my mind. I was unsure how to feel. It could be a wonderful opportunity, or it could end in hardship beyond my imagination. I was both afraid and excited. My passion was for herbs and healing, but I knew in my heart the trade of apothecary was too dangerous for me. Dressmaking was a good living. A familiar occupation that I could enjoy.

"We discussed your dressmaking skills shortly after you arrived, Isabelle. I suggested that you may be willing to sew garments for some of the immigrants who will struggle to pay for their fares. Are you still willing to do this? I will provide the makings for the scheme. This could be a way to keep your skills practised. Mrs Gretsch could allocate time during the week for the project."

"Yes, Mrs Chisholm, I would be very thankful to be creating children's clothes."

"How are you coping with the transition, Isabelle? You were crying, I believe, so please don't try to tell me it was nothing."

"I..." I hesitated, not knowing how to describe my state of mind without sounding deranged. "I cannot help but remember sometimes, and I find I get lost in the memories. To the exclusion of things happening around me."

I did not tell even that generous lady that I found myself frozen in time, and sometimes shaking. I became a statue and held my breath when surprised. I woke up with my nightshirt soaked in perspiration, though I could not quite remember the dream.

"I will keep you in my prayers, Isabelle. Sometimes it takes time to find healing. Perhaps you would like to come to prayers with me on Wednesday mornings. I can have you assigned to be my attendant for chapel visits. I do not think Rachel will mind. Rachel does not seem to take joy from the experience. It will be an early start. I attend the convent and share morning prayers with the sisters. Their quiet devotion imbues my soul with a peace that I find nowhere else. You will not be expected to participate. Simply to sit quietly and soak in the atmosphere."

"I would be pleased to join you on Wednesday mornings, Mrs Chisholm." I hoped that my hopeful smile went some way toward reassuring Mrs Chisholm.

"I know you are not a Catholic. I hope the experience will not be confronting for you. I only hope to offer you some time soaking in God's presence."

"Thank you." I was genuinely relieved to be offered the chance to be away from the house. And curious about the style of the Convent's prayers.

"You can go back to your day, Isabelle, as soon as you have finished your tea and cake. Please return the tray to the kitchen on your way. I have some letters to write. Can I tell the couple in Sydney Town that you will join them as soon as the ship arrives? You will need to change to a small packet in Port Melbourne; the *Slains Castle* will travel on to Adelaide rather than make the journey up the coast of New South Wales. I have agents in Sydney Town who will make the introductions."

It all sounded daunting! But I nodded my head in affirmation of the plan.

I finished my tea and cake as quickly as was polite and cleared the tray. My spirits were lifted after that small amount of human connection. Mrs Chisholm was a wise woman. It is all I needed in that moment of sadness. I was able to finish my day without becoming lost in thought again.

CHAPTER 6

Grief's Sting

"Holy, holy, holy, is the Lord God Almighty, who was and is and is to come!"

Revelation 4:8 ESV

Holy, Holy, Holy, Lord, God of power and might. Heaven and earth are filled with your glory. Hosanna in the highest. Even in the dark of night, my song will rise to thee.

End of May 1849. Clinterty, Scotland.

G 'Twas a monumental task that had been given me. Tae convince the stubborn Scots, I called relatives, into following me tae a faraway land. A very, far-away land. 'Twould take us maybe five months under sail tae arrive. That was if all went well. I began reading. I called at the parish tae ask the good Father if he had any material about the colonies of New South Wales. Father Xavier was very helpful. Seemingly, he had been studying the Colonies in the Great South Land. He even suggested that he might travel with us if the bishop approved.

Doug proved tae be the most difficult tae encourage. He had no objection. He simply had no care. He had no enthusiasm for life. Everything was too hard. Doug was me closest friend, and I didnae wish tae travel without him. He needed the change more than I.

Doug selling the land was an essential part of the Laird's offer, but I wouldne have encouraged Doug tae give up his family lands if I didnae believe it would be the best thing for him. The laird's selfishness played into the hands of God.

I knew I would travel regardless of Doug's decision. I needed tae plan our contributions tae the fare that month and speak tae Mr Foster about how tae organise the weekly contributions and banking arrangements. He had spoken of it, but I wasnae paying any heed tae such details at the time.

I did all I could tae encourage me family tae be at the gathering. It was time then tae find out how many would join me. I closed up shop and made me way tae the Craigieburn. I thought tae be early and have a pint before standing up tae talk. It has been said that I have a compelling way about me when I speak, but that night I felt an impression of importance tae what I would be saying.

It was with enthusiasm I was greeted as I entered the tavern. The surprise I felt was most likely unjustified. Perhaps it was tae be expected that many wanted tae hear about the possibility of a better future.

Even though I hadnae said what we were tae discuss, many had spent time in conjecture. There were noticeable absences. Like me, Ma and Da. People who couldne ever consider leaving ancestral lands for another county, let alone leaving the highlands for another continent at the opposite end of the world. I knew me closest family wouldne join me in the venture. I also knew that when I sailed, it would be the last time we would see each other in this lifetime. The duplicity of me feelings was confusing. I was confident of me belief in the venture, but also reluctant tae leave me nearest family behind.

I looked around the room, curious about who would put their hand up tae join me. Those people were tae be me new family. The family God placed in me care. I felt a sense of responsibility, but rather than oppress me, it energised me. The words began tae flow.

"Thank ye all for joining me this evening. Would ye mind if I get a drop tae lubricate me tongue before we start? I was unaware of me lateness." Some laughed. The barmaid placed a pint in front of me. Evidently, I was in position.

"Thankee. I suppose I am tae begin then. Following the funeral of our beloved Molly and so many others, Father Xavier informed me that I would be visitin' him at the rectory."

There were more sniggers and some elbowing in the ribs around the room. We all shared a similar reaction tae being summoned tae the rectory. There were also a few suggestions about the purpose of me instruction.

"And wasn't it a hearty surprise tae discover we were called tae share lunch and listen tae the tales of a man who has journeyed across the world. This, Mr Foster, painted a picture of great benefits tae be gained from hard work and skills of living on the land. He described creatures that were unimaginable. Nobody owns the land, so it is there for the taking. The original inhabitants have done nothing tae cultivate the land nor shepherd the creatures.[5]

"The English have implemented policies that make life here, for so many of us, a struggle.

"There is a society in London who aim tae aid family groups of twelve tae travel, and tae build a new life."

Those who had come tae listen rumbled with disquiet at that statement. There was never a joy tae be had with allowing the English tae win at anything.

"'Tis nae right, nor is it fair, but it is what it is." I breathed in deeply before continuing.

"I have been reading since Father Xavier introduced Doug and me tae Mr Foster. I have been praying all day as I worked. It is me firm belief that this could be a good opportunity tae secure a future for those willing tae undertake the venture. 'Tis me belief that our Heavenly Father is leading me tae make this journey and wants me tae lead a group of family members who are also looking for new opportunities.

"I am excited about the venture and wanted tae introduce the idea tae ye all at once. I know that many of ye, like me Ma and Da, would never leave the highlands that inhabit our souls. I am speaking today tae those among ye who are looking for an adventure. An adventure that promises tae bless the industrious."

The silence lasted for a full half minute before the first person spoke.

---

[5] This is a representation of 19th century beliefs rather than a representation of the truth. The original inhabitants did cultivate the land as well as care for flora & fauna. They did these things in a way not recognised by the newcomers. The Irish and Scottish were also being pushed off their land, but the correlation was not seen.

"Well, I have tae say lad, of all the possible stories I speculated aboot for tonight's gathering, that wasnae one of them."

"Nooh Uncle Jimmy, I expect it has come as a surprise tae ye."

"Bloody oath, lad, you've never talked of belief in a calling from God before."

"That's the message ye picked up here tonight, Uncle?"

"Yer different, lad, since Molly's passing. Won't ye wait before making such a life changing move?"

"Nae, Uncle Tommy. 'Tis sure I am about this being the right move for me. Yes, I did struggle with God following Molly's passing. But I found a peace when it was done."

"Well then, I will leave it tae the young tae make such a journey."

It was then time tae allow private consideration of the scheme.

"Please contemplate what I've said, everyone. I'm confident that there will be enough tae make a group of twelve. Come see me in the shop this week if yer interested. I need tae give Father Xavier a comment on intention before a fortnight passes."

"Isn't it a penal colony, lad? People are sent there for punishment. I'm thinking it may be a punishing place tae be."

"Adventure of a lifetime? I'm thinking it may be a lifetime sentence. What if ye change yer mind?"

"'Tis true that it will nae be easy. From what I have heard, there is much tae gain."

At that point, the meeting dissolved into many close conversations, all expressing an opinion. It was a necessary part of the process, and I thought it best tae allow a natural conclusion. Those who were truly interested would come see me when others who might disagree were not watching.

I finished me pint, ordered another and a pie tae go with, then settled at a table with Doug.

"'Tis good tae see ye finally made it. I'm glad tae see that ye roused yerself sufficiently tae join us. Have ye eaten today, friend?" No response. "I'm concerned for ye, Doug. I want ye tae be strong enough for the journey."

"Who said I would be going? I work from before dawn till late into the evening. There isnae anyone tae cook. I am the only one left, Gareth. There is nae reason left tae live."

"All good reasons tae take up this new adventure, brother."

"Molly has passed away. We're nae brothers."

"Best friend then. Regardless of what ye say, ye will always feel like family. I want ye tae join this venture with me, Doug. I believe it will be the best for us both."

"Aye! But me pride rankles at the idea of giving that bastard what he wants. Handing it tae him is like serving me enemy a delicacy. He came by today and offered a mighty good price. A price that is nae inspired by good business sense. An offer that shouts he wants tae rid Scotlain of vermin. The truth that the highlanders belong here as the natural heirs tae the land is nae considered. It wounds me tae give way tae his prejudice."

"So, this adventure I believe God wants us tae undertake can be bankrolled by the enemy. Let's squeeze the man for all we can and leave his judgment tae God. He will be held tae account for his wrongdoing."

"I just cannae give up me anger, friend. I dinnae want tae give up me anger."

"'Tis hurting ye, Doug. I dinnae want tae let him win by seeing ye pass away neither. Seeing how the anger is hurting yer health, I'm beginnin' tae think that we're told tae forgive for our own benefit Doug; nae for the benefit of the one who harms us."

"Sounds easy, Gareth. Ye make it look easy. Too easy! Maybe ye didnae love Molly so well after all."

With that barb, which penetrated all the way through my heart, Doug pushed back his chair and left; leaving a trail of injured people with whom he collided as he raced for the door. I was hurt, but I was most distressed about the lack of nourishment. Doug had left the pie I ordered for him untouched. I looked around the room for the next hungry person that I could see. Aunty Meaghan looked my way, so I waved her to join me. The pie was split into two pieces and shared with me cousin, Adeline.

"Let him have his grief, his way. He will work through it in time, lad. I know he loves ye like a brother."

"Ye heard that then? Aye, Aunty, I know 'tis true. I hope and pray that his grief will work through quickly enough for this opportunity tae be nae lost. It will take a lot more saving without the endorsement of the Laird."

"We will find a way tae join yer group, Gareth. There is little for us here. If we fail in this venture and pass away, at least it will be in the pursuit of a solution tae our problems. I would hate tae wither away, complacently accepting what is being done tae us. We want tae keep fighting tae the end. Who knows but that this is what God wants us tae do?"

We finished our meal in comfortable silence as the room around us stormed with discussion. I was glad tae hear some snippets of approval for the plan. We only needed twelve. I felt confident that twelve would be found in the fortnight. It was Doug that I was uncertain of. It was for sure wrong that the Laird was pushing him hard during a time of grief. Opportunistic bastard that he was. I felt a sudden remorse for me attitude but didnae understand the cause. What was wrong with calling something what it was, after all? I was then, yet tae learn that the Holy Ghost invading me soul could lead me into a better path.

N Gareth expected to sleep well following the gathering of the family. Talking and reminiscing about family who had passed, and better days that had also passed, left him with a feeling of acceptance and belonging that soothed his grieving soul. When he found himself wide awake before the moon had fully risen, Gareth climbed from bed and paced the room.

When he heard his mother's quiet voice, he knew he was disturbing the household. He left the house through the kitchen door, putting his hand to restorative cheese as he passed the pantry. He would not be greedy, so took only a small portion. *'Just enough tae keep the cold from seeping through tae bone.'* There was something about the night air that made the cold penetrate in a way it did not in the day. The dark and damp combined made a warm night feel cold, no matter the layers of cloth. A time when everyone should be by the fire or in bed.

"I'm nae sure why it is that I am awake in the middle of the night, but if ye have something tae say tae me, Jesus, could ye make it quick. I was seriously enjoying me bed just now."

Gareth walked further from the house, so he had no need to whisper in the quiet of the night. He walked toward the trail that led to the peak. Hoping the exertion of scaling the goat track would tire him out.

"I'm sure nae settled about the grand plan for me life at this time in the night."

G As I walked, the doubts that filled me heart bubbled tae the fore. I wasnae a great person that I should dare tae encourage me family tae follow me into a life far, far away. What if I failed in the venture?

Me Ma and Da wouldne leave the home they knew for the uncertain future tae be found in a foreign land. The thought wouldne leave me alone. '*Was I leading desperate people tae their destruction?*

"What am I thinking?"

"You are thinking of obedience. You are not leading your family, I Am."

The voice was so clear I nearly turned tae see who was talking tae me. But I also ken the voice was nae audible. The voice spoke inside of me. I ken the voice even though it was a new experience for me. The authority was unmistakable.

"Oh, so 'tis yer doing that I'm awake in the middle o' the night. Ye know I am nae good enough for this venture. Me Molly has passed; nae doubt I have sinned in some grievous way. I cannae take the burden of others' passing because of me own sinfulness. Maybe if Father Xavier joins us tae keep us on the straight and narrow. For the spiritual guidance that we will surely need. Then maybe others needn't pass over before their time."

"Fret not, Gareth. Your sins have been forgiven. I see you as a son without blemish. Be good for the benefit of your family and yourself. My promises will flow from your obedience. Your goodness will not determine who will be with me today and who will live for another hundred years."

"Sure, and who will wear the blame if things dinnae go well for those who travel with me? Can the responsibility nae be shared, Father? 'Tis a small thing tae ask for."

"I love you, Gareth. I am calling you to a new life. I want you to lead your family to a new place where I promise your life will prosper."

"'Tis such a long way, Father. And no way tae return if things fail."

"I keep my promises!"

"Sure, and for certain. That is the truth."

"Follow the Holy Spirit to the great southern land. I will not take away the free will of the lords who neglect and abuse your people. I will give you help and encouragement as you travel and build a new home."

"And Father Xavier?"

There wasnae an answer tae the last. God had finished speaking tae me. I was tae be satisfied with his promise. Logically, it was a big promise. I admitted that much tae meself and continued tae speak.

"And I will be holding ye tae that promise, Lord."

I kept scaling the craggy peak as I contemplated the conversation I had had with the almighty. *'For sure, and if I tell everyone about that conversation, I may find nae one wanting tae follow the mad man.'*

"Should I be tellin', or should I be keeping our conversation tae meself?"

I received nae answer! I was tae decide that for meself. Me conviction about travelling tae the southern land was firm. I felt me soul settle into peace as I accepted the path I would take. All I could do then was pray. As I stood on the summit, I offered up praise.

"Holy, Holy, Holy Lord. God of power and might. Even in the dark of night, my song will rise to thee."

I sang aloud with only the creatures of the night tae listen. I knew I would be finding the chapel in the coming week, so that I might light a candle for each one of the eleven companions who would travel with me.[6]

The walk down took less time than the ascent.

I found solid sleep as soon as the covers settled.

I woke surprisingly refreshed and ready for the week tae come. Ma noticed the missing cheese but offered no other comment about me journey into the dark of night.

"Would you take a hamper of food over tae Doug for me before making your way tae the workshop? 'Tis hard enough keeping the farm going on his own without having tae cook as well."

"For sure, Ma. I'm nae sure how much he will eat, but I know that if food is nae put under his nose, he will eat nothing. I couldne tempt him with a pie from Craigieburn yesterday. And that's saying somethin'."

I hurried me own breakfast: Scant as it was, it was over in three mouthfuls. I was glad for the opportunity tae speak further with Doug. I hadnae any idea what tae say, but I aimed tae keep trying. When I approached the farm, I couldne see smoke rising from the chimney. I could see nae sign of life. I began tae fret again until I remembered the walk during the night. There would be nae good

---

6 The lighting of the candle is a symbol of the faith with which we ask for God's help. We light a candle as we invite the Lord's presence into what we are praying for. The presence of God brings light. "Your kingdom come, your will be done, on earth as it is in heaven." Matthew 6:10 ESV

result from me fretting. I determined again tae visit the chapel at the first opportunity, so that I could pray and light the candles.

At that moment, Doug materialised beside me. "Oh, Hi. I didnae see ye on me approach. Where were ye?"

"The persecutor has just been. I've sold me soul and needed tae walk. I'll be joining ye on yer adventure. I've had nae sleep for three days, struggling over the right thing tae do. I have finally realised that I need tae do the best thing for me. I cannae live here with the memories. Hate for the usurper whose greed led tae the demise of me family is eating me alive. I need tae put some distance between meself and the memories. Maybe if I can forget, I willnae be filled with so much hate.

"I've just sold the farm tae Lord Ashley. Made him pay twice the value plus half the fare for twelve, and he still feels like he won. Bastard!" After a short pause, Doug looked me in the eye with nae thought of looking back. "When do we leave?"

"Ma sent ye some food. Will ye eat now? 'Twill spite him if ye grow strong."

"I am suddenly famished."

CHAPTER 7

An Introduction

"Be subject for the Lord's sake to every human institution, whether it be to the emperor as supreme, or to governors as sent by him to punish those who do evil and to praise those who do good. For this is the will of God, that by doing good you should put to silence the ignorance of foolish people. Live as people who are free, not using your freedom as a cover-up for evil, but living as servants of God. Honor everyone. Love the brotherhood. Fear God. Honor the emperor. Servants, be subject to your masters with all respect, not only to the good and gentle but also to the unjust. For this is a gracious thing, when, mindful of God, one endures sorrows while suffering unjustly."

1 Peter 2:13-19 ESV

November 1849, London

Three months had gone by, and I was finding it difficult to remember that there was a new life waiting for me at the end of the tunnel. I was in a bad mood more often than I was not. The grind of constant disfavour with the people in my daily life wore me down. I lived for the opportunity to breathe that came with every Monday. I had not found companionship in the church where I attended with my aunt. Maybe my fears got in the way. The service reminded me of home, and I found myself reluctant to share. Phillip and Chloe, on Monday evenings, were a balm to my wounded soul. Chloe's indomitable generosity of spirit refused to give way to my fear.

I had many a talk with Chloe about the need to be guarded, but she smiled and informed me that I would heal eventually, and then I would understand. It made no sense to me. I had told her naught about my past. But she persisted with her assertions. She seemed to see more in me than I had revealed. Something that would have made me uncomfortable if it had been from anyone else. I have come to understand that there was no need to warn Chloe about the evil of others. She was fully aware. She simply chose to overcome the knowledge. I longed to find out from her how it was done. My ongoing bad moods were evidence that I had not achieved the peace that Chloe had found.

A sound penetrated my cloud of self-musings. Heavy footsteps sounded in the corridor outside the room I was fixing for the imminent arrival of a guest. I needed to take control of myself, or I would be ensnared by one of the deadly duo's schemes. After four months, you would think that I could have maintained a state of alertness. Phillip's voice could be heard with more volume than was absolutely necessary. He was alerting me on purpose. Thanking him silently, I paid closer attention to what was happening outside the room where I was just finishing with the bed. The mantel was heavy to manage, but I found work went more smoothly if I worked alone.

"Psst…She's nearly done in the east room. Hurry!"

"D' 'and is tight. There, done!"

As I left the room, the clock at the end of the corridor chimed a quiet nine times. I cheered to know that I travelled through my work with record speed. Or so I thought. I took the old linens to the chute and decided to get a jump start on the next room before heading downstairs for brunch. There were to be guests for lunch, so I hoped to satisfy my grumbling insides before helping to convey the midday meal. When I arrived in the kitchen, I realised what the murmurings had been about. The servants' refreshments were finished, and I had missed the meal. It all seemed so petty. I despaired of them ever quitting. I told myself it would be only ten more months. I reminded myself that I had resilience. That was one of the days I did not feel like I had perseverance.

Phillip approached and talked to me in front of all the staff. His face hidden from their view freed him to give a sympathetic look as he delivered a message in a tone laced with long suffering. The long-suffering of having to work with me.

"The mistress would like you to serve in the dining room, so best hurry and change into a clean dress."

The room went silent. Only for a few seconds, but the message was clear. No one was happy about the development. I heard the room explode in conjecture as I hurried away to change my apron and seek some peace of mind. I felt like nothing good would come from the change in allocation. I was puzzled. Why would the mistress want me serving the guests?

It was not a fancy dinner. The mistress had purposely dressed in her plainest day dress. The meal was more hearty than extravagant. When the guests arrived, I saw the purpose of the tableware and dress. The guests were country farmers. Not poor farmers, but farmers, nonetheless. The clothes indicated that their farm produced well, and the roundness of their cheeks suggested that they were rarely left wanting. They were unusual guests. Not a social visit, then. My curiosity emerged. A trait usually reserved for the FCLS meetings.

With the reminder of the FCLS meetings, I felt my internal perspective change. I relaxed and became focused, without trepidation for the things transpiring around me. As the meal concluded, Mrs Chisholm turned to me and instructed me to join her in the library.

The staff paused for a heartbeat, then continued with their tasks.

I waited for Mrs Chisholm and her guests to vacate the room, then followed slowly, but not before seeing the sneer of disdain on the faces of my peers. Each time my separation from the normal was proclaimed by some small difference, I was made to pay a price. I knew it would come. The anticipation of their machinations enhanced the outcome they wished to achieve.

I entered the library to find Mrs Chisholm and her guests seated at the round reading table in the centre of the room. The business end of the lunch seemed to be about me.

"Come and sit with us, Isabelle." I approached the table and drew out the remaining chair. When I was seated, Mrs Chisholm continued. "This is Mr and Mrs Hill."

"It is a pleasure to meet you both." My mother's lessons returned swiftly. I compartmentalised and forgot that I was seated in the library with my mistress. I was transported to another space and adopted the persona of Isabelle, the dressmaker's daughter.

At that moment, Molly arrived with tea and cinnamon cake. I felt the malice and was momentarily shaken. But Molly would not dare to display her malice in front of the mistress, so I reframed my focus and compartmentalised.

"Do you remember that I spoke to you about a family that wanted a surrogate daughter for the journey to New South Wales? Normally, I would have arranged this introduction at the rooms of the FCLS, but Mr and Mrs Hill are farmers who live outside of town. They have been unable to be here on a Monday evening. Their sons…"

Molly's ears pricked up at that, and Mrs Chisholm took notice. Thankfully, she also decided that it was not ideal for my workmates to be listening in on the conversation.

"Thank you, Molly. I will pour the rest of the tea. You may return to other occupations. Please ask Mrs Gretsch to ensure that we are not disturbed for an hour."

My joy at reprieve was to be short-lived. I was torn. I felt joy at Molly leaving and fear of Mrs Gretsch's retaliation. When the door closed behind Molly's retreating form, I reminded myself again to compartmentalise. Saying to myself, *'I am Isabelle, the dressmaker's daughter.'* Mrs Chisholm went on.

"Their sons, William, Daniel, and Gerard, are managing the farm whilst their parents travel to meet you. Do you remember me telling you that the youngest, a daughter, passed away in the winter of '47 from the morbid throat? I think Isabelle, that you may be able to relate to Mrs Hill on this, as your brother Gregory passed away in a similar way."

The Hills had been studying me intently throughout the introduction, but at the mention of their daughter, their eyes misted over.

A silent drop formed a track down the side of Mrs Hill's face, and her lips quivered. Mr Hill was the first of the couple to speak to me.

"It is a pleasure to meet you, Isabelle. We have been told much about you. You understand we asked for the information not to invade, merely to ensure we would be able to offer a safe passage for you and a comfortable one for our family.

"This is an adventurous endeavour on which we plan to embark. Your aunt has told of your troubles in Ellesmere Port and also the information she has shared with most of the travellers. You will be safe with us, Isabelle. We do not hold with the superstitions that many do."

I was a little lost with what to say, but I knew I needed to say something. It was my turn to have a droplet travelling down my face. It surprised me, as I had stopped tearing up every time I thought of the events that took me from home. Maybe it was the compassion that I saw in his eyes. Maybe it was the slowly drying tear on Mrs Hill's face. Evidently, we all had a reason to run. I cleared my throat and chose to be brave.

"Thank you, Mr Hill. I am grateful that you are willing to invite a stranger into your family for the journey." Mrs Hill looked at me suddenly.

"Oh dear, please forgive me for becoming emotional. It has been more than a year since Aggie passed, but I am having difficulty moving ahead in life. Aggie was my only daughter, and I miss her terribly. It will be for my benefit that I ask you to travel with us. Do you think you could manage being my companion for the trip?"

I looked into Mrs Hill's eyes and searched her heart. I saw a kind lady who could not be much trouble to me.

"Yes, Mrs Hill. I can see my way to being a true companion to you for the voyage."

I made the statement as a promise. I had little choice anyway. My alternative options were few and mostly unpleasant. We then spent an hour getting to know each other with questions and answers both ways.

At the end of that first hour, it was decided that we could not gain enough insight into each other in just one hour. So, with Mrs Chisholm's help, we arranged for me to spend a few days at the farm. I was both excited and anxious about the prospect. Excited to be away from Mrs Gretsch and anxious about being vulnerable in a strange place.

So unlike, the Isabelle of Ellesmere Port.

CHAPTER 8

A Trip to the Country

"This Book of the Law shall not depart from your mouth, but you shall meditate on it day and night, so that you may be careful to do according to all that is written in it. For then you will make your way prosperous, and then you will have good success. Have I not commanded you? Be strong and courageous. Do not be frightened, and do not be dismayed, for the LORD your God is with you wherever you go."

Joshua 1:8-9 ESV

Late November 1849. Wembley

The day of my trip to the farm arrived with little fanfare. Mrs Gretsch was not pleased, but she did not begin any new tortures.

Perhaps she viewed the visit as a sign that I would be leaving soon. Whatever the reason, I was glad to be spared more agonies. The wagon was hitched, and my carpet bag loaded. Mrs Chisholm selected Phillip to be my coachman for the day. It was good for Phillip to meet fellow travellers also. I was uncertain who to thank. As things fell into place, I asked myself. *Was it God's design to place friends around me to protect me on the voyage? Or was the clever design instigated by Mrs Chisholm alone?* Then I grasped God's focus on relationship. Mrs Chisholm was a Godly woman, so her actions, always influenced by the Holy Spirit, were God's way of providing for me.

It was a day full of a promise to be pleasant. The sun was shining as we drove through the countryside. The leaves had turned to a kaleidoscope of amber and red. The fragrance of ripe grains wafted across our path sporadically. The fluffy white clouds moved above us without bringing more shade than we liked. I anticipated an amiable conversation between Phillip and me. A conversation not restrained by the possibility of being overheard.

"I apologise for my appearance of forbearance as we left the house. I did not wish to spoil today's outing by shifting the status quo in the house. I believe it is still best to give the appearance that we are not friends."

This hurt as usual, but I understood. A small part of me believed that Phillip adopted his approach more for his benefit than mine. Still, I understood.

"I forgive you again and always for the deception, Phillip. Let us enjoy the time we have to speak freely and put aside all thought of the household. I remind myself that it is not a personal dislike of me that they display. They were blocked in achieving a goal and act out of their resentment."

"For sure, and what topic should we discuss? The unusual fauna of the land to which we travel? I must admit, Isa, I am excited. Everything I read increases my curiosity."

"No, the creatures all seem so fanciful, I don't know where to start such a conversation."

"What then can we discuss?"

"I would like to discuss what we can expect from the people we are to travel with."

"It is gossip you are wanting, then. So, Isa shows a fault after all."

"Hush, I have many faults. Do not speak that I believe myself to be perfect."

"I was teasing Isa. You can see that. Yes? You must admit, though, you do everything so well that the others in the house suspect you to be arrant and so resent you all the more. It may not hurt to show them some mishap so that they can focus on that rather than thinking of ways to torture you."

"That is precisely why I do not show mishaps. I work extremely hard to make no mistake. I aim to avoid giving them ammunition. I thought we agreed to not discuss the household. I want a day of sweet relief."

"I meant only that if you show some weakness, they may grow sympathy rather than use it against you. People can be strange creatures. Of course, it is a risk that they would be incapable of growing sympathy for you. But what would you lose? Has giving them no ammunition worked for you? They use your *perfection* as ammunition."

Phillip stopped talking and studied the lane for a few minutes. I suspect he noticed my growing unhappiness and decided to converse on subjects that would return a smile to my face.

"The people we will be visiting with; are they to be your family unit then?"

I sighed and tried to regain my calm.

"Indeed, they are. They seem upright and are willing to extend grace."

Phillip's raised brows and intense eyes indicated to me that I had said too much. I went on quickly to avoid his question.

"I am to be a companion for the mother. Her only daughter passed away a year ago. I know what it is like to lose a child when they are young. Mrs Chisholm thinks that we will be able to understand each other."

Realising the ambiguity of my statement, I rushed forward trying to fix my mistake. I did not need Phillip to begin conjuring up explanations for the things I said. In my attempt to keep my life a secret, I had made some very misleading statements.

"I think I must tell you something of my life to avoid misinterpretation of my words."

"That may be beneficial. But think before you reveal things to me. I know that I am trustworthy. But Isa, ask, will you continually suspect me of telling others what you revealed?"

I thought on the possibility for a few minutes. I felt the need to speak freely with another person with whom I was journeying through life.

But!

Phillip denied me as a friend to all others in that life. Could he be trusted? When we were alone and when at the FCLS, he spoke to me, and of me, as a friend. So, not all others. My head hurt from contemplating the dilemma. I tried to force understanding and found no answer. In the fog, I surrendered and followed my heart. I hoped it was not another mistake.

But wait!

When did I start thinking of my life as a series of mistakes? I did not make a mistake that led me onto that path. It was imposed upon me by another. A jealous and uncaring person who did not consider the consequences that her actions had upon another. Or did not care.

Decision made!

I spoke for half an hour, telling Phillip about what had happened. For better or worse, the information was no longer mine alone. I hoped that he understood. I hoped that he was a rational man who denied superstition. But of course, Phillip's character was so steady, he would not give in to superstition.

Tears ran freely down my face as I described the hurt of Angus' betrayal. The grief of leaving all the people closest to me behind. At the end, I was empty. But also, a little refreshed. The retelling was good for me, I think.

After a time of plodding along in silence, where I suspect Phillip processed the information and came to a judgement of the story, he spoke to me in a gentle voice. The gentleness was perceptively genuine. My fear abated as I came to understand that blurting my story was not such a grave mistake.

"To be honest, none of the conjectures came close to the truth."

Another few minutes passed as I listened and marvelled at the birds we saw along the way.

"So, you know some of the healing arts then, young Isa. Will you tend my aunty sometime when you return? No! That may lead to giving your story away."

"You could give me your aunty's history. I may be able to recommend some tea. Would that help?" Phillip nodded his approval before we returned to some friendly banter and turned the conversation to the FCLS.

"What do you think of Chloe?"

Finally!

Phillip brought up the subject of Chloe. How long had he been trying to bring the conversation around to Chloe?

"It is my turn to reveal something of my heart. You may have noticed that I have been forming an attachment for Chloe. But I see no evidence that she has more interest in me than she has in every other person with whom we are to travel."

"Is this true?" I could not hide my smile as I prepared to tease Phillip. How could he not see that Chloe had him in her sights for a husband?

"You make jest of me."

"To be honest, I have seen no special regard coming from you toward Chloe. If you fancy her, then show her. A girl cannot reveal her heart before a man shows interest. He would run for cover or take advantage of her. It is a sad way to view things, but I have oft seen it happen. Take the risk of injury and speak with her. If Chloe has no interest, she will in the least be gentle as is her habit."

"Why cannot a girl be the first to reveal her heart?"

"Because, as I have seen, men are inclined to enjoy the challenge of winning something against the odds. If it is won before the race begins, the interest wanes."

The creases between Phillip's brows suggested to me that he had not previously contemplated the thought.

"That observation may be valid. I will need to think on the possibility some more. But you suggest that a wife is a prize to be won. How is she my helper if she is a prize for me to win, and so a possession for me to hold?"

What a thought! I had not previously contemplated his argument.

"Indeed, on that, I will need to spend time in thought. I have often seen men run for cover or take advantage of a woman who reveals her heart first. My thought is cynical, but also easily observable, often enough."

The remainder of the trip, we spent in conversation about the strengths of our FCLS companions. It was good to think about how we would be able to help each other in the mysterious place to which we would travel.

We arrived at the Hill's farm midmorning and were ushered into the parlour for tea and cake. It was new to be out visiting. Mr Hill and their three sons took time out from their daily schedule to join us for tea. The eldest, William, was a young man of fifteen, Daniel still an awkward teenager at thirteen, and the youngest, Gerard, a timid twelve-year-old.

I looked around the room to gain insight into the family I was to travel with. There were small paintings hung haphazardly on the walls. A few portraits, a landscape or two, and one or two very good paintings of birds. My eye settled on a portrait of a young girl with very dark hair, snowy white complexion, rosebud pink lips and vibrant blue eyes.

"That is my daughter Aggie," Mrs Hill offered in a soft voice.

"She is stunningly beautiful, Mrs Hill. The world is worse off for the loss of such a friendly face." A few moments of silence followed my comment. Everyone with an opinion, but none willing to go further into the conversation.

"The other paintings you see scattered around are my way of finding solace when things feel hard."

"That must explain why there is none of you." My observation brought a smile to Mrs Hill's face, and I saw a mother with a gentle heart. "I very much like the paintings of birds. Are they birds you see on the farm?"

"Yes, Isabelle, I enjoy walking in the meadow by the stream. Aggie and I would collect flowers and berries there on Sunday afternoons. I enjoy making my own tints for watercolour. Perhaps we could take a walk there this afternoon before we cook the evening meal."

I was thrilled at the prospect of learning how to make the tints, so responded with a huge smile. I saw Phillip glance my way and smile at my smile.

"Superb! We will plan a simple meal so that we can spend some time there."

Mrs Hill, then, was the cook for the household. It felt a little like home. Mr Hill took the conversation in another direction after closely observing Phillip whilst Mrs Hill and I made plans.

"Do you plan to travel to the colonies, Mr Manning?"

"Yes, I hope to be travelling on the same ship as Isabelle, it being the first ship to leave. I am certain that Mrs Chisholm selected me to accompany Isabelle today so that I might also be acquainted with fellow travellers. I am still looking for a family unit to which I may attach myself. A family needing to make up numbers to satisfy the FCLS."

"Are you fond of Isabelle then? It will be our responsibility to care for Isabelle during the journey. I understand that she will then be adopted into the household of a couple in Sydney town."

"That is a fast leap, Mr Hill. What gave you the impression that I was fond of Isa? We are friends, but my heart is drawn toward another."

"It was a look of fondness that you displayed when Isabelle smiled. It is good to know we will not need to be chaperoning during the journey. It would add another complexity."

"Isa and I both work for Mrs Chisholm and so spend some time in each other's company. Isa is becoming fast friends with the girl I have taken a liking to." My comment on the topic settled the matter.

"In truth, I do not think I could fall in love with another. I am aware now that Angus was inconstant, but it will take my heart longer to recover. I both grieve the loss and find myself angry with him. It will be hard to trust in someone being faithful to me. I am certain I could not look at another for a very long time."

"You say, Mr Manning, that you are looking for a family to travel with. We have recently had a young couple pull out of the venture. The young lady, when faced with leaving her mother behind forever, would not bring herself to leave." A sentiment I understood well. "Would you like to join with us on the journey?"

"And if I can convince Chloe to wed me, will there be space for her also?"

And the pieces all fell into place.

God was creating a ring of friends around me. But still, I was angry that the deliberate evil of others resulted in my being required to leave my family behind forever.

Following lunch, Mr Hill and his sons left us so they could put in a few hours of labour before sunset. For a farmer, there was always more work to be done.

Phillip wished me well and promised to retrieve me two days hence.

I felt a pervading peace in the Hill's home. A peace that I wished to enter; a peace of which I was also a little afraid, and so, resisted.

I felt restless, but I could not discern why. The Hills were all very accepting of me, and the boys included me like I had been their older sister all along. It was like a haven.

However, the haven also made me uncomfortable. I only had a vague awareness that I waited for the next disaster to happen.

That afternoon, Mrs Hill and I spent a few hours foraging for berries to press for pigment and scraping rocks for colourful sediment.

"How do we make green, Mrs Hill?"

"I would like you to call me Aunty Bev if that suits you. My nieces call me Aunty Bev. I think the title will establish a feel for family and discourage the boys from forming any unwanted attachment. We will be travelling in close quarters for several months. The familiar title will encourage appropriate closeness between us, I think.

"But to answer your question, there are some tints that I purchase. There is an emerald green tint made from copper that is not expensive. I am hoping that my order will arrive before we travel."

"Perhaps, Aunty Bev, we will need some blue also for a depiction from the bow of the ship." Mrs Hill smiled at me, taking on an enthusiasm for her activity.

"We will do well together, Isabelle. I noticed that Mr Manning called you Isa, do you prefer that name?"

"No. It is a name imposed upon me by an unfriendly housekeeper. My family call me Issy when they are feeling affection. Isabelle, when it suits them. I am happy to be named either."

After collecting some ingredients for the making of paints, we returned to prepare the evening meal. It was good to be in the kitchen creating smells that tantalised the palate. I have always enjoyed aromatic cooking. Mam insisted that I make the meal look good also, '*because some people are attracted by the vision more than the smell.*' I loved my Granda's shop because of the smell waiting to be identified as I lifted a lid on a jar. Well, maybe that was one reason. I also liked to see sick people made healthy. After washing the cooking equipment, Mrs Hill showed me a recipe for making homemade watercolour blocks.

"I do not use these when painting a portrait. These are for the many paintings of birds I produce to overcome the vapours. Perhaps on the ship, we will keep ourselves amused by painting what we see."

The men of the family spent their evenings planning the journey and discussing what seeds they thought best to transport with them to New South Wales. Mr Hill also nurtured cuttings from his best fruit trees in the hope of growing familiar food on their new property, which was to be located southwest of Sydney Town. I hoped that their venture was successful. The produce consumed around the dining table was very much to my liking. According to Mr Hill, the country on the southern slopes was thought to have a climate suitable for apricots and cherries. It was a pleasure listening to the plans.

The last evening, I was on the farm, the conversation turned toward the people travelling in the Hill's family group. There was to be another family of four, who were first cousins to Mr Hill. Their children, twelve and twelve. A 'pigeon pair' born in the same year, ten months apart. The other Mrs Hill had lost four other children in infancy. Such a tragedy. My heart ached for the family.

There is too much tragedy in life.

Nana always told me to look for the good and put my attention on that. At the time, I had forgotten the practice. I lived in the land of evil dramas all around. I shook my head and decided to listen to the voice of Nana speaking inside.

When Phillip arrived to retrieve me, I was feeling hopeful for the journey ahead. I could enjoy Mrs Hill's company. And I thought that working alongside her to care for the family would be a task that was appreciated. In all, I once again began to look forward to the journey with some enthusiasm for adventure.

CHAPTER 9

Chloe

"Bear one another's burdens, and so fulfill the law of Christ. For if anyone thinks he is something, when he is nothing, he deceives himself. But let each one test his own work, and then his reason to boast will be in himself alone and not in his neighbour. For each will have to bear his own load."

Galatians 6:2-5 ESV

Early December 1849, London

I One Monday early in December, as the temperatures plummeted toward a cold Christmas, Phillip and I arrived at the FCLS meeting to a fervent greeting from a distraught Chloe. I ushered

Chloe toward a secluded corner so that we could find out the why for her loss of composure.

"Calm yourself, Chloe, and tell us what is wrong."

Chloe glanced at Phillip and hiccoughed. Looked into her lap for a solid minute, then gave a small nod. Seemingly, Chloe had decided not to send Phillip away. I hoped that was a wise decision. But then, if they were to marry, Phillip would need to know the family secrets. Then I wondered if that was even true. Do we need to reveal our all? Maybe some things are better left in the past. Although apparently, this drama was well and truly in the present. I told myself to stop vacillating and listen.

A letter had been received informing Chloe's aunt that her uncle, who had been away for an extended voyage, would be returning home earlier than expected. Chloe had thought she would leave for the colonies before he returned. The letter said that Chloe's uncle would be home in less than three months. What was not yet clear was why this was a drama. The information came out slowly, with much hesitation from Chloe and determined quiet from me.

Phillip shuffled his weight from foot to foot and looked like he might bolt at any moment. In a breathy voice barely above a whisper, Chloe revealed the unexpected.

"I….my…uncle began to visit my room after I had retired for the night. … Maybe a month before he set sail last June. At first, he said he wanted to talk to a friendly soul. I was uncomfortable. He said that my aunt was already asleep, and he did not want to bother her."

I was surprised the situation had not made Chloe mistrust friendly people. Phillip's attention was fixed, his discomfort evident.

He looked like he did not know what to say. His fists clenched at his side.

"I did not want to appear ungrateful that he had allowed me to live under his roof when my mother and father died in an accident at the railway station. I tried to talk to my aunt, but I could not make her understand me. At first, he only demanded conversation. But slowly, he began to sit on my bed. Then to lie next to me. I tried to remain dressed and reading at my table until he would surely be in bed, but he always seemed to know when I had given up and retired for the night. He began to touch me and told me that he loved me more than my aunt because I would listen to him. I was too afraid not to listen."

There were, by then, silent tears rolling down Chloe's face. I passed her a handkerchief so that she might not have drops splattered on her poplin gown. I wanted to protect Chloe from gossip as much as possible. I was very thankful that no one had wandered close enough to overhear the story. Phillip's demeanour had turned dark. It was hard to know what conclusions he was drawing and with whom he was angry. For certain, he was angry.

"I begged a friend to let me visit, telling her that I wanted to allow my aunt to have my uncle's undivided attention for the weeks remaining before he set sail. I went to the docks to wave goodbye and then returned to live with my aunt. I felt betrayed. She had failed to protect me. It was as if she could not cope with knowing something ugly could happen between her husband and her niece. But I loved my aunt, and I loved spending time with her, doing the things we both love to do. We have much in common.

"I escaped from my uncle's home before I was ruined forever. But I am terrified of living under the same roof with him ever again.

I thought I had planned a method of escaping a dreadful future if I could leave for the colonies before he returned. His voyage was planned to be eighteen months. I expected to sail on the first FCLS ship, which is due to leave port three months before he was due to return. Now what am I to do?"

The Drysdale kicked and landed the blow with force enough to make me want to vomit. Hearing Chloe's rendition of trauma left us speechless. Phillip and I were silent for a full minute whilst we assimilated the new information with the Chloe we knew and loved. I suppose Phillip had more to consider than I. After all, he was planning to marry Chloe. A young lady whom he just learnt had been emotionally wounded by the man who was meant to protect her. A tough pill to swallow. Phillip walked away. Chloe watched him leave, then looked at me with renewed grief. Quickly, I absorbed what Chloe had revealed. I was uncomfortable. I felt lost to know what advice would help.

"I guess I can only expect Phillip to see me as damaged goods. I suppose there is little hope we will wed now. I have agonised over the need to tell him, but nothing happened beyond touching outside my clothing. I do not believe it will stop me from enjoying the touch of a loving husband."

"Phillip himself caused me to consider this month. Are we possessions that we could be considered goods? Damaged or otherwise? Wait, give him time. You will see that he is a better man than that."

"He has shown no special interest in me before. I do not see that I have progressed my cause."

"So, are you telling me then that you have set your sights on Phillip? You have not said as much previously? Has he not spoken to you yet?"

The tears stopped rolling down Chloe's face. There was barely a trace of distress visible on her face. She looked resigned and a little exhausted. My Aunt Alison walked toward us with a smile of greeting and paused when she saw Chloe's usually bubbly self, looking subdued. I wanted to tell Chloe that she had naught to fear. Phillip was looking to marry her, and that all would be well soon. He would digest this information, and his love would overcome. But in truth, I was not certain. It was hard to predict how someone would react to bad news. I simply did not know Phillip well enough to predict his response. I thought I had known Angus, and yet he had responded in a way that I did not foresee. People did what they did! Often with little rational consideration.

My faith in the male gender eroded a little more. I thought Chloe's story more debilitating than mine, and yet, until then, Chloe had shown nothing but acceptance and trust of the people around her. I thought, perhaps, she had mastered the game of compartmentalisation better than I.

My Aunt Alison looked between us and raised her brows.

"Can I help?"

It was not my story to tell, so I waited for Chloe to speak. After an embarrassingly long pause, I thought I would have to say something. My aunt patiently waited. Taking on the role of a mother hen. With her unmoving stance, my aunt made it clear that she would continue to wait until one of us spoke. Addressing Chloe, I began a conversation designed to provide her with a way out of her uncle's home. Desperate measures for desperate times.

"Aunt Alison, it is so good to see you. What marvellous timing. Did you not say that you are looking for a companion to travel with you when you visit the Scottish Highlands next month?"

My enthusiasm sounded false to my own ears, but my aunt picked up on the manoeuvre and chose to seek understanding for my statement later.

"Why yes, do you know of anyone who would enjoy a trip to the Scottish Highlands. I would not be very demanding."

A small glimmer of possibility sparked in Chloe's eyes.

"Wh..when do you leave, Mrs Lindsey?"

Chloe was a little hesitant in her speech. Perhaps thinking it was too good to be true. Perhaps not wanting to appear too desperate, even though in reality, desperation was a good description of her situation.

"And when do you plan to return? I may be interested if you depart soon." She rushed on. "So that we might return in time for our departure to the colonies."

"Would it be possible for you to be ready for departure in a fortnight? We plan to leave this month. I know it is soon. The companion I planned to travel with is unexpectedly required at home to care for her mother, who has, in the last week, become suddenly ill. It would be fortunate indeed if your own aunt could spare you. It will be a slow trip during the winter. We plan to return in the spring. It will be a long time to be away from family."

And so, God orchestrated another symphony. Turning bad to good for those in need. God's provision never failed to inspire awe.

"Oh, but I would have the opportunity to see Scotland before I leave for the colonies. And my uncle will be returning soon, so my aunt will not need me for company. But would you not prefer to take Isabelle?"

"I was approaching Issy now to invite her." Aunt Alison took that moment to see my wish before she added. "Although I think it could be too disruptive of her employment with Mrs Chisholm. This may be a much better plan. I promise that we will return in time for you to prepare your departure to the colonies."

Chloe's expression changed to one of relief mixed with enthusiasm for a new adventure.

I was astounded at the speed with which a drama developed and then was solved. It put me in mind of the Psalm that had been read during morning prayers at the convent.

> "Ego autem ad Deum clamavi, et Dominus salvabit me. Vespere, et mane, et meridie, narrabo, et annuntiabo; et exaudiet vocem meam. Redimet in pace animam meam ab his qui appropinquant mihi; quoniam inter multos erant mecum.
>
> Jacta super Dominum curam tuam, et ipse te enutriet; non dabit in æternum fluctuationem justo."
>
> LVC

Read in Latin. My Latin was still poor, so I memorised the translation whilst I went about my work in the afternoon.

> "As for me, I will call upon God, and the Lord shall save me.
>
> Evening and morning and at noon I will pray, and cry aloud, and He shall hear my voice.
>
> He has redeemed my soul in peace from the battle that was against me, for there were many against me.

Cast your burden on the Lord, and He shall sustain you; He shall never permit the righteous to be moved.

Psalms 55:16-18,22 NKJV [7]

It was good of Mrs Chisholm to invite me to be her attendant for morning prayers. I enjoyed sitting in the back and soaking up the peaceful presence I experienced in the chapel. The sisters were always quiet and offered me a smile whenever they passed. I had been finding more solace in the morning chapel than I had in the Sunday service, which I attended with my aunt. Maybe because it did not remind me in any way of the life I had left behind.

[7] Psalms 55:16-18,22 Latin Vulgate, then NKJV

CHAPTER 10

Phillip

"Blessed is the man who walks not in the counsel of the wicked, nor stands in the way of sinners, nor sits in the seat of scoffers; but his delight is in the law of the Lord, and on his law he meditates day and night. He is like a tree planted by streams of water that yields its fruit in its season, and its leaf does not wither. In all that he does, he prospers. The wicked are not so, but are like chaff that the wind drives away. Therefore the wicked will not stand in the judgment, nor sinners in the congregation of the righteous; for the Lord knows the way of the righteous, but the way of the wicked will perish."

Psalms 1 ESV

December 1849.

N Phillip ran his fingers through his hair, nearly pulling it out by the roots from the struggle to contain his overwhelming sense of inadequacy to save. Phillip paced as he thumped his hand into his fist. He looked heavenward, then to his feet. His expression changed with each thought that raced through his mind.

A latecomer to the meeting tipped his hat as he walked by, then turned to consider the strange behaviour before him. The latecomer then shook his head almost imperceptibly before turning to enter the building and begin greeting his fellow travellers. He turned a few times to witness Phillip's turmoil before he moved so far into the meeting that he could no longer see into the darkness outside.

Ph *'Chloeeee!'* I ran my fingers through my hair as my insides seethed in a cauldron of turmoil. I did not know how to think.

I was angry!

More angry than I had ever been.

With a man I had never met.

'*How could someone take advantage of such a generous soul?'*

I was afraid!

Afraid that Chloe might never be able to love me. Was that why she showed no preference for any man? Might she despise all men? Even as she showed respect and concern for all those same men.

I was grieved because I had already convinced myself that we could never marry. I was confused. I realised, when I thought I could not be with her, that she was more to me than I had imagined. I had thought myself fond of Chloe, but in that moment, I knew I loved her. It was not past tense, and yet I feared that it needed to be past tense. I wanted to marry her yet, and still, I was aware that

I did not. I was not sure I could know of her story and live with the consequences. Would it have been better if I had walked away and never known? But then, how could I understand any reluctance she might show?

N Phillip was grateful for the darkness that concealed most of his behaviour. But he also knew that he needed to cover over the turmoil and return to the meeting before others came to find him. He did not want to reveal the reasons for his odd behaviour. He knew that he looked extremely odd. Thankfully, he was not talking to himself. He could have been denied a place on a ship if he were deemed mentally unstable. He purposed to get a grip on himself and not jeopardise both their chances at a new life.

Phillip pasted a smile on his face and re-entered the meeting. The people were taking their seats to listen to the speaker, so he slipped into a seat at the rear. Chloe and Isa were visible from where he sat, but neither turned to look for him. They presented a studied attention toward the front.

The evening's topic was as informative as any other, but Phillip could not have told a soul what it had been about. He remembered listening but then could not recount what was said. *'In one ear and out the other,'* as his nana would have said. His frame of mind made conversation awkward during refreshments. That evening, for the first time, Phillip wished to leave the meeting early. The burden to speak to Chloe before departing was great. Finding words to say when he was so confused, a more difficult conversation than any he had faced before.

Phillip made his farewells to the group he was dithering with and backed away. He scanned the rooms for sight of Chloe and Isa as he moved toward the exit.

He avoided engaging in conversation.

He needed to find Isa before he could depart and assumed Isa and Chloe might still be together. He made his way from the auditorium, through the refreshment tables, toward the library. When he arrived at the library, he saw both Chloe and Isa sitting, talking to Mrs Chisholm in a small nook at the edge of the gathering. The novel sight of Mrs Chisholm sequestered away from the larger group impressed upon Phillip that private matters were being discussed.

He needed to be patient.

So that he could think alone and plan his words, he picked up a book, sat in an isolated wingback, and pretended to read.

Ph Honesty and humility are usually the best course of action. But then, Chloe did not need to know of my confusion. She must have been sorely offended by my sudden withdrawal. An apology first, then!

'I'm sorry for running from you.' I think not!

'Please forgive me, I was shocked.' Better, but did not say how I felt about her. But then, maybe it was better if Chloe did not know how I felt. I certainly did not know how I felt. I was destroyed by conflicting emotions. I did not know how to order my thoughts. I concluded it was best to say as little as possible.

Mrs Chisholm retreated from the enclave and made her way back to the larger groups for discussion. I took my opportunity quickly and claimed the seat recently occupied by our patron. Chloe and Isa did not look entirely comfortable with my approach.

"You seem to have successfully schooled your composure, Phillip."

"Yes, Isa." With some stern words to myself, I raced on before losing the opportunity. "Forgive me, please, Chloe. I do not understand my earlier reaction."

I stopped talking because I could not order my thoughts. Pride compelled me to avoid revealing my inadequacy.

"I forgive you, Phillip."

Chloe said this with a downcast demeanour. My heart broke when confronted with the lost and defeated look. But still, I did not know what to say. Isa watched me as I studied Chloe intently. I wanted to know Chloe, but I was unwilling to reveal myself.

"Are you nearly ready to leave, Isa? I do not want a late night."

"It seems that Phillip is anxious to depart." Isa made no effort to hide her disdain for my behaviour. "Where will you stay tonight, Chloe? Do you want me to find someone to sit with you?"

Chloe took a deep breath and lifted her ribs. Her action brought her face up to gaze at Isa appreciatively.

"No, thank you, Isa. I will be fine to mingle now. I will take up Mrs Chisholm's offer for me to stay with her tonight. I will ride with her and have a message sent to my aunt. Tomorrow I will make some decisions."

Chloe embraced Isa with the affection of a sister. She did not turn my way again. I stood and made my way to the exit.

I The following morning, Phillip came to find me as I dusted the library.

Chloe was still abed and had missed sitting down for breakfast with Mrs Chisholm.

Mrs Chisholm had sought and found me before leaving the house to visit with my Aunt Alison.

She indicated to me that she was going out to organise for Chloe; a sanctuary until the ship sailed.

In truth, I would have enjoyed a trip into the highlands of Scotland. The fact that I did not have an income with which to support myself on such a trip, made the arrangement for Chloe to travel with my aunt the best plan for all. I could see the logic. I was happy that Chloe could be safe from her amorous uncle. I also still felt the injustice and drudgery of life.

"That was a big sigh."

I jumped, as I was inclined to do if I did not see a person approach. A habit newly formed. I did my best to position myself so that I could be attentive to all angles, but when I slipped into the quagmire of my thoughts, my alertness was diminished. I reminded myself again to stay in the present moment, where I could avoid being surprised.

"You scared me, Phillip."

My heart rate returned to normal too slowly. My alertness was hard to dissipate. I had come to trust Phillip more since our trip to the Hill's farm, but when fright arrived, it took time to overcome.

"Are you truly always so afraid, Isa?"

He didn't wait for my answer of yes, but pushed on with the matter that caused worry lines to be evident between his brows.

"Chloe has not come down. Do you think she is afraid to run into me?" Phillip spoke in hushed tones, which did nothing to diminish the intensity of his expression.

"That is possible. You were not very pleasant last evening. Do we need to whisper?"

"Would you take a plate of breakfast in and check that she is alright? She may be feeling timid in this house. I know that a grand house would be usual for her, but this is a strange circumstance. When you think on it, we are not from the same class at all. Why would she consider marrying me? If it were not for the emigration, we could never be together. She has always worn such plain and simple attire, I thought her to be looking for a life built on the back of her own efforts, as I am. I did much thinking last night. Her manner of dress may have more to do with avoiding physical attention. I was unaware that she had an annuity."

Phillip then looked me in the eye with an apology for his behaviour. It was reminiscent of a lost English Sheepdog. With his chocolate brown eyes expressing his feelings of remorse far more than his voice betrayed.

"I overheard Mrs Chisholm talking with Chloe last night. I know, it was wrong of me to eavesdrop, but it was hard to avoid. I needed to function as the servant that I am. It took most of the night, but I have come to terms with her revelation of home life, and I love her more. Her generosity of spirit in the face of such diabolical circumstances! When she meets people, she is always so truly kind. But how can I ask her to marry me? I am a servant. And after last night, she probably thinks I am judgmental. You look at me like I am raving."

"To be honest, I think you are raving a little."

There was a smile in my whisper. It was a relief to have some levity in my day. I knew that Chloe was as interested in Phillip as he was in Chloe. I thought it best for them to discover that without my help. All in their own good time. I was happy to have something good to think about.

"But what is to be done about your dilemma? It is interesting that neither of us have previously considered the class difference. At the FCLS, we all seem to be from the same class. Emigrants! I could try to find out what Chloe is thinking on the subject. My impression, though, Phillip, is that Chloe holds you in high regard and is waiting for you to speak to her. After all, you do not have much to lose from speaking to her."

We were still whispering as Molly walked past with a quizzical look on her face. I said in a louder voice.

"Certainly, if Mrs Chisholm asked for me to take a breakfast tray up to Miss Higgins at ten o'clock, I will prepare it now."

Then I scurried off toward the kitchen, leaving Phillip, who had not seen Molly approach, wondering what new peculiarity had possessed me.

Mrs Shaw was busy organising lunch preparations when I entered her domain. Even though Cook was friends with Mrs Gretsch, she, for some reason, did not participate in the '*harass Isa*' campaign.

"Hello, Cook, Phillip has just told me that I am to take a breakfast tray to Miss Higgins at ten. Do you mind if I prepare the tray for her?"

"It is all good, love. You go get me a block of the cheddar from the cellar while Beth prepares the tray. "'Ave yourself a glass of milk whilst you're there, you look peaked."

"Thank you, Mrs Shaw."

I could not say more, even though I would have liked to be more friendly. Mrs Shaw always had a friendly demeanour, but I found her charm disarming and was afraid of saying too much. I had tried asking about the health of her family in the past, but even that had turned into a quagmire when she started talking about her daughter's interest in Phillip. I made my way to the cellar after giving Mrs Shaw a smile of appreciation and returned just as the tray was ready.

I placed the tray on a small table in the hall while I knocked on the door to Chloe's room. There was a muffled response from inside, so I announced my purpose.

"'Tis I, Chloe, come with a breakfast tray for you. May I enter?"

The door flew open, and a fully dressed Chloe pulled me into the room and went to shut the door.

"Will you not let me bring the tray in?"

"Oh! Of course, although I am not famished. In truth, I am not sure I can eat."

I retrieved the tray from the hall and placed it on the small table by the window.

"Then you can talk, and I can listen. I cannot dally long, Mrs Gretsch will not accept any tardiness from me."

"Oh! I am so sorry, Issy. I forget that you must live like this. Little wonder it is sometimes so hard to get a smile from you."

Chloe meant no harm, but I was confronted by the knowledge of how I was perceived. My proficiency at not reacting was increased each day I lived under Mrs Gretsche's authority. I avoided reacting to little hurts and did not let the comment penetrate the shield I had constructed. I planned to think on it later. I did give a look of impatience, though, when the clock chimed the hour. The intense awareness for the passing of time was difficult to contain. Chloe looked at me with desperation.

"Yes."

Chloe then rushed on in an all-too-similar fashion to Phillip's. They really needed to talk to each other.

"I slept so well after praying with Mrs Chisholm that I was surprised; when, after dressing, I went to leave the room and descend for breakfast, only to be suddenly filled with trepidation."

Chloe started to rock on her feet.

"For what? I asked myself. There is naught to fear in this house."

I disagreed but kept the thought to myself. Chloe began to pace, two steps to the left, two to the right.

"But then it came to me that I do not know how to behave with Phillip in this situation."

The delicate hands of a person who did little real housework began to twist, separate, and join in the opposite aspect at an alarming rate. Chloe was more distressed than I had previously understood.

"What is it in this situation that bothers you most, Chloe?"

The next answer divulged more about Chloe's heart than anything else she had said.

"The multifacetedness of it all. I know that is not a real word, but I cannot be correct while I am like this. Phillip finding out about my history, and me being unsure of his feelings, has made me realise that I care more about him than I intended."

I lifted my shoulders, then heaved a quiet sigh. Chloe did not notice. She was on the outward leg of her pacing.

"The awkwardness of being in a home where my friends are servants, and I am a guest. At the FCLS, we can all be equal in society. I am learning from you all the things I will need to learn to survive in a colony where I will have no servants. Even though I could not afford to employ servants myself, I am used to having people wash and cook for me. Thankfully, I know how to dress myself."

A small, shy smile accompanied a gentle look my way before Chloe returned to squeezing her hands as she paced.

"Staying in this house has forced me to confront an important issue. How can I learn more? I cannot ask to do the washing at home. My Aunt would become suspicious. It is true, I have not told her of my plans to leave. It would only mean months of my aunt trying to find me a suitable husband. Something I feel that I have already done. But how do I convince Phillip that I would be a good wife for him? I sound like I am ranting, but my thoughts keep chasing in circles, and I cannot see what I should do next."

"Next, you will be leaving with my Aunt Alison for an adventure in Scotland."

"Which will not increase my competence in caring for myself in the colonies."

I had a spark of an idea.

"You will need somewhere safe to stay on your return to London. It is to be expected that your uncle will still be in residence."

"That is another issue I cannot keep from my mind."

Renewed pacing followed.

"I could write to the Hill family and ask if you could take on an apprenticeship in farming life until the *Slains Castle* sails. Mrs Hill is lovely, and her three sons are too young and too well-behaved to be a problem for you."

"But why would they say yes to that scheme?"

I knew why, but how to explain to Chloe? Instead of confronting the issue of Phillip and Chloe, I took another route.

"Have you solidified a family to travel with yet, Chloe? I know the Hills have a place in their family for one more. This could be a good reason for them to say yes to the scheme."

The look of relief transformed Chloe's face.

"Oh! Would you, Issy? Please write to them as soon as you can. I would love to have the issue of my accommodation following my travels sorted before I leave with your aunt. One less small problem to be concerned about."

Chloe then launched herself and gave me an affectionate hug of gratitude.

"In this hopeful frame of mind, may I encourage you to eat something and then find your way to the library? Phillip has told me that he also feels awkward. But I think it would be best if you confront your fears on that small issue. You are both generous people; you can find a way to relate to each other, strange though it may be. I must return to work before I am missed. And work extra fast to make up the time so that I can avoid as much torture as possible."

"I am so sorry, Issy. I will pray for you."

I sighed for all the good I thought it would do and went back to my work. Although, to be honest, things could have been worse. I could have been charred remains by then if God had not looked after me. But then, a little more comfort would not have gone astray.

When Mrs Chisholm returned, I was summoned to the library. I had learnt to trust in the generous spirit that belonged to Mrs Chisholm, so I had no fear for the encounter. Rachel, who was seated next to me at the nuncheon table, smirked, intimating some horrible outcome for me. I ignored her attempt to instil trepidation where none belonged and made my way to the library with a light step. If I had known the topic of conversation, I might have been more hesitant. But then I probably should have guessed.

"Thank you for coming so promptly, Isabelle. Please close the door. I want to discuss something of a delicate nature and would like to avoid being overheard."

"Yes, Mrs Chisholm."

I took a seat, as directed by hand signals, across from a small round refreshment table set next to the window. Far enough from the fire to avoid the direct radiated heat, but close enough to be cosy. The usual pot of tea and cinnamon cakes were already on the table. Rachel had known that there was naught to fear and had simply been trying to sabotage my encounter.

"I have been gallivanting around town this morning trying to do what I could for poor Chloe in this most difficult circumstance. I visited her aunt to see if I could broach the subject with her. With Chloe's consent, of course. But with no good result. It is, as Chloe says. Her aunt is in denial. At least she did not accuse Chloe of lying or worse of being a seductress, as so often happens. It was the strangest conversation I have ever had. Every time I tried to bring up the topic, it was either ignored or deflected somehow. It is as if Mrs Mortimer has blinkers on. She was completely unable to recognise the subject. It was incredibly frustrating, but I concluded there would be no help from that quarter.

"Then I went to visit your Aunt Alison. We have known each other for many years through our husbands' acquaintance. I enjoy visiting with your aunt to discuss the goings-on between the Protestants and Catholics. I converted to Catholicism just before my marriage. My husband and I needed to be in the same church to avoid conflict, and it meant more to Archie than it did to me. I do enjoy prayers at the convent. It centres me in the midweek." Mrs Chisholm then brought herself back to the imperative topic at hand.

"Your aunt and I had a thorough conversation about the best way forward. I agree with the plan for Chloe to accompany your aunt to Scotland. There should be ample time for the travel to be completed before Chloe is due to join you on the *Slains Castle.* But what to do until then and afterwards? Your aunt tells me that there is a growing attachment between our Phillip and Chloe. It was a surprise for me as they are from such different backgrounds."

Mrs Chisholm's comment created in me a realisation that I knew little of Phillip's background. A circumstance I needed to rectify.

"After consideration and some discussion with Alison, I can see the advantage to both in such a match. But this does mean that Chloe cannot stay here until her departure. Neither now, nor when she returns. As her uncle has not yet arrived, I think Chloe should be safe with Mrs Mortimer until she leaves for Scotland."

I wondered why I had been called in. Mrs Chisholm continued her monologue. Why did I need to be included in the deliberations?

"But Isabelle, there is a dilemma to be solved for when she returns."

At that pause, I took the opportunity to share my idea.

"I have had a short talk with Chloe this morning. It seems she is afraid her skills in the home are lacking for survival in the colony. Phillip discussed with Mr Hill when he transported me to the farm, the possibility of joining the Hill family group for the voyage and beyond. I thought perhaps to ask Mrs Hill if Chloe could be apprenticed with them to learn how to be a farmer's wife. Phillip was a little presumptuous and did verify that there would be a place for a wife. Just quietly, Phillip and Chloe have confided in me separately, their interest in each other. I thought it could be a good situation all around."

"That is a plan that could work very well, Isabelle. How has so much been going on, and I have not been aware? Hectic with public speaking and wooing politicians, I suppose. It is good that God pays attention to the details of our lives."

I was taught that was the truth. But I disliked the details of my own life immensely. So, I withheld a willingness to trust God for myself.

"Would you like me to write to the Hill's also?"

I nodded my head in assent and prepared to rise.

"But this is not why I called you in. I wanted to make sure of your feelings on the subject, as it must seem like you are being neglected to make way for the needs of another."

The compassion brought tears to my eyes as I sank back into the chair.

"Oh, Isabelle, I am sorry. Would you like to share how you feel? I know this cannot be easy for you. But think, there must be something grand that our Heavenly Father would like you to do in the time before you leave. He will give you rest at the right time.

"And that puts me in mind of another project. How are you coming along with sewing garments for other travellers? Summer frocks and short pants for boys. It is quite warm in New South Wales for most of the year. They have a very long summer."

In truth, I could not see anything grand that I might be doing. My circumstances were something to be endured with the hope of future reprieve. There was no direct good to be had.

"I spend what little time I have sewing. I have completed but a few dresses so far. I would do more but find I have very little time."

"I will tell Mrs Gretsch to allocate Wednesday mornings when we return from the convent. Will that give you time to enjoy your dressmaking?"

The thought of spending several hours following the prayers to sew and contemplate brought joy to my heart and elicited a spontaneous smile.

"Well, now, that makes me think that I do not see you smile often, Isabelle. I will be praying that you can find peace within the storm that has raged around you."

"Thank you, Mrs Chisholm."

With the quiet that followed, I knew the chat was over, so I made my way back to the beds that needed to be made. As I walked the hall of bedrooms, Chloe emerged, apparently ready to confront the day. Chloe told me that Mrs Chisholm had arranged a short meeting for her with Phillip in the Library before she left for home. Phillip apologised again, and Chloe accepted his apology, but not much else was said. I was a little disappointed that they had not shared their hearts. I hoped they would not take too long to build up courage. Chloe was due to depart in just a few short weeks.

Later that night, I wrote a short missive to Mrs and Mr Hill explaining some of Chloe's situation, leaving out the difficulties with her uncle, and requested that they invite her to stay so that she could learn the art of keeping house on a farm. As they would not return until the spring, and we would be leaving early in the next autumn, it would not allow Chloe to experience much of the harvest. However, she would have the opportunity to preserve some of the summer fruits and learn how to run a home, doing much of the work herself. It would no doubt be a mountain of learning and would seem like back-breaking work to the uninitiated. I had confidence that Chloe would face the opportunity as an adventure.

The next meeting of the FCLS brought a return to the previous routine, with Chloe and Phillip behaving in much the same manner as they had before. Both were still filled with deep insecurities and not brave enough to declare themselves. I found it all rather frustrating and seriously considered interfering. Or more overt encouragement in the least. Encouragement like 'She loves you, speak to her.' Instead, I proved a coward myself and would not become involved in something that could lead to the same heartbreak that I was still experiencing myself.

So, everything simply continued.

At the FCLS, a few days before Chloe's departure, my Aunt Alison ambled toward Phillip and me as we discussed the large meeting we had seen depicted in the newspaper. The drawing showed people looking through windows and doorways to catch a glimpse of the speakers within. Seemingly, many people were interested in emigration. I felt privileged for the first time to be included in such a well-planned venture.

"Hello, possums." We all looked at my aunt with boggled eyes.

"I beg your pardon, Aunt?" Before I could say more, she laughed. "I have just now heard one of the returned emigrants use that term. I thought it was so unusual, I had to give it a try. Have you come across the possum in the books of drawings yet? It is a funny-looking creature with big eyes, a pointy nose, and a very bushy tail. Not very big and runs around at night helping itself to seedlings and crops."

"One of the creatures we will need to contend with then." Phillip offered. "I'm not sure how that can be a friendly greeting, though. Is it not like calling us thieves? And I read that the locals eat them. That would make us prey as well as thieves."

"Oh! I did not think of that. I think I will forget the term. I do not want to speak ill over people." Chloe walked through the front door and joined our conclave.

"Hello, Mrs Lindsay. I am finished with my packing and am ready to have my luggage removed to your home. I am so glad that we will be leaving this week. I am concerned every day that my uncle's ship will pull into port."

Chloe spoke with such enthusiasm I had to again remind myself not to fall into the pit of envy.

Phillip developed a more intense look of panic the longer Chloe spoke.

"Packing? Luggage? Leaving? Where are you going?"

Apparently, Phillip was not aware of the arrangements to keep Chloe safe. They had not spoken at all. It was time to do something.

"Yes, Phillip. It has been arranged for Chloe to accompany my Aunt Alison as a companion when she travels through Scotland. They leave on Thursday."

Once again, Phillip walked off when confronted with unpleasant news. And it did seem he thought it unpleasant news. I followed him. It was time to have a say in what I considered a ridiculous situation.

"Hold Phillip!"

I was unsure if I was pleased or apprehensive about Phillip turning to wait for me to catch up. His waiting meant that I was required to have my say.

"Please come sit in a corner with me. There is much to be said."

I could not then change my mind. I certainly lacked enthusiasm. But I could not have such a hard heart that I left two friends who had been good to me floundering in their inability to connect, even though they both desperately wanted that very thing. After all, some marriages were good. My parents, and Mr and Mrs Chisholm, to think of two very good examples. I was disturbed by how my fears led me into twisted thinking.

"This is an unhelpful habit you have, Phillip. That you walk away when you are distressed. It leaves others thinking that you are angry with them. Is this the case? Are you angry with us? With Chloe?"

"Yes. No. What I mean is, I am both. I am glad that Chloe will have a safe place when her uncle returns. I have been worrying over this and trying to think of solutions but have not found a truly good solution. I was aiming to ask her to marry me, but I have no home to place her in until we reach the colony and build our own. Even that seems pathetic, but at least I know it is what she always planned to do. I am still unsure that she would accept one such as me for husband. I am a coal miner's son after all."

That was the first I had heard of Phillip's beginnings. Little wonder he was unsure.

"If you were planning to ask her, then ask her before she leaves. Tonight even. The worst that can happen is that she say no."

"But when would we wed?"

"Phillip, that is tomorrow's trouble. Find out first if she will have you. Then work out how to make it happen at the right time. Chloe has her escape from her uncle's house planned out. With some help from others. I am disappointed that neither of you have spoken about those plans, as you are both so interested in each other." Keenly, Phillip looked at me with a directness unusual for him.

"You know this then?"

With a great sigh from me and a spark of pleasure in Phillip's eye, I nodded. His smile widened.

"Yes, I do. But it is up to both of you to do something about it. Chloe has her well-founded insecurities, also remember."

Phillip took on a look of introspection.

"You are right. I need to check my pride and risk rejection."

I winced! How could I encourage another to risk rejection when it hurts so much?

"If I do not take the risk, then I have not the possibility of joy."

Oh! Of course, I had forgotten that since my own situation had not ended in joy.

"You do not speak in a way that would make me think you are a coal miner's son."

"When I was ten years old, my best friend, the son of the mine owner, fell from a rock into the ocean. He was set to drown had I not jumped in and helped him swim to shore. I did not think to be brave; he was my best friend; I could not leave him to flounder.

"Together, we made our way to shore. We were exhausted and cold when we struggled onto the pebbly beach, but we were both alive. My sister, who had seen us enter the ocean, ran for help. When we pulled onto the beach, there were night shift miners ready to haul us home.

"They went first to the great house with the owner's son, then planned to continue on to the village. We were both blue from the cold when we arrived at the big house. The owner, Mr Black, was so grateful that he brought me in to sit by the fire. We talked, and I had my first-ever drink of hot chocolate."

He smiled with his memory and glanced at me conspiratorially.

"Have you ever had hot chocolate, Isa?"

"Once, my grandfather brought some chocolate back from Spain after a mission to purchase healing herbs and inspect the farms where they are grown. I agree, it is an amazing experience."

"After the rescue, Mr Black must have approved of my character. I was invited to work as a servant in his household. I was given time to study with my friend Adrian. His tutors became my tutors also. Mr Black told me that he was training me to be a steward. I was taught to read and write, and also to count and calculate. I decided to mimic Adrian's pattern of speech and so sound less like my brothers."

"How did you come to be here in this household, Phillip?"

"Adrian wanted to attend a meeting that he said would be good for a lark. He had far more time for wandering than I did. By then, I only saw Adrian when he was home from the university. I spent most of my time helping Mr Black's steward. With the mines being so successful, there was a lot of work involved in the management. The meeting was an FCLS meeting, and I was inspired from the very first. I spoke to Mr Black about my interest; he was more than happy to make enquiries and help me to realise what had become a dream for me. He wrote to Mrs Chisholm, whom he was acquainted with through her political machinations. I was offered a position here, and Mr Black has paid for my passage. I save and will take a loan for a start in the colony."

"So, you are very skilled, Phillip. Why would Chloe reject you? I suppose you have not told her any of this."

"True. I have not."

"What of your family, Phillip?"

"Most have passed away. Coal mining does not make you live a long life. I have a sister whose husband is still with the living. He is a butcher, so does not breathe the dust, nor does a butcher get caught in a mine collapse. I am very grateful to Mr Black for helping me to climb out of that pit. All my family were also very grateful. My parents were happy that at least one of their sons would not have to contend with life as they did."

"If you will stay here, I am going to bring Chloe this way. I want you to share some of this with her and ask her to marry you before boarding the *Slains Castle*. And truly, ask her to tell you of her plans until our ship sails."

The following morning, my Aunt Alison arrived for an unexpected visit with Mrs Chisholm. Bringing Chloe with her. Whilst the two matrons were sequestered in the library, Chloe was left to seek out Phillip. I observed this from my post, polishing handles in the entrance hall. Chloe was so preoccupied that she did not notice me evaluating her progress. Phillip, walking from the kitchens with purpose written into his features, found Chloe as she was preparing to open a door to the morning room. He walked up close and found a silent communication as he looked into her eyes with studied intent. Purposely reaching past Chloe, who held her ground as the distance between them diminished, he opened the door and allowed Chloe to enter before following closely behind. The suggestion of shared intimacy was charged.

I did not witness what followed, but when they both emerged ten minutes later and caught me still looking at the doorway, they came directly over to share what looked to be very happy circumstances. I felt relief at the release of frustration, joy at the news that they would wed before the ship sailed, and envy that I had no such happy news of my own. Seemingly, I had grown green eyes. I despaired that my life could ever again hold such joy. I had become a sad creature. Not a creature to be envied.

"I recommend that the banns be read on this very Sunday."

They looked at each other with a surprised look.

"Oh! In which church?" They said simultaneously.

They were destined to forever struggle with communication! They had not yet discussed which church they each attended. I had to wonder if they had ever talked about their differences. They didn't know it, but they were both Catholics who had never met in church.

"I think both may be best. You might even consider visiting each other's church. I think you will both need to do much letter writing while Chloe is away."

At that, they turned to each other and smiled an intimate smile, then made their way over to the library, hesitated momentarily, then knocked to gain access. They disappeared into the room, and I went back to my work. When I left to sit for morning refreshments in the kitchen, they still had not emerged. I hoped all would go well for them.

CHAPTER 11

Winter

"The counsel of the LORD stands forever,
the plans of his heart to all generations.
Blessed is the nation whose
God is the LORD,
the people whom he has chosen as his heritage!
The LORD looks down from heaven;
he sees all the children of man;
from where he sits enthroned
he looks out on all the inhabitants of the earth,
he who fashions the hearts of them
all and observes all their deeds."

Psalms 33:11-15 ESV

January 1850, London.

It was bleak in the house through the winter. Such short hours of sunlight and so much rain. I missed sitting around the fire with my family at home, sharing stories, new and old. I missed Chloe even though I had only seen her on Monday evenings.

With my Aunt Alison away, I stopped attending the non-conformist church and began attending Mass with Phillip. I found that I enjoyed the ritual of the Catholic service, and I enjoyed learning more Latin. A useful skill when reading about herbs and medicine.

With Mrs Chisholm's permission, I read all the medical and botany books in her library. When I had read all the books from her library, she borrowed more from friends so that I could learn more. I was careful not to let Rachel, Molly or Mrs Gretsch catch me reading those volumes. I had no wish to repeat the experiences of Ellesmere.

I discovered one evening, the treacherous trio: Mrs Gretsch, Rachel, and Molly, chanting around candles in the cellar. It was odd! With small straw figurines, bowls of scented water over a brazier, and a large book on a pedestal. I had the briefest glimpse before scurrying away in fright, so I can neither say what they were chanting nor the purpose of their meeting. It was enough, though, for me to think that they were in fellowship together over some purpose.

It was not like any Bible study I had ever seen. The atmosphere felt thick, pressing, and compelling. It felt like I was being drawn into the will of others. The heaviness and compulsion lifted with each step I took away from their enclave. I never returned to that room in the cellar and purposely avoided the attention of the three women.

I received confirmation from the Hills regarding Chloe's secondment to the farm. It was all arranged for her return. Phillip and Chloe managed to correspond even though Chloe was often on the road, moving from town to town.

The wedding was planned for August. A midsummer wedding with many flowers to adorn the bride. They were then to have a short honeymoon trip. A trip to the shore so they could focus on each other before undertaking the adventure of emigration.

I was very happy for them but found it increasingly difficult to feel any happiness in my own life. All felt very mundane when it was not threatening.

One cold and bleak morning in January, Phillip came to me and gave me a letter from Chloe. It was the first letter I had received from Chloe. It had not occurred to me that we could be corresponding. I pulled the shawl around my shoulders to ward off the winter chill that I could not conquer. I tipped my head to the right and managed a small smile of thanks as I looked up into Phillip's concerned face.

"Thank you, Phillip."

I sounded forlorn even to my own ears. Sometimes it was just too much to maintain a cheery demeanour.

"It will be so nice to read about someone else's life. I do not seem to get enough letters from home. I mean that I do not think any amount would be enough."

"Enjoy! And thank you for the tea and rub you recommended for my aunty. She is much improved. You have a talent for healing tonics, Isa. I have seen you put many hours of reading into the study of medical and botany books."

"Yes, it reminds me of my grandfather. I have been considering the need to take seeds for medicinal plants to the colony. I have written and asked Granda to send me a starter box. I hope to collect the package next time I walk into the post office. But please keep this information to yourself. I live in dread of Rachel or Mrs Gretsch using such knowledge against me."

"Understood. Can you not get past what happened and begin to trust again? That was an unusual circumstance that surely would not be repeated. I, for one, am glad that we will have someone experienced in healing arts."

"Well read, rather than experienced, Phillip. I enjoy the reading, and I am enthusiastic about planting a medicinal garden in my new life. As enthusiastic as I can be about anything these days. I admit that I feel a little better and somewhat warmer after talking to you. I have spent too much time embedded in my head these past seven months. Only eight more till our ship sails. I can manage that. I despair of my personality, though. I seem to be a different person from the Isabelle of Ellesmere."

"I have noticed that you are withdrawn. If talking helps, I will seek you out more often."

With that, Phillip headed back to whatever work he had been doing before the mail arrived. I placed Chloe's letter into a pocket so that I might read it slowly and enjoy the stories she had to tell. I for a surety needed some good stories to enjoy.

21 January 1850, Clinterty, Scotland

To my dear friend Isabelle

I am sorry that I have not written sooner. There is no excuse. I admit that I have been caught up in my own delight at becoming engaged to marry Phillip. Also, your Aunt Alison has been like a whirlwind on this journey.

After the first few waypoints, where we arrived at an inn within hours of the same couple, I realised there was more to our trip than recreation. I forced myself to be more observant and discovered there were FCLS meetings while we were in each town. I purposed myself to talk with Mrs Lindsay about the happenstance. I wanted in! I found enthusiasm for the travel that had been previously insipid.

I was unaware that this trip is for more than pleasure. It is also an information dissemination for the FCLS. Did you know before we left that we would be arranging meetings in each town along the way? It has certainly kept me busy. I have greatly enjoyed meeting so many interesting people.

We are currently in Clinterty, Northwest of Aberdeen. It is a quaint village. Not overly friendly with us. I am told there is still some resentment toward the English in these parts. They seem to have long memories. We dined with Lord Ashley yesterday eve, and I must say, I came away with my skin crawling. There was something about his comments that left me very uneasy. He seems to have no respect for the people who belong here. I hope there will not be many like him in New South Wales. He even boasted that he was 'aiding' a family to leave for the sole purpose of taking their land. He talked of them by name, *so that the following day, when I met the very same people at the organised meeting, I felt very awkward conversing with them. It was like having knowledge about them that I should not have had. It made me feel embarrassed. That I was somehow complicit in the machinations of lording it over others and manipulating their circumstances for personal gain. It somehow seemed worse when it was personal.*

The representative of this group was a man of impressive height and breadth. Though he did also have the look of someone who never quite had enough to eat. A tradesman of some sort, as evidenced by the calluses on his hands. He impressed me with the care he took to speak well of his family and the insight he seemed to have of the journey ahead. He has obviously done his research. He is seemingly well-read. A rarity in a tradesman, I am told.

I had to pause at that statement. I felt an immediate kinship with another who had had their life manipulated for the personal gain of an evil person. I was also a little offended at Chloe's assumption that tradespeople did not read. It was surprising how easily the opinions of others could be influenced when they sat down to share a meal. I decided in that moment to guard myself against falling prey to such folly from that time forward.

Your Aunt Alison endeavoured to introduce us, as our two groups will be travelling to the same area south of Sydney in New South Wales. The plan is to encourage the two family groups to support each other with their ventures. When your aunt told me of this, I did my best to learn something of the family. They have experienced an excessive amount of personal tragedy in recent years. I suppose it is to be expected that our fellow travellers would have stories of woe in the same way that we do. Of course, we know Phillip is an exception to this. He travels to better himself rather than to run away. I feel so blessed to be promised to Phillip. If my uncle had not behaved badly, I would not have been planning to emigrate and thus would never have met Phillip. I can now be thankful for the dramas of my life because without them, I would not have this blessing.

How are you progressing with your own dramas, Isabelle? Please write to me and share with me what is happening in your life. I miss you. Phillip knows how to send the missive when it is written. Mrs Chisholm sends a packet forward to our next location. She helped to plan the itinerary, so knows where we will be. Weather permitting.

Mr Forbes, the family representative I was telling you about, is a tradesman, but most of his family are farmers. As they forgave my Englishness, they began to share. I think they will be of much help to us as we settle into a new way of living.

I long to hear about all the happenings at the FCLS meetings. I am enamoured with Phillip, but he does not write very much about the people we enjoy observing. Please write soon.

With Much Love from your friend
Chloe Higgins

I sat and looked out the window into the grey drizzle that surrounded my life that winter. I pulled my shawl closer, even though the room was not especially cold. As I enfolded myself in the shawl, I enfolded myself emotionally in a blanket of sorrow. I fluctuated between moments of hope and moments of despair. I knew that I could help myself by taking control of my thinking. I just did not have the desire and strength to take control. The household had worn me down. First, I was discarded by my community, then I was maintained as an outsider in the home where I lived.

The horrible despair was about to consume me when I thought of the family Chloe had written about in her letter. There was comfort in knowing that I was not the only person being persecuted. Again, I decided to paste a smile on my face and keep counting down the days till my release. Such a strange household. Mrs Chisholm was benevolence itself, but there were persons within her household who could be described as nothing other than evil.

May 1850, London

The day of Aunt Alison's and Chloe's return finally arrived. After four long months, it was good to see them both. Two allies in a harsh world. Chloe descended from the carriage, which had pulled up to the front door and helped my aunt to arrange herself before entering the house. Chloe looked so happy. It lifted my soul before it came crashing down to earth with a load of envy and resentment. How could I be so happy for my friend but also so resentful? I was conflicted and needed to school my features before moving to greet her. I had time, Chloe was entering through the front door, and I had taken only a moment from my work to gaze out an upstairs window.

Sooner than expected, I heard footsteps in the hall leading to the room in which I was occupied cleaning. The door blasted open, and in rushed Chloe. I was so surprised my mouth hung open. Chloe rushed across the room with so much enthusiasm I had no option but to accept the embrace I was treated with. Not very stoic of her. Seemingly, Chloe's time had been as joyful as mine had been miserable. The bubble of pleasure was contagious, and for a moment, my heart was comforted.

"I have received permission from Mrs Chisholm to steal you away from your duties and take you for a walk. I am so happy, and I have much to plan with you. I leave for the Hill farm the day after tomorrow. My Aunt Gertrude writes that my uncle is home. I will not stay in her house while he is there. I have chosen not to tell her of my return to London. I will tell her that I have been taken directly to the Hill farm to avoid fruitless explanations. But we can talk as we walk. I will wait in the foyer for you to collect your walking shoes. Molly has already been sent to inform Mrs Gretsch." I groaned audibly before I quickly covered my mouth.

"I do not want to seem ungracious. All I can think of is the punishment that will be extracted later."

I took a deep breath and exhaled slowly behind closed eyes. With a weak smile and a small voice, I accepted the inevitable and added,

"I will be with you shortly."

When we returned, and after enjoying tea in the garden with my aunt, I went to fetch a book that Mrs Chisholm wanted to lend to my aunt. As I approached the garden from the back of the house, I overheard Chloe speaking with Aunt Alison.

"When I met Isabelle, she was a little subdued by sadness and fear, but now she oozes resentment and despair. I had no idea just how bad things were for her in this household. Instead of healing, Isabelle has found more trauma to deal with. Her laugh, when it happens, has lost its spontaneous effervescence. I challenged Phillip because he had not told me in his letters. He said to me he had not noticed the extent of despair until I brought it to his mind. Then he proceeded to talk about placing a frog in cold water and bringing it to the boil slowly so that it would sit and allow itself to be boiled alive. I am very unhappy with him about it."

Aunt Alison's reply was more disturbing even than Chloe's comments.

"And I am unhappy with myself. The Isabelle that I knew as a child; the smiling, jesting, and generous girl who had a kind word for everyone who crossed her path, has been replaced by a pinched-lipped mouse that says as little as possible even when asked a direct question. I had some knowledge of her struggles. Isabelle asked me not to interfere, but now I think it was a mistake to stay silent. I fear I have not helped her during this most difficult time in her life."

I made my presence known before I could hear more. There was no point in being reminded about what was happening to my character. I could feel every bit of what they were saying. I knew it to be true. I just could not see my way to forgiving people who intentionally caused me harm. I huffed a small sigh before I came close.

"It has been good to see you both. I am glad you stopped to spend some time with me, even though I will be required to pay a price later. I need more positive company. I am counting the days until we leave for Australia."

With an inadequate smile, I handed Aunt Alison the book I had retrieved for her and then walked away. I could feel their concern for me as I left but felt it only as pity. I have discovered that being pitied by others is not an experience to be enjoyed.

Chloe left for the Hill farm the following day, and life returned to the normal I had been living for almost a year. Aunt Alison did challenge me about attending the papist church, but I asked her to leave the topic alone. After all, I was finding some comfort in the services at the Catholic church with both Mrs Chisholm and Phillip. I simply said that if I could meet God there, what did it matter which congregation I attended? Aunt Alison nodded and left it alone, but I could see her great concern for me. It only made me angrier. I knew that my aunt was not the enemy, yet I could not prevent myself from being a little rude when talking to her.

The concern began to filter back to Ellesmere. The letters from my family became epistles of encouragement. A fact that I found very discouraging. I knew it to be so very unreasonable of me, and yet still, I could not prevent myself from displaying a curtness of manner that had never previously been a part of my nature. The only thing that kept me going was sitting in the peaceful environment of others in prayer. I could not find my way to participate but found that those around me did not notice nor insist upon my participation because they inhabited their own joy or struggle.

CHAPTER 12

Intermission

"On my bed by night
I sought him whom my soul loves;
I sought him, but found him not.
I will rise now and go about the city,
in the streets and in the squares;
I will seek him whom my soul loves.
I sought him, but found him not.
The watchmen found me
as they went about in the city.
"Have you seen him whom my soul loves?"
Scarcely had I passed them
when I found him whom my soul loves.
I held him, and would not let him go
until I had brought him into my mother's house,
and into the chamber of her who conceived me.
I adjure you, O daughters of Jerusalem,
by the gazelles or the does of the field,

that you not stir up or awaken love
until it pleases."

Song of Songs 3:1-5 ESV

August 1850, London

After thirteen long months in service, Mrs Chisholm devised a grand plan of having a party to introduce the two family groups travelling on to New South Wales: The date was set, the invitations sent, the arrangements made. I found that my excitement grew despite my attempts to suppress the emotion and avoid the risk of disappointed hope.

My focus slowly began to shift toward physical planning for my departure. Chloe and Phillip were to be wed in only a few weeks. The FCLS meetings became more crowded as families arrived in London to secure arrangements before the ship sailed.

With light from a crack to the tomb in which I lived filtering into my life, I shed some of the gloom that had settled on my personality. With the warmer weather and longer days of summer, I was even found to smile on occasion.

Chloe arrived from the Hill farm to stay for a few days and assist in arranging the party, which would also be her wedding feast. It seemed appropriate somehow to celebrate with our new community. Our new family. A family that I had only half met. Not even half met to be truthful with myself. Chloe was much more familiar with so many more of the family; I almost caught myself slipping into the envy I had sworn to avoid. It was a constant struggle. I knew I needed relationships that could edify me. But my mood seemed to rule itself, leading me onto paths of dark thinking. Or did my dark thinking lead to my mood? Both, I suppose! And they both led me to behave defensively. A mode of conduct that was uncomfortable for others. It was no way to build new, edifying relationships.

I threw myself into a frenzy of preparation, hoping that my heart would follow and rejoice in what I dispassionately knew to be very good circumstances. My strategy was effective until each time a new source of envy presented itself before me. I was determined not to allow it to win. One look into the eyes of Mrs Gretsch and Rachel, something I avoided most of the time, and I could see what I did not wish to become. There was something dark and disturbing boiling beneath the surface of each. I did not want to allow Mrs Gretsch and company to win in their task of vengeance on my soul. When I looked into the eyes and soul of Mrs Chisholm or Chloe, I could see a contrast that was as dramatic as it was refreshing. I knew which way I wanted to grow. I simply did not know how to achieve my goal.

The day of the wedding feast arrived.

I was impressed with the simple elegance of the day. Neither very expensive nor flashy. Chloe had purposely produced a feast that would fit into the class she was entering rather than the one she was leaving.

There was an abundance of summer flowers donated by the many people who loved her. Cook enjoyed the preparation of good aromatic food rather than opulent fare. The smell of lamb and rosemary mingled with a softer aroma of vanilla and cinnamon. I found myself inhaling deeply from the many aromas as I set up tables in the garden, as well as any available nook that could be found. The straining of the strings squealed as the fiddlers tuned their instruments. My feet tapped in time to both imagined and remembered music.

I ran my fingers through the ribbons of satin adorning the balustrade as I walked past to collect more table settings for the outside. I could only think that Chloe's Aunt Gertrude must have hired the use of extra table settings. I had never seen so many stored inside the Chisholm home. The enthusiasm for the occasion was contagious, and I saw nearly everyone in attendance smiling broadly. I felt my heart swell and decided to give way to risk for the day. Like a warm spring breeze blowing through a house that has been opened after a long, cold winter: The sensation of pleasure, so foreign to me now, filled me with intense euphoria.

As the guests arrived, I could see the eclectic manner of dress and thought how apt it was in representing our new community of travellers. People, with many differences, united with a common cause. I was busily trying to put some finishing touches on the table settings when Mrs Chisholm came to me and suggested that I change my hat. When I gave her a perplexed look, she smiled and went on in a soft voice filled with generosity.

"Go and change your clothes so that you can change your perspective and take your place amongst the guests. This party is for you, also, Isabelle. I want you to enjoy yourself."

As it was then late August, only weeks before we were to set sail, I squared my shoulders, looked Mrs Chisholm in the eye, smiled broadly and replied.

"Thank you, Mrs Chisholm, for your generosity and all you have done for me."

With that, I turned quickly and fled up the stairs in the main foyer. I felt eyes on me, so turned as I ascended. A very large man with dark hair and a red beard, wearing a kilt of all things, was looking at me intently. A look of inquisition and curiosity. But there was also an element of astonishment and a spark of admiration. It had been so long since I had seen such a look that I quickly turned to look in the direction I travelled. Not wanting to trip over my long skirts as I made my way to my room.

It did not take long to change into the best dress in my possession. A soft sage green with tiny marigolds embroidered by my mother around the neckline and hem. My mother had said when she made the dress that it both matched and enhanced the vibrancy of my hair and the cheerfulness of my personality. As if the red and yellow blend created the shimmering copper colour of my hair.

Mrs Chisholm had been right in her estimation. Changing my clothes had allowed me to change my view of the world. I had changed my hat from servant to guest and was ready to join the party. Hope for the future began to heal my heart. Soon, very soon, we would set sail for a new life in a new land. It was up to me to make the choices that would influence my success.

N Gareth bumped Doug's shoulder, with the roughness of a brother, to gain his attention away from Cousin Adeline. Doug followed the direction of Gareth's gaze with a complaint dying on his lips.

"And what kind of servant climbs the main stairway in full view of the receiving line?"

"One that ye find stunning. Apparently. Close yer mouth, Gareth. I was wondering how long it would take yer tae notice a woman again. Now it seems I have me answer. It is time, brother."

"Nae! 'Tisn't like that. I am merely curious and surprised at the audacity of the chit."

The thickening of Gareth's brogue suggested that he was in denial about his attraction.

"Curious and surprised tae find yerself drawn tae the charms of a girl with hair the colour of an orange sunset?"

"That hair seems tae change colour as she moves under the light of candles. Ye could be right, Doug. Perhaps I was more drawn tae her than curious about her audacious behaviour. A pity tae find meself coming back tae life and be unable tae pursue that which inspired the stirrings."

"Why cannae she be pursued? Are you too good tae pursue a servant? A badly behaved servant?"

"'Tis nae that. We sail in just a few short weeks. 'Tis unlikely the copper bell is set tae sail with us."

Gareth followed Isabelle with his eyes until she disappeared from view. She was intriguing.

"Could be! We are, after all, at a party tae meet others that will be sailing tae New South Wales with us."

"As for the servant comment, ye know me better than that. I will be seeking her out somehow this day."

Gareth and Doug reached the line to greet and congratulate the bride.

"It is good tae see ye again, Miss Higgins."

"Soon to be Mrs Manning. I would like to introduce you to my soon to be husband. Mr Phillip Manning." Chloe turned to Phillip. "Phillip, this is Mr Gareth Forbes and his soul brother, Mr Douglas Robertson. Mr Forbes is the representative for the other family travelling on to New South Wales."

"It is a great pleasure to meet you, Mr Forbes. I look forward to many hearty conversations about our adventure. But first, I aim to marry and take my Chloe on a short trip into Derbyshire."

Gareth and Doug moved into the hall and waited for Aunty Meaghan and Cousin Adeline to catch up.

G "Yer lookin' lovely today, Adeline, lavender is yer colour."

"And I have tae say it is smashing tae see ye both wearing the tartans."

"I'm nae sure how comfortable I am wearing a skirt in London. It feels out of place in England."

As the party progressed, I caught glimpses of the translucent hair that seemed tae be many shades of copper and bronze. I caught glimpses through the crowd, but I couldne find the servant from the stairs. When I had given up and counted it as lost, I turned tae speak tae Cousin Adeline and found her conversing with the copper bell who was now dressed like every other guest. That could explain her ascending the main stairs. The dress she wore was extravagant in comparison tae her previous attire. The fit was perfection and looked tae be purpose-built for her by a quality dressmaker. Cannae have been inexpensive. The colour and embroidery made tae draw attention tae her vibrant hair. But how did that fit with the servant's clothes she wore earlier? An enigma that inspired curiosity.

"Hello, cousin, I havnae seen ye since arriving."

"I've been meet'n many people who we are tae know well in the years tae come."

I could feel the copper bell's eyes upon me, but didnae dare look tae see what she was think'n. I seemed tae be very affected by her spirit, which I could feel standing next to me.

"Well then, cousin, have ye met Miss Isabelle Lindsay yet? Miss Lindsay, this is me bear of a cousin who will be our representative with the FCLS for the next two years. He fancies himself a leader. One that speaks tae God no less."

When me cousin introduced us, I couldne any longer delay the admission of me inner stirrings. I turned and was immediately engrossed in the depth of her spirit. I drew breath slowly.

"Adeline, there is nae need tae scare off every person we meet with such descriptions. It is a pleasure tae meet ye, Miss Lindsay. I fear me cousin has left out the most important part of the introduction. What ye are tae call me that is. For *Bear* is a nickname I could well lose without grief." I gave a small nod of me head and without losing eye contact, proclaimed, "Me name is Mr Gareth Forbes. I look forward tae travelling with yer family."

The veil fell back from her eyes ever so briefly. I could see a gentleness and generosity, but also a mountain of hurt. For the briefest second, I felt us connect. Then it was gone. As it should be. We were yet strangers after all. Doug chose that moment tae join us, and I shuffled the encounter tae the back recesses of me mind. Tae be brought out and contemplated on at a time when I could give it me full attention and hear what God had tae say on the topic.

"Hello, Adeline, Gareth. Would ye please introduce me tae yer new acquaintance? Ye seem tae have become fast friends from what I could see from across the room."

Could me family never stop causing me embarrassment? I didnae need tae be encouraging any romantic attachments. I needed tae have me attention focused on keeping us all safe in our venture. Miss Lindsay looked uncomfortable, so me guess was that she was concluding the wrong thing.

But then I considered that Doug's attention may have been for his own interest. Me insides knotted at the possibility. Although I wasnae prepared tae form an attachment, I wasnae prepared tae tolerate watching someone else claim the attentions of Miss Lindsay. Nae very fair-minded of me. Thankfully, Adeline covered the awkwardness of me contemplations by introducing Doug tae Miss Lindsay herself, from where they started up a lively and congruent conversation about their opinions on shipboard travel in close quarters.

I lagged in the conversation and moved on tae another group of travellers I hadnae met. A location from where I could watch Miss Lindsay without divulging me innermost thoughts. A situation that seemed imminent had I stayed close by for much longer. I couldne remember ever being so distracted by a person in the past.

We left the gathering as the sun was setting. It had been a fruitful afternoon, meeting almost all the people who would form our new community in the colony. The warm late summer evenings of August, with the sunset still being late in the day, made for a good time tae walk with Doug and Adeline. I was glad the venue couldne allow for dancing, I didnae cherish twirling in a skirt. Somehow, a fling belonged only in the highlands, over swords that would cut a mistake.

We talked of what we expected from the people we met. We made plans for the journey and plans for what we needed tae transport as luggage tae aid our new life. Seeds, a spinning wheel, and me own woodwork crafting tools. I had me focus back and wouldne allow any feminine distractions tae prevent me from completing me responsibilities as a representative for me family.

CHAPTER 13

Sails Unfurl

"Do not be deceived: God is not mocked, for whatever one sows, that will he also reap. For the one who sows to his own flesh will from the flesh reap corruption, but the one who sows to the Spirit will from the Spirit reap eternal life."

Galatians 6:7-8 ESV

September 25, 1850

I spent a week at my Aunt Alison's home waiting for the weather and tides to be ideal for leaving Gravesend. Aunt Alison accompanied me to the docks to ensure my safety until I could board the ship. We arrived on the dock to find a milling crowd waiting to be transported by tender boat to the ship that was moored in the river. I joined the queue only to give up my position when Chloe and Phillip arrived a quarter hour after me. My moving back in the queue to stand with my friends caused less outrage with the other travellers than would have occurred if I had invited my friends to join me further forward. I greeted Chloe with an exuberant hug that was not quite socially acceptable. And sent a smile Phillip's way that said, *Don't dare deny me as a friend anymore.*

Chole was her usual elegant self, which made a sight to behold because Phillip had gone out of his way to look as much like a pirate as he possibly could. With a scarf tied around his head to keep his long hair out of his face and a tan that had developed on his trip to the coast. Phillip enveloped me in a hug like I hadn't received since leaving my brothers behind in Ellesmere.

"We can truly be friends now, Isabelle. No more housekeeper to be guarded around."

G We began boarding but a few days before the ship planned tae set sail. We waited on the weather and tides for the best opportunity tae leave port. With our cargo stowed, we found a berth in the cramped steerage compartment allocated tae our family before returning tae the main deck. As I stepped over the edge of the hatch onto the deck, I saw the copper bell arrive on the dock, ready tae board the tender.

A profound distraction manifested immediately. I couldne have that. 'Twould be a long journey if me thoughts were consumed with desire. I decided 'twould be better tae meet her as she boarded. The plan being tae build a friendship. Me thinking was 'twould be easier tae maintain separation from her in me mind that way. Rather than allowing me heart tae run free with fancy. 'Twould help keep me emotions under control, where they belonged.

† The briny smell of the ocean, only eight miles away, alternated with the stench of the docks as the breeze changed directions. Seabirds squawked overhead as they competed for scavenged food. The tender bounced on the churning surface of the water, swollen from recent rains. My excitement alternated with trepidation as I struggled to bring my emotions under control. I had arranged for what little cargo I had, to be loaded and stowed, two days before.

We pulled up alongside the tall ship that was to carry us away. One hull bounced off the side of the other even though the ropes were pulled tight and were secured by the sailors tasked with transporting the passengers from shore. A ladder was put down from the main deck of the ship that was anchored in the river. It was a very unladylike way to board a ship, but the *Slains Castle* had limited time at the dock to load the first-class passengers and cargo. The able-bodied steerage were allotted a boat ride and a climb.

When I had recovered from the inglorious method of boarding the ship and taken a few steps onto the deck, I was struck with awe at being on such a large vessel. The only travel I had previously made on the waterways was by barge. A very different sensation. I felt the ship move and was aware that my feet did not fully agree with my sight. I looked up into the rigging at the height of the main mast and saw small men climbing over the furled sails. I was again consumed by both excitement and trepidation. In the river, the feelings were not extreme, but I wondered how intense my feelings would become when surrounded by a roiling ocean, and no land was in sight. Not that the sight of land would mean very much. I could not swim. The danger of that swiftly became relevant to me.

"'Tis an awesome sight and feeling, is it nae? We sailed from Aberdeen tae London on a smaller packet. Even though I could see land most o' the way, and the seas were calm, I had a very real sense of vulnerability. I was glad of the swimming me da compelled us tae learn even though the water was often frigid."

I was surprised to hear my thoughts echoed back to me. I turned to see the tall bear of a man. Now, what was his name? It took some effort, but I managed to recall.

"Good afternoon, Mr Forbes. It seems that you were given the opportunity to board before me. I agree, it is an impressive sight. I look forward to setting sail so that I might see the ship at full sail. I have been told it is a spectacular sight. But I also find myself somewhat fearful of being vulnerable to the sea. Where I grew, there were many a widow whose husband had been lost to the depths."

"'Tis true, it is nae a method of transport for the faint of heart. Ye though, dinnae have the look of one who is faint of heart."

I looked at Mr Forbes and saw a man who was perceptive and yet not judgemental. I thought we would be able to get along well with a group led by him.

"I detect there is a faint smell of human emesis that no amount of scrubbing can eradicate. I have some tea and needles that my grandfather taught me how to use. I am hoping that we will not need either. Let me know if your family struggle in adjusting to life on a bobbing ship."

I waited to see his reaction to my statement. I felt the need to establish where my healing skills fit into his estimation. I had heard the Scots were a superstitious people. I wanted to know where I stood from the beginning. His reply did not fully satisfy my curiosity.

"There is a ship's surgeon, I suppose ye know that."

He did not seem to take issue with my gender, but more so with my lack of qualifications. This was a fair and reasonable reservation. I had never met a woman admitted to medical education.

"They can be waylaid treating the wealthy and leave the lower decks to fend for themselves."

"True." He drew the word out as he considered what I had said.

"I have no qualifications except that I learnt much from my grandfather, who is an apothecary. And I have read many medical books. A simple tea that can do no harm is what I offer."

"And the needles?" The sceptical look on his face was almost comical; it was mixed with so much distaste.

"A Chinese treatment my grandfather learnt on one of his trading journeys. I have heard many reports of its effectiveness. But as I have never been on a ship before, I cannot verify the claim anecdotally. I am told that if anyone is desperate enough from severe and lasting seasickness, they will try anything. It offers no pain but is hard to explain."

"I will keep it in mind, Miss Lindsay. It was a pleasure tae chat. I must away and ensure that me party are settled and that we willnae need tae request anythin' from the shore."

With that, he gave a small nod of his head and a smile that felt too familiar. As if he considered us to be fast friends. I found his mindset a little baffling. It was only the second conversation we had ever had.

Isabelle and Phillip joined me at the railing while we waited for the rest of our party to board and a steward to direct us to our allocated quarters. As we made our way, single file down ladders and along passageways, the distinctive smell of oiled wood, brass polish, brine, vinegar, and the faintest stench of bodily fluids made me wonder how long it would be before I became so used to the smell of the ship that it no longer consumed my notice.

I felt the ship move under my feet, but my eyes did not agree. My knees bent, but the bulkheads did not change their angle. It was an unusual sensation, but I felt confident that with calm seas, it would not be a problem for me. Everything that I had read suggested that most passengers would become accustomed and not have ongoing sickness. Even though it felt hypocritical, I asked God for his blessing of health throughout the journey for my fellow travellers as well as myself. I told myself it could do no harm.

With only small portholes and an open hatch for the infiltration of light. The light became dimmer as we travelled into the lower decks. The steward walked us through the sailors' mess, which had a solid table in the centre, bench seats, and hammocks hanging above. All spotlessly clean. The galley was not visible as we passed, but I saw a few first-class cabins in the bow with a feel of spaciousness and light compared to our destination in the depths of the ship. We descended the last ladder into the steerage compartment, which held bunks three high, placed very close together. Some of the passengers who had already boarded busied themselves erecting makeshift tents by tucking linens into the top bunks and between bunks within their allocation. A small amount of privacy was afforded that way. I could see the benefit. But truly, privacy was an illusion. We could hear and smell everything that went on throughout the compartment.

The hull berth contained a table running along the spine of the ship between the married couples' bunks. We were not allotted any of those bunks but instead were given narrow tri-deck bunks that were placed in the stern and bow. Listening to my cousins over the years, I understood that the ship would roll side to side more than pitch and toss. They said that the pitch and toss were the worst for sickness. The placement of our bunks meant that we rolled left to right when the ship pitched in heavy seas and headup-headdown when the ship rolled on calmer oceans. Hard to say what would have been better.

The triple-deck couples' bunks, allocated to couples with babies, were placed perpendicular to the single bunks and lengthwise to the hull. This allowed some space in the centre of the compartment for the long table and bench seats. The steward informed us that the centre table was our dining area. The ship's cook provided the cooked food in what could only be described as buckets. We were forbidden any flame. I have been told that the food served on the *Slains Castle* was better than what was served on most emigrant ships.

The only light was what filtered through the tiny portholes near the top of the bulkhead and through the open hatch when the weather was fine. Aside from stormy weather and rough seas, we were free to walk on deck to take in fresh air. I greatly valued the time spent on deck. The compartment felt cramped and smelled bad even before all of the passengers were loaded.

We were told how to find the privy, and it was described to us the need to flush with a bucket of seawater after use. When I asked if there was a hole for the contents to escape into the sea, the steward gave me a long-suffering look and informed us that it would escape only to the bilge, which was placed directly below our sleeping and eating quarters. He smiled broadly at the horrified look on my face. Five long months we needed to endure those conditions. All I could think was that I went from one bad situation to another. We did later learn that the steward was having some fun at our expense. Most of the waste dropped straight into the ocean and was flushed out by the waves that hit the hull whilst the ship was in motion.

My aunt had gifted me a journal with pencils for the trip. I realised on that first day, it was a well thought out gift. With no ink to spill and the ability to write without a desk being two necessities I had not previously considered. I made a swift decision to again start marking out the days of the trip whenever we had light.

Mr Hill planned and allocated Chloe, Mrs Hill, and me a triple bunk. The women were allocated to sleep on the two centre stands of bunks, and the men on the external bunks. In such close quarters, married life was awkward for the bashful. As I was a little taller than Chloe, I volunteered to take the top bunk. Beverly asked to take the centre, and Chloe was happy with the bottom bunk; saying that she would not fall when she rolled. The thought had not occurred to me. However, once the thought was suggested, I looked to see the net that could be fixed in place with well-placed hooks.

The thought of needing the net made my stomach turn. I reminded myself that my eyes, my ears, and my feet were in disagreement, and that was acceptable. My stomach settled immediately. I knew from what I had read that not everyone would be able to settle their innards so easily, and in heavy seas, I might not either. I wondered who in our group would suffer the most.

We worked on transforming our set of four triple bunks into a space that would be our home for the next five months. We had brought on board an extra blanket each, and I had made woollen hats for each of us that could be worn even when sleeping, when in the southern polar regions. I was glad that Mrs Chisholm had encouraged us to do extensive research into what we could expect. I had not included much research about the voyage, but I had read a very detailed journal written by a young lady who had made the same voyage five years before us. She had omitted the information about the bilge, but it was probably better not to know in advance about something I had no power to change.

In all, my spirits were elevated to happiness on that first day because we were starting a new adventure, and the people I was with both accepted me into their family and were considerate of everyone in the group. No one person stood out as being overly self-interested or malicious toward others. At least in that small space, I felt safe. Something I had not felt for over a year.

Mr Hill called us to gather and then prayed for the journey ahead. The practice seemed novel to me after a year and a half of sharing close quarters with the Wiccans who served in Mrs Chisholm's home. I had concluded that Mrs Chisholm was either unaware of her servants' beliefs or tolerant of their right to choose. I had needed to deal with their devious manipulation, but they were generous enough with others. I was still struggling with why God allowed those circumstances to ruin my life. Well, that was my perspective as we entered into prayer. I therefore derived little comfort from the group joining together to pray.

The following day, the *Slains Castle* docked at the quay for the first-class passengers to board. We were advised that it would be best for the steerage passengers to stay below deck for the duration of the process. To allow space for the first-class passengers to board unimpeded. The advice felt both condescending and reasonable. I was disappointed to miss satisfying my curiosity about the first-class passengers. The assumption that we would crowd to see them irked the most. I must admit, though, the asking that we do not avail ourselves of the deck while at the dock gave me the desire to do that very thing. Perhaps it was evidence of a rebellious spirit? Something I had not considered in myself before.

The following day dawned with news that we were to set sail with the next outgoing tide. I saw the sailors scurrying around preparing the ship. We did not need to wait long. The ship sailed slowly down the Thames with the help of steam-powered tugboats. Once past the mouth of the river, she was brought about, and the main sails unfurled. With so many sailors on deck and above in the rigging, tying and untying ropes attached to the railings, booms, and sails, it was hard to find a safe place away from the action. The sailors did not hesitate to scold any who got in their way.

The sensation of hurtling along the top of the water was intense. I smelt the brine as waves splashed against the hull and created a mist that stayed with us for the first leg of the journey. I can honestly say that when it was my turn to stand at the most forward part of the deck that was available to us, I felt invigorated by the feeling of wind and sea spray that became our constant companion. I learnt later that it was not always as pleasant as it was on that first day.

The journey began with calm seas, good winds, and fine weather. Once we achieved stability in the ship's routine of cleaning and daily life, we found some free time for setting up our painting on the sheltered portion of the deck. We were allocated limited time for the activity as we needed to share the spaces with many passengers. I experienced some of my best memories when painting on deck with Chloe and Mrs Hill. Until one day, we came to the attention of a first-class passenger by the name of Violet.

"Hello! My name is Violet. I know it may seem forward of me to introduce myself, but we are all out of our usual comfortable society, and I am in need of companionship."

This was said with a practised smoothness that I found alarming. However, I could not say why I was disturbed by the young lady who appeared to be so very sweet and friendly. Maybe it was the friendliness of someone outside our usual social class, although class differentiation was less observed on the ship than was usual in London.

Her accent did not fit with the sound of the English upper class. I couldn't place the accent, though. It sounded like someone had mixed in many different locations to come up with something new. The quality of her dress demonstrated that she, or at least her family, had money. Her hands were gloved, so we could not see if she possessed calluses. Later in the journey, when we saw her hands, it was easy to see that she did little physical work. It was true that she had few first-class passengers to be friendly with.

"Hello to you also." Mrs Hill offered once she overcame her surprise. "I am Mrs Hill. My companions are Chloe and Isabelle."

I assumed that Mrs Hill chose to introduce us in such an informal way to match the informality that 'Violet' began with. As we were of a similar age and Mrs Hill was not, the informality did not extend to herself.

"I love to paint. Would you mind if I join you the next time you set up to capture a beautiful sight at sea? I have all the necessary equipment with me in my cabin, but have not yet had the courage to set up on deck."

It all seemed very innocent, but also a little unusual. My time in service had left me suspicious when there was no need for suspicion. I decided it would be best to allow Mrs Hill to discern the genuineness of the young lady, because my senses were skewed by misadventure.

"It's a pleasure to meet you, Violet."

I used her given name to mark a willingness to be '*as friends*' even though we did not know each other. When Violet turned to me, I sucked in my breath. Intentionally, I chose to breathe out slowly and get a grip on myself; I thought the flicker of malevolence must have been imagined. After all, what reason could Violet have to be my enemy? I decided then to seek out the priest that I had seen travelling with the Scottish families. For a chat and a request to pray for my damaged soul.

The window into the young lady's soul closed quickly, and we were left with a vision of beauty not often seen. With hair the colour of dark coal, sparkling blue eyes that reminded me of early twilight, porcelain white skin without a single blemish, and rosebud pink lips, Violet was stunning. The practised smile and gentle demeanour defied what I had momentarily seen, so I dismissed my misgiving as having arisen from my damaged heart.

Each day gave way to the next in a monotonous march of sameness until, one day, as the four of us were painting on deck, a young officer pulled alongside my painting and commented on the way I had captured the colours of the many sunsets we had seen into *one fine painting*. I felt a surge of animosity driven my way, but I could not place where it came from. Violet had decided to join us on many occasions, and the four of us had developed a camaraderie that made those days of monotony bearable. I looked up to see the officer glance at Violet before quickly looking back toward my canvas.

"How did you manage to find those tints available?"

I was taken aback that a stranger was attempting to engage me in conversation. I looked toward Mrs Hill to gauge what expectation would be on my reply but found no guidance in the way I would have found guidance from my mother. I missed my family when it came to awkward situations. My mother always seemed to know what to do. Thankfully, Chloe answered for me. I'm sure my friend sensed my unease.

"Mrs Hill has been teaching us how to make tints and how to mix those tints to create a palette. Isabelle does seem to have taken to the art well. I'm afraid my efforts have not produced the same results."

Then the officer shocked us all by addressing Violet in a very familiar manner, but he was not complimentary. It sounded both intentionally offensive and unnaturally possessive. It left me wondering what the two could be to each other, and if things were well for Violet.

"Miss Whyte, I thought you might have learnt a little more by now. You have been working with these passengers for a whole month with little change in your ability to mix colour."

Three things were evident from his remark. The officer had a previous acquaintance with Violet, whose surname was apparently Whyte. It struck me that we had not yet learnt that detail. He did not approve of her spending time with passengers from the lower decks. And there was some disdain for both Miss Whyte and passengers from the lower deck. If I had been tempted to take pride in my work from his flattery, I no longer could. His good opinion was reluctantly given, and it seemed only given to pierce Violet with a barb. It also showed that he was keeping watch on Miss Whyte. There was obviously more going on there than we knew. Even more surprising was Miss Whyte's response. It was sassy rather than humiliated or embarrassed.

"Well then, you have finally condescended to show me some attention."

"Violet, you know I have duties to which I must attend."

"And dinners to share with any but me."

"I have no say over who dines at the captain's table."

We waited for an introduction, but none was forthcoming. We were to be privy to a personal conversation. Not included. It was very awkward because we could not easily move on with our paints set out as they were. We all added extra focus to our works of art with no improvement at all. The officer's parting comment was even more baffling.

"Such nice work, little Christmas Bell."[8]

This he said as he looked at my painting and walked onto the bridge. I felt an imperative to talk with the good father. I was uncertain if I was sensing things that did not exist or if there was a real danger in those two individuals.

In the afternoon of the following day, I walked on deck with Chloe for exercise and simply to enjoy the breeze after the extreme heat that accompanied the midday hours. Mr Hill had informed us after the last passenger's report, as delivered to the leaders of the groups by the first officer, that we were nearing the equator. We were to make port in Freetown, Sierra Leone, to deliver mail as well as take on supplies and freshwater before heading into the southern oceans. It was certain that the lower-deck passengers would not be allowed to disembark even for a short walk. We were to remain shipbound so that the ship could be ready to sail at the whim of the weather.

As we walked, I noticed the Catholic Priest also walking the deck and thought then was a good time to meet him. I obstructed his journey around us and put to him a simple request that I hoped was in keeping with his mandate as a priest of the papist church. I knew little about the mores for the common people in his church.

---

[8] Blandfordia nobilis – is colloquially known as a Christmas bell because it is shaped like a bell, is red and gold in colour, and flowers in December.

As I made it obvious to him that I intended to speak with him, he stopped his walk and sent a smile our way. For a change, Chloe looked shy, a mystery I needed to investigate at a later time. The good Father waited without saying anything.

"Excuse me, please, Father. I am not a papist, but I enjoyed the services at the parish of St John Evangelist in Islington before we set sail. I am in need of some counsel. Would it be an imposition to ask for your attention when you have time?"

I saw that Chloe was shocked. I had neglected to begin the encounter with the usual social small talk, not to mention introductions. The corners of the priest's mouth twitched as he held back a smile before he replied.

"The answer is yes, of course, I can be available to listen to your troubles. You may call me Father Xavier."

He then waited for me to introduce myself. Thankfully, Chloe had gained her usual composure and, after giving me a quizzical look, responded.

"It is good to meet you, Father. I am Chloe Manning, and this is my non-conformist friend," this was said with a sad smile directed at the Catholic Priest, "Isabelle Lindsay. Please forgive her, I do not think she even knows what she said."

"I would be happy to talk to you, Miss Lindsay. I am due to meet with someone shortly, but I would be happy to arrange a time to talk with you. Would you like to walk the deck with me tomorrow morning before the heat drives us all into the shade? Just after sunup is probably the best time."

"Yes, thank you, Father Xavier." I could hardly barter the time as I was demanding enough.

"I will find you then. Have a good afternoon."

Father Xavier stepped around my immobile stance and walked briskly to catch up with another man. I think that very large Scottish man who continued to be both friendly and aloof at the same time.

"Have you lost your sanity?"

Chloe turned to face me fully as I gazed down the deck in the direction Father Xavier had gone. When I turned back to her, she was looking at me as if I were a simpleton.

"Did you think it might be an idea to speak to me first before revealing your secrets to one who may very well turn out to be our parish priest?" She shook her head slowly. "No, I can see that you do not have the experience of a parish priest. Perhaps your non-conformist ministers are different. Be very sure you want to reveal your secrets to the good Father before you meet tomorrow, for it is certain that he will know all before the walk is over."

"I am puzzled by your response. What can there be to fear in telling my story to Father Xavier? Is he not trained to help? Is it not his calling?"

"Once you tell him, he will know, and he will not forget."

"We do not have a priest in our congregations. We have elders. And I would truly like the advice of one of those elders right now."

"I advise caution until we know his character. Not all priests have entered the *'calling'* because God called them. Some have had a different motivation altogether."

I had made up my mind, though. I wanted to talk to someone who I hoped at least knew his scriptures well. And someone who would be compelled to keep any revelations close. However, after Choe's reaction to my request for counsel, I decided to establish his convictions regarding witches before I revealed too much. What a ridiculous thought! Or so I had thought, before the tempest created by Lilith in Ellesmere.

On the following day, Father Xavier found me before breakfast. Defying any sense of subtlety, I began our conversation with…

"Have you read of the happenings that occurred in the Salem of the Americas?"

"Why yes, Isabelle. What an interesting place to start." He spoke with the gentlest of smiles adorning his face. "I spent some time in the Americas before taking up a mission in New Caledonia. I was sent home to Scotland when most of my family passed away, leaving my youngest sister by herself. She has married now, so I am once again free to join an expedition to the far reaches of the known world. I think Terra Australis can be thought of that way."

I do not know how Father Xavier managed to so effectively loose my tongue. I blurted in detail against the backdrop of briny spray and a gentle wind, as the ship arrowed through the smooth morning waters of the Atlantic Ocean. I told of my shock at my community believing the lies told of me by Lilith. Of my anguish at the betrayal of Angus and the depth of my grief as I was separated from my beloved, as well as from everyone I had ever known. I even described my last eighteen months in Mrs Chisholm's household working under the Wiccans. Then I finished with…

"I do not know why I feel this fear. Nor why I have such a sense of foreboding. I am uncertain if I am imagining things or if there is indeed something to fear. I have always had a keen intuition, seen people's motives and known what to expect from them. But my current fears seem irrational. I do not want to be the person who acts on irrational emotions. I do not want to become as irrational as a mob."

"Job, when in the pit of despair, proclaimed,

> "For the thing that I fear comes upon me, and what I dread befalls me." [9]

"I think, Isabelle, that this may be some of your current trouble. When we are afraid, we draw the thing we are afraid of from the people around us. It is like they can smell the fear and so know on whom to perpetrate their favourite sin. Perhaps it is the demons whispering in the ear of those who would listen. Suggestions that they could do this or that to the vulnerable. Whispering of vulnerabilities that they would not otherwise know about.

"The only antidote is to place all your trust in the Father of life. The one who loves you and cherishes you and who wants to bless you in all things. And remember,

> "Blessed is the man who remains steadfast under trial, for when he has stood the test he will receive the crown of life, which God has promised to those who love him." [10]

"The mob was irrational once it had started, Father. I do not know when it could suddenly start again. I cannot understand the behaviour. I am certain I would not have behaved in the same way."

"Be careful, Isabelle, of judging those around you for their sins. Of thinking that you, in your own strength, could never do such. If unrepented, that kind of self-righteousness will lead you to do the very thing for which you have judged others."

---

[9] Job 3:25 ESV

[10] James 1:12 ESV

"What an interesting thought, Father. I cannot imagine such a process."

"Remember, for today, to intentionally put your trust in God. He saved you in Ellesmere. He will keep you close to himself in whatever comes before you. It is the only answer for finding freedom from the bondage of your fears. For bondage it is, to live in fear."

"Thank you, Father. You have given me much to think about."

As I walked away to begin the day's work, I felt more confused than reassured. I could see the truth in what Father Xavier was saying, but I could not see the workings in my own mind and heart.

After Chloe and I had finished most of the tasks assigned to us that day, we walked the deck and talked. I chose not to discuss with her my conversation with Father Xavier. After we walked, it was my time for too much thought whilst lying on a cramped bunk. It was both hot and humid, with little breeze making its way into the cabin. We had packed the petticoats that kept us warm further north into cotton bags to use as pillows, until we once again were faced with extreme cold. I could neither decide which I preferred nor which I disliked most. To feel stifled with the fatigue brought on by extreme heat or the bone-aching cold, where no matter how many layers you donned, it was impossible to feel warm. My irritable musings were interrupted by a plea from Mrs Hill.

"Isabelle, dear, would you please go to the galley and retrieve our last ration of water for today? It is early, but Mr Hill is sweating a fever and needs to replace his fluids. Would you also bring back a small container of cool seawater to dampen a cloth so that I can give him a cooling sponge bath? I do hope he is not developing a serious illness."

When I came back, I placed two drops of a formula made from essential oils that my grandfather had given to me before leaving

London, into the palm of Mr Hill's hand and instructed him to press his thumb into the oil and then to press his thumb up into his upper palate. I had used the formula myself when starting a fever and had recovered quickly every time. Granda thought much of the formulation and recommended direct administration into the mouth. I then gave Mr Hill a dollop of balm to spread the remaining oil across his hands. The scent was very heady and mildly uplifting. Beverly's curiosity was easy to see.

"What is in that, Isabelle? It smells so fresh."

'It may smell good, but the taste is bitter beyond belief. I admit, though, it is now dispersing into a crispness I can feel in my whole head. I will stop complaining. Such a foul taste must be good for me."

"Rosemary, wild orange, clove, and cinnamon. It is costly to produce, so we use it in small quantities. It is quite a lengthy process to distil the oils. I have found the formula to be very helpful. I can also make some tea if you think we can spare the water. Perhaps it would be better to add some of our turmeric to the evening meal and give all of us some protection. The water is in short supply."

As I approached the deck that same afternoon, I could hear many of the sailors and passengers grumbling in small groups. We had been moving toward Sierra Leone, not at great speed, but moving through the water with wind in the sails. I had not noticed, as I tended Mr Hill, that the rocking of the ship calmed. As I engaged my senses, I realised that it was not simply calm. No movement at all could be felt. Emerging from the hatch, I saw that the sails hung limp and were being furled by numerous sailors. The ocean was flat, without peaks or waves. There was no froth in sight. With the stillness, the scent of the latrines began to hang in the air. I could see the silent and ever observant large Scotsman leaning by the rail with me in his sights. I ventured to have a conversation that would end his quiet perusal.

"Hello, Mr Forbes, how has your morning been?"

"It was a fine morning till the becalming caught us."

"Is that not a mixed-up metaphor, Mr Forbes? Does not the very nature of becalming mean that it could not catch a thing?"

"If it's precision ye like then, I was enjoying the breeze that was moving us toward our destination in such a pleasant way till we were cursed with a becalming."

"A becalming?"

"Aye! That is what the sailors have called it. They say we could be trapped for weeks wit' nary a breeze tae fill the sails. Nae movement at all; in this heat and with little water. They say it is unusual this side of Sierra Leone. But we must wait it out. I, for one, will make the moost of the extended deck time as I understand when we arrive in the very southern latitudes, 'twill be both cold and blowing a gale. Nae good nor safe for time on the deck."

"I am not sure which I will prefer. The cold and rocking or the stagnant, oppressive heat."

"I hope it isnae the heat ye despise, for ye are heading tae a town that is known tae be much hotter than home." I felt a little like I was being lectured, so I prickled.

"I did my research also, Mr Forbes, I believe that Sydney Town is to be milder than this most of the year."

"I will ask ye in a week what ye think. The *Squatter* who spoke tae us about his time in New South Wales told that the summer would give several weeks of extreme heat with nae respite overnight."

"Then I suppose I will need to enjoy the many weeks of cooler weather when they are upon us."

"'Tis a beautiful climate that we are heading for then."

Mr Forbes looked disappointed rather than annoyed by my prickles. I did not understand why I was prickly. I simply felt annoyed. With him! Without reason. I was anxious for no reason and took it out on whoever was around.

Mr Forbes displayed more forbearance than I would have. He did not walk away but simply waited. When my conscience pricked, I attempted a new topic of conversation.

"Will you be travelling on to Port Adelaide? I disembark in Port Phillip myself."

"As will I. I am headed tae Sydney town. Well, twenty-four miles south of Sydney, in the Cumberland area. Most of me family group are farmers. I am a cabinet maker and will set up shop close tae their farms."

"I will be travelling to Sydney town also. I am to apprentice with a couple who have no children. I am uncertain in which part of Sydney their business is located. I suppose it is remiss of me not to have asked that question. But then, it was not a factor in the decision to travel." My voice dropped to a tone with a sad cadence. "I had little choice. Decisions were made for me in my fugue."

Gareth told me later that he could not place the meaning for my use of the root word for fugitive, but he did not comment; he decided not to pursue a better understanding. He said I sported a fragility that was easy to see.

"'Tis a long way to travel from home for an apprenticeship."

"I was not given a choice in the '*travelling a long way from home*'. As it was, I needed to leave my community behind."

An intense sadness came across me and permeated the air around us. The spark of resentment in my tone was easy to hear. Gareth, ever observant, understood my mood and matched me for sadness, but I could not see in him any anger or resentment about leaving his home behind. Perhaps he was more an emigrant than a refugee.

"My mother is a dressmaker; my training is almost complete. The couple are looking for someone to do life with as much as help in the shop."

"'Tis a sad thing we must leave our loved ones behind. Nae matter the circumstances that bring us tae that place."

I could see that Gareth was speaking from experience, but neither one of us wanted to share the details of our circumstances.

"I am glad to be looking forward to better things, Mr Forbes. I have done much reading about the colony of New South Wales and the things we can expect. What is to be found twenty-four miles south of Sydney?"

"Me family are headed tae Sydney Town first. Then, we will be heading south tae a similar location where the Hill family will be settlin'. Southwest of Botany Bay. They have opened up an area eccentrically called Bottle Forest. There are currently tall cedar trees in the area that are good for making furniture, and parcels of land for farming."

"You know then that I travel with the Hills? A simple deduction, I suppose, as I am with them much and share bunks with the family. There is no privacy in the steerage compartment."

"I have talked at length with Mr Hill, as the leader of his group, when we meet tae receive updates from the first officer. We've built a good rapport with each other. God has provided ye with a good man tae watch out for ye in yer new life."

The longer we talked, the more relaxed we became, but it felt like he knew more about me than I knew of him. I felt vulnerable, so remained internally prickly.

N Isabelle walked away, leaving Gareth with a feeling that he had been viewed with suppressed animosity. He remained at the rail, hoping for a breeze, though none was to be had.

Doug was often at a loose end on what he viewed as an horrendous voyage. He was one of those unfortunate souls who remained sick at sea throughout the journey, except in very still waters.

Doug came to rest beside Gareth in a mood better than Gareth had seen since setting sail.

G "What a lovely day tae be alive. Not an iota of sickness. If only it meant we were getting closer tae our destination."

"'Tis surprised I am to see yer so chirpy, Doug. So now you look forward tae reaching New South Wales?"

"Nooo, I cannae claim that. I am anxious tae depart this living hell of a tiny home bobbing in a vast expanse of ocean."

I was relieved tae feel some amusement after the last conversation, which I had found so unsettling.

"Yer finally talking tae the lass then. 'Tis about time. When I saw ye together, I walked an extra lap of the deck tae give ye time tae chat. It appeared a close tete-a-tete. Will she be settling anywhere near us, do you know?"

"Ye know full well I've done me research. I have found out much from Mr Hill, hopefully without appearing tae be the hunter." Doug laughed at me own expense.

"'Tis good tae see yer discomfort. It takes me mind off me loss. And I know Molly wouldne have ye pine forever."

"I'll admit I have moments of guilt. I know Molly wouldne have me pine. She was too merciful for that. But still, it makes me reluctant tae pursue me interest. It feels a little like I'm putting Molly out of this life by thinking less aboot her. It makes me reluctant tae find a new life. Tae diminish the memory by creating new ones without her. And I dinnae want tae be living with comparisons."

"And I'm sure yer future wife, whoever she may be, will nae want that either."

"We have too many things tae be expending our attention on once we arrive in Sydney. I have nae space tae be courting a lass. From what I understand, she is still a lass. Very young. I cannae deny I feel drawn tae her, though. She doesnae know the area tae which she is headed. I also cannae deny I hope it will be close tae where we settle."

N Gareth and Doug sank to the shade in the lee of the railing on the deck. There was no point in going below where it was hotter than above.

CHAPTER 14

Crossing Over

"Those whom I love, I reprove and discipline, so be zealous and repent. Behold, I stand at the door and knock. If anyone hears my voice and opens the door, I will come in to him and eat with him, and he with me. The one who conquers, I will grant him to sit with me on my throne, as I also conquered and sat down with my Father on his throne."

- Revelation 3:19-21 ESV

November 1850, Sierra Leone

It was a full week before we had sufficient breeze to fill the sails enough for movement toward Freetown. The ship pulled into port in Freetown to deliver cargo, post, and packages from London. The first-class passengers disembarked for a few days, leaving the steerage to barter for some supplies with traders who were allowed onto the ship.

Mrs Hill, Chloe, and I found the bright colours of African fabrics and tints appealing. We purchased a new shirtfront each that was more suited to the climate and discarded the same quantity of clothing that was worn and washed to death. The tints were different to what we had seen before, so we set up to paint a scene of the harbour. Making a short competition of the effort.

As we were painting, Violet approached the ship escorted by the officer who had seemed so malevolent when he insinuated himself into our group weeks before. Under her bonnet, Violet was red-cheeked and angry. The officer attempted to placate her, but he also wore a grin. The officer stopped the procession of dock workers who were carrying loads across the gangway. He tipped his hat with an ever so slight bow, and Violet pranced past him to come on board. The officer then winked at me with a smile and departed the scene as the workers once again utilised the gangway. Violet, having seen us, made her way toward our location.

"It seems that in this town, we are seen as less than human. I think I may now have some notion of how the blacks feel in London. I was made to wait behind every black person to be served in the marketplace and was shown to an outside seating area behind the restaurant. If they don't like the way they have been treated, why do they insist on treating others in the same way?" Mrs Hill took up the challenge first.

"Perhaps to give us an understanding." Violet's response was fractious.

"Perhaps for revenge."

"That is also possible. What would you do, Violet, if the tables had been turned?" Violet chose not to answer.

I shared some insights that I had gained from my extensive reading through Mrs Chisholm's library.

"With that reasoning, Violet, things would never end. I have read that before white people made slaves of black Africans, the Africans from the Barbary coast abducted Europeans for the very same purpose."

Chloe weighed in on the conversation then.

"And before that, the Romans took people from all over to feed their slave market."

"That is interesting. I did not know that. So, you are saying then that white people abducting Africans was payback?"

Violet huffed at the convoluted reasoning.

"This is an unnatural place. No civilised society would treat the fair-complexioned people in that way. Every educated person knows that the blacks are less capable of governing."

"It seems you will be better to stay on the ship then, Violet."

"Yes, that is what my fiancée has just said as he escorted me back to the ship. I did not appreciate his amusement at my discomfort." Violet turned to Beverly. "Would you mind, Mrs Hill, if I join you in painting the harbour? It is very picturesque. I have acquired some new tints in the market. But I can see you also have acquired new tints. However, did you manage that without leaving the ship?"

We explained that the vendors had been allowed onboard, and Violet commented that that was probably more pleasant than her own experience. I, for one, would have preferred to experience the local population as they were. We spent the remainder of the afternoon creating our impressions of the port. Each piece showed the mood of the artist in the colours and emphatic view. I voted that Chloe's was the happiest of paintings.

"Could we attach your work to the bulkhead somehow? Do you think the captain would mind?"

"I'm certain we could do that, Miss Lindsay." I nearly jumped out of my skin when the deep, thick brogue spoke behind me.

"I was unaware that you had joined us, Mr Forbes."

"I have some small tacks which we could utilise to display the art. The paper is thin, and the bulkhead strong. 'Twould be good for all our spirits."

Violet studied us as we interacted.

Mrs Hill accepted Mr Forbes' offer and suggested we tack more than one piece of art to the uprights near the dining bench.

"We can get started this afternoon."

Mr Forbes stayed to chat with each of us before making his way to a group of men playing cards.

"You have a beau then, Isabelle?"

The comment startled me into turning my view back to Violet. I saw both Chloe and Mrs Hill exchange glances.

"No!" I said far too adamantly. "We are barely acquaintances, and he is not much to my liking."

I almost explained that Angus was nothing like Mr Forbes but caught myself before speaking it aloud. After all, Angus had not been a shining example of masculine virtue. I needed to review what I would value in a spouse. The comment did, however, cause me to consider whether Mr Forbes was showing interest. But I concluded that he was equally polite to all of us and spent the same amount of time talking to each of us.

The voices on the port side of the ship, where Mr Forbes had gone to talk to the passengers playing a friendly game of cards, started to rise in volume and tone. There was an argument underway, and when we turned to view the goings on, we could see Mr Forbes holding two passengers apart. I did not know either of the passengers to talk with but had of course seen them around. The dark-haired, short man was often seen taking the food and drink ration from the tall, slender man who had copper coloured hair and an abundance of freckles. I often considered myself fortunate to not have the freckles that commonly accompany the orange hair.

I could never understand the bigger man giving way. But we were to be eyewitnesses to the reason why. Mr Forbes had a hand on the head and the chest of the dark-haired man, holding him back effortlessly, while the small, angry man threw ineffective punches. As the small man began to calm, Father Xavier came and stood beside Mr Forbes to lend his authority to the situation. But I could see that Mr Forbes had it well in control. After speaking a few words to the angry man, he returned to the victim what he had previously swiped from his hand. With no fuss, the men parted, no doubt to pick up the altercation once again at a later time.

Father Xavier made his way over to the red-headed man and settled in for a lengthy conversation. It was refreshing to see a person stand with the timid to give aid. I had to admit to myself a stirring of attraction for the big Scotsman. If only Angus had stood with me.

I was plunged once again into regret for the past and sadness for my loss. I could not find cohesion in my emotions regarding Angus. I both still loved him, so grieved his loss, and hated him for deserting me. I never wanted to set eyes on him again and yet missed talking to him about the things that mattered.

A good thing, I suppose, given that I never would see him again. Attraction or no attraction, I was not ready to risk the hurt again, so put the emotion aside. Violet, however, was not slow to voice her impression. With a cat smelling the milk look on her face and a purring smoothness to her voice, we were left with no doubt.

"Well then, now that is an impressive man. Do you think he has a future as a landowner in the colony? You did say, Isabelle, that he is not your beau?"

"It was my understanding, Violet, that you are engaged to Mr Garret, the second officer. Are we mistaken?" Chloe was always aware of and could abridge the centrality of a matter. The perfect diplomat.

"Mr Garret is simply the best choice from a bad lot. My father insisted that I marry on my return to Sydney because I ran away from my governess in France and insisted on travelling home alone. I am certain my father's choice of groom would not be to my liking. Mr Garret wants to settle in Melbourne. There is talk of gold, and he plans to become very rich. He thinks that my father can help set him up in business in the country around Melbourne. We have a business agreement, that is all."

"I suppose that explains why he shows interest in all the pretty girls on board." Violet prickled at the stab. I was surprised at the unexpected barb from Chloe.

"Perhaps he should mend his ways, then, if he hopes to retain my interest. My father is a merchant in Melbourne who can make or break Mr Garret."

An awkward silence fell as we all searched out other topics of conversation. Extraordinarily, I was the first to offer the new topic.

"Do you like to sew, Violet? We have each purchased some fabric from the traders allowed on board and plan to sew ourselves a new shirtfront."

"I embroider. I leave the mundane sewing to the dressmaker. She does a commendable job. Far better than I could do. Mrs Butler has a way of making my figure look its best."

"Then she must be a good dressmaker."

"Are you insulting my figure, Isabelle? I thought you sweeter than that."

Surprise at my comment being misunderstood led me to reinforce the lesson I was learning: That I needed to remain silent!

"I only sought to compliment the dressmaker. A good dressmaker knows how to enhance natural beauty as well as cover the flaws a person perceives in themselves."

With a flick of her head, Violet turned to Chloe, angling her body to exclude me from further conversation. I was at a loss to understand her intention. Not sure I had done anything to warrant her disregard. Once Violet had left our company, I had to ask Chloe what she thought of the encounter.

"I think that you may be her competition with both gentlemen. Have you not noticed the regard paid to you by both Mr Garret and Mr Forbes?"

"Mr Garret is secured by her, and I can be no competition as I will be an immigrant who owes money; and so would have no way to advance his desire of being rich. Violet is beautiful. Why would he look elsewhere?"

"It seems that he plays games with her. He knows he has an upper hand and seems to behave disrespectfully. It is probably Violet's own insecurity rather than rational deduction. Mr Forbes is another thing. He is an ordinary tradesman; I am not sure why she could be genuinely interested in him. But her interest was plain to see when he was conversing with you and when he gallantly stepped in to aid the lanky copper-top."

"Yes, but Chloe, although I see that Mr Garret plays games by paying attention to me in Violet's company, Mr Forbes treats me like all other passengers headed in the same direction. There is no special regard."

And so, Mrs Hill joined the conversation.

"I believe, Isabelle, that he hides it well by treating those around you with special regard so that his regard for you is not obvious. According to Mr Hill, he has asked a lot of questions about where you are going and who will be your guardian. He has also commented that you are still very young. Through our few encounters, I have seen that he is drawn to you. I am not sure why he seems to have decided not to act on that attraction. At least for the time being."

That set me to thinking about what I thought. Truly, I was reluctant to consider any romantic entanglement after Angus. My heart still hurt very badly. How could I trust another after the betrayal of Angus? I decided to discourage any interest from anyone.

Two weeks following our arrival in Freetown, the *Slains Castle* was restored, and minor repairs were made. We were ready to set sail, so the first-class passengers were recalled to the ship. Before we could get underway, another ship came into port from the south and disseminated reports of the doldrums south of Freetown. The captain called the leaders to a meeting and explained the situation of the winds. He then informed the family leaders of the need to cross the Atlantic to the coast of South America before catching the winds that would take us south. There was general acceptance of the plan. No one was keen to be in the doldrums again.

As we approached the equator, the sailors began to prepare for a celebration on deck. We were told that the sailors crossing the equator for the first time would undergo a ritual. And if the male passengers did not wish to undergo the same ritual, they should make themselves invisible for the day. The fun and frivolity made for a refreshing incursion into the boredom of such a long journey with so small a group of people. What had seemed like a large group at the beginning of the journey now seemed very limited in social interaction.

A few days after leaving Freetown, the crew began to display signs of having contracted a fever whilst in port. No one seemed to be extremely ill, but the fever progressed from the crew to the passengers in the steerage hold. Our group added the protective spices to our meals and seemed to be recovering easily. I was sitting on deck, enjoying the breeze as I wrote in my journal, when Chloe came to me with concern on her face. It was her turn to care for the members of our group who were laid low.

"Isabelle, do you have any of that remedy left that you used to treat Mr Hill? I fear that Mrs Hill is worse off than the younger of us have been."

By then, Chloe was becoming familiar with the remedies that I carried and had seen me use them.

"Yes, it is in the box of oils. Do you need me to come and help?"

"No, Issy, you take your rest, I know which bottle, and I know what to do."

I smiled gratefully and knew that I could trust Chloe, so I chose to stay put and finish my journal entry. As Chloe moved back to the hatch, I saw that Violet had paused in her conversation with Samuel. We had not had the pleasure of Violet's company since the outbreak of fever had begun. It seemed sensible to me that she was keeping a distance whilst so many from below decks were ill. Violet gave me a look of simpering satisfaction. I took a moment to wonder what could be behind the look but decided that I did not need to know. I considered that it could not be important and returned to my writing.

The winds across to Brazil were slow and not always in our favour, but we made headway and were treated with the added experience of South America that we would not have otherwise seen on our voyage. We came into port once again to replenish supplies and glean information from other ships travelling the Atlantic Ocean.

The lower deck passengers were allowed to disembark for a day trip into Macau, Rio Grande Do Norte, where the Hill family and I found great interest in the dress of the natives. The Portuguese influence was to be seen all over. The locals did not speak English, so we relied upon interpreters whom we had no choice but to trust; their loyalty bought by the highest bidder. I had not seen any native Americans before, and as they were so different to the Africans, I wondered how different again the indigenous population of New South Wales would be. I had read many books, but there were few portraits included in those books. My anticipation of interest in new things increased the further we went from England. The grief of leaving my family was still there but did not occupy my thoughts as constantly. I began to feel joy in life and at the possibility of adventure.

The unexpected sensation of each place smelling so different was surprising. The aromatics that I studied with my grandfather could have given me an expectation for this, but somehow, I didn't correlate the extracted oils with the possibility of that scent hanging in the air of the locations where those trees were found. The scent hanging in the air of Brazil was a complex combination that shifted with the breeze. I would have liked the opportunity to visit the forests that I heard the ship's surgeon talking about with Father Xavier. It was apparent that they had both previously visited Brazil.[11]

[11] Trees of South America/ Brazil. Myrcia (Myrtaceae) high in linalool, a- & b- pineanes, sesquiterpenes, -bisabolol, selinenes and valerianol, germacrene D, b- caryophyllene. And the scent of brine.

CHAPTER 15

Tempest

"Blessed be the God and Father of our Lord Jesus Christ, who has blessed us in Christ with every spiritual blessing in the heavenly places, even as he chose us in him before the foundation of the world, that we should be holy and blameless before him. In love he predestined us for adoption to himself as sons through Jesus Christ, according to the purpose of his will, to the praise of his glorious grace, with which he has blessed us in the Beloved."

Ephesians 1:3-6 ESV

November 1850, Heading South-South-East

The ship's supplies were replenished in only a few days. We again set sail into a NNW headwind. Tacking with a heading of SSE, the ship appeared to change direction often. The sailors worked constantly with the ropes on the deck. It became a hazardous place to relax, so we spent more of our time below decks. The ship being battered by waves caused renewed sea sickness for the vulnerable passengers. We were told that would be the way of it until we reached the winds that would take us down into the southern regions. I noticed that more people began to show signs of sickness. Chloe and one of the Hill boys again felt nauseous. They managed to keep their food down, though, so I made some soothing tea when we were given hot water and added some ginger to our meals. One afternoon, the ship picked up speed and stopped changing direction so often. The sun consistently rose to the port side and set to the starboard. I felt an elevation of excitement as we travelled into places unknown.

Violet again joined us on deck to paint. Seemingly, the assumption of her keeping a distance due to the illness plaguing the lower decks was correct. We had a week's reprieve from drama and once again found the humdrum of life in a very confined space on an expanse that seemed to have no end.

We began to don our warmer clothes, but the weather did not become as cold as I expected. We left home in the autumn and then travelled into the tropical regions. As we progressed into what would have been the winter months at home, we had been travelling into the summer months of the southern hemisphere. It created in us a sense of perpetual summer. An unexpected byproduct of leaving England in September. I found some joy in the experience. Perhaps I would suit the climate of Sydney, where a winter low was like a spring high in England.

To avoid ribbing from the big Scotsman, I decided to keep the sentiment to myself. We had been building a friendship of sorts.

Walking the deck to converse after our morning work was done. I found our conversations stimulating. Mr Forbes was well read, so we debated and challenged each other's wit on many occasions.

Unless Violet joined us.

Then the conversation turned to the mundane. I could not understand why the dynamic changed so much. Violet was not a silly chit. We had had many healthy, investigative conversations with her in our art group. Violet began to come upon us more often. I think by design rather than by accident. I was slow to realise Violet's intention. Not searching for a husband myself, it took me many encounters to realise that Violet had set her cap at Mr Forbes. She displayed a demure expression and hid her intellect. I was baffled that she wanted to lead Mr Forbes on and that she considered those arts a way to draw forth an attraction.

"Do you not think it a beautiful morning today, Mr Forbes? With the temperature just right. Not too hot like the tropics, and not too cold like a winter in England?"

"Aye, lovely it is. I look forward tae the climate of the home for which we are headed. Ye have said that ye grew up in Melbourne. The climate there must be very similar tae Sydney."

"Melbourne is five hundred and forty-five miles southwest of Sydney. Mostly south. Other than Christmas being in the heat of summer, the climates are not that similar. I have only travelled to Sydney a few times, but speaking to friends who did their schooling there, I understand that the weather is predictably milder than in Melbourne. My home often delivers four seasons in a day.

"Melbourne has more of the riches from the gold that has been found. So has good prospects for anyone immigrating. Would you not consider settling closer to Melbourne? You are the leader of your group, are you not, Mr Forbes?"

"Aye, I am the one stepping up tae that responsibility. But I dinnae tell me family, which way tae go. They listen tae me because I do most of the reading, but we discuss and make a mutual decision on things of import."

"You do not see yourself as a leader of men, then, Mr Forbes? It is my belief that a leader leads."

"Well then, on this we dinnae agree. I believe that a leader inspires and demonstrates the best way tae live. I lead by example and allow those who come with me tae offer their own pearls of wisdom for the group tae consider whenever they choose tae be that generous. We vote on decisions of import. We delay a decision if possible until we all agree if 'tis practical tae wait."

It was my turn to weigh in on the discussion. It was refreshing to have a real conversation with Violet along for the walk.

"That must take a lot of discussion, Mr Forbes. For you to wait until you are all in agreement?"

"True enough, some of us like tae spend a lot of time sharin' our opinions. If done respectfully, there can be nae harm in that."

"Do you think it possible, that some choose to agree against their first inclination, just to bring the discussion to an end?"

My comment drew a large smile from Mr Forbes and a subsequent scowl from Violet. Not that she allowed Mr Forbes to see the scowl. That was for my benefit alone.

"Oh, aye, 'tis true. I meself have capitulated on occasion tae simply see the discussion come tae an end. Not on things close tae me heart though. And I think that can be an important part of a group dynamic also."

"How so?"

"The person who holds something close tae their heart is more likely tae make trouble if the decision doesnae agree with their heart's choice. Mostly, community harmony is more important than the logistical choices being made."

"That is an interesting perspective, Mr Forbes. I will have to think on that."

It was easy to discern that Violet wanted to wrestle back dominance in the conversation.

"Can there not be harmony in a group being told what is expected of them and then choosing to comply with those directions? Decisions are made easily and quickly. The masses only need to comply. It is simplicity."

"The crown would certainly agree with ye. But do they have harmony, with so many prison ships as evidence of discontent? And consider, they miss out on the valuable input of those masses who dinnae need it tae be simple. Who dinnae want tae be simply **told** what tae do."

"You sound like a radical, Mr Forbes."

"Subjugation and submission are nae the same thing. I prefer me community tae choose submission rather than tae live where subjugation is forced upon the community. Tae choose submission, we each need tae own the decisions and rules. This is achieved by all being involved in the process of creating those decisions and rules.

"If ye discuss the need tae create a safeguard tae protect pedestrians from horses on the street. And, as a group, come up with a decision tae have raised boardwalks with cordons tae delineate the pedestrian walkway where no horse should walk. Then, even though the horse could be led by its rider tae walk on the pedestrian access, those people who were involved in the decision-making process are more likely tae comply with the new guideline than if a leader at the top simply decided and then told all that yer had tae comply. Or else!"

Violet struggled with the conversation. Not because she did not understand. But because she was used to being the one making the decision and did not like the idea of losing that power. Mind you, as a woman, the only power she had was to convince the man with whom she was intimately acquainted, being father, brother, or husband, to make the decision she wanted. I liked what I was hearing and only wondered if the women were included in the decision-making process.

"I think also, Mr Forbes, we can choose to submit because we trust the leader. We submit to God because we know that he loves us, and as the Creator of all, he can take care of us. In much the same way, the people God ordains to be leaders can take care of the people they lead. If it's known that they respect and love the people they lead, then trust can be placed in them."

Violet's view sounded too idealistic for me, so I contributed my distrust.

"Sadly, although God can be trusted, people are not always so reliable. I think it is true that mutual respect is encouraged by open communication, but unfortunately, power corrupts. People are not always so loving as God in heaven is loving, nor are they capable, even if willing, to take such excellent care of us."

I did not share my personal struggles with the way God had been 'taking care of me.'

My comment was too much for Violet. She made a hasty retreat.

"Good day, Mr Forbes. Perhaps we could walk and talk with just two of us one day, so that we can talk about more pleasant things. Perhaps tomorrow morning?"

Mr Forbes seemed unsure what to do with that request. A request that was so intentionally designed to exclude me. And which was stated in front of me.

"I would be glad tae walk and talk with ye on another occasion, Miss Whyte. I cannae ever guarantee that we will nae come across another soul hungry for conversation, though. As ye were yerself when you joined us today. I am appointed tae spend some time with me cousin Adeline tomorrow morning, though, so it will have tae be at another time."

And just like that, Mr Forbes both accepted and rejected Violet's invitation. I was hurt, flabbergasted, and then impressed. Violet smiled, turned, and walked away.

"'Tis hard tae say if I just made an enemy. I am truly uncertain of what is happening there."

"Mrs Hill and Mrs Manning both say that Miss Whyte has set her cap for you. As she has a fiancé, I could not understand what they were saying. But perhaps they are correct."

"I hope 'tis nae true. I cannae be thinking about courting whilst trying tae establish me family in our new home. Past grief is still too fresh for me."

I looked to see the emotion underneath his words and took note of a soft melancholy.

"We are kindred spirits on that, then, Mr Forbes. I could not yet look at another either."

He looked a little stunned at my statement.

“Ye hardly seem old enough tae have lost someone. But then I suppose Molly and I had been courtin’ since she was only fifteen. We were only waiting for me tae prepare a house for us. Not always easy when space is scarce. A room above the shop didnae seem suitable for a family. And sure enough, a family always follows a wedding.”

“Angus and I had to wait until I was turned seventeen. To be safe; because a family usually does follow a wedding. The banns were to be read the week I lost him.”

I didn’t explain how I lost Angus, as it didn’t make any difference to my feeling of loss. Mr Forbes and I were not destined to be together. We were forming a friendship, but we both knew it was for the duration of the voyage only. When we arrived in New South Wales, we were headed to new locations which could be far, one from the other.

“Will ye call me Gareth? Mr Forbes seems too formal after months stuck on a ship bobbing in this vast expanse of ocean.”

“Yes, I think you are right on that, Gareth. Please call me Isabelle.”

We walked our separate ways for the day, and I realised that I would miss walking with Gareth the next day. It was nice to have that feeling of friendship with another. Violet did not get her way, but she had managed to upset my next discussion with Gareth. I suppose she achieved half of her goal.

G ‘Tis good to see ye out walking, Doug. It can only do ye well.”

“The seas have a relative calm today, and the doctor assures me I will feel less ill if I can see the horizon. Nothing helps, though, when the sea is rough. Ye looked tae be having a good conversation with the young ladies. Which one is yer favourite?”

“Ye know I’m nae thinking in that way, Doug. I want tae establish our community before I become distracted.”

Doug gave Gareth a smirk of all smirks. "Noo, I dinnae know that at all."

Me brows lifted with disdain for his comment. "I am concerned that Miss Whyte may have some intentions that involve me. That cannae be a good thing. Mr Garrett has made his claim tae that young lady clear tae us all. I can sense trouble brewing."

Doug winced. "Ouch! Hopefully, we will have calm seas so that I can keep an eye on ye. I'll do me best tae run interference."

"The clouds I can see tae the southwest dinnae bode well for that promise."

Doug turned and followed me gaze, only tae take on a look of despair.

"Each reprieve is so short-lived. I had best face north so that I can enjoy this moment for as long as possible."

We stood for an hour waiting for the next thing. When the ship lurched, Doug headed tae his bunk. The winds pushing us tae the south picked up speed, and the clouds rushed in our direction faster than we were travelling south. From where I stood, it felt like the wind was blowing toward them, but the clouds moved in the opposite direction. Toward us. How is that possible?

By the end of the day, the wind was erratic, gusting in all directions, and the sea was nae better, with odd peaks of white foam all over. The top of the waves met the wind, sending creatures of white mist dancing from the peaks. The sailors worked furiously. We were all ordered below deck, and the hatch was closed. I made me way to Doug's bunk to see how he was faring and arrived in time tae see him hurl the contents of his stomach into a bucket that he kept beside his bunk. It had been decided early tae give Doug the bottom bunk due tae his ongoing hurling.

"I suppose this is one way tae keep me close, Doug. Will ye be right while I empty that thing?"

"At least we will be movin' quickly. And we have the added advantage of Miss Whyte having nae access tae us."

'Ye have lost weight, Doug. I hope ye are still healthy when we arrive."

"'Tis a sure thing that I will never travel back tae Scotlain. I couldne voluntarily do this again. 'Tis ye I blame, 'cause 'tis ye who convinced me tae this living hell."

"I feel bad aboot it, but it will come tae an end. Has the doctor nae been able tae help?"

"Nothin' he's given me has helped. In honesty, looking at the horizon does help. 'Tis a pity we are locked below decks when the worst of the motions are upon us."

"Young Isabelle offered her assistance on the first day of the voyage…"

Doug's eyebrows went up. "Isabelle, is it? And ye with nae plans at all in that direction."

"We enjoy debating with each other, she has a keen mind, 'tis all. Isabelle offered aid on the first day of the voyage, but I thought she couldne know more than the doctor. I have seen that none of her group suffers as badly as ye. Could be a coincidence, but Mr Hill praises her treatments. Even the bizarre needles. Would ye be willing tae give it a go, Doug? I'm nae sure I like the sound of needles."

"That would be because yer nae feeling the torture of the motion sickness. I am in a place where I will try anythin'."

"I will ask her tae join us."

I knew where tae find Isabelle. She was in the process of treating her own companions. I observed what she was doing; it seemed cruel. But the individuals were nae showing any signs of pain. Mrs Manning was even smiling at her as the needles went into the site on her ear. She seemed tae have other needles hanging out of her hands. I was still uncertain. Doug needed help, though, and the doctor was on the upper decks treating the first-class passengers. I cleared me throat tae make Isabelle aware of me presence. She seemed deep in concentration, and I didnae want tae make her startle.

"Isabelle," I said quietly.

"Speak, Gareth, I can listen and work at the same time. However, I cannot needle and look away." I saw the logic in what she said.

"Would ye be kind enough tae help Doug when ye have done helping yer own group?"

"I am glad you have finally asked. I have been concerned for Mr Robertson. It is best to start these treatments a day in advance of expected rough seas. This weather has come on unexpectedly, though, so we are late, but it should still help. I have finished here now, so we can see to Mr Robertson. I have some more needles. I will remove the needles from Chloe when I return."

Isabelle spoke as she stood and collected her little box of tricks. When we got back tae Doug, he was once again hurling into the bucket. When he was done, I took the bucket tae empty into a larger vessel kept closer tae the hatch. When I returned, Isabelle had gotten straight tae work and needles hung from Doug in strange places. Scepticism and a small measure of horror must have shown on me face. Isabelle gave me a smirking smile and added with cheek.

"It is fortunate you do not suffer from the motion sickness, Gareth. It seems that you would be unconscious before seeking my aid for yourself."

"Wherever did you learn this?"

"My grandfather travelled to China on one of his merchandise trips. He learnt a lot of unusual cures from them while he was there. He did not take up recommending the use of all, but this he taught to me." Isabelle turned tae Doug and added. "The effect will not be instantaneous, Mr Robertson. Close your eyes and concentrate on which way you think the ship is moving."

"Surely that could only make it worse."

"No, truly, I have come to realise that the acceptance of what your senses are telling you can help. Right now, your eyes and ears are in disagreement. You can stop them from arguing so much by denying one of the senses any input of information. You cannot deny your ear, so deny your eyes. Try! Close your eyes." Doug glared at her, then slowly closed his eyes.

"Take a deep breath in through your nose. Good, now focus on that as you let it out slowly. Good. Count as you breathe out."

Doug seemed tae visibly relax. Isabelle kept up the breath coaching for a few turns, then went quiet. I stepped close and put my hand on Doug's chest as I sent up a prayer. I felt him find ease from his symptoms. Then, amazingly, he drifted into sleep. Isabelle stood slowly, stepped away and spoke quietly.

"I will return to remove the needles when I have done with Chloe. You look a little stunned, Gareth."

I turned tae her and spoke quietly as if from a far-off place.

"I admit, I am surprised. I'm uncertain which part of that helped."

"Does it matter? Probably all of it worked synergistically. I hope that by the time Mr Robertson awakens, the needling will have a lasting effect."

‡ The storm worsened quickly. It was then every man for himself. I could no longer rise from my bunk without slipping along the deck and smashing into bulkheads and uprights. I lay on my bunk, which seemed to rotate on an axis in gyroscopic precession. It was dark, pitch black in fact. The stench of unwashed bodies and vomit was enough to cause me nausea for the first time.

Thankfully, the sick feeling turned me away from eating. A good thing, as our food was not delivered, and I had only a few dry biscuits to nibble on. I sucked on some of the crystalline ginger, which my granda had suggested I pack.

It was cold!

So very cold. Our blanket and hat helped but could never be sufficient. It had seemed like we travelled into a perpetual summer, but with the loss of the sun and the wind blasting us straight from the southern pole, it quickly became extremely cold.

The dampness, the lack of light, and the lack of activity brought about by the restriction to our bunks contributed to the feeling of cold. We were not told to stay on our bunks; it simply became the practical alternative to bumping into bunks, slipping on the vomit that rolled around the deck underfoot, and falling to roll in the wet grime that by then covered the deck. There was no hope of helping others. Self-sufficiency and endurance were the only options. It was every man for themselves until the storm ceased its angry barrage. I could hear that my fellow travellers were in dire need of help and felt bad that I was unable, and in truth, unwilling to help.

An understanding of desperate fear filled me to the core of my being. The storm that raged outside of what seemed like our communal coffin set afloat was fierce and terrifying. All that was left to me was to pray. I sent up some half-hearted prayer that became more sincere at the sound of splitting wood and the crashing of heavy objects above. I could not feel close to God, but I prayed anyway and hoped that the prayers of those close to God would be effective. The fear of shipwreck grew, and as I faced my mortality with the expectation of imminent demise, I cried out to the one who had blessed me with His presence in Ellesmere. Once again, I was filled with his peace in the middle of the storm. This time, a literal storm.

The storm only lasted hours, but the damage above and below decks was severe. I ventured off my bunk and tiptoed between the worst of the debris on the deck. I ascended above in search of fresh water, for myself, and for my family, who remained weak. The sight on the upper deck was truly frightening. With all three masts broken, we struggled to make headway. The sailors scurried to create some order from the chaos. The captain yelled orders, which were then relayed by the coxswain. From piecing together what I heard, I learnt we would make our way to Cape Town. Ostensibly, an achievable goal.

It took the passengers who travelled below deck days to clean the filth and return the cabin to a liveable environment. My arms and shoulders hurt from dipping the bucket into the ocean for water to clean the decks. I checked on the people to whom I had ministered. Mr Robertson had fared better than many. He was heard telling other passengers and thanking me often. I was gladdened to hear that I had been of some help.

On that slow limp toward Cape Town, Gareth and I were commonly found talking by the railing at the bow of the ship. Our conversation about books we had each read in preparation for a new life was ever stimulating. The storm had passed over, and the wind was in our faces as the ship glided slowly through the water. With three masts down, our journey toward Cape Town to effect repairs was like waiting for the first shoots of spring after a long, cold winter.

December 1850

After we left Cape Town, where the ship underwent repairs and we all had an opportunity for shore time, I began to hear whispers that would cease when the whisperers caught sight of me or viewed me from the corner of their eyes. I could see that I was being studied with suspicion. Imputed for an unknown crime. I was baffled! One day, when doing our morning chores, Chloe looked hesitant, then began to speak.

"Isabelle, do not fret." Naturally, I became immediately wary. "I have been hearing some comments that alarm me. People are saying crazy things like: '*I heard she was sent out because she makes potions*', and '*she has brought them with her.*' '*Do you think she might be a witch?*"

My heart pumped harder and faster: The fear corporeal. My hands began to shake as I looked intently at Chloe's speaking form.

"Our group knows it is not true. But we do not know where it is coming from, so that we may put an end to it."

"I am afraid, Chloe. I do not think I can manage this."

"Why is your fear so intense? It is only a little gossip."

I left and made my way to my bunk without looking anyone in the eye. I needed some time alone to regain an outward semblance of self-control.

I had not told Chloe about what happened in Ellesmere. The only person to whom I had told the whole story was the Catholic priest. I then understood Chloe's warning about speaking to Father

Xavier. I did not truly know what his beliefs were about such things. I fretted over how the gossip could have hit so close to the truth of why I had been compelled to leave my home. It could not have come from the priest, though, or it would have been more specific. The accusations were similar rather than the same. I became jumpy and suspicious. Ready to defend myself at any moment. But I also lacked the skills to defend myself. I felt vulnerable and afraid most of the time. I began to avoid eye contact and could feel that people no longer trusted me.

My mind would not stop reliving the events of my past, and I could not focus on what happened around me. I began to find myself drifting when people were talking to me. One such occurrence happened as I walked on deck with Gareth.

"Did ye hear what I said, Isabelle? Ye seem unusually distracted."

I dragged my attention back to the moment. With my gaze on the deck, I tried to both answer and avoid answering the question.

"I am distracted, Gareth. I have heard there is some gossip being spread about me, and I am concerned."

"I have heard the gossip. 'Tis ridiculous speculation created for entertainment by people who are bored with the travel. 'Twill all blow over. And remember, you willnae be seeing most again once we reach the colony. Not many of us will be travelling North. And those who will, ken ye well enough to see the lie,"

"Still, it is distracting me."

"Perhaps the good Father could give ye some advice on how tae manage yer distraction. I have found him tae be genuine and full of Godly advice."

"I am afraid it could worsen the situation. Do you think he can be trusted? The Catholic church has been known to treat those accused of witchery both unfairly and harshly."

"'Tis a ridiculous accusation and I've heard only one or two give voice tae the concept of witchery. Ye would think people could've grown past such with the advent of science. But 'tis still a young study for sure, and gossips enjoy the thrill of making baseless accusations. I'm certain Father Xavier can be trusted on the topic. I've seen evidence that he can be trusted tae be both full of grace and sensible. I dinnae believe he would consider there tae be any truth in the gossip. I might try tae discover where the gossip is coming from so that we can put an end tae it. Do I have your permission tae butt in on that?"

I felt the cold wind of the southern latitudes biting through my skirts. The ship travelled at increased knots in the constant winds that I heard the sailors refer to as the roaring forties.

"I think I will go below. I am shaking as much from the cold as I am from the fear, Gareth. I will seek out Father Xavier a little later, I think. I will trust your judgement, though I have no real reason. I think I may have seen enough of your character. Experience has taught me, though, that people can be unpredictable."

G Isabelle walked away with her head down. There was a remarkable change in her behaviour which I couldne understand. But Doug was right, I had become a small bit attached tae the lass. I planned an investigation. Before I could set about me business for the day, though, Miss Whyte caught me by the rail still gazing out tae sea.

"Why, Hello, Mr Forbes. What a pleasure to run into you today."

"Greetings, Miss Whyte. I have observed that ye dinnae join the other ladies in their painting on deck any longer."

"The weather is too miserable for such pursuits. The other women do not persist themselves for very long anymore."

Miss Whyte looked a small bit awkward as I offered nae further comment. Wanting tae get about me business but nae wanting tae offend, I tried tae think of what tae say that would extricate me from the conversation. 'Twas nae very generous of me, but I found Miss Whyte's flirting increasingly uncomfortable. There could be no good purpose in accepting her behaviour as I couldne form any genuine relationship with her. She being of a different social standing and destined for a different location. I had been biding me time. Expecting circumstances tae separate us soon enough. I saw a desperate edge form around her behaviour. An edge that heightened each day. She chose tae continue the conversation without me encouragement.

"Have you not heard that Miss Lindsay is a dangerous character, Mr Forbes? It is said that she offers potions and strange remedies to the sick. The ship's surgeon is concerned that an untrained 'healer' is interfering with his patients."

There was, by then, a simpering smirk on Miss Whyte's face that matched the downturn of her chin, and her looking at me through her lashes. A demeanour that didnae inspire trust. All I could ask meself, though, was whether Miss Whyte was only repeating the talk of others?' The talk needed tae be dammed. But I was at a loss tae know how tae accomplish the task. If enough mud is thrown, then some of it will stick. Nae matter how clean the recipient was prior tae the talk, the reputation somehow ended up tainted.

"Ye have a close knowledge of Isabelle's character, Miss Whyte. How can ye pay credence tae such talk?"

By the flash of annoyance on Miss Whyte's face and the tension in her stance, I saw that I had offended in some way. I was, however, uncertain about the manner of the offence. Me uncertainty grew into understanding the longer Violet spoke, and I considered the subject at the core of her annoyance.

"You call Isabelle by her first name, then. And yet you persist in calling me Miss Whyte even though I have asked you to call me Violet."

"'Tis respect for yer future husband and yer station in life compared tae me own that leads me tae address you more formally, Miss Whyte."

My explanation angered her more.

"I sought to elevate you and offer you an alternative to drudgery. I wanted to help you escape a life destined for drudgery by offering my father's support, so we could have a more equal future together."

I was astonished at the almost proposal. I couldne be certain, but I thought that was her surreptitious intention.

"I would be a much more advantageous choice for you than Miss Lindsay, who has nothing to offer but strife with the community."

Nae so surreptitious after all.

"I willnae be considering such things for years tae come, Miss Whyte. Nae with any lass. I have made a commitment tae me family. Tae focus on building our community. 'Tis me understandin' that neither is Isabelle interested in such things. This is perhaps why we can be friends."

Miss Whyte turned and walked away. With nae obvious anger. She simply walked away sedately and slowly. Greeting those she passed as she went.

After that encounter, I was concerned that maybe I should be afraid. For meself, and for Isabelle. It occurred tae me that Miss Whyte could be behind the malicious gossip, so I set about talking and listening tae what other passengers were saying. I was led by what I heard tae seek out the ship's surgeon. More than one person was saying that the talk came from that quarter. The surgeon had seemed like a reasonable man when I spoke tae him about Doug, and I thought it incongruent that he would be superstitious.

"G'day tae ye, Doctor. Would ye be having time for a chat?"

"Yes, Mr Forbes, you have caught me on a day of rare, good health for the ship. Shall we get ourselves a cup of tea from the galley and find an uninhabited corner of the deck? The cook is always happy to provide me with tea. A small advantage to helping people. Sometimes they love you for it, even though you would give the same care to those who do not."

We settled into the lee, out of the direct wind on deck. There wasnae many passengers on deck because the wind was cold, even though it was then the summer months.

"The wind chill factor is challenging, but we can talk here without being disturbed. I think it was the look on your face, Mr Forbes, that gave me the impression your discussion might be of a serious nature. How can I help you?" He touched his ears and added, "I am all ears."

I was impressed that the doctor was so aware. Many of his colleagues were only interested in the science of medicine. I wanted tae be careful tae make nae accusation without knowing the facts. The ever-present danger of gossip.

"I'm uncertain if ye have noticed the rise of some malicious gossip respecting one of the lower-deck passengers. I'm concerned that the talk could lead tae behaviours that might be harmful. Though I must say, I consider gossip tae be inherently harmful. I have seen a change in the demeanour of the passenger who is the subject of the gossip."

"You must be talking about young Miss Lindsay. I have had many passengers coming to me concerned about the consequences of having taken some of her remedies during the voyage."

I began tae bristle. I thought the Doctor was confirming the talk that I had heard and was about tae explain tae me the bad effects of Isabelle's treatments.

"I have done my best to allay their fears. I have gone to Miss Lindsay for a supply of some herbs on a few occasions. Her box was well supplied by her grandfather when we set sail. It is somewhat depleted now. She is an impressive young lady and has come to ask that I see several passengers from below decks. Passengers who were afraid they would need to pay me so would not seek my services without me first seeking them out and explaining that, in paying passage on the ship, they had already paid for their care. Miss Lindsay has not once tried to treat a patient with a serious complaint without consulting with me."

"The gossip is saying that ye are yerself telling people that '*her potions are as witchcraft.*' From what ye have told me now, this cannae be the case."

"Correct, Mr Forbes. That is something I would never say. Although there are people who dabble in strange religious practices. I am a man of science, I do not believe there is any power in such things other than the power of suggestion."

"I would be interested tae know where such talk is coming from then."

"And why have they claimed my name in the talk? I have allayed the fears of some but others believe what they want to believe."

"Thank ye, doc. There isnae a great deal of the voyage left. There is probably little that can be done tae rectify the travesty, but at least it will come tae an end."

'Twas the following day I came upon a huddle of people slinging insults. There seemed tae be a single person with their back against the bulkhead. I felt an urging from God tae investigate, so I drew up behind tae see what I could see. When I saw Isabelle was the individual being attacked, and attacked was the only way tae describe what was happening, me sense of protectiveness leapt tae attention. I became suddenly aware of how far our friendship had come. And how dangerous the situation had become.

I pushed through and stood next tae Isabelle. I looked each person in the eye before they disbanded slowly. I escorted a silent Isabelle back tae the Hill Family bunks, where I left Isabelle in the care of Mrs Manning. Mr Hill looked at Isabelle and then tae me, but before he could finish formulating the impression that I was tae blame for Isabelle's obvious distress, I requested tae have a chat with him.

"Could I have a word with ye, Mr Hill, while Mrs Manning cares for Isabelle?" Mr Hill jumped at the offer.

"I would have insisted on the same if you had not requested Mr Forbes. I think right now would be appropriate."

He moved toward the hatch with the expectation that I would follow. As soon as we had gained a modicum of privacy on the upper deck, Mr Hill took the upper hand.

"What is happening, Mr Forbes? Isabelle is obviously distressed."

"I think we may need tae protect Isabelle from the other passengers until we reach Melbourne. I just came upon her being reviled by a group that had her backed against the wall. I suppose ye've heard the gossip that is goin' around. I have nae been able tae establish the source, but I am beginnin' tae think it an intentional act tae cast aspersion on Isabelle. With a design to draw me attention away. So that the other might have a chance. I havnae any evidence for that, Mr Hill. I have spoken tae the doctor, and I am certain it doesnae come from that quarter, even though the talk says it does. Some of the comments made by Miss Whyte have led me tae suspect her involvement. I plan tae give the appearance of distance from Isabelle in the hope of removing the motive. Would ye please explain this tae her? I dinnae wish her tae be hurt by what may seem like a slight."

"Are you sure of your own motive, Gareth?"

"I am sure. I will also be distancing meself from Miss Whyte, with great relief, as I dinnae want her thinking her scheme successful. In truth, it all seems very far-fetched and nae very believable. None of it makes very much sense. It is irrational and nonsensical"

† The wooden planks below my feet were all I could see as we made our way back to the modicum of safety offered by the Hill family berth. The very penetrable blankets erected as makeshift walls felt flimsy. They were opaque but not solid. I could not be seen, but neither could I see what approached. I was grateful for the escort given by Gareth. He was never less than a formidable presence. I had experienced instant fear in the moment I recognised the danger. Extreme alertness came next. Then gut-wrenching trauma brought to me, a nausea that made bile rise to my throat.

My fear of things turning ugly was manifested physically in the perspiration running down the channel of my back and the twitch around my left eye. I could look no one in the eye. Whilst the mob were hurling insults and accusations, I stood there frozen, with a deadpan expression. Too afraid to speak or move for fear of inciting more aggression. I pushed the fear to the back and forced a calm exterior, detached from the reality of immediate danger.

As Gareth walked with me to my berth, my dejection increased with every step. I felt hopeless to overcome what seemed a repeat of the past. I could find no understanding of my circumstances. I felt confused, my mind in a fog. I could not make my thoughts correlate or coalesce.

Even though the Holy Spirit had helped me during the mob assault in Ellesmere, I did not seek his help. I cannot explain it. Other than to say that I still felt resentment toward that mob. I forgave Lilith and Angus. But can you forgive a mob? Is not forgiveness for the benefit of the sinner? To be a sinner, you must be a person. I could try to forgive each person who was there, but I only saw the faces of a few. I blocked the seeing of many. I knew that I still felt resentment though, maybe even of God himself for allowing the situation. For allowing the situation to repeat. How could I then ask God to stand with me and comfort me?

By the time a view of Chloe's feet came into sight, tears trickled down my face in a silent march. I found a seat on the edge of her bunk. I sank into a corner. I resisted crawling backward and pulling up my knees. I was aware, so very aware of everything around me. I made a conscious choice to lift my chin and not cower. I knew when Mr Hill walked away with Gareth. I took note of Mr Hill's tone of voice, which indicated he suspected Gareth of wrongdoing. I was unable then to defend him. I was unable yet to speak at all. *Soon,* I told myself. *Soon, I will explain what transpired on the upper deck.*

It was then certain in my mind that Violet was behind the gossip. I couldn't understand why it would happen again in so similar a way. Did I do things to inspire becoming the target of a girl wanting the attention of a man? Gareth and I were merely friends. If Violet had set her cap at Gareth, I would have been no obstacle. The malicious gossip could gain her nothing.

Chloe sat next to me in silence until I took a few deep breaths and glanced up to see her face. She took that as a sign I was ready to be consoled and so put her arms around me. We remained in that position for several minutes until I pulled away, ready to face my dilemma.

"Thank you, Chloe. I needed that. We have become very good friends, I think."

"Friends forever. Whatever the enemy may throw at us."

Pensively, I commented with a true understatement and the smallest of smiles at my facileness.

"I dislike that whenever I draw close to God, trials happen."

Chloe smiled with me and placed her hand on my hand. I still could not answer the question of why things seemed to repeat. And why they happened to me? Was there a sign on my forehead?

"I think for the remainder of the journey I will not walk alone again."

Mrs Hill joined us when she saw events unfold. We both looked up as Beverly approached.

"I am glad to hear you say that, Isabelle. I was having the same thought myself. I hope it does not make you feel a prisoner. It will be for only a short time. There cannot be much of the journey left."

I looked up at Mrs Hill and silently nodded my head as I accepted my fate for the next few weeks. The remainder of the trip looked to be unpleasant, but I consoled myself with the knowledge that there was an end date.

What I did not expect was Gareth's solution to the problem. Nor how his solution affected me. I missed our conversations. They had become an integral part of my days on the long journey. I could not help but feel rejected, even though I knew logically it was for a good reason, and there was no real rejection in his avoidance of me. In some small measure, it felt like Violet had achieved her goal.

Chloe would no longer talk to Violet. She said, *'As Violet could not be trusted to represent the truth in anything. It would be best to have no association that could later be misrepresented.'*

Our family went about our lives doing all the same things. We just did those things with me in the company of other family members. I spent a great deal of time in the company of Chloe and Phillip. And nearly as much time in the company of Aunt Beverly and Uncle Thomas. I did not miss the implication that whenever I was with Chloe or Beverly, their husbands were also with us. For added protection, I suppose. The result of their plan was peace for the remainder of the trip.

I was not hungry for time alone, so felt only appreciation for their care. Having the men with us when we worked at our daily tasks did cause me to consider that I had been socialising mostly with the women and girls. Chloe and Phillip would walk together. Beverly and Thomas would walk together. But until that day, I had mostly spent time with the women in our group.

We had all become family to each other over the long journey. The mutually experienced hardships braided us together.

Some of the other passengers avoided our group.

Others behaved like they had heard nothing of the drama.

No one spoke openly of what had happened.

I saw Violet laughing on deck with other passengers, and I saw her flirting with many of the unmarried men. Mr Garrett always showed up and ran interference. His claim was well marked, and the male passengers began to change direction if Violet was seen in their path. I could not expend my energy worrying about what might happen to Violet. She had taken herself away from my sphere of concern. For me, Violet was a perilous person.

I missed talking with Isabelle as we walked about the ship. The conversation had always been stimulating. Leaning with my elbows against the side rail on the downward list of the ship, I accepted the misty spray that caught me every so often. The wake of the ship mesmerised me as I battled tae find understanding for the things that had occurred. The good Father found me gazing into the wake with me hair blowing in me face.

"I find looking forward is often more helpful than looking back, Gareth. What has your attention so fiercely that you did not hear me approach?"

I made a small start when he first spoke. In truth, I had been so deep in thought I missed that he stopped tae talk with me. I considered me answer as I turned toward the bow of the ship where he had stopped beside me. The wind cleared the hair from me face, just as salt mist covered me lashes.

"Ooh! I was taking most of the water tae the back of me head rather than tae me face. 'Tis true I was deep in thought. 'Tis another person's dilemma I was contemplating. I cannae understand the recent happenings around Isabelle and Violet." I gave no explanation as I expected the priest tae know all of what occurred in his sphere. "Nor Isabelle's extreme reaction. Mind ye, the other passengers had her trapped whilst firing accusations her way. She mumbled as I escorted her back tae Mr and Mrs Hill.

"She seemed tae forget that she was speaking aloud. That she was nae alone. As if she lost awareness of me presence. She said, '*Why do the same things keep happening to me?*' I dinnae know that she had a history of being attacked by a mob. If that is what she meant. I am curious also, Father. Why would the same bad things happen tae people unless they do something tae provoke?"

It took Father Xavier a minute tae construct his reply. No doubt making sure he didnae reveal another person's secrets. Then he started by telling me stories about strangers far away.

"Over the years, I have had a few evil people come to me for confession. Not the regular sinner. People who prey on the vulnerable for pleasure. I'm not suggesting that this is what has happened here, but I think the observation still applies. More than one of those predators has said to me that they blame their victims in part because they are so easy to identify in a room full of people. When they scan a room, they can see who is vulnerable to their advances. They cannot explain their perception. Some say that it is like someone whispers in their ear. Some say they try to resist, but the whispers get louder. Others say that the potentials react to people in a consistent way. They think they can perceive nuances in their behaviour. Then they test out their perception before proceeding. If the potential has the skill to resist, then they are turned away.

"It is possible that demons whisper into the ears of those who have an ear to listen. The demons know what has worked in the past to draw a person away from God. It is also possible that whatever Isabelle has experienced in the past has made her fearful, and so vulnerable. Leaving her without the skills to resist. She is very young."

“’Tis possible, Father. I dinnae have the answer tae her question. I find that I feel her distress, though. I need tae pray on it.”

We stood there together looking at the water pass, then took up a conversation about the transfer from the *Slains Castle* tae another smaller clipper that would carry us up the east coast of New South Wales.

The journey from Cape Town along the roaring forties, as it is called in the latitude of strong, cold winds, is over. As we passed the one-hundred-and-thirty-degree east longitude, the sailors cheered. We were told that unless there was a storm system brewing off the east coast of *Terra Australis,* we would make landfall in a few days. Our perspective of the sun had shifted. Shining mostly on the starboard side in the mornings and to port in the afternoons. The cold lessened, and our bones began to thaw. The joy the news brought to my heart made me smile the broadest smile that had spontaneously bubbled forth since the day I had become engaged to Angus.

I no longer felt devastation when the thought came to mind. It pleased me to know I was healing. A renewed hope was released in my mind and my heart to match the new faith that I had found whilst lying and listening to the masts fall and my fellow emigrants hurl their insides onto the deck. And without asking, God had protected me in that calamitous trouble. My new attitude of thankfulness then transformed me in a way I did not expect.

At some time during the trip, we had all begun spontaneously to address each other by familial, familiar names. It happened without planning or acknowledgement. It happened without our notice. We had been knit together as a family over the five-month trip, in very close quarters, during very trying circumstances.

CHAPTER 16

Terra Australis

"Have I not commanded you? Be strong and courageous. Do not be frightened, and do not be dismayed, for the LORD your God is with you wherever you go."

Joshua 1:9 ESV

January 1851

Once, through the heads, the surprise of a wide blue harbour opened before us. Port Phillip was larger than I expected. The trip across to Hobsons Bay over calmer waters in the one-hundred-and-five-degree heat of late morning was stifling. The breeze stopped as we came to our mooring, which made the heat even harder to tolerate. There was a clear rusty stain to the water, which intensified as we travelled up the river. I could see a thick reddish cloud cover to the northeast that gave an eerie glow to the sunlight filtering through. My undergarments became wet from perspiration as we waited, for what felt like an age, to be allocated a transfer to shore. After such a long journey, we were keen to disembark, so any waiting felt unjust.

It was announced that we must wait for the authorities to send the health inspectors aboard to assess the risk of disease that we might carry. We were also informed that a tax collector would assess the arrival taxes that would need to be paid. We had not been told about those in England before we sailed. It was apparently a new thing born from the advent of a gold rush. I felt lost as to how I would pay the taxes and hoped that they would not be high. Mr Hill assured me that he would arrange payment, and we could organise reimbursement later. I was truly fortunate to have had a person of Mr Hill's character caring for me throughout the trip.

Violet's father boarded the ship with the health inspector and whisked her away on the same boat when the inspector left. Violet briefly introduced Samuel Garret, the second officer. Mr Whyte looked down his nose but relented to meet Mr Garret over a pint after the ship was safely docked. The look of harshness on Mr Whyte's face inspired me to pray for blessings to be heaped on Violet. She had wronged me, but I saw in her father, and the treatment she accepted from Mr Garret, that she was a desperate person looking for an escape from confinement.

I asked my Heavenly Father in that moment to bless Violet with a close relationship with himself. To forgive her and to save her from the bad choices that she was making, and to draw her close. To fill her with the Holy Spirit so that she would be better able to discern the truth of his word in the scriptures. As I prayed for her to be blessed, I felt released from a measure of my own pain.

The acrid air seared the insides of my nostrils. There was a strangely astringent and oddly stimulating scent in the air that cleared my nasal passages and was replaced in waves as the breeze shifted. Shifting between astringent searing; a fetid stench of streets where rotting refuse had accumulated, and then the smell of burning far away. The Yarra River, in which we anchored, was bordered by a marsh filled with birdlife that took to flight with a deafening noise of bird calls. Loud and screeching rather than song-like. The river was an opaque, dark, rusty colour with burnt leaves from upriver floating in swirls. Later, we found out that there had been a bushfire upriver, followed by intense rain.

The people speaking of the rain told us that we could have no idea of the rainstorms until we had witnessed them for ourselves. We were told that the rain drenched through to your underwear in seconds, was gone in ten minutes, and then left you feeling hotter than before the storm. Nothing like the gentle mists of home. The wharves looked ordinary and new. Much busier than I had expected. And it all seemed incongruent with the pastureland that could be seen just a short distance away.

After the inspectors boarded and completed their reports, it only took an hour to bring the ship into dock with the help of a steam tug. We had been deemed low risk and were in luck that a ship had departed that morning, leaving a berth for us. As we disembarked, I had the odd sensation that the ground was moving. We were lined up on shore before tables with government officials. The FCLS had expended effort to make the process as short as possible by providing the authorities with our personal information, trades, and destinations. We were required to organise payment of the taxes and were then sent on our way. From speaking to other immigrants later, I understand that this could have been a much longer process. Once released, we walked the distance of a mile from the dock past a low waterfall to come upon the town itself.

The flat, wide streets of dirt had few carriages. There were new, somewhat spectacularly ostentatious buildings being constructed. The veteran sailors informed us that this was because gold had been found in the countryside within walking distance from the port. The authorities had gone as far as offering a reward for the discovery of gold closer to Melbourne so that the town could avoid losing its population. From what I saw, I thought that the township had more people than they knew how to house in a sanitary manner.

We walked through the dusty market street close to the wharves on our way to the boarding house that had been recommended. The market displayed goods from many foreign lands, brought in by the arriving ships. It was surprisingly small compared to the markets at home, Africa, and Brazil. But what it lacked in quantity was made up for in variety.

There were strings of Chinese men with long ponytails lining up as if in a work party, preparing to walk the seventy miles to the gold field, pushing ungainly burrows before them. The journey was said to take three days. We also saw men and families from all over the world, brimming with excitement, wearing unusual styles of clothing, preparing to make the journey. Some of our veteran sailors were planning to leave the ship and take the journey themselves. It brought to mind God's warnings about storing up treasures on earth, as happiness is not to be found in treasure. I estimated there was an equal number of forlorn souls approaching the warrant officers, looking to work their passage home.

We overheard complaints as we passed by groups of men suffering obvious deprivation on our way to the boarding house. Our lodging for a short stay in Melbourne, New South Wales.

"The landing tax broke me at the start!"

"Water to drink was scarce 'cause those dammed yella fellas would dump their refuse in the stream."

"We had to choose between hunt'n for food and pann'n for gold."

"Got some colour, but not enough to pay the price of the vendors."

"I'm heading to Bathurst, I hear they have found a good strike up there."

The walk to the boarding house was more arduous for me than I expected. Whereas I had no trouble from the sea sickness when on the ship, I found that extreme nausea assailed me once we were on dry land. It felt like the ground was moving under my legs, and my eyes told me that the stationary trees were moving. My eyes and my ears were in agreement, but my mind would not accept the information that the ground did not move. For the first time, I wished for a cup of my Granda's tea.

The plan was to spend a few days in Melbourne before meeting the captain of the small clipper that would take us to Sydney. We needed to wait on weather and tide. The Bass Strait is a treacherous stretch of water. I had no understanding of what was explained to us. How could the next port be so many miles distance? It was inconceivable that Sydney would be so far from Melbourne. We were to have another sea journey that could take weeks, depending on the prevailing winds.

We boarded the clipper only two days after disembarking from the *Slains Castle*. It was to take us all the way to Port Jackson. We were underway early as the weather and tides became favourable. I never saw Melbourne again. The countryside that I only saw from a distance and the wetlands, which I had had no opportunity to explore, were beautiful, but the town had not impressed me. I had no sense of loss as we once again sailed through the heads of Port Phillip Bay.

The weather was calm. But still, the headwinds when we exited Port Phillip were very strong. We had an uneventful journey through Bass Strait, then once again began to head north. The sailors worked hard for the first day before we pulled into Port Franklin. When we rounded Cape Howe, we again had strong headwinds, which may have explained the expected duration of the journey.

The coastline alternated between sandy beaches, sparsely treed parkland, and heavily treed landscape, separated by escarpments of rocky outcrops that looked like colourful vertical beaches. We sailed far enough to sea for deep water but close enough to call into several ports along the way. With cargo and passengers disembarking and embarking at each port.

The sealing ships were in every port with rough sailors spilling from the ale houses. It was good that we had the opportunity to eat meals cooked in kitchens rather than a galley, but we were told to sleep on the ship because they would not round up stray passengers when leaving port on an early tide. We were also filled with tales of woe about previous passengers who had been robbed or murdered by the unlawful in a place with a high percentage of the population as ex-convicts. Criminals who had learnt to retaliate rather than change their ways.

The captain who shared this information with us was young and did not inspire the same level of confidence as the captain of the *Slains Castle.* Listening to talk amongst the crew, we concluded that it was his first voyage along that coastline. He was newly arrived from New Zealand. It seemed like easy sailing, so we did not have any concerns. The crew were all old hands. 'Old salts', as my father would have said. There was also one dark brown man who was indigenous to the Sydney area.

He introduced himself as Wangi without making eye contact and told us that he was '*Guri from Camaraigal fam'ly*'. He had a sing-song way of talking that sounded like a bubbling brook and fired words so fast it was hard to keep up with the story. We all found him very entertaining because he told funny stories about the exploits of his companions and mimicked the captain and other sailors when they were not watching. No one took offence but instead laughed at the characterisations Wangi represented. They were clever and insightful; they demonstrated how aware Wangi was of the people around him and what motivated them.

A week after setting sail from Melbourne, we noticed an increase in the sailors' activity on deck. With those off duty hastily ascending the ladders.

Wangi moved around the ship, securing some of the luggage. Preparing other pieces of luggage for a trip overboard. Yelling at passengers to lash their wrists to the centre grate; ordering them to stay under the thick canvas and stay low. The captain, taking in the commotion that he had not given orders for, turned slowly to Alexander, the first officer, with a perplexed look on his face. The crew member who had climbed to the crow's nest shouted,

"There! Green!"

Then lithely and quickly dropped to the deck. Wangi came forward and started proclaiming to the captain and gesticulating that they needed to enter the bay after next.

"Go straight, then come about into next bay. Not far. Good shelter."

The captain turned to Alexander with obvious anger that his ship was acting without his authority. After all, everything was ostensibly calm.

With his face turned red, he demanded.

"Explain yourself, First."

Wangi danced and gesticulated that they needed to move out to sea rather than enter the cove just ahead.

Alexander, in a measured voice, informed the captain.

"It's a low-pressure system coming fast, and the clouds are green."

He was about to describe what they were expecting, but the captain interrupted with a yell.

"The meaning, Alexander!"

"Wind to sixty knots, swell to twelve feet, and hail."

Was his quiet response.

"And our black man, Alexander, what is he doing?"

"Wangi is a generational sailor of these waters, sir. He alerted us to the pressure before we took readings." The captain once more interrupted.

"How could he possibly know? The wind is calm, the 'swell' is not to be seen, and if Ivan had not climbed to the crow's nest without orders, then we would know nothing about clouds that must be too far away to be of concern, given that I can feel no breeze blowing them this way."

As the captain spoke, a single gust of cold air caught the sail, and the boat lurched north.

"You can thank him later, sir. We must come about, or we will not be able to pass the northern headland of the cove on our way to a much safer bay. We need to head out to sea to clear the rocks ahead before we turn into the bay that is north of that promontory. Otherwise, the winds will drive us into a dangerous cove. Wangi knows this coast better than anyone else I know."

In the background, being completely ignored by the captain, Wangi literally hopped from one foot to the other as he gesticulated his recommendation.

"Geh nee la. Geh Nee La. Mr Captain, look, see south, now. Come about. Hard starboard or we not make safe Cooyong. We go round the head into much better bay. Go between the middle and north head. Wind picking up in earnest now, gusts coming closer together like contractions when Mrs has baby."

Looking down his nose, the captain spotted a couple of small coves that looked to provide shelter and a channel that looked promising. Wangi gesticulated and yelled atop the wind as the ship began to heave in the increasing swell.

"Nooo! Captain, north of headland, not south. Wind too strong to avoid Wreck Bay. Come about, Head to sea, then back through next heads."

But it was too late by then to avoid the cove without being thrown against the rocks of St George's Head and the sheer sandstone so common along the coast. As the captain fought the wind and tried to bring the ship into the cove, Wangi began to unleash the passengers and rip the big skirts off the women.

"What is that crazy bugger doing. I will have him lashed when we are safely in the harbour."

"He is unconcerned about that captain. There will likely be few survivors." Alexander's comment was said with a fatalistic acceptance of the situation. Reminiscent of Jonah's suggestion that he be thrown overboard.[12]

By then, Wangi was throwing luggage overboard with the help of passengers. We could see that we were in extreme danger.

To the north, we saw mist along the bluffs. The waves crashed against the rocks at the base of the sheer cliff wall that extended for as far as we could see into the diminishing visibility. As we entered the cove, we saw a couple of small beaches between the rocky outcrops, but by then the wind and waves were pushing us forward at a speed that could not avoid collision.

Wangi kept saying, "We are headed for Booderie, not Cararma."

And somehow that was very bad.

Where the captain was taking us looked passable, but I was convinced that Wangi had knowledge of the area that the captain did not. I admit that I did not understand what was happening. But as Wangi had been ahead of our white crew at every step, I chose to follow his lead.

The ship broke up on rocks as it was pushed toward the shore. Those of us who could reach for floating debris and kick were washed up onto a beach. Battered and bruised, we crawled out of the water and collapsed onto the sand. But our new best friend would not leave us alone. He had bare feet and had removed his shirt. He yelled at us in his musical voice. Instilling an urgency that I did not understand.

---

[12] Jonah 1:1-12

We had gained the beach, and it was not cold. What could be the urgency?

"No stop, people, until you reach trees. Big rocks will fall from sky."

All I could think was *How ridiculous*. Then I was struck by what could only be described as a rock that had fallen from the sky. *How had he known?*

"From where did he gain his knowledge and power to forecast?"

I mumbled under my breath as we picked ourselves up and scrambled as best we could to the trees. When we tried to continue our scramble, deeper into the bushland, Wangi insisted we turn around. He shouted that the trees would kill us if we went too deep. We finally comprehended and hugged the base of a tree very close to the beach. We looked out to see falling rocks of ice move as a wall in a north-westerly direction. It was both beautiful and terrifying. Thankfully, the trees gave us protection from the worst.

But then Wangi compelled us to leave the somewhat dry space under the tree canopy as he herded us back onto the beach. We were told to lie flat on the soft sand and be quick to roll if needed. I could not understand the urgency of his demands until a bolt of lightning hit a tree. The tree burst into flame and fell to the ground, where previously a family with children had taken cover from the icy rock storm. The hail had come down in sizes I had not previously imagined. Some of the slowly melting hail still lay on the beach. It felt cold to the touch, so I pushed as much as possible away and pulled my hands in close to my side.

The rain slowed into a light constant. The strong winds that buffeted us rolled away to the north along with the thunder. It took about half an hour of solid prayer before we all relaxed into waiting out the storm. I lay there and finally smiled to myself because giving in to the feel of rain splotching my face rather than fighting the situation was surprisingly releasing. Like I said, it was warm enough that we did not feel cold.

I remembered Wangi vividly because he was so integral in our survival. He had such a musical voice and humorous demeanour when he was not trying to save our lives.

Not all made it ashore. I hoped that the missing crew members and the captain were able to swim ashore on another of the beaches.

There was no mention at our onboarding meeting that the whole coastline was susceptible to sudden, dangerous storms. We thought we had passed the '*danger of shipwreck*' portion of our journey. A foolish thought I now understand. The ocean can always be treacherous.

When the rain stopped, we picked ourselves up and looked around for our travelling companions. There were family members missing. Daniel, one of the Hill boys, could not be found. Ainsley, a cousin of Gareth, was also missing. The captain and most of the crew were not with us. We prayed that they would all be safe on a different beach.

Whilst we were still mesmerised following the drama, Wangi was hard at work collecting fallen branches that he believed would become a fire by some magic. He set a space away from the trees and higher than the high tide mark on the beach. I watched as he then went to the fallen tree and picked up a burning splinter. I was amazed that he succeeded in transferring the flame to his damp fireplace with a splinter from the burning tree. To call the wood wet was a stretch, even with so much rain. When the clouds rolled north with the wind and thunder, the sun beat down on us with so much intensity that the clothes that remained on my person began to dry. One look at our group, and I concluded that we needed to spend time on the beach recovering. I estimated that it was by then late afternoon, so I picked myself up and walked over to ask Wangi for information.

"Hello, Mr Guri. What is the best thing for us to do now?" I got straight to the point; there was no good reason to approach the subject slowly.

"Just Wangi, lady. We're not like English. No, mister, and no call me by last name. Disrespectful."

He smiled at me as he spoke but did not look directly into my eyes. It was somehow not offensive. It seemed a natural way for him to have a conversation. He all the while tended the fire.

"We make fire to cook fish or possum. When locals come, we ask to stay for one night, maybe two. Depends, if we can salvage from broken ship."

"Is this not your country? Is there a chief whom we need to ask for permission to stay?" I looked around sceptically. "Do you mean that, to stay on the beach, we need to ask permission? We were shipwrecked."

I said the last statement with evident incredulity. After all, the weather had given us no choice.

"You ask a lot of questions."

He then paused whilst he tended the fledgling fire. I thought I was not going to get an answer, but he was in no hurry, and he did eventually answer.

"This not my country. I from up north. Different people, different elders, different stories."

I think I would have understood his explanation better if I had the knowledge then that I have gained now. At the time, I only understood that he was not a local.

"So, how do we find this chief so that we can ask permission?"

"No chief. They find us. They see smoke. They already see shipwreck." He was a man of few words when not telling a story. Ostensibly, normal life did not require many words. "When they arrive, we ask, then we ask best place to camp."

"Why light a fire then?"

"Light this fire safe distance from trees. Then we put that fire out."

I gazed over at the burning tree. It was not a large fire, but we had no buckets. He followed my gaze and shook his head. I could see that he did not want to have to explain. He quickly looked my way, then looked away again.

"You ask men, come see me. I need help."

And with that, I could tell that the conversation was over. I walked over to Gareth and Mr Hill, who were consoling the members of their respective groups who were by then looking out toward the shipwreck. Searching the waves with the hope of sighting missing loved ones. At least there were no bodies floating face down. The waves continued to pound the shoreline. The noise and the wind took our voices away and made it hard to have a quiet conversation. As one of the Hill boys was amongst the missing, I gave the message to Gareth, then turned to take Beverly into my arms so that Mr Hill could do what needed to be done despite his fear and grief.

When I gazed back, I saw that the men had begun shovelling sand onto the smouldering tree with stiff bark scoops. At the same time, I noticed some black men without what I would call clothing, standing at the edge of the tree line.[13] Observing our goings on and waiting. One of the mob swung something from a string, and I heard a low whistling noise. They watched for several minutes before Wangi looked up and made his way over to them. Wangi made some kind of greeting that involved his whole body. Not quite a dance. He had a short conversation with them, and they then handed him a spear before he made his way back to the men of our group.

Then followed a short instruction, that concluded with downed tools and a procession over to the fire that Wangi had set on the beach. The locals made their way over to the burning tree to inspect the site. My curiosity was so piqued that I had to make my way over to the men's group to find out what was happening. When I drew close, I could hear Wangi giving the men a report that utilised far more words than he had been prepared to use when speaking to me.

"They take care of fire now. It's their country, and they have plans for fire. They not tell me their plans 'cause I not need to know. They give me one spear to hunt food for us and say we can stay for a few days. They keep watch, so no need to tell them when we leave. Cave up the beach for shelter if rain come back. Tomorrow, we swim to wreck to see if we can salvage useful cargo. Otherwise, all gone. We need to make our way to South Huskisson and find passage to Sydney. Not sure how we pay for that." He winked and added, waving his hand toward the women and children, "Maybe we can sell some."

---

[13] I acknowledge the Traditional Custodians of the land on which this portion of the story is set. And I pay my respects to Elders past and present. The Jerrinja people of the Dharawal- Dhurga language group.
Cultural heritage We Come From The Land – Huskisson Heritage Association Inc. A Brief History of Jervis Bay | Jervis Bay Wild

He then had a huge grin on his face. In some way, the situation was amusing to him. Gareth and Mr Hill looked at each other, shook their heads and then gave a small nod. The situation for us was dire, and we needed Wangi's help regardless of his levity. Mr Hill spoke first.

"I think we may need more firewood for the night ahead."

Gareth added, "Perhaps we can also investigate the cave that we have been offered as shelter. We may be better moving closer to there." They both looked at Wangi for his opinion. Wangi smiled.

"Hop to it then," he said as he turned and ran back into the water.

When he returned, he was carrying several fish, which he carried in a makeshift basket made from seaweed. As he approached us, he announced.

"Good tucker," and threw the fish into the sand. He then looked toward where the smouldering tree lay and waved his hands from the women to the tree.

"You can git the bark and bring here?"

The *request* was in the friendly tone of his voice rather than the words spoken. It was a very rough meal. He collected some vegetation and claimed that it was food. The flavour was bland and the quantity sparse, but we were thankful not to starve.

By that time, it was getting late, so we all bedded down as best we could for a night, sleeping under the stars with no blankets and minimal clothing. I think Chloe and Phillip were happy to be finally lying next to each other, and I noticed them disappear for a while into the bush. The night turned out to be clear and balmy, warm until around five am, just before the sun came up. The day following the shipwreck proved to be one of the hardest I can remember.

The salvage was not very successful until the Aborigines arrived with some nawi, the name Wangi used for the small boats made from bark. They were not very large, but they were fast when controlled by the locals. They helped our men bring ashore what they could for the price of selecting items from each haul to keep for themselves. It seemed like a fair bargain as they chose items that were less essential to us. We all wanted at least one set of clothes and the best footwear to be had. None of us possessed gold, so there was no battle there. If they found liquor on the wreck, they were welcome to it, as we did not think it could be very helpful to us except as a fire accelerant.

My medical box was salvaged. I was very glad about that, because I had some basic instruments that would have been hard to replace, and the bottles of essential oils were always tightly sealed, so they remained useful. Each one of us had to select carefully what we were prepared to carry. We were to start our new life with little more than the clothes on our backs. Thankfully, we knew that if we could make it to the office of the Family Colonisation Loan Society, our grants were already organised. Our beginnings would be a struggle, but not impossible.

That night, the local Aboriginal family played host and invited us to share in their meal as well as their campfire. The young ones were not allowed to leave the firelight. One of them explained that the Hairyman might get them if they wandered. They all seemed content to stay and listen to the stories that were told by the older women and men. Unfortunately, there was no translation, but I enjoyed watching the movement that accompanied the stories. We moved back to our campsite together and were so exhausted that most of us were asleep without remembering how we got there.

The following day, we formed makeshift packs from torn sails so that we could carry our salvaged possessions. Only the very important, irreplaceable things from our salvage were kept. My medicinals were heavy even after I discarded what could be replaced later. I therefore chose to take only one change of clothing. I would need to wash and wear damp clothing until we could reach civilisation.

Wangi explained that we would need to walk to the nearest town, along tracks used by the indigenous peoples. He was not familiar with the tracks, but he was confident we would find our way well enough. What choice did we have? He kept using the word adventure. The word adventure quickly became something of which to be wary. The nearest town was a nine-mile walk through scrub, sparse forest, and along beaches. Wangi was uncertain what we would find there because the railway had been replacing the shipping route that transported produce from the mountains in the west to the ports in Sydney.

"Should be some steamers. Wool still need get to Sydney. You prepare to work the cost of your passage, hauling wool? Heavy work. Not sure how ladies travel. You think on it. Come up with something." He then split a big grin and added, "or sell some to pay passage for others."

We knew he was being humorous, but how do you come up with that as a joke?

What was normal in his life?

G The sojourn on the beach could have been a holiday full of fishing and frolicking in an ocean that felt warm in comparison tae home; if we hadnae feared for our very survival. Those of us who could swim took up spearfishing lessons with Wangi. I was very pleased with meself when I caught me first edible fish. Wangi also tried tae show the women how tae find suitable vegetation for eating. And nae tae take overly much from any one plant. He explained that this was nae his country, so he didnae have the knowledge of where things were tae be found. The women were relegated tae this task as their clothing made swimming difficult.

In all, fresh water was the rarest commodity. We relied on the locals tae supply us with water for drinking. From what I understood, they supplied us with drinking water tae keep us away from their water supply. Nae trusting us! Tae keep it safe for their own drinking. Wangi told us stories of white people defecating close tae the water, washing in the drinking water, and deliberately poisoning the water. None of those things sounded appealing, so I was happy for them tae guard the supply. It did serve tae remind us that we were visitors and nae welcome tae stay any length of time.

I helped me family tae select only the most important things tae carry. Nine miles was nae so very far if yer walked on a well-made path, but I understood from Wangi that we would be on terrain tae which we had nae familiarity.

The salvage went as well as could be expected with waves pounding the hull. Wangi said that the seas were calm following the storm, but still, the waves made for hard work. We managed tae salvage sewing equipment that the ship kept for repairing sails, so we made canvas bags for the shoulder or back. We didnae see any sign of our lost shipmates attempting tae salvage, so we feared the worst for their safety.

We started our trek the day after we finished sewing our packs. I was thankful that we were nae alone. God had provided us with a guide who had a sense of humour and who was happy tae help us.

He could've left us and made his own way tae the port with much less trouble for himself. We walked four miles through the bush that first day and came upon a beautiful lake. Wangi decided tae set camp there for the night, which allowed us time tae collect wood and find food. The rocks we cleared from our sleeping spaces, we added to the ring we found for previous fires. We camped in a commonly used space, with permission from the family of people who lived there. Or so Wangi explained when he gave us the rules of engagement for the space. Places we couldne go and instructions for safety. Mostly regarding how tae manage fire. Apparently, it was a serious thing. Something tae be afraid of if nae managed well. We were told that the men were responsible for managing the fire. We were responsible for keeping everyone safe. It was a strange emphasis, but we accepted what he said. We had chosen, after discussion amongst ourselves, tae follow Wangi's lead until we again reached civilisation.

Wangi took a few of the men with him into the bush after explaining tae everyone tae nae touch the snakes or spiders. The women had horrified looks on their faces when this was said. I got the impression that touching either of those things was nae on their list of must-do.

"Make lots of noise." He smiled and added, "They run away cause you very scary."

I joined Wangi in the hunt for a *goanna*. From the description, I understood it tae be a big lizard. I was nae confident that a lizard would be large enough tae feed us all until I saw the creature on the side of a tree. It was huge, with very long claws and the ugliest face I could remember seeing. We followed instructions and before long we were carrying the lizard back tae camp after removing its innards and tying its legs with grass. Grass, like none that would be found at home. Strong, wiry, and long enough tae tie. Wangi threw the whole lizard onto the fire. There was no extra effort put into preparing a meal.

With nae hint of rain, we didnae fear spending the night without shelter. The sleeping spaces were set close tae the fire. We used our bags for pillows and had nae blankets. The weather was hot enough tae feel relief at the drop in temperature overnight rather than fearing the cold. Protection from the insects was found only in the smoke and clothing that covered our arms and legs. Most of us by morning had found an extra shirt tae cover our heads.

The infernal buzzing of insects in me ear quickly became a fearful thing when it was followed by a sting. The night was filled with an intermittent roar of insect noise. When asked about this, Wangi pulled a black insect from a tree and shook it whilst cocooned in one hand till it produced a single voice from that roar. He then opened his hand and let it fly with no harm done. They were nae tae be feared then, except for the disturbance of peace and no quiet time tae sleep. The noise also came and went throughout the hot day.

We packed up camp and started our walk the next day without breakfasting. Most of us, unwilling tae eat the goanna flesh left from last night's meal, threw the remains into the fire when we boiled water for tea. Me cousin had salvaged some tea, considering it tae be a necessity of life. Another nephew had salvaged a small boiler. Wangi called it a billy. Wangi walked up while it was boiling and threw in a fresh leaf from a gum tree. The flavour was both appealing and refreshing. I had tae agree with Adeline that morning, it was the only thing that helped me tae keep moving, and tae keep encouraging our party tae keep moving. We were glad tae share with the Hill family. We had become like family tae each other by then.

We helped each other to keep moving despite the grief of walking away from our missing family members. It was one of the hardest things we had ever done. We prayed that they had survived and would be able tae find their way back tae us somehow. We had another long walk in front of us that day, but Wangi assured us we would be able to reach South Huskisson by late evening if we 'pushed hard'.

As we walked along, I noticed some magenta-pink berries about the size of a Persian grape. Elongated rather than round. When I pointed them out to Wangi, he responded with a wide smile.

"Here Miss. *Lilli Pilli*. They gib you less thirst for walk. Best to eat from ground if you can find one not preeblously chewed."

When I bit into the flesh of a berry untainted by insects, there was an immediate sour and tart flavour with little sugar. But Wangi was right, it somehow made my mouth feel refreshed and started the saliva, which then masked my thirst. That, in turn, made me feel energised. I took to eating one berry every time we came to a bush with fruit ripened enough to fall from the tree.

It became more difficult to see as the sun sank behind the mountain to the west of where we walked. I heard some rustling in the undergrowth and turned to see a furry creature with a not-quite-pointy snout, round girth, small pointy ears at the top of its head, and beady yet sleepy eyes. It ignored us as it slowly munched on the green shoots coming up through the charred surface under the trees. There seemed to be a patch of burned ground, approximately twenty feet in diameter. The creature looked so cuddly that I began to approach without thinking there could be any danger. As I turned and stepped out to approach the creature for which I had no name, a spear came down in front of me to halt my progress. I looked up to see Wangi looking at me. He gave a slight shake of his head without taking his gaze from me.

"No, miss, him have big claws. No touchy. No good for eating, so we leave him. We camp over there. Kangaroos be here soon. We spear and eat one. Ground is good now for bringing the kangaroo."

I caught the main meaning of his words but felt that I did not quite understand everything he meant to communicate. He had such an unusual way of expressing himself. He seemed to use as few words as possible to gain my compliance. And then, with one word and a hand signal, the rest of our group set up camp not far away. Perhaps he thought I understood his full meaning.

Gareth came alongside me with a concerned look.

"It was my understanding that we would reach the town today."

"Aye, it was tae be so, but we havnae made good time, with some of us nae able tae walk fast. It does indeed seem we are tae spend another night around a campfire. How are ye after the spear came down in front of ye like that? I fear that me own heart is still pounding. Wangi seems tae enjoy shocking us, one way or another."

Gareth offered a smile with his compassionate words. However, when I looked over at Wangi, I could see a much larger grin splitting his face. I couldn't decide if I should feel fear, amusement at being the target of his joke, or just plain annoyed. The spear had not landed very close to me, just close enough to give me a start. The ponderous creature moved off slowly. Evidently, not concerned about the intruders.

"Thank you for asking, Gareth. It seems I need to avoid taking things seriously when Wangi is involved. And hope we come to no harm. Do you think he can be trusted?"

"Aye. I trust in God tae see us through. We have little choice but tae trust Wangi. He is currently helping us tae survive a situation we would struggle much harder with if he were nae with us. I'm choosing tae be thankful. He communicates with the men more than the women. Cannae say as I understand why that would be."

I felt reassured. Or at least acknowledged. It seemed like Gareth could understand how strange it all felt for the women. But then I suppose his cousins had been expressing concerns similar to my own.

I emerged from slumber the next day with a feeling that I had been stared awake. Through slitted openings of my eyelids, I saw that our group had been surrounded by Aborigines standing on one leg holding spears. I was rigid until I heard Wangi talking to them from a position by the fire, where he sat on his heels without his knees touching the ground, apparently unconcerned. He talked to the men surrounding us in their language, so we had to wait for a translation of their demands. After about a quarter hour, Wangi switched to his version of English.

"We sleep close to hunting ground, and they want us to move. They already knew we trabling through them country, so not mad. They invite us to hunt with them for breakfast. We get up now. Move!"

At that statement, we all rose quickly. We had all been sufficiently startled, to not insist on finding a drink. Nor relieve ourselves in the nearby bush. We donned our packs, cleaned up the area that we had disturbed and followed the natives back to the patch of ground that had been blackened by fire.

As we watched the mob '*hunt*', I began to understand more of what Wangi had said the day before. The animals that were good for eating were themselves munching vigorously at the green shoots that could be seen emerging from the burned patch. The men slaughtered simultaneously the animals they had selected for eating. The *kangaroos,* which I guessed was the name of the creatures, were eating without concern for the men who slowly surrounded them.

One very large creature stood on its hind legs and gazed at the hunters, ears twitching and alert, while the others continued to eat. As the first spear flew, the animals startled and hopped in different directions. One came straight toward me. I, like a startled rabbit, stood my ground. Thankfully, at the last moment, it dodged on a tangent around me. Wangi shook his head as he looked at me sprawled on the ground. He then shared a joke in the language of his group, and they all laughed.

"No catch for wrestle, spear to eat."

I laughed also, my pride could not sink any lower, so was content to be of service in adding humour to the morning. They only killed three *kangaroos*. I thought their success had been limited but gained an inkling of the truth that they had purposely only killed three of the hopping creatures when it came time to carry them back to the camp.

We then stopped only a mile from our previous location, and the men began to set the space alight. I was stunned, then a little panicked. It was not a hot day, and the breeze was gentle. I could see no good reason to be setting the place alight. And I could not get the men to answer my questions of why. We were told to sit under the shade of a distant tree and not leave that shade until instructed. I thought the whole thing very high-handed of them and did not like the feeling of vulnerability as the fire spread. They purposely spread the fire by brushing the ground at the base of the fire with fresh cuttings of green leafy branches. I was raised to be afraid of fire unless it was contained in a brick fireplace, so thought it was very risky behaviour. We sat for what felt like hours whilst the locals played with fire.

When they had finished their game, and I admit it was a game of which they maintained absolute control, they called us with a hand signal to follow them. No words of explanation were offered. They signalled in a manner that indicated they were the masters of their location and we the interlopers. The signal was their only invitation for us to follow them to their camp.

As I walked with the local women to the shoreline from the women's camp that afternoon, and as we sat eating the oysters we were collecting, they explained the practice of farming with fire. They deliberately set fire to a patch of undergrowth so that when it began to grow back, the wildlife were attracted to the new growth and became easy targets. They then described how they caught a possum by lighting the underneath of a tree to smoke the climbing creature out of its hole so that a man who had climbed the tree could then club it over the head. I immediately looked to the trees and was baffled that anyone could climb those tall trees. They had no low branches on which to cling. I decided that I would like to see that one day. Guessing that there must be a trick other than pure physicality.

We had another night by the campfire listening to stories told in an unknown language. The stories had a singsong sound to them that I enjoyed, and body language that was almost a dance. It cooled off enough at night for us to sleep comfortably without a blanket. As I looked up at the stars that were different to what was seen from home, I knew that I needed to stop thinking of England as home. I knew that I needed to start thinking of this colony as my home, or I would remain forever homesick. But I lay there beside the fire, looking up into the unfamiliar constellations, and allowed myself to be lulled into a sense of foreign melancholy. The hurt was refreshed in my soul as I remembered the injustice perpetrated against me.

I pleaded with God to help me forgive those who had hurt me. I knew that I was succumbing to bitterness and suspicion. I viewed every circumstance with an expectation of how it could turn against me.

Would that make a difference to the way I behaved?

Would it make a difference to the way people perceived me?

I forgave my enemies afresh and asked God to punish them for me, as it was not my place to seek revenge. I felt some relief, but I knew the suspicion remained. I could not shake the expectation that similar things could happen at any time in the future.

I could not bother Mrs Hill with my emotional state. The anguish over Daniel still being missing, possibly dead, was plain to see. The whole family, including me, would start crying at random moments, whenever we thought about what young Daniel would have done in this or that situation.

> "But my eyes are toward you, O GOD, my Lord; in you I seek refuge; leave me not defenceless! Keep me from the trap that they have laid for me and from the snares of evildoers! Let the wicked fall into their own nets, while I pass by safely." [14]

The following day, we arrived in South Huskisson before the nooning meal. The largest proportion of our group found the shade of a tree under which to sit, whilst Gareth, Mr Hill, Wangi, and

[14] Psalms 141:8-10 ESV

Father Xavier went scouting for information. They planned also to tell the authorities of the shipwreck and the missing travellers.

It was a rustic settlement with but a few buildings. The stench of animals waiting in a holding yard hung in the air until the wind changed to an onshore breeze early in the afternoon. There was a hotel close by, but we had no funds with which to purchase water or food. Just as my parched mouth started to protest with the cracking of lips, a woman and her daughters approached with a bucket and two mugs for us to share. It would have been good to know the source of the water so that we could help ourselves. We thanked the woman so profusely that she began to apologise for not thinking of it earlier.

"I shoulda' thought on it sooner. As it says in the good book, '*Verily I say unto you, in as much as ye have done it unto one of the least of these my brethren, ye have done it unto me.'* Forgive me for thinking on it so long. I was afeared. We don' get visitors wanderin' out o' the bush on a daily basis. Exceptin' for the blacks that is. *'A pound of sugar, Mrs'*, is what they ask, and then they leave right quickly. Without a trouble. The whites that come out o' the bush are more a problem. Escaped convicts and the like. They that built the wool road. It was easy to see, though, that yur group is not the like. And I must admit it was only when me curiosity overcome me fear that I 'membered the scripture. Now I'm talkin' too much and tellin' yu all my secrets. I'm Saddie."

There was a short pause then, when none of us began to talk. For myself, I was too stunned. Before any of us could overcome our surprise, Saddie began talking again.

"I blame the lack o' women to talk to for my propensity to run on when a pair o' ears presents itself. The men are not much for talkin', are they?"

Adeline managed to jump into the conversation there, if you can call a monologue a conversation, but then, as Adeline had had success, and Saddie looked relieved, it had become a conversation.

"For sure, and who wouldne want to be meetin' the newcomers to find out the important information firsthand." Adeline then added with a smile and a wink, "Me name is Adeline Robertson, and as ye can hear, I'm from Scotlain. Just arrived, with a wee bit of a rough landing."

Then Adeline managed to turn the conversation back to Saddie. It was remarkably well done. The Celts were masters at divulging little and becoming informed of much.

"Can ye tell us a little about the settlement, Saddie?"

"Weell, I don't have much time to spare as I need to prepare dinner for the crews when they're ashore."

Saddie stated as she enthusiastically found herself a place to sit under the tree. She began a history of the town that could only mean the sailors would be eating simply that night.

She explained!

The smell that hung in the air came from the sheep waiting to be sent to Sydney for slaughter. The warehouse was full of wool that would be sent to England via Sydney. The southern railway that had just been built would mean less and less wool transported down the wool road from the highlands. The only thing she told us about the blacks was that it was customary to give them a pound of sugar or flour when they came to the kitchen door. She didn't seem to know much else about them, even when we asked probing questions.

The men returned just as Saddie, satisfied with using as many of her allotted daily words as possible, returned to the kitchen. She had looked up and seen a ship move away from the wharf, then let out an '*ooh*,' made her apologies and hurried away. Her companions she had sent back earlier with instructions to cut up chokos. We had been fed chokos when visiting ports in the warmer climates along our journey. Gareth and Mr Hill gave us a rundown of our situation as a duet.

There was a workers' cottage available, but we needed to sleep on the floor. At least it had a wooden floor and a kitchen with an outhouse out the back. We did not spend sufficient time there during the day to become insulted with the rudimentary accommodation. We all worked long hours to save for our passage. I was able to be thankful that we had a roof over our heads when I saw low, dark clouds approaching across the water from the north. They did not look greatly menacing, but my apprehension was fuelled by the last experience we had had with rain in the colony.

We dragged our weary bones up, collected the few belongings that we had and walked the half mile to our allocated cottage. Wangi was nowhere to be seen, and I wondered what had become of him. I managed to find a corner in one of the rooms allocated to the women and children. There were three rooms in total. All the men slept in the living room, which had a table and basic kitchen supplies. With the overflow sleeping on the veranda. At least they would be cool. The heat inside was stifling. The next problem to solve was food.

After depositing our meagre belongings and laying out our blankets as a bed, we set off for the beach. The drizzle of rain was more refreshing than drenching. The men brought the spears that Wangi had helped Gareth to make and took to the water. Only a few could swim, so the spears brought a trifling amount of success. The native women had taught us to make small baskets from the grasses. The non-swimmers used our baskets to 'net' some of the smaller fish that swam in schools close to shore. A small group took their knives to the rocks and collected crustaceans. When a small meal had been collected, we headed back to the cookfire at the rear of our accommodation. We were sadly lacking anything but seafood. But we were thankful not to starve that day.

The outhouse was gruesome with a rickety door that had a large gap top and bottom. We were thankful that there was at least a lid covering the top of the pit. The spider webs needed to be cleared, and a basin with soap found for cleaning. I set about looking for this basic household item in the one cupboard found in the house. I caught Gerard Hill exiting the outhouse as I returned with the basin and convinced him to help me find a stump for a stand while I returned to the beach for saltwater and sand. Concluding that it would have to be sufficient until soap could be purchased. Thankfully, the house was not far from the beach.

The shacks dotted along the beach, buffeted by strong salty wind, all looked the same. They were very simple dwellings on the outskirts of town.

I needed to hitch up my skirts to fill the basin and avoid drenching my hem. The cool water that ran over my shoeless feet held a refreshing that I wasn't aware I needed till I felt the release of heat and tension. Far from cold, I re-entered the water after placing the basin on the white sandy beach, just to stand and pray. Though the sun had gone behind clouds, the air was warm. I couldn't resist taking a moment to feel the sadness wash over me and ask my Heavenly Father where he was in all that had happened. I felt lost and alone. I knew he was there, and although I felt some comfort in my sadness, I could not feel the closeness I used to experience before all the dramas.

I was startled when a grey fin breached the surface. Then another, and another. Five in total, but not all at once. Fear produced a stunned stillness until a nose came out of the water and then dived again. They were so close and yet I had not seen them till they breached the surface of the water. The rain had stopped, the sun was behind me, and clouds still covered the seaward horizon. With the sun setting in the west and reflecting off the clouds to the east, the water looked golden. I felt like I could stand there forever. A small glimpse of paradise.

"'Tis a beautiful sight. Makes me want tae praise God with everything I am."

I hadn't heard Gareth arrive on the beach but felt no startle at his words. The sight was so awe-inspiring that all I could feel was peace. In a dreamy voice, I replied with as few words as possible.

"Yes!"

We stood there with our own thoughts for I have no idea how long. Then reality had to be revisited.

"I came tae check that there were no unexpected dramas tae be had on the beach. Gerard said where ye had gone and yer task for the walk. When ye didnae return, I thought tae check on yer safety. I can see ye had unexpected visitors but nae the dangerous kind."

"They were marvellous. So close. I did not expect dolphins."

"Aye, they were much closer than when they swam with the ship."

We turned and made our way back to the cottage. Gareth picked up the basin of sand and water to carry. I no longer felt the compunction to return shoes to my feet. I knew that I would need to return to a civilised mode of behaviour as we had reached town, but I was in no burning hurry.

The simple meal had been portioned out into large oyster shells by the time we returned. Just enough to prevent starvation. The men given larger portions for the hard labour they needed to do the next day. We sat around after dinner singing some a cappella tunes from memory. The English and Scottish learnt each other's folk songs.

The onshore breeze had cooled the evening into a sultry atmosphere disturbed only by the buzz and zing of mosquitoes that dived toward our exposed skin. Wangi had offered a natural remedy that we had all found far too repugnant to consider. He had told us that his ancestors smeared fish guts into their hair. I could not see how that would deter the stingers. We determined that if any tried, they would be exiled.

The next three weeks were a blur of working, scrounging for food, and trying to sleep. We discovered that the vine with large green fruit growing over what the locals called the dunny was a choko vine. Although not delicious, it was edible and filling. Not much that we recognised as food grew in the area. Once a day, we used some of our hard-earned cash to eat at the community kitchen. One relatively nourishing meal a day. It was also necessary to buy drinking water as a freshwater supply was a long walk away. Most of the drinking water transported from a distance inland.

I cannot say I enjoyed that time of deprivation, but it did come to an end. Some of the local families donated clothing that they no longer needed. We looked like a very ragtag bunch. Messages had been sent to Sydney on a steamer that left the day after our arrival. When it returned, it arrived with an agent of the FCLS. The agent came with documents to help him identify the passengers listed as missing following their departure from Melbourne. We were fortunate that our listed descriptions were thorough and complete. If we had wanted to go missing to avoid repaying our debt, we could have done so. However, we were all of a mindset to be found. We hungered for the plans that we had before leaving England. I was even keen to meet my new *parents*. A stranger feeling I had never experienced before; curiosity, excitement, trepidation, and uncertainty, warred for attention within.

CHAPTER 17

Sails Left Behind

"Peace be with you. As the Father has sent me, even so I am sending you....Receive the Holy Spirit. If you forgive the sins of any, they are forgiven them; if you withhold forgiveness from any, it is withheld."

John 20:19-23 ESV

February 1851, Huskisson

The FCLS agent organised our passage to Sydney on the steamer's return trip. The fare was paid by insurance, which was a prerequisite of the FCLS's agreement with each traveller. We were grateful we had been required to pay the insurance premium before leaving England. We had thought it could only be to prevent loss of funds for the FCLS.

The grief we experienced at leaving people we had only known for such a short time was surprising. I suppose we had bonded during adversity with any who had helped us.

As we boarded the ship, we saw Wangi mimicking a handsomely dressed man and receiving giggles from a group of girls sitting along a bench at the bow of the ship. When Wangi caught sight of us, he came to greet us with his usual happy manner but offered no immediate explanation as to where he had been for the intervening three weeks. Catriona could not resist asking him about his scarcity and was given a reply with a '*Well, where do you think I was?*' incredulity that laced his expression.

"I walk, miss!" He said as if it explained all.

Speechless, we continued onto the deck to avoid a bottleneck developing with other passengers boarding. The complement of paying passengers was made up mostly of the FCLS castaways, but not entirely. With favourable seas and wind from behind, we expected to dock in Sydney before midnight. As it was now only five in the morning, I dreaded the long day without a berth. There were comfortable chairs in the saloon and a bar for purchasing refreshments. But nowhere to lie down when sleepy. Very different to the ocean voyage under sail. The only weather that we would need to be anxious about for this trip was storms, which the captain assured us would not happen today. We murmured to each other, '*That would be a pleasant change.*'

We had little to amuse ourselves besides a game that an African worker on the wharves had shown to us. A game that required only that we collect rocks or shells and carve out a wooden block with seven bowls down each side and one larger at each end. Thankfully, we had a cabinet maker with us who knew well how to work with wood and borrowed tools. Gareth even made a few extra boards for a fee. The rules were simple, and the winner could keep the rocks or shells they won. There was some skill to the game that did not rely on chance to win. None of us had much to lose, so the risk was minimal.

We dropped in and out of playing as the boredom of the day frazzled our nerves. The vibration of the ship powered by steam engines left me feeling exhausted, and I found that my head bobbed if I sat too long. Gareth walked with me on a few laps of the deck. A pastime we had had no opportunity to enjoy since Violet's interference.

G "'Tis good tae be walking with ye again, Isabelle. I've missed our walking and talking in the last month. 'Tis also a shame that we are nae likely tae be living near enough tae continue the practice when our new lives begin. We may very well go our separate ways as early as tomorrow. I expect yer new family will be keen tae meet ye when the ship docks."

I had only just thought of the possibility and decided tae take the opportunity tae wish Isabelle well and let her know that I would miss her company. I had grown a respect and a regard for the hardworking and loving person that we had travelled with for so long.

"It had not occurred to me that the Beaumonts would meet the ship. I have a sudden trepidation. What if we do not get along?"

Following this comment, Isabelle became distant and distracted, nae responding tae questions. 'Twas concerning. I noticed that she spent minutes at a time staring transfixed into space. And yet she would put her hand on the rail tae steady herself if the ship had a sudden jolt.

"Do ye think ye would benefit from talking tae Father Xavier? I could find him for ye. Last I saw, he was playing at the Mancala. And doing well, I might add. Giving the prettiest shells tae the wee lasses for the making of necklaces, and the knuckle bones tae the lads for playing jacks." Isabelle turned tae me slowly and, with a sad smile, nodded her head.

"Yes, maybe that would be a good idea. I don't understand why I become disturbed by the simplest things."

I left Isabelle in her silence while I went tae fetch the good Father. She looked forlorn as she stood beside the rail, the wind pulling her bright hair back from a face marked with sadness. I couldne help wonderin' if the winds of change would be difficult for Isabelle. I had tae admit that me feelings made me want tae bear the burden of that difficulty for her. I knew I couldne. I didnae know all what her sadness was about, but I knew she would need tae work it out for herself. I trusted Father Xavier would help her. I had had many helpful conversations with him during the voyage.

I found Father Xavier amid the lively games taking place in the saloon. There was only one board for the Mancala, so only two played at a time, with a group behind them spruiking advice. A smaller group of the younger members of our families played a game of jacks with the bones scavenged from the kitchens, with Sadie's encouragement. Another group were involved in an excited conversation with some locals regarding the climate and water supply in the country surrounding Sydney. Me cousins and the Hills ate up any information they could garner. They talked about recent drought conditions and the need tae slaughter livestock tae preserve the fields. Nae something we experienced a lot at home, where we had centuries of experience managing the level of stock our country could carry. We needed tae listen closely if we wanted tae have success. I was glad our elders were paying close attention and put sufficient questions forward tae keep the conversation going.

The noise level in the saloon was high, which is why I had sought the outside for some moments of peace. I spoke close into Father Xavier's ear, not because I was trying tae be private, but because it was the only way I could be heard. As he wasnae currently one of the players but simply fulfilling the role of spruiker, he indicated with signs that we should exit the room so we could be heard by each other, and thankfully not by others. When we stepped onto the deck, the breeze made me realise just how hot it was inside the cabin. The sun glared. One of the stewards recommended tae us that the wind would deceive us and belay our knowing the sun burned our skin 'til it was too late. The burn wouldne show until the sun began tae sink behind the land tae the west.

"Best find yourselves a hat. I've just taken one to the red-headed lady standing at the bow of the ship. I couldn't let a complexion such as hers find out the hard way. She'd have been blistered all over by sunset. The pain of which you don't even want to imagine. She seemed to be a little dazed. If you are of her group, you might want to take her a drink. There is some tea available at the bar. Complementary for all paying passengers."

"Thankee for yer help. I will take her a drink shortly." Well, I planned to get a drink for Father Xavier tae take tae her. "'Tis Isabelle I have come tae see ye about. She looks tae need some spiritual consolation. I know she has spoken tae ye about what troubles her from her past. She has nae spoken tae me about all that she has in her past, so I thought it best tae ask ye if ye could speak tae her now. I will get that drink and bring it tae her. Would ye like one yourself?"

"I will go and find her. By the time you bring the drink, I expect we will be nearly concluding the preliminary niceties designed to set a person at ease. Do not get waylaid, Gareth. I would appreciate a drink also. Be direct in your procurement and delivery."

"Aye, Father. I'm hearing ye. I willnae be disrupting yer counsel."

X As the steward had indicated that Isabelle was on the bow at the western side of the ship, I approached from the starboard so that Isabelle would be able to see me approach. The breeze in the bow was strong enough for me to be grateful that I had anchored my Capello. Uncertain how easy it would be to replace in a colony so far from home. And a colony not in favour of the Roman Church. There were cathedrals, but I was uncertain how many of my brothers would be wearing the broad-brimmed hat.

Isabelle had tied a scarf around the brimmed straw hat that the steward had lent to her. The ends of her colourful hair whipped in the breeze. It would take some time to untangle when next it saw a brush. The smell of brine was strong in the air from the waves smashing against the hull. But not enough for us to feel the water on our skin. I drew up alongside her and waited in silence to see if she would begin a conversation.

She did not.

We were still standing in silence when our tea arrived. Isabelle held out her hand and gave a downcast smile to Gareth in thanks. I accepted my drink and gave a soft thank you before Gareth departed.

"The steward has told us that we must drink as we will not notice the sun and wind taking our water until we have a pounding headache. I learnt this the hard way when I lived in New Caledonia." Silently, Isabelle began to sip the drink. "Can you tell me what is bothering you, Miss Lindsay?" It took Isabelle several false starts before she began to speak.

"I feel a sudden trepidation at the thought that I will be meeting the couple who are to adopt me. It makes no sense. I have known this would happen since it was explained to me in Ellesmere, and yet, of a sudden, the fear has overtaken me. It has only just occurred to me that we may not get along well with each other, and this fills me with dread. I know it is disproportionate, but I cannot reason with myself. What am I to do if I find myself in another bad situation? All this time, I have been travelling toward a solution. What if the solution does not work? I will then have no further solution." Isabelle's trembling increased the further she went into her speech.

"You are borrowing tomorrow's troubles. Troubles that may never be an issue. I can tell you all the reasons that what you fear is unlikely to happen. The couple will be responsible for you, so will try to protect you. They are planning to love you, and given that you are so lovable, why would they not? And many other logical arguments against your fear, but I suspect that none of those arguments will allay your fear because your fear is anchored in the past, not the future. You need to work out, Isabelle, why your past still has such a hold on you. Would you like me to do what I can to help? We still have hours of travel time. We could utilise some of that time, but I think you will need more than one conversation to resolve this in yourself. I can hope that I will be stationed close to your billeting, but if I am not, would you allow me to send a brother or sister who is close by to call on you?"

Isabelle turned to look me in the eye. After an intense assessing gaze, she replied, "Would a sister be compelled to silence as you are,

Father? And would it be someone who would not easily judge me a witch when she hears that people in my past have done so?"

"Yes, to not repeating what you say to another, and I can be careful to make sure it is a sister who would not assess according to other people's opinions, both now and from the past. Shall we find a seat out of the wind and sun, and probably a distance from the engines, so that we can talk? I can give you some simple exercises that may help. I would also like to pray with you if that is acceptable. I must admit, though, if you say no to the last, I will pray anyway. Just silently. I will not be able to help myself."

I walked to the starboard side of the stern, where we would have shade and some privacy. Isabelle followed and sat with only a four-foot distance between us.

"As the apostle Paul said, and remember he was one who experienced suffering.

> "For the rest, brethren, whatsoever things are true, whatsoever modest, whatsoever just, whatsoever holy, whatsoever lovely, whatsoever of good fame, if there be any virtue, if any praise of discipline: think on these things. The things which you have both learned and received and heard and seen in me, these do ye: and the God of peace shall be with you." [15]

"I want to recommend that you use a notebook to write down the blessings God has sent your way. Daily, as soon as we can get you a notebook and a pencil. For now, we can use some water on the deck. It will fade quickly, but the benefit will come from the

---

[15] Phillipians 4:8-9 DRB

action of writing, not the keeping of your notes. I would also like to teach you some breathing practices our brothers use in contemplative prayer. You may find them beneficial in accepting the moment you are currently living, rather than distressing over what may or may not come to pass in the future. What say you, Isabelle? Do you want to give it a try? We can start with the simple things?" Isabelle gave me a small nod, then another with conviction.

"Yes, Father, I do not want to be paralysed by the things that have happened to me. I want to be happy as I was before Lilith took a liking to Angus, and a hate for me."

"Do you remember us talking of forgiveness, Miss Lindsay?"

"Yes, I remember. I have forgiven them both more than once. And left them for God to punish. I plan no revenge, myself. I leave it to God to vindicate me."

"I would like you to try a third thing, Miss Lindsay. Ask that God reveal himself to Lilith and Angus, so that they may be blessed with closeness to Him."

"Should they not pay a price for wickedness? I have paid a price for their wickedness. Should I not be vindicated? They may still be with God in heaven, but here and now they should reap consequences."

"The apostle John tells us,

> 'He said therefore to them again: Peace be to you. As the Father hath sent me, I also send you. When he had said this, he breathed on them; and he said to them: Receive ye the Holy Ghost. Whose sins you shall forgive, they are forgiven

them: and whose sins you shall retain, they are retained.'[16]

"Do you want to be responsible for their souls, Miss Lindsay?"

I could see that the offence would return over and again until Isabelle could bring herself to accept, even ask, that they be released from God's punishment through grace. Just as we all need. Just as she had herself accepted. A tall order that Isabelle did not yet seem ready for me to challenge her on. She understood that she needed to forgive but was not yet ready for them to be blessed with God's forgiveness. We spent some time going through the breathing exercises the brothers use in their contemplative prayer, and I recommended that Isabelle practice them often.

"Thank you, Father, I can feel more of God's peace upon me now. I will find a time in the day to practice in the hope I can put all the nastiness behind me."

Isabelle went in search of her companions, and I sat and prayed a little longer. I could see that Miss Lindsay's troubles would not be finished until she could learn to forgive as Jesus forgave. I purposed in myself to follow up on the young woman's situation in the colony.

It was a lovely afternoon for being on the water. The rocking and dipping of the ship as it moved toward our destination. The only thing that marred the peace was the constant vibration and noise of the engines. The sailing ships, though dependent on the wind, were a more peaceful way to travel. I stretched out my legs, pulled my Capello over my eyes and began to nod off for the last afternoon snooze I would be blessed with for a long time.

---

[16] John 20:21-23 DRB

The conversation with Father Xavier was both settling and unsettling. I learnt that it was possible to be tremendously torn emotionally. I longed for the peace and internal happiness I had had before the death of the boys in Ellesmere. I found that in a moment, I could become distracted by thinking about the situation of then. And of the then of working under Mrs Gretsch's authority. And the then of travelling with Violet Whyte. I wanted peace, but the things that happened in the past seemed determined to invade my present. I asked myself, was I doing something that caused the situations to happen? I could not see anything in my behaviour that was different to the behaviour of others. Nothing that would mean I deserved to be treated as those groups of people seemed determined to treat me. I resolved to practice the exercises given to me by Father Xavier. He seemed wise. I thought, in the very least, they could do no harm.

I walked and contemplated until I found Mrs Hill seated in the shade at the stern of the ship.

"I enjoy looking into the wake. It gives me the best sense of moving toward my destination. Perhaps because at the bow, I cannot yet see the end of the journey."

"I can see how looking for a destination that you cannot yet see could make you feel despair rather than satisfied that your journey is underway."

"I am finding this journey more tiring than any of the days under sail. Do you think it could be the constant noise and vibration?"

I sat next to Beverly and joined hands with her. It felt good to have the positive touch of another person in whose company I felt safe.

"I am praying for all our futures. Yours with a new family, ours in a new location with much work to be done, and Daniel wherever he may be. I do not FEEL that he has passed. Do you think that you can feel these things, Isabelle?" This was said with silent tears slowly sliding down Beverly's face.

"I was sitting next to Agnus when she passed, and I could see her spirit leave. It is so different with Daniel; I am uncertain of his future, so look for ways that the truth may be known. We were struggling so hard not to drown that we may simply have not been aware of FEELING his passing. I came here partly to escape the loss of my daughter. Now I have lost a son also."

Beverly's distress helped me to exit my own worries. We sat there and held each other's hand. There really was nothing to be said. We both missed Daniel. Beverly, more than I. We drew comfort from simply sitting and sharing in the grief.

Watching wake waves.

Smelling the brine in the air as we travelled away from where we had last seen Daniel.

"I join my prayers with yours, Beverly. That if Daniel is still alive, God will send to him, people who will help him survive. More than to simply survive. To grow, and to be brought back to you. To us. So that we might once again enjoy his company." Mrs Hill gave my hand a small squeeze.

"Thank you, Isabelle. You are a treasure."

I was uncertain of her proclamation but said nothing. We sat in silence until the sun began to set, and the air began to cool. Psalm twenty-three came to mind.

> "Nam, etsi ambulavero in medio umbræ mortis, non timebo mala, quoniam tu mecum es. Virga tua, et baculus tuus, ipsa me consolata sunt." (LVC)
>
> "Even when I walk through the darkest valley, I will not be afraid, for you are close beside me. Your rod and your staff protect and comfort me." [17]

† When the cool in the wind became uncomfortable, we went looking for the others in our family with the thought of sharing a meal.

'Fear not! God is with you always!'

The refrain kept popping into my mind throughout the remainder of the journey.

[17] Psalms 23:4 NLT

CHAPTER 18

The Billeting

"You whom I took from the ends of the earth, and called from its farthest corners, saying to you, 'You are my servant, I have chosen you and not cast you off'; fear not, for I am with you; be not dismayed, for I am your God; I will strengthen you, I will help you, I will uphold you with my righteous right hand."

Isaiah 41:9-10 ESV

February 1851, Port Jackson

It was announced that we were approaching the entrance to Sydney Harbour. All I could see were more sandy beaches interspersed between cliffs that looked like they crumbled often. The sand and cliffs had the colour of caramel confection with oranges and berries mixed through. Unexpectedly, though perhaps due to the announcement, I should have had an expectation, I saw an opening between the cliffs through which I could see an expanse of blue-green water.

The sun was in our eyes as we approached the high cliffs. The westerly approach was necessary as the captain navigated the steamer through what he called the *Heads*. After months at sea, I needed to adjust my understanding of the word and thought he must have been talking about the head of a river rather than the lavatory. I thought, '*No, wait, wrong end, we would be at the mouth of a river. So why did he call the cliffs the Heads?*'

Phillip and Chloe were standing with me, entranced by the unfolding scene. We were engaged in a frivolous conversation, and I voiced my nonsense aloud. When I exposed my gaps in knowledge, they laughed at me. I found no offence in their amusement. I was secure in their love and smiled at the awareness. I felt both sad at soon losing them and filled with joy at having such good friends. I prayed that God would not separate us entirely.

"A headland is land that juts out from the coast and is surrounded by water on three sides. There must be some more solid rock as well as the sandstone in those headlands."

Of course, Phillip had an understanding of rock; he was, after all, trained to manage a coal mine. As we sailed between the headlands, a harbour with the most intriguingly irregular shoreline opened before us. The sun was setting, leaving the gold and red hues in the sky reflected off the water. When I looked overboard, the water close to the hull had an unusual viridian colour. The air was warm and had a strangely astringent scent that I found refreshing.

Our ship anchored close to the north head and waited for a tug to pull alongside. The officer who climbed aboard grilled the captain and walked the length of the ship, observing the crew and passengers. I felt quite unnerved by the scrutiny. We were not allowed to approach the docks until every person on board had been *inspected.* As we had only travelled from Huskisson and there was no sign of illness aboard, we were given permission to dock at the wharves in Darling Harbour.

As we tugged our way toward the south side of the harbour, I saw very small boats with one or two occupants and smoke rising from the centre, making their way toward the opposite shore. The tiny boats were very narrow and made of wood. Or so it seemed. I learnt later that the boats, which the locals called nawi, were made from bark rather than wood. They were very similar to the small boats used by the natives near where we shipwrecked. With the addition of smoke. About which no one seemed concerned.

'How then do they not burn a fire through the bottom of their nawi with the fire that produced the smoke?'

The closer we went toward the docks, the refreshing scent in the air alternated with a stench of refuse. It was dismaying that we travelled toward the stench rather than the fresh smell that I supposed emanated from the trees dotting the northern shore.

As we docked alongside the wharf in Darling Harbour, Gareth came up to me and handed me a small sheet of paper with a verse,[18] written on one side and a prayer for my blessing written on the other.

---

[18] Isaiah 41:9-10 DRB

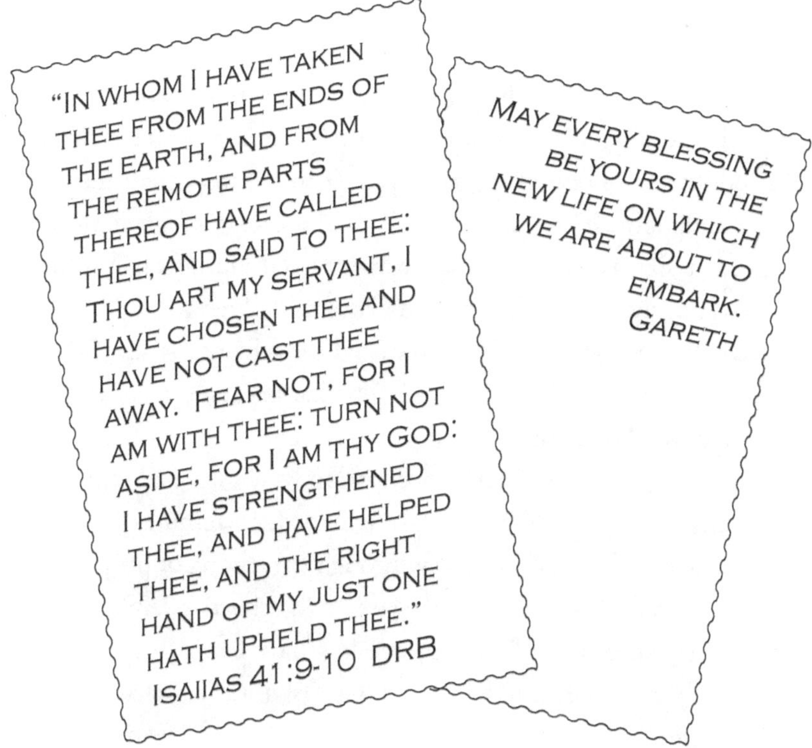

It felt overly familiar and at the same time an acknowledgement that we may not see each other again once we went in different directions the next day.

Sad!

Another loss to manage as I descended the walkway toward a new life. I looked through the twilight onto the shore at the people milling about, waiting to greet the passengers as they came ashore and knew that they were all strangers to me.

G Enthusiasm was at the forefront of me mind as the ship docked and the gangway was put in place. I could see the people gatherin' on the shore and wondered who would be there tae meet us. With the uncertainty of our arrival following the shipwreck, the original plans were altered. They had always been a little fluid, though. Travel by sail was never a certain thing, and the message of our arrival in Melbourne had been on the same packet that transported the arriving immigrants. The only method for the agency tae ken we had arrived at all was by the message we sent from Huskisson. I studied the faces in the crowd till I spotted a face that I knew.

Mr Foster, the man who introduced the scheme tae us, had singled me out and was waving his scrappy hat back and forth tae gain me attention. His clothes looked well-worn and tough for hard work. I didnae recall what manner of occupation Mr Foster had said made his living, but I was soon tae be enlightened. In minutes, he stood before me after barrelling his way through the throng of people.

"It is well pleased I am that you have arrived safely at last. I was dismayed to hear of the shipwreck. I have come from the mill directly to meet the steamer so as to give ye a warm welcome. Our community is in sore need of your skills, Mr Forbes. We have many families building houses and wanting to turn them into homes. Ye will have an abundance of business for yerself and an apprentice, I think. There are many a lad that is suitable, it be just for ye to settle on a candidate."

Mr Foster paused to breathe and gave me the opportunity tae turn the meeting from a monologue tae a conversation.

"'Tis good to see a familiar face, Mr Foster; it has been a long and arduous trip, as ye would be familiar with. The shipwreck near the end capsized all our expectations. From what ye say, some of our plans will remain the same. 'Tis glad I am to hear of it."

"Please call me Seamus, we are not as formal in the colonies."

"Then please call me Gareth. We aim to start our new life by taking on the local customs. Where do ye fit into the community we are headed for, Seamus?"

"Straight to business. I can respect that. I began in this colony as a lumberjack, but now I own and operate the sawmill south of here. There are a lot of trees coming down and a lot of houses going up."

"And my part will be tae furnish the houses. This sounds like a beneficial partnership."

"We can talk more on the 'morrow, there is a welcome party planned for ye all at the FCLS boarding house in town. There is lodging organised for ye all. Tomorrow, ye will begin to separate for different locations. All to the south. There are places there with new development. I understand that there is an experienced coal miner with the other group. There is a coal mine further south than we are going, and the owner aims to convince that young man to manage the site for him. Not so far that he will be isolated from the family he travelled with. We all need to find our own path, though." Seamus really knew how tae talk. I needed only tae repeat a few key words tae keep him talking as we walked tae the boarding house up the hill.

The boarding house had male and female dormitories where we stashed the very few belongings we had left before heading to the refectory. There had been several volunteer staff members at the docks tae answer questions and help us tae make our way tae the house. The long bench tables were laid out with cold meats and vegetables for a dinner we needed but didnae expect. The fruits in bowls were also a welcome sight. I hadnae seen an apple in some time, and I wondered where they had been grown. I made me way tae sit with the Hill family as I was certain we would part company the next day. Most people were trying the same thing, so there was a case of musical chairs until the grace was said, and the plates piled high. It was the best meal I had ever had! Every bite had more flavour than I remembered the same foods ever having in the past. We had finally arrived on solid land once again. I thought I had tae agree with Doug. I planned never tae undertake such a journey again.

I found Chloe sitting with Beitidh, Gareth's younger sister, and invited myself to join them. Chloe was in the middle of explaining the new plans that she and Phillip were to embark upon. It was the first I heard of it, also. Surprise was evident on my whole being. Chloe reached for my hand to offer the connection I needed in that moment. Realisation that I had to let go of Chloe hit hard. But I had to let her go to make her way with her husband. The awareness that I would soon be adrift with strangers unsettled me, and I became overly talkative. Frenetic in my conversation as I tried to hold onto something that would soon be gone. Something of which I had to let go.

"You will not be staying with the Hill family, then? I do not know why I would expect you to do so. After all, the arrangement was for the journey. Not for us all to stay together forever. You and Phillip must, of course, start your new life. I had hoped it would be in the same town. I did not anticipate that we would not be nearby. Of course, you must go where you can best make a life for yourselves."

I stopped talking with some effort. My mind knew, but my heart was in rebellion. I put into practice the breathing taught to me by Father Xavier. I listened rather than talked and focused on my breath for the count of ten. I noted the sounds in the room and the way the candlelight created shadows on the walls. All while being able to hear Chloe's story unfold as she explained the situation to us. The Hill family, wanting to grow stone fruits, would be settling further up the mountain in the southwest. In the same general direction as Gareth's family, but not close enough for regular visits. Our communication would be limited to letters, as it was with my family at home.

More loss!

The breathing helped me to calm myself and think on the verse given to me by Gareth. To be aware of my new situation. Accept what was to come. And even to face the unknown with less fear. Chloe faced a similar circumstance. She was travelling to a location, hours distance by horseback, where she was unknown to others. Where *they* were unknown.

There was that difference.

For Chloe and Phillip, it was they. Coalcliff, although not greatly distant, was remote for travel. Most traffic came and went via the wharf built to transport the coal to Botany Bay and Port Jackson. I could see Chloe's trepidation even though she told her story with calm and assurance. There would be very few women in her new home. Listening to the story of my friend's future unfold helped me to bring my own story back into perspective.

I was to meet my new adoptive parents the next day. Before the Hills left. They assured me that if they were not comfortable with the character of my new family, they would not let me leave with them and would instead make a way for me to join them in their new home. I was overwhelmed with gratitude when they approached me and explained their benevolence to me before we gathered in the refectory. It took much of the fear away. There was so much happening all at once, I found it difficult to keep my thoughts from scattering.

When I stopped interspersing Father Xavier's breathing exercises into the evening, I got lost in my thoughts. Without fail, being lost in my thoughts led me to worry and fear. Before leaving England, Mrs Chisholm assured me that the character of my new family had been investigated, and she was confident it would be a good match. She had personally spent enough time in their company to be certain of a good outcome. I decided amid the chaos of the evening to put my trust in Mrs Chisholm's guidance. And what should have come first, I chose to put my trust in God's plans for me. I remembered one of my Mam's favourite promises.

> "For I know the thoughts that I think toward you, saith the LORD, thoughts of peace, and not of evil, to give you an expected end." [19]

We retired for the evening in the early hours of the morning. After taking our time to meet with each person we had travelled with and been shipwrecked with. The people we would possibly not see again. For some, that was a few. For Chloe, Phillip, and me, it was everyone. We were the last to bed and fell asleep finally in the middle of sentences, in bunks next to each other. The following day, we slept past sunup but not so late that we missed breakfast. Gareth's family had finished breakfast and were preparing to leave when Chloe and I arrived in the refectory. I could see that Gareth employed delaying tactics until we, the last comers for breakfast, had arrived. I was glad that he had held his party up by helping with the clean-up from breakfast and by holding discussions with Mr Hill. I could see his sad smile as he caught sight of me and came toward me with a fidgetiness

[19] Jeremiah 29:11 KJV

I had not seen him display before. He held his hat and turned it in circles as he paused before saying…

"I aim tae see ye again, Isabelle. I dinnae know how, nor where, nor when. I lay awake when I finally made me way tae me bunk. I prayed for peace and for sleep, but there was none tae be had 'til I heard God saying as much."

He took my hand as we stood before each other and, for the first time, looked into each other's eyes.

"I am certain we will meet again, and I look forward tae that event with happy anticipation."

With that said, he let go of my hand, turned and walked away to the wagon that Mr Foster had brought for transporting Gareth's family before they reached the trail that had no space for wagons. I stood and watched as they started moving. I waved when they took turns, turning to wave goodbye. Gareth was the first, the middle, and the last of his family to wave a parting. Only stopping when Doug laughed and elbowed him in the ribs.

Chloe took my hand and led me to the bench where the remains of breakfast were still laid out. Eggs and bacon, a luxury we had not enjoyed since leaving Melbourne. We gave ourselves a good helping and ate slowly as we talked about what had transpired.

Chloe laughingly said, "It's all over. He left! Not that it ever started. How do you feel, Issy?"

"I am stunned. I do not know how I feel. I do not know what he meant by what he said. He has never shown any interest in pursuing anything more than a friendship. Why would God speak to him about us meeting again?"

"It is a mystery for sure, but I have heard that his family undertook this venture because he heard God talking. Some say it was simply his grief talking, his fiancée having died tragically."

"He told me the story of his devastation when Molly passed and then of his coming close to God. I think his faith is genuine, and he listens for direction from God. If so, why would God have him tell me that we would see each other again? For what purpose? I think God only speaks to us in that way when there is a need for us to hear what he has to say."

"Do you not think he showed interest in you himself when he took your hand and essentially promised that he would be in your future?"

"No, Chloe, I do not want to think on things that are so uncertain. I do not want to begin a fantasy in my mind. It would not be helpful for me. Please help me by not talking that way. Instead, talk to me about what you expect to find in Coalcliff."

"Mostly, black coal dust being cleaned from our cabin continually. And being afraid that when Phillip goes into a mine, he may not return. I can hope that most of his work will be conducted outside the mine. We have been assured a cabin and a female servant. I am glad for Phillip's time in service, as it will make it easier for me to find a friend in the woman. Although in truth, I do not know the age. She could be very young, or she could be very old. I mean to make a friend of her regardless. And I hope the refectory and laundry servants are women whom I can befriend. It would be hard if I could not see all the women as potential friends. Imagine Violet in such a place!"

I had to laugh at the reminder of our companion on board the *Slains Castle.* Violet deemed us appropriate on occasion and inappropriate on other occasions. I could see that Chloe would be able to navigate her situation better than most. Having a heart of grace and love for the people less fortunate than herself. An attitude born from her own story.

"I wonder how much we will be living beside the native population, such as Wangi?"

"The mine owner made no mention of the natives living close by. It did not occur to me to ask, but surely, they will be a part of the community as they were in Huskisson."

"I am yet to find out the exact location where I am to settle."

Despondency was easy to see on my face. Chloe chose to delve into the topic in her understanding way.

"Keep it in your mind that the Hills will have you to live with them if you need. You would be able to take up dressmaking even without the sponsorship of the couple coming to meet you. You have years of experience learnt at your mother's side. Promise me, if there is any trouble, you will write them and ask to go to them. Please do not wait for another invitation. Let the first invitation be claimed as a standing invite. Sometimes we do not need to wait for the second or third invite before it is polite to accept."

"Hmm." Chloe saw that I was coy about what she said, so she immediately found Beverly and dragged her to where I was still eating. I have to say, Beverly did not look reluctant and delved straight into conversation.

"Isabelle, I want to make sure you understand that you are invited to come to us any time you need."

"I take it that was a 'second' invite?" The smirk on Chloe's face matched the raising of her chin and the smile on both our faces.

"And a third; please do not hesitate to write us and ask us to come and find you, to aid in your travels, and to stay with us as long as you need." Beverly looked pleased with herself, and we all laughed at our traditions.

"Noted, Aunt Beverly. I will not hesitate to contact you one way or another if I am in need or not in need. I promise. And I am very grateful to count you among my friends."

As we settled in for a second cup of tea, we heard a commotion at the entrance to the building. Before we took our second sip, the matron of the boarding house entered the refectory, followed by a couple in the middle years of life. They were of a similar height and build. Slight! And looked almost frail in their lack of muscle mass. But also, energetic and quick to smile. The woman had luscious brown hair with natural waves falling from the pins and binding on the left of her head.

The man had little hair at all. The remaining half circle that surrounded at ear level was a closely cropped fuzz of grey. Even though his hair was grey and her hair a honey brown, they appeared to be of a similar age with very few wrinkles or blemishes. They each had a natural rose colour to their cheeks and lips, which for him were only just visible through the abundance of red brown hair on his face. Clearly grown to make up for the deficit aloft.

They were well dressed in finely tailored but simple garments. I guessed that it must have been the couple who were coming to fetch me. Their clothing was the kind of clothing my mother insisted that all her workers wear. Inexpensive and well-made to indicate both professional skill and humility as one looking to serve others with that skill.

The woman pulled to the fore in her enthusiasm to meet me. The Matron made a quick introduction and left us *to get acquainted* as she had much work to organise with so many residents overnight and so many comings and goings on that day. The one introduced as Mrs Iris Beaumont came forward to offer her hand to me in greeting. I was not used to the forward, almost masculine style of greeting, so it took me a moment of hesitation before I matched her greeting in kind and offered my hand.

"I am so pleased to meet you finally, Miss Lindsay. We have waited and worried for nearly a year as you journeyed here. It is such a long way. I remember our own journey almost twenty years past. Malcolm and I look forward to forming a friendship with you. We can sort out what we are to call each other later, but I would like you to start by calling me Iris. I will leave you and Malcolm to sort out between yourselves how you would like to address each other."

With this said, the baton was somehow passed to Mr Beaumont. They had an understanding for communal communication that they had established over years of cooperation. I immediately felt comfortable with the slightly unusual couple.

"My wife does like to talk first, but she never talks for me. It's an agreement we have. Please call me Malcolm for the time being. We like to be a thoroughly modern couple. Equal in our rights and responsibilities to manage a home and business."

Perhaps more than slightly unusual. More, highly unusual. I had never heard of such a thing. A husband ruled by law, a woman by manipulation. It was simply the way things worked. Granted, sometimes the man ruled by physical force as well as by law. I gave a broad smile as my heart jumped into the possibility of a new kind of environment.

"Thank you for your generosity in taking me in. I hope my circumstances have been explained to you. I am still young and need help establishing a life in a new place. The place where I belonged before was ripped away from me."

I had divulged far more than I intended in only a few moments of knowing the couple. They inspired wholesome trust. I desperately hoped that it was not some kind of deception, and my trust misplaced.

"And please call me Isabelle. You are right that more formal modes of address would quickly become cumbersome." I turned to Beverly and raised my brows. "What do you think, Mrs Hill, do we have time for us all to sit for tea before you depart?"

"I will go find Mr Hill, Isabelle, I am sure he will be glad to meet Mr and Mrs Beaumont."

I then went to fill a fresh pot with tea and retrieve cups for us all, as the Beaumonts settled into seats and started a conversation with Chloe. It was a pleasant time of fellowship before the inevitable parting that rushed toward us. The Hills all came along, one by one, until it was a large party around the refectory room table.

As pleasant as the time was, we all needed to start our journey before it was too late to reach the day's destination. I was pleased to learn that the Beaumonts had recently set up shop to the south, not more than a day's journey from where the Hills would be founding a farm. I was heading to a place called Hurstville. The settlement was the township where both the Hill's group and Gareth's group would shop for things they could not grow or make. Even Chloe and Phillip might come to town on occasion, though most of their supplies would be transported directly in by ship. It was disappointing to find out later that the journey to Camden would be a much easier trip for the Hill family when they needed supplies, so we would not see them often at all.

I felt comfortable going with the Beaumonts to their home. But I also longed for the familiarity of friends with whom I had invested so much time in everyday life. A bitter taste of sadness and a sweet taste of possibilities. I would not say that I was unhappy. My fears had been pushed away from my awareness. The future offered much promise.

CHAPTER 19

Beginnings

"For I know the plans I have for you," says the LORD. "They are plans for good and not for disaster, to give you a future and a hope."

Jeremiah 29:11 NLT

February 1851, Hurstville

I

A beginning!

The road was dusty.

The coach stifling!

We had hours of rough, dusty road ahead.

The dry, earthy smell of dust in the air was not unpleasant but it did create consequences. A layer of red dust slowly formed on my dark coloured dress. There was sense in Iris and Malcolm wearing beige coloured linen. Each of them had a beautifully made suit.

The dust kicked up by the horses on the dry road began to tickle my throat. Iris explained that blocking the breeze that came through the windows would be worse than dealing with the dust. Malcolm passed me a soft, oiled-canvas water bag to ease my dusty mouth. When I only took a sip of the warm liquid, I was told to drink deeply or risk a bad headache.

Why did everyone encourage me to drink tepid liquid by warning of a headache? I was not in the sun and not working hard. I struggled with drowsiness and could not sleep due to the sway and bounce, but I was not working. To tell the truth, though, the soaking of my underclothes with perspiration was a loss of fluids to which I was unaccustomed. I felt like I had walked a long distance when I had only sat. I felt the dust on my eyeballs, in my nostrils, and in the canal of my ear as well, but I was too fascinated to close my eyes as Iris suggested.

The view from the window changed from densely built townhouses to larger, sparsely separated big houses surrounded by parkland. Then slowly gave way to large homestead houses with many smaller buildings built close to the main house. I had not seen more than a mile from the coast of New South Wales before that day. The colour of the grass was not a real green. Neither were the trees a green like home, except for a few English trees that had been planted close to the big houses. The grass was almost brown. Malcolm explained that they needed rain.

When we stepped outside the carriage to give the horses water, the grass crunched under my feet. The shade of the trees, if you could call the patchy shadow shade, offered little coolness. The leaves felt stiff and waxy. There were brown spots and easily seen yellow veins on the otherwise blue-green leaves. On closer inspection, I saw chandeliers of a more lime coloured leaf with orange veins that hung from a limb of the very same tree. The tree that otherwise had masses of the almost blue leaves. The strangeness was that it was not a symbiotic vine. It appeared to be of the same tree. The trunks had blackened bark around the base and fresh growth low to the ground.

The astringent scent in the air was oddly uplifting, with an almost freshness when the dust settled enough to smell the scent. The drawings from the books in London had not fully prepared me for the circus style bizarreness. I could hear crackling as something moved in the dry underbrush around the tree but could not understand why Malcolm and Iris made the occasional stomping movement. The quizzical look on my face inspired an explanation.

"We do not want to surprise or be surprised by any snakes. They can be extremely deadly. Be careful of sitting, Isabelle. Also, look closely to ensure no ants are using the ground as a trail."

"I have been sitting for too long, so I am happy to stand."

When I took their suggestion to heart and looked down at the ground, I saw very large orange and red ants scurrying around. And large black ants on my boots. Iris followed my gaze. With one look at my boots, Iris started stepping without changing location. She gave me a small smile as I copied her antics. Malcolm bent to brush away the ants that had already taken up residence on my boots.

"Their bite is unpleasant. You don't want them travelling to the nether regions." Was his only comment.

A different form of travel.

At least no rain.

Until suddenly there was.

A lot of rain. A downpour that lasted only ten minutes but left puddles around us, a rivulet running down the track, and the carriage dripping. We had made it inside the carriage with only surface drenching and were then reluctant to exit again until the puddles and rivulets had soaked into the ground. The heat of the day seemed worse rather than better following what Iris and Malcolm called a little sun shower.

"Not enough, I am afraid, the farmers will be wanting more than that. Much prayer is needed."

Malcolm did most of the talking while we travelled. I wondered if the paleness of Iris' complexion was caused by motion sickness. The trip across the ocean must have been bad for Iris if that was the result of a carriage ride.

"Do you feel unwell, Iris? If I had known of your motion sickness, I would have offered some of my grandfather's tea before we left."

"You are very observant, Isabelle. Yes, the carriage ride makes me feel ill. I think the stifling heat, as well as the motion, combine to take all enjoyment of travel away from me. I prefer to ride the back of a horse, but that would not have been practical for today's journey. You will have to tell the story of your grandfather when I am able to pay attention."

Thankfully, we needed only a few stops for the horses on the way to the Beaumonts' shop. Their living quarters were above the shop located on a dusty street that ran perpendicular to the main road. Three shops back from the intersection.

The hired carriage stopped on the main road and let us down with the minimal luggage I had. We ambled past the haberdashers and the button shop before coming to a halt in front of a red brick building with wrought iron latticework on the upstairs balcony. The large picture windows at the front allowed for a display of a fashionable dress with accessories on one side of the burgundy door and a tailored ensemble of frock coat and trousers in the window on the other side of the door. The windows were framed with a deep forest green that enhanced the linen curtains, which were pulled back to allow potential customers a view of the work taking place inside.

Within, I saw a young woman talking to a customer. Iris opened the door and entered ahead of Malcolm and myself. A thoroughly modern couple indeed. I was to learn that apart from customers, both men and women, we were expected to behave as equals and open our own doors as well as rise to give aid as equals when there was need of help. An adjustment that at first caused me to feel slighted but then gave me a sense of empowerment.

As we entered the shop, the tall woman with the darkest of brown hair and fairest of skin tone, with steel grey eyes and rosebud lips, sent me a forced smile. A smile that showed all her perfect teeth but did not display a natural upturn. The almost straight line of the smile denied a true sense of happiness. Not the owner's fault, simply a trick of nature. So unlike Chloe's smile, which even when slight, gave the impression of intense happiness.

"Isabelle, I would like you to meet Miss Macauley. Heather has been my apprentice for the last five years as she learnt her trade."

I could not help wondering why the Beaumonts needed to adopt me when they had Heather to work with them. But then the answer to my internal question came immediately.

"Heather is the daughter of our town constable. We hope that you will learn to love each other. There is more than enough work with the growing population to keep us all busy. We may even be able to keep up with the demand for clothing."

It was unspoken, but I thought the mention of Heather's family was an indication of why they sought an adoptive daughter. I would likely never see my family again, so there would be no daily competition for my affections.

"It is a pleasure to meet you, Heather." I offered as Heather came around the counter.

She extended her hand as she greeted me with an accent like some of the locally born people we had met in Sydney. A little too much breath in the nose and an added sing-song tonal quality that varied the pitch more than at home. The words ran together, making it difficult to separate one word from another.

"It's good to finally meet the competition for employee of the year. I thought I had won hands down when you shipwrecked off the south coast. But here you are, looking healthy and ready to start the race."

I was stunned. I struggled to determine if she was being honest in issuing a challenge. Perhaps she attempted satire with herself as the target? Bringing attention to her flaw to remove the sting of the truth, and so, strangely, made it null and void?

"OK, Heather, enough of that. At least you have given Isabelle an understanding of how things stand from the outset. But can we have dinner and let Isabelle settle in before we begin the competition that truly does not exist? You know from our conversations that there is no competition. Isabelle is to be thought of and respected as our daughter. Isabelle has travelled a long way to become a member of our family. There can be no competition in that, Heather."

"So you say, Malcolm, but we will see."

I was not sure what to make of the confident young woman who appeared to be only a few years older than myself. I extended my hand to the hand she still held before her and accepted both her greeting and her challenge.

Even though the Beaumonts said there was no competition. The characters of Lilith and Violet in my past had taught me that if Heather meant to compete, I had better be ready to take the competition seriously. I had no way of knowing how dirty she would fight to win a competition for which I did not even know the prize. I suspected that it was more than the affections of the older couple. There had to be more at stake than affection. Affection I assumed, she had from her own family. A family that lived in the same town.

Iris gave me a tour of the house as Malcolm prepared a simple dinner. The master bedroom and the family parlour both had French doors onto the upstairs balcony. It was a simple home with simple furniture. The fireplaces in the master bedroom and the parlour shared a chimney stack. The stairwell separated the rear of the house into two rooms. One was used as a study and the other as a second bedroom. My new bedroom.

It had a window looking out over the kitchen garden to the rear of the house. I placed my small bag onto the single-size bed in the centre of the room. I took in the set of drawers plus a standing wardrobe along one wall. I saw through the only window a small wooden building at the end of a short, paved walkway in the yard. The choko vine growing over the top showed the purpose of the very small building. Our stay in Huskisson had given us knowledge of where to expect the lavatory to be located. Out of the house and covered with vines. There was no fireplace in my room, but the brick chimney from the kitchen was visible on the internal wall. The study was a mirror image of my room, but with different furniture.

"There is no fireplace in your room, Isabelle, but as your window faces north, I think you will find it comfortable year-round. It never gets very cold here. The heat is more of a problem. You will need to leave your bedroom door open to achieve some flow-through breeze, some nights in the summer, so that you can sleep. You will see. Please be sure to talk to us if the room is uncomfortable. We cannot fix what we do not understand. There is also an attic upstairs that runs the length of the upper story with no internal walls. We use this space mostly for storage. You are welcome to explore when the fancy takes you. If you want to clear a space for your own study, it can be arranged."

I turned in a slow circle, taking in my new home. It was a blank slate waiting to be personalised. The bed coverings were white with only a small amount of fine lace on the top cover. The walls were the colour of fresh cream, and the curtains were made from a lilac hessian. I appreciated the simplicity of the room and turned to see Iris studying my reaction. Our eyes met and held as I offered her a smile drawn from the sense of peace that was invading my soul. I felt that I would enjoy living there. How I knew that was a mystery. But I was reminded of the feeling I had when my Granda and I stood before the mob and prayed. A sense of influence from without. An influence that indwelled. An influence I was happy to allow.

"Do the fixings of the room suit you for now, Isabelle? I am certain that soon enough, you will have altered things to your preferences. You are free to use any of the off-cuts from the workroom to make cushions and hangings that give the room a more personal feel."

"Thank you, Iris. I think I like the current simplicity. The lack of busyness is calming."

"Let's take ourselves to the kitchen, then. We do not have the space for a formal dining room, so we eat our meals in the kitchen or the garden when the weather allows or dictates. It is probably too hot for eating indoors this evening. We will have to battle the flies."

We each served a plate of food from the serving dishes set out by Malcolm and carried the same to a table set up on the back veranda. The veranda was a wooden deck with a canopy of grape vines, only eight feet deep and had a shallow stairway that led down into the garden.

The veranda was just large enough to house a narrow table with two benches running lengthwise. There were also three wicker lounge chairs on the other side of the doorway. Beyond which I saw a door leading into what I guessed was a laundry. I took a seat on the bench facing the garden, with Iris and Malcolm each sliding along the same bench. Malcolm placed a pitcher of water on the table and turned up the glasses from a tray that seemed to have its permanent home on the table.

"We like to sit looking at the birds that come to share our produce. I hope you do not mind. With three, it may make conversation more difficult. I have given Heather an early mark, so she has returned home for the day. It will be just us for dinner. This will give us time to form ourselves into a family."

"Heather has a loving family and so has no need for us in the evenings."

I sensed a feeling of grief underlying the comment, though no malice was displayed. I was too young to understand the loss Iris and Malcolm felt at not being able to procreate their own family. We ate in silence for a quarter of an hour. Enjoying the song of the birds until a cacophony of noise assaulted my ears. First, one drumroll croak that increased in intensity. Then a multitude beyond count joined in the chorus. I could not see where the noise came from, though I looked intently. The sound seemed to emanate from everywhere. The Beaumonts must have noted the wide eyes and open mouth as my neck became like rubber, turning this way and that. Iris gave me the explanation I sought.

"Ohh! The cicadas. It took me a while to work out what you were looking for. We are so accustomed to the noise that we don't notice it very much anymore. It will stop and start as the night falls."

And at that, the noise stopped suddenly, before a solo cicada started up again, encouraging the others to join in its song.

"The children from the button shop next door are probably out looking for the different colours. That makes them stop and start their song. It's too warm inside for them to be put to bed yet."

"I, I cannot claim to think it a pleasant sound," I stuttered. They both laughed softly.

"Nor could anyone. Though it does suggest the pleasure of warm summer evenings."

We then sat in silence and enjoyed the soft, cool breeze that came at the end of the day. There was a peace in the air, despite the noise of the cicadas. The Beaumonts left me to my thoughts as they enjoyed time in their own. A pervading sense of happiness and contentment invaded my heart.

We woke early as the first rays of sunlight penetrated the windows left uncovered to allow for cool air during the night. A new experience for me. At home, we would never allow the nighttime miasma to enter our home through open windows. Iris assured me that the only thing to fear in the nighttime air of the colony was the buzzing in your ear and occasional sting from the mosquitoes. We had mosquito nets hung from the ceiling that formed a canopy over our beds to prevent the sting, but nothing prevented the buzz of the mosquitoes trying to get through. I had slept as well as could be expected in a new place with an awareness of my surroundings that kept me in a shallow sleep. Iris came into my room with a jug of warmed water.

"I will show you today how to find things so that you can fend for yourself unless unwell. When you have finished washing and dressing, you will find us in the kitchen preparing breakfast. You will find your place in the work schedule soon enough. We do not have designated roles. We pitch in as the need arises. I hope this little bit of strangeness won't cause you any angst. It is not the way most homes operate, but it works well for us. Mostly, Malcolm prefers to be the cook, and I am happy with that. If you want to be the cook, you will have to race him to the kitchen."

From the Kitchen, we heard Malcolm's loud response.

"I heard that. I think I do most of the cooking because my stomach grumbles first."

With that, Iris smiled and left me to dress. I saw her looking at my limited wardrobe and expected a comment. Iris simply closed the door for me as she left the room. I dressed quickly and carefully made my way down the steep staircase.

When I entered the kitchen, Iris was setting three places at the table and Malcolm was placing in the centre, a platter of eggs, bacon, toast, and jam. Blackberry jam, I think. Malcolm said a reverent prayer of thanks, using few words, as he placed the food on the table. He was then seated in a flash and created a sandwich with all the ingredients. I felt inspired to try the same and was pleasantly surprised that blackberry jam and bacon together created a fulfilling sensation of completeness to the meal. Iris chose to eat from her plate with a knife and fork. Malcolm winked and Iris smirked.

"Teaching our young charge your ordinary habits already, I see." The comment was made without malice, and I felt that there was a sense of approval rather than disdain. "The shipwreck must have taken most of your luggage, Isabelle. Today, we will start with making a few new outfits for you. Our customers can wait a few more days. No one is in a huge hurry for their orders."

"That is very generous of you, Iris. But I assure you, I do not want to be a bother. I can sew for myself in my spare time. The evenings are long in the summer. I can earn the fabric over time."

"Nonsense, what kind of adoptive parents would we be if we did not want to help and provide for you. The evenings will not be as long as they are in England, just as the winter days will not be as short. Please let us enjoy having you here. We will be a team to be envied."

Iris' last comment, ever so briefly, made me worry over being envied. It had never gone well for me in the past. Ordinary was my new goal.

"Then I would very much like to have more than one dress to wear. Thank you, Iris."

"I think we will start with a pale olive linen. What do you think, Isabelle? Not too bright for a summer's day."

"Linen sounds expensive. I would be happy with a poplin print."

"Linen will be more comfortable, though. And suitable for church on Sunday. You can show me the level of your skills as we make a pattern and sew. It will be good to know how far your mother has progressed with your training. We can make the second dress from a poplin print if you like. What colour would you like?"

"I think I am partial to lilac or lavender at the moment. My training has been hampered by my interest in Granda's apothecary shop. I absconded at every opportunity. I enjoyed working with the healing herbs."

"You mentioned that in the carriage ride. You can tell me some of your story over our work today."

Life settled into a rhythm of breakfast in the kitchen. A time set aside by the Beaumonts for individual devotions and reflection, where we all went our different ways. Then we met in the shop, which was divided into two sides, men's wear on the west and ladies' wear on the east. Heather arrived as we settled into our tasks for the day. We all lunched together after fixing sandwiches with bread from the local bakery that was collected and delivered each day by our errand boy. Iris claimed that the baking of bread was too time consuming for a working couple to manage. Heather left for the day around five in the evening. That was the signal for us to down-tools unless there was an urgent order to complete. Something Iris informed me they did their best to avoid.

We took it in turns to prepare dinner, with Malcolm telling me that I needed to learn all the skills for life. We ate on the back veranda unless it was pouring with rain from a *Southerly Buster* or when very cold in the winter. After dinner each evening, we walked as a family to the grove. As winter came round, we turned back when the sun began to set. Walking to the waterfront in the evenings was my favourite part of the day. We talked about the day and what had meant most to us that day.

CHAPTER 20

Beginnings

"For I know the plans I have for you," says the LORD. "They are plans for good and not for disaster, to give you a future and a hope."

Jeremiah 29:11 NLT

February 1851, Bottle Forest

G "I foond meself woond'rin', what 'twoold'v been like tae bring Molly tae this place. Nae, I aim tae sound more like the locals. I foond meself wonderin' what it would have been like tae bring Molly tae this place. I am no certain she would have liked it much. She was so comfortable in the highlands, and this place is so veree different."

"Oh, aye, I know what ye mean. Yer speech didnae change so much. Points for trying. She loved the cool air in the winter, always wantin' the windows open nae matter how cold outside."

Doug and Gareth both swatted the flies from their faces between sentences.

"These blasted flies are worse than I've seen anywhere so far."

"We didnae go into the farmlands in Africa. 'Tis certain they would've been bad there also."

"Welcome to a new life." Gareth laughed. "'Tis me ye will blame for this in the future."

"I do like the warm air, Gareth. I thought tae find that a torture but am pleased tae thank ye for that aspect of the destination ye chose."

"I believe God responsible for both makin' this place and for sendin' us here."

"And nae mention of the one who thought himself a god worthy of worship."

Bitterness still dripped from Doug's tone when the Englishman was mentioned.

"I hadnae thought o' Lord Ashley since leavin' Clinterty."

"Nor I, but the mention of Molly brought it all tae mind. The mawkit grievous time on the ship seems tae have put all me emotions of that time intae the past. Some benefit derived from the suffering."

"I didnae have your bad journey, but still, I cannae imagine wantin' tae repeat such a long, treacherous journey. I willnae be returning home. The shipwreck off the coast reminded me how perilous the journey was. God brought us through, but truly, anythin' could've happened. From disease, tae lost at sea. Or a terrible accident. The masts comin' doon in the storm could've left one of us washed overboard. We may never know what happened to Cousin Ainsley. 'Tis a loss, but also a blessing that we're only missin' one of us after such a long journey."

"Oh aye, 'tis true that."

It was a blessing Mr Foster purchased his supplies the day before. The overland journey was long and nae very comfortable. There was nae cover over the wagon. Seamus advised us to keep our sleeves rolled down and the hats he supplied on our heads. He said he couldne have us burnt to a shrivel before we even arrived. What little breeze was tae be had was nae blocked by canvas, but the sun on exposed skin felt almost painful by the midday, so we all did our best tae keep it covered or in the shade when stopped tae rest and water the horses. Mr Foster had also supplied cheese sandwiches that he recommended we eat before they were spoiled by the heat of the day.

The water in the canvas bags was warm and unappealing. We were told there was no time tae boil water for tea and the lighting of a fire could be treacherous on such a day. We all drank from the unappealing bag, taking frequent sips tae clear the dust from our throats. We were given cut-up yellow and green fruit after the mid-day. I couldne say I knew what the fruit was, but it was juicy, sweet and unspoiled.

Mostly we sat facing each other across a channel of supplies with our eyes closed tae minimise the dust and glare. I thought we would all need a good wash when we arrived at our destination. The thought no sooner came into me head and the heavens opened up tae give us a drenching. Unlike us, the supplies were under a canvas tarp tae protect them from both the dust and the rain. We all began tae laugh at the rivulets of rusty brown seeping from behind ears and down necks. We removed our hats tae clean our faces and enjoy the short respite from the sun.

The rain didnae last. Steam began tae rise from our backs as well as the canvas covering the supplies at our feet. The steam turned our wash into a Turkish bath. I suspected that we would all smell equally bad by the end of the day. Seamus must have seen the looks we were giving each other as the steam began tae rise.

"Never fear, we will be camping beside a river where you can all have a wash before nightfall. We need to cross the river today, then make camp to spare the horses. We will not have far to travel tomorrow, but we will need to walk or ride horseback for the last few miles. 'Tis not a trip for the faint of heart. At least we will not be cold, and we will be able to light a fire. I have organised for the local blacks to provide a meal and a story. Traded with them for flour and sugar, as well as a little of the rum. There are not many still living on the land, but there are some. We will be sleeping under the stars, so let's hope the stars are on show so that we can keep dry. We won't dry as quickly at night if we get wet. It could also leave us a little cold."

The thought of being cold, even if wet, was beyond most of us. Even in the night, we had not needed a blanket for some time. Lying on top was more comfortable than underneath.

"Thank ye, Mr Forbes, 'tis good tae have some idea of what tae expect." This was said by me sister, Beitidh, who was sitting just behind Seamus.

"I always think so. Have you seen any of the blacks yet, Miss Beitidh?"

"Oh aye, 'twas a black man who helped us survive the shipwreck. And a local family group from the area. They were very generous. It was good tae meet them and see a different way of living. We owe them some debt. I'm not sure how we will be able tae repay."

"Start by treating the family we stay with tonight with respect. They are different from us for sure. 'Twould be good to learn from them rather than copy those who try to eradicate them and call them animals. We know what it is like to have foreigners push us from our country. And yet many of our countrymen are doing the same here." [20]

I looked tae Doug and could see his turmoil at the idea. We had traded places with Lord Ashley. And yet I couldne see a way tae make it right. If we didnae buy the land, another would. I determined then tae pray on it.

"Will there be many of the locals near our selections?"

I was curious about what tae expect sharing the country. From what I had seen near Huskisson, they were nomads without permanent dwellings. Nae dwellings that we saw anyway.

"They are about. They'll come calling, asking for sugar or flour. Best tae share with them. It's the way they are. They will share information with you."

"What kind of information will they be sharing?"

"Some about fires, some about water, some about what plants not to disturb. It's worth paying attention, they have lived here for a long time. They willnae share how they know mind. They just give advice, some call it commands, on a seasonal basis. If they say 'tis a bad place to put your house, listen. Else, you are likely to have no house in a few years. Likewise, don't let the livestock eat just anywhere. Fence

---

20 "I acknowledge the Traditional Custodians of the land on which this portion of the story is set. And I pay my respects to Elders past and present. The Gweagal people of the Dharawal language group.
Cultural heritage Aboriginal History - Sutherland Shire

exclusion zones when the elders say to keep certain plants. As you can imagine, the ones who call it commands don't get along with the natives and look to remove them. I found peace with them by sharing. I advise you to do likewise."

I was not sure what Seamus really meant by sharing, but I was tae find out. Beitidh, always curious, took up the talking.

"Do ye share many meals with them then, Mr Foster?"

Beitidh was showing a lot of interest, but then she had always been the first tae welcome strangers tae the community.

"Here and there, here and there."

And that was the end of the conversation. Those of us who took Seamus' advice tae heart discovered a different way to view the world from the people who were here before us. Life was nae about owning the land but rather about caring for the land.

We arrived at the crossing of the Georges River mid-afternoon and took a break tae give the horses a rest and water as we waited for the punt tae cross back tae the north side. The trees didnae look much. From a distance, the spindly leaves of the sheoak looked like they would be nae better for shade than the gum trees we had tried tae shelter under earlier in the day. It was stiflingly hot, so we were glad tae find the shade under the sheoaks that were found close tae the river's bank was much cooler than it had been under the gum trees earlier.

There were too many of us for the one crossing. Mr Foster took the wagon across with the first trip and left the people tae cross separately. We were told this was tae calm the horses and avoid them becoming unsettled. The task of driving the rig onto the punt was enough evidence that the horses didnae like the trip and preferred tae stay on solid ground.

We could see the bank on the other side with a narrow stream of smoke rising from a cook fire and muscular natives lounging alongside the river. Sitting in the shade of sheoaks, swatting flies as they talked. We could hear the occasional laughter that followed them looking our way. When the punt arrived on the opposite shore, the group of men ambled across tae help Seamus unload the then restless horses. To their credit, they had the horses settled quickly and the wagon moving toward a clearing from where the smoke rose. They appeared tae put little effort into their work but achieved all that needed tae be achieved. I was tae learn that this was a part of their character. Try less, achieve more. The heat made me wish that I could simply swim across and meet the ladies on the opposite shore. When I made this suggestion, the dockman from the north shore looked at me quizzically.

"If you wanna be shark food, go ahead."

"Oh! In that case, I think I will wait tae ride the punt. Thank ye for yer advice."

There was something irreverent about all the colonials. They seemed tae be laughing at what they saw as our foolishness. With no fear. They didn't care what the new chums thought of them. Yet when confronted with a Mounted Patrolman or Colonial policeman, their eyes wouldne be still in gaze. I saw it on a few occasions whilst walking the streets of Sydney earlier that day. They would not look them in the eye. Another peculiarity tae contemplate so we could avoid pitfalls in our new home. Our new home it was, and I was determined tae make it a good home.

The punt returned tae collect us, and after our own crossing, the afternoon was filled with collecting firewood, oysters and fishing. The local family showed me how tae make me own spear from the centre stalk of a grass mound. A lesson I learnt readily. The woodwork being a task that was nae new tae me. The fibres collected for fixing the barbed bone to the head, was the information that was truly new to me. Beitidh told me later that the women had shown her some of the grasses, flowers, and leaves they collected tae go with the meal. Nae enough information tae survive, but interesting. The mention of collecting herbs made me think of Isabelle, and I felt a sense of loss creep into me heart. I quickly put the thought aside. There was nae use thinking on things out of reach.

The screeching of insects kept us awake into the night. The noise went from deafening tae an irritating quiet buzz by morning. Many of us were forced tae climb under the blanket tae protect against the welts that itched infernally when scratched. Seamus offered us a salve the next morning as he apologised for nae warning us about the savagery of mosquitoes living near the river.

"Best to ignore the itch and resist touching the welts."

"More easily said than done, I think. At least now I know why ye dived under the blanket when the fire was doused. And there was me thinkin' ye felt the cold that didnae exist."

"First to muffle the noise of the cicada, then the buzz of the mozzie," Seamus explained. "I hate the dive bomb on the ear. King Mulway,[21] over there, suggests the application of some fish paste, but I cannot come at that."

[21] The English assigned the term King onto a native they designated king of a people group. The term king was an English construct. The Indigenous people of NSW did not have kings or chiefs. The English gave breastplates to 'Duchess' the natives. Many today would say that this was the English disrespecting the indigenous cultures. Rather than a sign of respect for an individual. To 'Duchess' someone is to sideboard them.

"Is that what that smell was?" I screwed up me face. "Maybe it would be worth it." As I scratched the welt, I was told tae leave be.

"Those born here seem to have less problem with them. My daughter says she decided when she was twelve never to scratch at a bite again. Now they rarely sting her, and she only gets a red dot if they do. Says, she still needs to cover her ears, though, because they hover overhead unless there is another person close by. Then the blighters attack the other person."

"That seems very far-fetched. And do you believe her story?"

"'Tis no story. I've seen no welt on her in many years. Only the tiny red dot."

As we spoke, we had been packing our belongings onto pack horses. We were tae walk from the river. Seamus added tae each horse a small bag that contained tools he had purchased in Sydney.

"To share the burden," he said, "and to make up for your losses in the wreck. I am thinking you lost the tools of trade that you brought from home."

"Most all of them."

We finished our work in silence after that and were ready to leave in the half hour. We were grateful for the FCLS insisting that we purchase shoes and stockings with the cost tae be added tae the loan. Some of us still battled blisters from the wearing-in of new shoes. The dilemma then, tae choose between cuts from going shoeless, or blisters from wearing new shoes. 'Twas a ten-mile walk. Nae that many miles of walking, but we made slow progress and didnae arrive till after the midday.

Famished, we dropped under a tree and removed the shoes from our tortured feet.

Mrs Foster and her daughter carried basins of water for us to wash our feet at the first sight of a blister on young Dierdre. Correctly guessing that we all suffered from the same malady.

We hobbled over to the table set for lunch under the one Red Cedar tree left standing in the Fosters' home yard. An interesting tree, very tall with a wide trunk reaching straight to heaven. There were fan-shaped roots above ground that gave the feel of a fairies' parlour. And leaves that made me think of feathers. The bark was tough and scaly and had moss on the southern aspect of the fan-shaped roots. The moss looked dried out from the summer heat.

The water flavoured with lavender flowers was the most popular offering on the table. Mr Foster's daughter, Sophie, made several trips to refill the jug. When our thirst was sated, we were able to converse with our hosts over a cold lunch of roast lamb and mint jelly sandwiches. Sophie explained the preparations that had been made for us while we ate.

"We have prepared a space in the community hall for you all to bed down tonight. Seamus has prepared tents for you to take to your selections tomorrow. With the necessities for setting up camp. If you work together, it should not take long to build a basic cabin for each allotment. It will be rough for a time, but the weather is mostly good. The biggest fear in the summer is fire. Be very careful you do not walk away from a fire still burning, nor still smouldering. Our local mob of aborigines, the Gweagals, will drop by, no doubt, to keep an eye on you."

The following day, we found our selections and marked out our boundaries with the help of the local surveyor. Then the task was tae set about choosing a place for the cabins. We aimed tae locate the homes as close together as possible so that we could support each other. There was a nice hill not too far from a stream that had all four selections enjoying some higher ground. Our homes would be within a mile's distance, all around.

Seamus told us right that the Gweagal people would visit soon enough tae point out the errors in the placement of our homes. We didnae have tae listen, but I felt the Lord prompting me tae take some advice and move the foundation of our first cottage up the hill, further from the creek that had barely a flow of water. The elder pointed out the leaf litter high in a tree. I scratched me head as I looked around and at the trickle flowing along an almost dry creek bed. I couldne conceive that the water would get that high. I scratched me head and ran me fingers through me hair before nodding in agreement. The wasted effort we had put into the started foundation was a loss. But there was nothing for it, we moved and began levelling a site further uphill. Years later, when the trickle became a huge raging river torrent for a week, we sought out the elder to thank him.

We set our home above a sandstone outcropping and resigned ourselves tae carting water until we could improve the situation with a water tank and dam. Maybe a pump? A difficulty we needed tae solve. I added the issue tae the list of questions we were jotting down for the next time we saw Seamus.

Two weeks after we started, Seamus paid us a visit and asked me tae travel into the mill and fashion some furniture, with the intention of paying me in lumber for the cabin. As we were then camped together, there was no issue leaving Beitidh while I worked at the mill. I planned tae eventually create me own workshop, but we needed at least one house first. I left the rest of the men tae fell a few trees with the help of a local lumberjack. Again, for the promise of furniture. And the women tae begin a kitchen garden. The soil needed some improving, but with time we hoped tae plant market crops. The climate was different tae Scotlain but nae so different we couldne cope. If we thought in terms of season rather than month, it wasnae too confusing. The topsy-turvy of Christmas in summer turned out tae be a more difficult transition.

It took an hour tae walk between the farm and the mill each day. I would have preferred tae work on our land, but I wasnae essential. It benefited everyone most for me tae be the cabinet maker I was trained tae be so that we could buy needed supplies. Mr Foster's workshop was well equipped, and the work in the shop progressed well. Patrons paid well in goods and services for the furniture that, until then, had been very rough from what I saw. In time, I needed tae demand cash, but at the beginning, the barter worked well for us. I built a chook pen on me days at home and brought home the beginnings of a brood of hens for Beitidh tae care for. She liked working with the livestock, and the droppings supplied much needed fertiliser for the garden that was dug and tended by Doug with the help of

Meaghan and Adeline. With the addition of a rooster, when I completed a separate coop for him, the brood grew.

I came home with a milking ewe one afternoon, at which Beitidh screwed up her nose. But there were nae milking coos tae be had that year. We had tae make do if we wanted cheese. A task taken on by Catriona with Dierdre as apprentice after her school lessons were finished for the day. A second ewe was given as payment the next week, which allowed for milk in tea and damper. Life began tae take shape only a month into our settlement.

We built a simple four room house with the lumber given in payment. The tin roof was costly and took much work, as well as a promissory note on purchase. The cascading rain on the tin roof made the summer storms deafening and paused all non-shouted conversation during the downpour. We built the house with a hall down the centre, front door facing east, and rear door facing west to allow for fast cooling when the breeze arrived midafternoon. Hessian covered the windows until glass could be had. The fireplace was built on the east wall of the parlour, which was the southern back room. The chimney we made with bricks brought down from Sydney.

We built a kitchen extending from the south side of the back veranda with an outside dining area set on the back veranda. The laundry and bathhouse were built out from the north side of the veranda, with an outhouse fifty yards beyond the bathhouse. The fence for the kitchen garden we made higher each time a kangaroo was found within. The height eventually contained the fruit trees to keep the birds and bats away. We constructed the garden '*cage*' with tall posts and surrounded all with chicken wire as roof and walls.

The family met each Sunday for prayers tae mark the passing of the week. And we celebrated when the itinerate priest came to visit, telling us about the mass available in Hurstville. After two months, we were ready for the company of others. We were too small a group tae nae get irritable with each other if there was nae variety in companions. I was thankful tae Mrs Chisholm for insisting that family groups of no less than twelve undertook the journey together.

We met and decided tae make the journey once each month. The walk tae Hurstville was four hours of walking plus riding the punt. The first trip we walked tae *The Roasted Pumpkin* Inn Saturday afternoon and stayed the night. Beginning early again the next morn, the plan brought us tae arrive at Mass before the bells rang. Following the first trip, I prevailed in convincing the family that the next time we would be best walking on Friday afternoon tae visit the shops for supplies. Then stay at an Inn in Hurstville for the two nights rather than one, before heading home after the Mass. We scouted out a suitable inn and ate lunch before leaving that day. *The Miners' Hope* was a new establishment that looked clean and sold quality pies with ale.

Convincing the Priest tae hold a Mass in Bottle Forest became a mission for all who found the walk arduous. Meeting other Catholic families at Mass who regularly made the journey built a sense of community in the area. They were nae all from Scotlain. Some were from Ireland. A contentious relationship, but with time we looked tae be Australians so learnt tae exist side by side with the Grace of God as our help. We sought to

> "Follow peace with all men and holiness: without which no man shall see God." [22]

[22] Hebrews 12:14 DRB

We even found other European settlers who had come for the gold but chose tae farm instead. A melting pot of cultures that was tae be made into something new.

A stream of itinerants began moving into the area to whom Beitidh sold eggs and Catriona cheese. At ridiculously high prices as the consumers offered a higher price tae nae go without. Gold had been found in the area, and many tents went up. This made it necessary tae keep a watchman awake overnight and all tae be ever in company. The payment in gold became less desirable as the trip into Hurstville tae unload the dangerous commodity was arduous and fraught with danger from the ever-present bush rangers. Many of whom were escaped convicts who preferred tae take the fruits of another person's labour rather than bring forth their own harvest. [23]

It was decided that the accumulation of gold on the home property was more treacherous than frequent trips, as it created a larger target. Wherever there was gold, human society declined. It was a pattern repeated in all instances of which I had read. Thankfully, none of our family succumbed tae the temptation and allure of quick, *easy* money. From what we could see, the life of the miners was nae at all *easy*.

Once the first house was built, we as a group, voted tae live under the one roof and work on the market garden and growing stock. Selling felled trees tae the mill and creating a foundation from where tae increase. We planned tae build a new house each year over the

---

[23] On the road to Ballarat in 1853, Ned Kelly described a common kit for those travelling to the goldfields. Many carried only a pair of socks, a revolver, and a shillelagh. The preferred pistol was the machine-produced revolver of Samuel Colt because of the interchangeable parts and relative ease of repair. https://collections.museumsvictoria.com.au/articles/2810: Firearms in Gold Rush Victoria, 1850s

next four years. We needed four houses in under five years. One on each allotment.

I began running supply trips tae Hurstville with Seamus. It was on these trips that we began riding with loaded guns in hand, and another two left behind for the homestead. Our unexpected prosperity, brought about by settling close but not on a goldfield, brought both good and bad. What had seemed almost utopian at the start became an uncertain environment. The finance helped us tae start but also made us afraid of attack. We were developing a heightened awareness of our vulnerability.

Reading the newspapers when they could be had didnae help. As they were cut into squares for use in the outhouse, neither could they be kept from the women and children. Reading material whilst sitting became the topic of conversation and fodder for active imaginations. The weekly lay sermons focused on trusting God tae work all things together for good, a necessary part of keeping fear under control.

We kept a gun in the kitchen but were generous with any who came asking with hat in hand. The Gweagals were always polite and, on occasion, shared with us a kangaroo which they had slaughtered. I arranged with them tae trade some possum furs as the temperatures began tae fall at night. We were in nae danger of succumbing tae the cold, but the furs used tae make bed coverings ensured a comfortable night's sleep.

They all spoke their own, lyrical form of English, but I endeavoured tae learn some of their wodiwodi language also. When they started talking amongst themselves, I had little hope of distinguishing the words that I knew. They rattled it all off so very fast and with very different inflections; I couldne separate the words.

The Gweagals told us that they needed tae burn patches of land, telling us that it was important for keeping the country healthy. As I had seen the competence of the blacks near Huskisson, I couldne be afraid of the practice. They showed a gracefulness in their absolute control of fire as it moved slowly along the ground without consuming trees. I felt led tae listen and paid the men tae keep our land, or from the Gweagals' perspective, their land, safe. They told us where they would burn next and advised us tae move our livestock. It was a strange dynamic, they told us what tae do, sounding like ancient wisdom, and we thought we gave them permission.

Other settlers didnae have such a mutually beneficial relationship with the local aboriginals.

They *cleared* them off *their* land.

A group of them camped near our creek where they had told us nae tae build.

They were not always there; they came and went.

When they arrived, they came tae say hello, offered meat and took sugar and flour. Then told us if they planned tae burn. They killed some sheep tae eat, but asked which animal they could have.

It was on one of the supply trips tae Hurstville, which I had begun taking with Seamus, where I again came across Isabelle. Beitidh gave me a letter for the dressmaker with instructions on what tae order. Measurements, fabric choices, colour, and apparently an instruction tae send me tae the tailor for new pants. I expected tae simply drop the letter and return next month tae take receipt of the order. When I stepped into the dressmaker's shop, I was stunned by an awareness of God's goodness and a more organic sense of delight. I crossed the room with a large smile. Me hat turning circles in my hands.

"No, Gareth."

This was said as I sought tae make me escape. I wore an awkwardness because I was lost for words in me surprise at learning Isabelle lived so close.

"You are to cross the room and see the tailor for measurements." Isabelle smiled. "Did Beitidh not tell you what she wrote. I suspect she planned tae catch you off guard."

I withdrew my hand from the door and returned tae read Beitidh's letter.

"Nae! She didnae tell me her plan. I have limited time; can this be achieved post haste? We will need tae leave in the half hour if we are tae be home today."

"Mr Beaumont is out currently. Would you mind, Miss Macauley, doing the measurements?"

At the prospect of a miss doing the measurements, me discomfort was visible. I looked across the room at an attractive young woman and felt reluctant tae have her hands close enough tae measure me. I couldne wait, though, so I gave way and submitted tae the embarrassment. When done, I left so quickly that I neglected tae say goodbye. An action I came to regret.

CHAPTER 21

Not Again

"For God gave us a spirit not of fear but of power and love and self-control."

2 Timothy 1:7 ESV

August 1851, Hurstville

I Heather had finished her training with Iris and was then undergoing a traineeship with Malcolm for the tailoring side of the business. I needed to first work beside Iris so that I could complete my dressmaking apprenticeship before I moved on to the tailoring.

One afternoon, Heather was working in the tailoring side of the shop, and I, in the dressmaking. The Beaumonts had left us in charge when they went to share an anniversary lunch with each other. They had been married for twenty years. They seemed young for being married so long.

The Beaumonts had emigrated shortly after they married. Leaving England behind to escape the ex-convict stigma Iris had gained when she was jailed for her efforts in the suffragette movement. The thought being that in a place with so many ex-convicts, there would be less of a stigma attached. As their business was so successful, I can only think their strategy worked. I learnt that it was common for women to be the business owners in the colony. A leftover from the wives following their convict husbands and setting up a business.

With financial independence, women had more control over their lives, even though they did not have the vote. Iris remained an activist but went about her cause with paper and pen. Writing articles for the newspapers. The government in England decreed against any change to the status of women's suffrage in the colonies. Afraid to allow practices in the colonies that might influence home affairs. But Iris stated often that she was like the widow in Luke.[24] "Never give up, girls! It will come about."

I looked up from my thoughts to see Gareth standing just inside the doorway, with hesitation and a stunned look on his face.

He wore a heavy coat made from wool, as it was then in the winter months. It felt strange to have winter with no festive season. But then there was no frost or snow either. He removed his broad-brimmed felt hat and smiled a celebratory smile as he walked my way.

"Isabelle, I hadnae thought o' seeing ye. 'Tis a pleasure indeed."

Unbuttoning his coat to pull a sheet of paper from his pocket as he spoke, I could see the gun that had been hidden under his coat.

---

[24] Luke 18:1-8 ESV

The sight was becoming commonplace, or so Heather told, knowing only because she worked in the men's side of the business. All travelling in from the south had begun to wear guns.

"I would not have thought to see you in a dressmaker's shop either. The tailoring is to be found across the other side of the shop."

"I'm here with a note from Beitidh." At that, he handed the paper to me and continued to talk as he turned for the door.

"I cannae stay, but if yer happy I'll call in tae see ye earlier in the day next time we come tae toon."

I nodded my approval and smiled a smile that set my face to aching. I scanned the document before me as he walked to the door and set him straight about Beitidh's intentions. I watched as he awkwardly made his way toward Heather, who was giving me a considered look as she appraised the newcomer. I could see the appreciation that she had no hesitation in displaying for all to see.

Gareth left so fast following the measurements that my immediate response to his lack of farewell left me feeling rejected and thinking that he couldn't get away from me fast enough. The remainder of the day was spent nursing a melancholy encouraged by dark thoughts. It was in that atmosphere of distraction that Heather found purchase for the negative comments she seemed determined to push my way.

"I suppose he knows you well enough to not like you." Heather paused to add weight to what she said. "Like some of the other customers I've heard talking in the meetings on Sundays."

Heather's family being non-conformist, she attended the Congregational church but seemed not to have any convictions herself. I knew her intention was to condemn me for some unknown fault, but I had no way of defending myself. I had not managed to form many good friendships. Every time I enjoyed a fulsome conversation with one of the other young women in the congregation, the next time we met, the conversation was superficial and cut short because they needed to be somewhere else.

It happened on numerous occasions. I could only think the slights were intentional. The hurt I felt from a singular occurrence began to accumulate with every manifestation. Each time it happened, the hurt was greater. I became suspicious but also wondered if I imagined a slight when there was none intended. I did not understand it, and so began to delve into self-assessment. My confidence waned even further than my London experiences had caused. I became defensive and looked to blame others for what was happening to me. I convinced myself that there must be something other than my own actions and reactions at play in the situation.

But then I would react to a hurt with resentment or anger, and that in turn convinced me that if I could only behave differently, I might find a friend. No, that's not quite right. I had a friend in Sally. Sally was a wondrously generous person who gifted me her smiles and her time often. It was fewer enemies, I wanted. And I did feel like I had enemies. I was uncertain how much influence the comments Heather fired my way had on the behaviour of others.

From Heather, I could discern intention. Her unguarded comments, which were few, informed me that before I came, she had expected to inherit the business in which she worked. Iris and Malcolm wanted a daughter more than another apprentice. Their delight in having someone to parent was there to be seen. I was young enough to still need a parent, and I enjoyed the attention and care they lavished on me.

The relationship that developed with the Beaumonts was the saving grace that made my new life better than only bearable. I loved receiving letters from my family, but they were few and far between. Three letters from one individual would arrive at the same time because the letters had to wait for a ship travelling to the southern oceans. The dates at the head of the letters were invaluable for the aid in reading them in the correct order. But then, sometimes a tattered letter would arrive out of sequence, and comments within letters would indicate that I had never received some missives. My family wrote that the same was true of the letters I sent home. I was grateful that my family persisted in writing, even though any news sent was old news by the time it was received. I could not be there to celebrate the births nor share the grief of Grandma passing. The letters brought tears and joy. Leaving me to shed many tears on a roller coaster of sad and happy.

I felt lost and adrift. I wondered if I would ever feel truly at home again. My emotions started to fluctuate with extremes. Another reason for people to dislike me. My answer was to keep my feelings hidden. I went so far as to detach from them in myself, so that I could react after filtering the emotions through a sieve of acceptability. The drawback was that I did not feel spontaneous joy any more than I felt spontaneous hurt. There was always a lag so that I could be in control of what I allowed to show. Sally told me that I seemed to be becoming more distant, and she missed the sudden laugh or cry that I gave her when we first met. I had started to appear fake. Sally delved to uncover the truth because she was generous with her love. I wanted to be fearless in loving, as both Chloe and Sally were fearless. When I tried, the hurt within made me afraid. My hesitation was interpreted as reluctance, and so my love appeared fake. I sank deeper and deeper into despair. On the surface, I seemed bored but happy.

I would lay awake at night destroying my bedding as I constantly changed positions. I relived the hurtful events that had brought me to that place. The demons whispered lies into my mind as I rehashed the hurtful events. I created untrue beliefs, formed from those lies, and then began to live my life founded on the wrong beliefs. The whispers continued until lies seemed to be truth, and fear distorted my view of the world. Some started to call me paranoid, but there was always a grain of truth hidden in the lie to make it believable.

Iris and Malcolm started to worry for me. Others began to talk about me and create a distance. My fear generated in other people the very behaviour of which I was afraid. They could sense my fear, and Heather was there waiting to take advantage. To make comments that reinforced my faulty beliefs about myself, to me, and to others. Sad, sad life! I appeared to have everything but felt little blessing. I knew I needed help. I wanted Iris and Malcolm to feel gratitude from me, so I couldn't tell them how I felt. I began to hide those parts of myself as best I could, whilst still enjoying the family times we spent walking to the river.

CHAPTER 22

Pariah

"So I say, walk by the Spirit, and you will not gratify the desires of the flesh. For the flesh desires what is contrary to the Spirit, and the Spirit what is contrary to the flesh. They are in conflict with each other, so that you are not to do whatever you want. But if you are led by the Spirit, you are not under the law. The acts of the flesh are obvious: sexual immorality, impurity and debauchery; idolatry and witchcraft; hatred, discord, jealousy, fits of rage, selfish ambition, dissensions, factions and envy; drunkenness, orgies, and the like."

Galatians 5:16-21 NIV

October 1851, Hurstville

I Sally was huddled talking intimately with a small group of women outside the Sunday meeting. When she saw us arrive, she waved me over to join them. As each woman caught sight of my approach, they made their excuses and walked away. By the time I joined Sally, only Deborah remained engaged in conversation with Sally. When Sally paused in the conversation to greet me, Deborah quickly made her excuses.

"Sally, I really must go and help Mum with the Books. They were taken from the pews for refurbishment last week and need to be distributed."

With no acknowledgement of me, she walked up the stairs and into the chapel.

"I'm so sorry, Isabelle. I had no idea the gossip had led you so far into exile. It's a cruel thing to be so slandered. Do you have any idea where it started?"

My expression was crestfallen before I shut down the emotional response. I placed a winsome smile on my face before responding with a measured and steady voice. I could hear the forced calm and had no doubt that Sally could hear it also.

"I am certain it has been started by Heather. She has told me as much on more than one occasion. Not in the hearing of another person, though. The Beaumonts know of her animosity, but I have not told them of her malice. I am so grateful to them for their love and kindness that I want to appear happy for them. On Sundays, they are busy talking to the older couples, so have not seen that the young people walk away from me. In truth, I don't even know what people say about me. And I can't battle the unknown.

"I aim to be friendly but never get past the first interaction. The first conversation always seems to be a happy one. Increasingly, I find that the first conversation is stilted by others wanting to leave. Or they turn away as soon as they see my approach."

I took time to prevent tears from erupting, and time to force more internal calm.

"I have no idea what I can do differently. There must be something unappealing about me, I just don't know what it is."

The stunned look on Sally's face caused her to hesitate and choose words carefully.

"I am fairly certain that is not the case. If a person resists the first conversation, it cannot have anything to do with your behaviour. You are a lovely person. God made you a generous and kind-hearted person who often shares good things with others. I've not seen you judge another person harshly."

I interrupted the praise Sally was determined to heap on me. I could not hear what she was saying. I doubted the veracity of what she said. My doubt about my goodness left me feeling the need to reject and argue.

"I have forgiven some people only to turn around and judge them again when the memory intrudes into my day or night. I think I have become harsh in my thoughts." Bitterness was evident in my voice.

I forgave with my lips but retained the resentment. After all, where was my justice? I was waiting for God to make it all right again. Why did my enemies continue to prosper when I was faced doggedly with similar scenarios of an enemy destroying my reputation? I did not even know what accusation was brought against me, so could not defend myself. The lives of others seemed more important to God than my own. The mob always won, and God had not demonstrated to me any goodness wrought from the circumstances in which I found myself. How could there be any good purpose in a mob being deceived into believing lies spread for malicious intent?

I saw the compassion that emanated from Sally. She was genuine and not afraid of anyone. I asked myself, '*How did she retain the loving attitude?*' What difference in me caused people to hate me rather than love me the way Sally was loved? I had seen that her association with me had not damaged other people's opinion of her. Why did so many accept the lies told about me rather than rely on their own discernment? Sally quietly linked arms with me and sat with me through the service. When the singing and preaching finished, I clung to Iris and Malcolm until we left for home.

The following day, Jeremy and Susan Russell, Deborah's parents, came into the shop and asked to speak with Iris and Malcolm privately. A sense of foreboding entered the shop with them. I felt the antipathy like a pea soup fog, even though they smiled beautifully and spoke most gently.

"Good morning, Isabelle, Heather." The eye contact had the appearance of genuine pleasure at seeing us both. "How are you both on such a God given beautiful day?"

Heather jumped right in with a response, moving with bounce and verve from the other side of the shop. My anxiety increased with the enthusiasm Heather displayed in her greeting. Something was fomenting. I suspected the ingredients had been mixed and left to sit while the leaven raised the intended trouble.

"I am also well, Mrs Russell. Can I help you with anything this morning?"

There was no need to ask about the Russells' well-being as the conversation with Heather was lively and right before me.

"We have come to talk with Iris and Malcolm. Are they about?"

"They are looking at the stores upstairs. I can give them a message from you if you like. I am sure they did not mention any meeting scheduled for this morning."

"Yes, Isabelle, please let them know that we are waiting for them downstairs. It is important that we talk to them sooner rather than later."

I was stunned by their forceful manner and hesitated before responding.

"I... will... go let them know. I am sure they will put aside their work for an important talk with you, Mr and Mrs Russell."

I sedately walked through the door between the shop and the living quarters. When out of sight, I took a deep breath and took the stairs two at a time, skirts around my calves. On the landing of the second floor, I stopped to take a few more deep breaths. Iris had heard me bounding up the stairs and popped her head through the storeroom doorway. With a smile, she began to talk.

"Your youthful strength inspires me to walk up and down the stairs more often, Isabelle." But after looking more closely at me, the smile dropped from her face. "Whatever is the matter, Isabelle? I can smell no smoke. Your manner suggests to me some catastrophe."

With that said, Iris put her arms around me and waited for me to share. Malcolm joined us, then before I could deliver the message, he descended to the shopfront to investigate. Haltingly, I passed the message to Iris.

"Mr and Mrs Russell .... are here to have an... important ... talk with you. I felt the room change when they walked into the shop. It was so much like the dream I woke to this morning. I fear it can be nothing good. In the dream, a dark-haired girl was telling lies about me. I know it sounds like memories surfacing in my dreams, but I think it was a warning of things to come. I know it sounds like I am hysterical, but I have told you of my dreams before. This had the clarity of the prophetic dreams I have had in the past."

The concerned look on Iris' face turned to a benevolent and gentle smile as she comforted me.

"If it is a prophetic dream, then you know that whatever happens is no surprise to God. He will always comfort us if we dare to surrender and ask him for comfort."

With that reminder, I felt peace creep into my heart.

"Thank you, Iris." I held to her hands for a short while before releasing her to follow Malcolm. "I will put the kettle on for you."

I raced down the stairs at the same rate I had ascended. Once the kettle was set to heat on the stove, which I stoked, I made my way back to the shop, passing the Russells in the hall. Mrs Russell cringed as our skirts touched. An action not missed by Iris. Creases formed between her brows as she followed the Russells to the kitchen.

"Please have a seat on the back veranda whilst I prepare the tea."

That was the last I heard of the conversation as the Russells took up their station outside, and I re-entered the shop. Whilst the conversation was in progress on the back veranda and Heather hummed to herself whilst she worked, I fretted. With rigid hands, I worked on an elaborate dress for one of the young girls due to have her first communion in the Catholic church.

Such a fancy white dress for a seven-year-old. The eldest daughter of a local hotelier. Not a dress the girl would be able to play in after the event, with much lace for catching as she climbed a tree. It was very pretty, though. Her long black curls and porcelain skin contrasted and made her seem an angel. I understood the day to be a celebration with a party to follow the sacrament.

The little girl, Bernadette, giggled and chatted her way through the fitting. I learnt much about what she expected from the day. Bernadette went so far as to demonstrate her ritualistic first confession that was to take place the day before her communion. Little wonder the priests knew so much about the lives of their parishioners. The pleasant musings lifted my mood so that when Gareth walked through the door, tinkling the bell above, I had a smile on my face and no sign of distress. God had once again brought comfort to me in an unexpected way.

"'Tis good to see you once again, Isabelle. And a good morning to you also, Miss Macauley."

Gareth darted his eyes toward the tailoring and nodded his head in greeting before drawing closer to me for conversation. Heather lifted her head and looked miffed by Gareth not addressing her first.

Gareth leant against the counter, close to where I worked, and turned the felt hat in his hands. After turning his back to Heather, he began a conversation that he had planned to be a leisurely chat between friends who had been separated by circumstances not of their choosing. Once again, my soul soared. I had been sorely lacking friends at that time. Sally was the only companion in town, close to me in age.

"It seems you have come to the shop with time to spare for conversation this time, Gareth. It was disappointing not to catch up on the family gossip when you were last here. How is everyone?"

Our eyes connected as I spoke. I think it was the first time I had truly looked closely enough into his eyes to notice they were blue like the sky in the late afternoon.

"'Tis an apology I owe for me hasty retreat when I was here last. I claim discommodity due tae the unexpected embarrassment of a measuring. I hope you can forgive me for leaving without a, by your leave. Beitidh reprimanded me sorely for me bad behaviour. I learnt the contrition of it."

The sheepish smile he exhibited did not demonstrate a great deal of contrition. Enough though, for me to put the slight aside.

"Of course, I forgive you, Gareth. But still, you have not told the story of how your family fares. I apologise that I cannot offer you tea at present, the Beaumonts are in an important conversation next to the kitchen that I am reluctant to disturb."

"Parched I am, but as I've come tae see Mr and Mrs Beaumont as well as yerself, I will need tae wait for them. 'Tis early yet, so I can wait for tea and enjoy hearing of yer experiences since ye arrived."

"I will be more specific then. How is Beitidh?" He darted a look at me, then smiled at being caught, answering my enquiry with a question of his own.

"Beitidh is doin' fine. She is setting the livestock tae rights and producing eggs and milk aplenty for Catriona and Dierdre tae turn to cheese. I suspect she fancies me new apprentice. A local, part Aboriginal boy by the name of Joseph. He is old tae be apprenticed, but his family has been good tae us, so I wanted tae offer him a way tae learn a trade. I didnae expect Beitidh tae take a fancy. He seems tae return the fancy, but the women he calls aunties are nae pleased. He informs us he is told the girls he's allowed tae marry and will need tae convince the older women that his choice is a good one for their community.

"He is learning quickly and has a gift with the wood. He works hard. I like him, but he is inclined tae disappear for a few days without informing me. Teaching him this information is important tae share with me 'tis difficult. He simply says he thought I wouldha' ken he needed tae go burn the country when the weather suits. He seems tae think I should read the weather as he does. This I cannae do. The weather here is too new tae me."

My eyes grew larger and larger as he spoke. The townspeople talked much on their opinion of the blacks. None of it good. Gareth seemed to have a very different experience.

"You have an Aborigine for an apprentice? Are you not afraid?"

"Nae! I have found that we can come tae arrangements for our differences. We have been working well together. He has a tanned olive skin, honey brown wavy hair, and grey eyes. He doesnae look so diff'rent from the Italians ye see aroond. He attends the Mass when Father Xavier rides down tae the Bottle Forest once a month."

I was not convinced. I had heard too many stories for my opinion to be so easily changed.

It was at that moment that the Russells returned through the store, glaring at me and smiling at Heather as they left. Gareth noticed the look they sent my way and stood straight with a challenge in his eyes as they departed the store. Iris and Malcolm walked in through the internal door to the back as the Russells went through the front door. They each displayed a face of extreme sour. Iris turned to me when they had made certain the intruders had departed. When they noticed Gareth glaring at the Russells' backs, they offered me a benevolent look.

"Mr Forbes, it is good of you to come. We did not know when to expect your next visit to town. We have just had an unpleasant interview and need to calm ourselves before discussing business. Would you be agreeable if Isabelle offered you tea and cake whilst we take a few minutes to discuss an important matter between ourselves?" They turned to me.

"Isabelle, would you mind taking Mr Forbes through to the back veranda and organising the tea things?" They then turned to Heather.

"You are free to leave for the day, Heather. We will come and see you at home this afternoon."

I noticed a stunned and possibly resentful look on Heather's face as I turned toward the kitchen.

I led Gareth through the corridor to the kitchen in silence but did not hear any more of what happened. I was in turmoil over the possibilities and blocked hearing any threat of hurt. I walked straight to the beaded curtain that led from the kitchen to the veranda.

"Please take a seat in the sun on the veranda, Gareth, whilst I put the kettle on."

Gareth looked at me with sympathy. He could see trouble was afoot, and as he had experienced my succumbing to trouble aboard the *Slains Castle*, he concluded that the trouble was aimed at me. He reached a hand toward me and placed it on my shoulder. He gently stroked with his thumb.

"Isabelle, I want ye tae ken that come what may ye are always welcome with Beitidh and I out at the farm."

He then dropped his hand and took a seat in the larger of the rocking chairs to wait whilst I prepared tea things. I heard the sincerity in his words and took a measure of comfort that felt foreign. Rather than comfort me, this created a kernel of panic. Fear that I might rely on something that could evaporate in an instant if someone accused me of the very thing Gareth would not be able to forgive. It was irrelevant that I did not know what that could be. There was always something a person would not forgive. Or so I thought in my twisted, stinking thinking.

Iris and Malcolm joined me in the kitchen before I had finished preparing a tray of tea things. Iris gave me a hug, to which Malcolm joined in. I knew they cared for me. I trusted that they would stand by me. We had come a long way in the nine months we had been living together. Nine months of learning about each other's character. They were every bit as loving as my parents in England. It did not occur to me that I might doubt them. The reassurance helped.

"We will talk about this after our business meeting with Mr Forbes. I know that you will be burning with curiosity, but it is best we talk with you privately to decide how best you want to handle the situation. Is that acceptable to you, Isabelle?"

"I suppose that is best, as I do not know what has been said, and you do. I trust you both. Gareth is a good friend and showed himself to be of good character on the journey from England. More than once, I saw him stand up for the *set-upon* in a conflict. I feel certain that he can be trusted."

And yet I retained a niggle, despite my words of affirmation, that no one could be fully trusted before they were family.

G I prayed as I waited on the veranda for the cuppa tea and the Beaumonts tae join me. The message sent tae me had told of a plan for the shop tae have new shelves, so I knew 'twas business we were tae discuss. Arriving in the centre of a brewing storm had tae be God's plan. I trusted he would let me know the plan at the right time. Mr and Mrs Beaumont came through the beads and held them for Isabelle tae bring through a tray.

"We have closed the shop for the rest of the morning so that Isabelle can participate in the discussions. We had planned for Heather to attend the shop whilst we met, but it has been necessary to let her go."

I saw the surprise on Isabelle's face at that statement and concluded it was news tae her. I suspected the Beaumonts had not yet had time tae inform Isabelle of the details about what happened in their recent meeting with town elders.

"We will be advertising in Sydney town for a tailor's apprentice. The shop has sufficient work to support such."

Iris took up the conversation at that point in the way the couple had of co-leading the business.

"Some of this is surprising to Isabelle. The recent meeting was a surprise to us also. Circumstances this very morning have led us to make quick changes to our plans. We have a peace about the changes and trust that God approves of the decisions we have made. All of this is only mildly relevant to you, Mr Forbes, as we have been hoping to employ your services in refitting the shelving in the shop and to commission a few pieces of furniture for the upstairs. We have a larger family now, so we need a few more pieces of furniture." Iris then turned to Isabelle and continued.

"This was to be a surprise for you, Isabelle. Unfortunately, it has now become blurred with other happenings. But you can see that we had made this appointment with Mr Forbes before the events of today."

The reference tae family could only have been meant tae reinforce Isabelle's feeling of being in a family. I think I liked the Beaumonts. Before the events of that morning, I would have been reluctant tae spend so much time in town when there was still much tae do at home. Malcolm took up the conversation again as I paused tae consider.

"We will, of course, pay for lodging for the duration of the work, for you and your apprentice." I had nae reason tae hesitate in me response.

"Aye, I will commit tae the task. Would ye call me Gareth, though? Isabelle and I became friends on the journey across the vast ocean and decided tae drop the formality. I hope this is alright with ye. There is nae disrespect intended."

"Yes, Gareth, we had noticed that Isabelle called you Gareth. It might be worth retaining you calling us, Mr and Mrs Beaumont, for the time being. We do expect that you will be a moral man. We have heard nothing to the contrary."

"In the current climate, though, we request that you both address each other more formally in company. That includes the shop. We would like to avoid anyone claiming that you are *close* friends."

Once again, Isabelle showed surprise. I sensed that the Beaumonts had good reason for the request.

"Aye! I will do as ye say." This I said with a cooperative smile. "Now, do ye have any plans for me tae see before I take measurements and provide for ye a quote?"

Mr Beaumont retrieved the drawings he had made from the office alongside the kitchen.

"Thank you, Gareth. Could we ask one other thing of you? Please do not mention the happenings of this morning to any, other than we three."

"Aye, ye can count on me for that. I will keep the dealings close. I willnae mention the like even tae Father Xavier. Has Isabelle mentioned that the good Father helped her somewhat when on the *Slains Castle*?"

The couple looked tae Isabelle before Mrs Beaumont replied.

"Yes, we have had many long conversations with Isabelle about things she has endured. Thank you, Gareth, for reminding us. Is Father Xavier local to Hurstville now?"

"Aye, he rides a circuit that takes in our Heathcote area, and quarters in Hurstville when not riding. He is a good man. Better than many priests. Genuine in his faith, ye ken. 'Tis unfortunate that cannae be said for all priests."

After a lengthy pause, I thought it time tae move me bones. I still had much tae do before finding Mr Foster and heading home.

"Can I measure the room now? I have much tae accomplish before meeting Mr Foster and heading home. I will see ye next time we come tae toon tae provide the quote. Then if acceptable, we can arrange a time for the work tae start." Mr Beaumont stood tae show me out. "Good day tae ye, Mrs Beaumont, and ye Isabelle. I look forward tae seeing ye both again soon."

Isabelle looked tae be in shock as I had seen her before. Lost in her own world. But she pulled herself into the present tae say her farewell before I followed Mr Beaumont tae the front door. I noticed that he left the closed sign on the door as I left.

I watched Gareth walk through the beaded curtain toward the front entrance, then laid my head back on the chair, closed my eyes and hoped that when I opened them again, it would all not be real. I drifted into imagining a world where people trusted me to be the person I thought I was. Where people praised me for generosity and included me in conversation.

"Hello Sally, what a lovely hat, did you do the trimmings yourself?" Sally stood with Rebecca and Ester discussing last weekend's fete. They all turned to me with smiles of welcome.

"My sisters all raved with giggles about the cakes you gave them at the fete last week. Now I know why you kept buying your own creations."

I had only just begun this fantasy when Iris pulled me back to the present.

"It is probably best we talk now rather than leaving this morning's events to fester. Malcolm and I will need to visit Heather this afternoon, and I would like to reassure you before we leave."

Malcolm returned and took a seat on the other side of me. Each placed a hand gently on mine before sitting back and diving into what we all knew would not be pleasant, so might as well be done with. Iris, with her gentle and loving voice, started.

"It has been said, Isabelle, that you have been running around with multiple lads. The Russells came to tell us with the outward intention of making us aware so that we can put a stop to it before you find yourself in the family way. So that we could cast you aside and save ourselves from the embarrassment of public censure. We were surprised by the willingness of the Russells to act in such a way in response to gossip. We have never been close friends, but it is disturbing to us that respected members of our congregation could take such an attitude toward you.

"There can be no evidence to substantiate the gossip, and even if there were, that would not be God's way of handling the situation. We know this to be false witness and asked that they tell us who said those things to them. They claimed that they had heard the tale from many sources and could not possibly know who the original witness was. They said they thought perhaps the lads themselves had been bragging and were overheard by sisters who then talked to other young ladies. We know that none of it is the truth, Isabelle. We see the malicious gossip for what it is, but we cannot fathom the motivation for the gossip. Be that as it may, I think it is an unhealthy environment for you in the congregation, and we need to work out the best course of action."

My head fell into my hands, then into my lap as I caved into despair. From this doubled-over place, I wept. I hid my face from scrutiny. Iris and Malcolm gave me time to settle. They waited for me to sit up before continuing. I did not sit straight; however, even though I remained a little hunched, I had sufficient height to look into their eyes sporadically.

"I don't know what to say."

"There is nothing for you to say, but we do need to work out a plan of action. We think Heather is behind the gossip. The motive being simple jealousy. She had hoped to inherit the shop as we became too infirm to continue. You arriving then being such a success in all - skill, comeliness, and the development of a genuinely deep relationship with us has foiled her hopes. She has mentioned that you are too good to be true. There must be some hidden fault that caused you to leave England."

"Heather saw the solicitor arrive last week and may have eavesdropped on part of the discussion. The truth is, we asked the solicitor to draw up a will leaving the shop to you both equally. We thought it would be too much for one alone. Now we will need to change that. It is apparent that Heather cannot be trusted as a business partner. We will be advertising for an apprentice tailor in the Sydney paper as early as next week. I hope you can see the wisdom in this, Isabelle."

"Yes. Really?" Furrows of bafflement appeared between my brows. "I know that Heather has not liked me. She has wasted no effort since I arrived to send barbs my way. But this is extreme."

"We will go and see her with her parents present to tell her of her dismissal. Perhaps she will convince us that she was not behind the gossip. The workload will be heavy until we can find a good apprentice for Malcolm."

"What would you like to do about church, Isabelle? It is our opinion that these things are oft best not avoided. It will be hard to face a congregation when you know they have been saying false and malicious things about you. We are grieved that they have been so ready to forget the grace they have been given and heap judgement onto another. Right or wrong matters not. Now, Iris and I will need to spend time on our knees to not judge those who have judged. To forgive those who listened to gossip. Oh, to be naturally like Jesus."

The expression of disappointment changed to one of longing on the faces of my two best advocates.

I sat there in the silence as they waited and could feel the anger they directed at others, rather than at me.

I felt secure in their loyalty, but afraid of a mob's behaviour. Why me? Why again? I had forgiven the people of Ellesmere. I had forgiven the servants in Mrs Chisholm's house. I had forgiven the passengers of the *Slains Castle*. What was there about me that inspired so much hate? For them to hate me again? When would God vindicate me and give me justice?

"I will do as you advise. Please stay close to me. I hope that Sally will not also abandon me due to the hazard of being ostracised herself."

It was not till Heather was gone from the shop that I realised how oppressive her presence had been.

The meeting Iris and Malcolm had with Heather and her parents did not go smoothly. Iris and Malcolm made every effort to be diplomatic. To be gentler than the Russells had been. Casting no blame but allowing for possibilities. Unfortunately, the Macauleys viewed the dismissal as an accusation and assigned guilt to the trollop who had usurped their dear Heather's place.

A warning was issued by the constable that any *foot stepped out of place* by Isabelle would be seen and reported. Her every move would be evaluated according to the reprobate she was. He planned to write to the Watch back in Ellesmere for any information that would shed light on the dubious character of Miss Lindsay. The silence of the room with the last piece of information told, made my quick intake of breath both noticeable and revealing. My fear clearly seen.

Sally came to speak to me as usual on Sunday next. It was good to see that her friendliness had not changed. As for everyone else, they whispered to each other as they looked my way. They walked away when I approached.

So, not very different from previous weeks. The most significant difference was that now Iris and Malcolm saw every slight because they never left my side.

CHAPTER 23

Judgement or Healing

"Therefore it says, "God opposes the proud but gives grace to the humble." Submit yourselves therefore to God. Resist the devil, and he will flee from you. Draw near to God, and he will draw near to you. Cleanse your hands, you sinners, and purify your hearts, you double-minded. Be wretched and mourn and weep. Let your laughter be turned to mourning and your joy to gloom. Humble yourselves before the Lord, and he will exalt you. Do not speak evil against one another, brothers. The one who speaks against a brother or judges his brother, speaks evil against the law and judges the law. But if you judge the law, you are not a doer of the law but a judge. There is only one lawgiver and judge, he who is able to save and to destroy. But who are you to judge your neighbour?"[25]

James 4:6-12 ESV

December 1851, Hurstville

G Isabelle was working in the shopfront next time I visited toon with the purpose of taking a quote around tae the Beaumonts. As I entered the shopfront just behind a young man I didnae know, I was surprised tae see him saunter tae the dressmaking counter rather than the tailor's side of the shop where Mr Beaumont worked. I removed me hat as I waited tae see what would happen next, and tae me surprise, the young man dressed in a suit, boldly asked Isabelle tae have lunch with him. With an incredulous voice, Isabelle was prompt in her reply.

"I hardly know you, Mr Trent. We have never spoken a word to each other these last ten months, even though we attend meetings together. I fail to understand your sudden change of heart in wanting to spend a whole meal talking to me. The answer must be a no, Mr Trent."

I noticed Mr Beaumont move toward the exchange, so kept me place near the door.

---

[25] Humble yourself and let God worry about the good and evil of other people. The judge is a lawgiver. There can be only one Judge and lawgiver. God alone! It is not for people to say if the law is good or bad; nor to judge another person as good or bad.

"How can I help you today, Mr Trent? Miss Lindsay does not work the men's side of the shop. If you are after something for your sister, perhaps we could both help you."

Mr Trent looked Mr Beaumont squarely in the face as he placed his hat on his head.

"That's not what I've heard, Mr Beaumont."

With that cryptic statement, he turned and made haste for the door. I stepped sideways for him tae exit and received another cryptic comment just before the door slammed behind him.

"Maybe not as easy as said."

I felt the implication like a punch tae the gut and looked toward Isabelle tae see confusion in her eyes, but not in Mr Beaumont's. He seemed tae understand well what the exchange had meant. His countenance, accordingly stormy.

"Isabelle, would you please go and make the morning tea. I will put the '*back in five minutes*' sign out. I'm sure Gareth would like some refreshments while Iris and I go over the quote."

"Aye, Mr Beaumont, I would at that. Thank ye."

When Isabelle had moved toward the kitchen, Mr Beaumont held me back by standing in me egress.

"I can see you understood that, Gareth. I hope you know that there is no foundation to the gossip but only intentional malice. Isabelle seems to be a little slow at understanding their full implications until she has had time to contemplate the interactions. We no longer think it wise for Isabelle to attend the Congregational church with us. You mentioned a Father Xavier from the ship is housed in Hurstville. Isabelle has told us that she enjoyed the peace of attending Mass with Mrs Chisholm before she set sail for Australia. Could we impose upon you to look out for Isabelle if she attends the Catholic church here?"

"Aye, ye can!"

Mr Beaumont went on quickly before I could say more.

"Do you attend church in Hurstville very often?"

"Only once in a month, usually. 'Tis a long journey for the family. We dinnae have enough horses for all, and there is nae road for a wagon. We will be due tae attend this coming Sunday. I was going tae suggest starting work then if the quote is tae yer satisfaction."

"Excellent! Will you introduce her to some suitable young ladies? We do not have many dealings with the Catholics in town, apart from the making of white dresses, and most of those customers are a little young to become friends for her." This was said with an acquiescent smile. "Do you mind if we suggest this over morning tea? Or would you rather put forward an invitation?"

"Aye, I hear yer meaning, Mr Beaumont. I will invite her tae come tae Mass with me and me family. Father Xavier will be delighted tae see her also."

With that understanding, we both made our way tae the veranda where Mrs Beaumont and Isabelle had set the table and were awaiting us. A beehive cake with cream atop sat in the centre of the table and brought a very broad smile tae me face. "How did I get so lucky?"

"It is my beloved Malcolm's birthday today."

"Oh well then, happy birthday tae ye Mr Beaumont. Now I understand the closing of the shop for morning tea." As Isabelle handed me a slice of cake, I took the opportunity as it presented. I was ne'er one tae prevaricate. "I met with Father Xavier last week, Isabelle. When I mentioned possibly being in toon for the work on the shop, he asked after ye. He made me promise tae bring ye around tae visit with him. I did mention tae the good Father that he couldne summon ye as he can his parishioners."

I was jesting. Thinking that Isabelle would understand, but I saw me audience of three didnae understand the intricacies of me aspersions. I continued, trying tae extricate meself from a blunder.

"It made him laugh and he told me I was tae invite ye tae take tea with him at yer convenience. He said ye could bring whomever ye like with ye. Should I tell him ye will send aroond a note?"

Isabelle enlivened. "Why yes, I would like to see Father Xavier again. He had high hopes for talking to the wayward settlers and the indigenous alike. I would love to share stories with him."

"Would ye also be int'rested in attending Mass with Beitidh and me this Sunday? The family will be coming tae toon on Saturday tae attend confession before the service on Sunday."

Isabelle looked tae the Beaumonts before she answered with enthusiasm. "Yes, I would love to catch up with your family. It has been a long time, and I would like to see our new environment through their eyes." Turnin' tae Mr and Mrs Beaumont, she added, "Do you mind if I go to the Catholic church with Gareth and his family? They were good friends on the journey to Australia. The shipwreck and working together for survival formed us into somewhat of a community."

I respected that she asked for her adoptive parents' opinion on her attending a church outside their own preferred denomination. There having been so much angst over the centuries between the Catholics and the Protestants.

Iris answered quickly. I saw that the Beaumonts had discussed the need for Isabelle tae find a safe place tae worship.

"Of course, Isabelle, perhaps we could go with you to have tea with this Father Xavier. I'm not sure I like the idea of a parishioner being *summoned*."

I squirmed in me seat at this, as all eyes turned tae me.

"I shoudne ha' suggested such a thing. It is merely an attitude brought over from Scotlain. We joke aboot such things. There are some priests who behave in an imperious manner, but Father Xavier is nae one o' them. I'm sure he would love tae meet ye though."

Me sheepish look helped tae mollify Mr and Mrs Beaumont, and it was decided that Isabelle would pen a note before I left. She went upstairs for paper and pen, whilst we discussed the details of the new shelving. It didnae take long for the Beaumonts tae accept the quote. They seemed satisfied with the fairness of the cost and told me they would book a room at the local hotel for meself and Joseph. Isabelle returned as we were finalising the arrangements.

"I will need tae return tae the Bottle Forest and return with me family Saturday before mass on Sunday. I will need tae organise things at home for me tae be away for the week it takes us tae complete the task here. I'm told it is too hot and dry for the burning at present, so I expect Joseph willnae go missing."

I saw perplexed looks on the faces of the Beaumonts and a concerned look in Isabelle's eyes. I thought tae explain, but Isabelle jumped in.

"You plan to bring your darky apprentice. Will we be safe?" The tone indicated a self-righteous prejudice. An attitude I didnae like.

"Aye, Joseph is very civilised. He even eats with a knife and fork. And wears clothes. Ye willnae be needing to sew up any britches for him to don whilst here."

It was easy tae hear from me tone that I had taken offence. We each felt awkward whilst we overcame our prickly attitudes. Mr and Mrs Beaumont gave Isabelle a look that said they would be having a lengthy discussion when I was gone.

"Forgive me. You are right. I have allowed my respect for the people down south to be superseded by the stories that are spread in town. I can see that the talk is truly only fear mongering and gossipy tales designed for entertainment. And I suppose to make an excuse for treating the local aborigines badly."

"I forgive ye, Isabelle. I hope that ye will give Joseph nae need tae forgive yerself."

"I allowed my fears to invade my thoughts. A talk with Father Xavier is probably long overdue."

"Father Xavier Isabelle?" Mrs Beaumont showed her scepticism at this.

"I found him to be helpful on board the *Slains Castle*. His counsel seems to be based in much education and experience. It was always very biblical and Christ centred."

"Did he quote from the King James then?"

"Nae, Mrs Beaumont, usually from the Douay-Rheims for the lay person. Most of us dinnae know much Latin."

"I look forward to meeting Father Xavier, Isabelle"

We finished Malcolm's birthday morning tea discussing the chaos caused by the influx of gold miners tae the area and with me describing what we had been doing on the farm. We had built the second house, so half the family moved tae that house. We built the second tae mimic the first. The gold mining had brought a small boom tae the area, which helped us tae pay off the Family Colonisation Loan

Society. We had naught left tae pay and could use our increase tae build and invest in a future that looked promising.

Father Xavier sent a note around the following day.

Dearest Isabelle,

I am so pleased to hear from you. I am glad that Gareth passed on my message and would love to catch up with you over morning tea. Would next Tuesday, at nine am, suit you? It is, unfortunately, the only time that can suit me. I am sorry that I cannot be flexible. I leave for my circuit ride early on Wednesday and will be gone a month. This is my current mission. To ride a great distance, visiting families in the southern areas.

I look forward to seeing you again.

Yours faithfully

Father Xavier

I gave the note to Iris when she finished with the fitting she was doing, and we conspired to arrange our work so that we could meet with the priest at the time he requested.

"And yet, Isabelle, it still smells a little like a summons. I think I am beginning to understand Gareth's jest."

This did bring a smile to my lips and made me think of Chloe's reaction to my *speaking* with the priest aboard ship.

"Perhaps they see themselves as a parent, and so the congregation also see them as a parent."

Chloe had only been to town for one week in the year since we arrived. It was good to catch up, but I felt the loss of her. The loss of her needing to live in a mining town so isolated that I could not visit. And I could feel her loss living in a town with so few ladies for company.

Her last letter spoke of the friendship she encouraged with the settlement's cook and with her housekeeper. But I read loneliness between the lines of her communication. She shared with me her excitement about the news of her coming confinement and that she would be arriving in Hurstville six weeks before the baby was due. The plan was to stay in town close to a midwife and surgeon until after the delivery. The mining company rented a small house for her to live in for three months. I knew that Phillip would sorely miss Chloe, but I was to be blessed. When Chloe arrived, I could boast of two friends in town rather than one.

It was decided that Malcolm would stay at the shop, and I would visit Father Xavier with Iris to keep me company. I was grateful. It prevented others from approaching me as we made our way along the street.

"It will blow over, Isabelle." Iris commented on the looks that were sent my way as we walked without hurry toward our morning tea. "I speak from my experience following the release from incarceration. People will find a new topic to occupy their shallow minds soon enough. Trust me on this. I think it best for you to stay with us. There is no physical danger here, and most of the population have things in their past they wish to keep hidden. They may scoff when together, but they know in their hearts that but for the grace of God, they would be themselves condemned."

"It is the mob mentality again. When they come together, they feel they must agree with each other no matter their private convictions."

"Very true, Isabelle. A crying shame we are so influenced by the possibility of embarrassment."

Whilst I daydreamed about Chloe coming to town, we had traversed the distance of the main street and the ascent up the hill to the rectory of the church where Father Xavier resided. I had been so lost in the contemplation of pleasant things, I could not remember most of the walk. We approached the front door of the two-story residence along a paved walkway between hedges of lavender and roses. Both the lavender and roses were in bloom and gave off a heady scent of heaven touching earth.

The vow of poverty did not seem to mean living without comfort. The door was opened by a housekeeper wearing civilian clothes. For some reason, I had expected a habit-clad nun. I realised that was silly. They would hardly reside under the same roof as the brothers and priests.

"Hello, Miss Lindsay, Mrs Beaumont, I am Mrs Bellefonte. Father Xavier will meet you in the conservatory. Please follow me. He does love to cultivate his tropical plants. It is quite humid in the conservatory this time of year; I hope you have brought a fan. You may need it even though it is still quite early."

The housekeeper had not exaggerated the climate of the conservatory. The sun coming through the windows and the large pond on the south side created a tropical zone. There was a table with a tea service set out, close to the entrance and in the shade of some rather lovely flowering Tea Trees. The scent was a new sensation for me, astringent, almost citrus, but woodier. Father Xavier approached from out of the jungle within seconds of our stepping through the door. He walked straight to me and greeted me by placing both hands on my shoulders and kissing both cheeks.

"It is so good to see you, Isabelle." With some surprise at the warmth of his greeting, I responded with a smile.

"It is good to see you also, Father Xavier."

"Please forgive me, the European greeting, Isabelle. I forget sometimes, living in this multicultural home, that we are still in the British Empire."

Iris, with a look of surprise remaining on her face, extended her hand swiftly as I introduced her, taking no risk for a similar embrace.

"It is a pleasure to meet you, Father Xavier. Isabelle has told us much about the help you have been to her."

"It is a pleasure for me also to meet the woman generous enough to take an unknown character into her home and be God's blessing to her. Shall we take tea? There is a candle under the Samovar, keeping it piping hot. I hope you will enjoy a spiced tea. I know it is not common here, but I thought Isabelle adventurous enough to try my favourite. Mrs Bellefonte can bring an English tea service if it is not to your liking. The scones are regular, with cream and strawberry jam. It is hard to best them, and Mrs Bellefonte has made the jam herself."

At this, Father Xavier first pulled out a chair for Iris, then for me, before taking his own seat around the small garden setting under the trees. The bubbling fountain on the pond and the sound of bees in the flowers gave a relaxing and immersive experience. We enjoyed the silence as Father Xavier gave us time to soak up the atmosphere.

There was a pervading peace in the space that felt like the presence of God which I experienced during prayers. The silence felt comfortable rather than strained. Before any burden could be felt, Father Xavier started with a gentle but probing question.

"Am I right to assume, Isabelle, that you explained at length your experiences in England and aboard ship to your new family?" At my mellow nod, he continued.

"Would you like to share with me then how you have been managing your fears of late?"

He gave me no quarter to turn the chat into a casual, superficial meeting over tea. Without his straightforward approach, I think I would have avoided talking about any real issues. My Heavenly Father knew that I needed help. He sent that help in the form of Father Xavier. Iris' eyebrows nearly met her hairline at the very delving question, but she remained silent and allowed the priest to draw me out.

"I have been managing well, I think."

I knew I was avoiding some of the issue, but it was not easy to open a window into my inner workings. Father Xavier waited for me to continue without saying a word. I could read the look he gave me as his not being fully convinced. He might have also waited for a prompting from the Holy Spirit before he would continue.

"I have been having unpleasant dreams, though. And I freeze occasionally. And I get lost in daydreams sometimes until someone calls my name several times to get my attention. It makes me feel better. Not the freezing. That disturbs me. I can see what is happening. I can continue to work and respond. But I cannot blink or engage properly until I return. I can only describe it as returning. It is like I am viewing and controlling my actions from a distance."

I looked around the garden as I spoke, knowing that I sounded disjointed and confused in the rush of words that came forth. I glanced at Iris before I returned my gaze to Father Xavier.

"I am sorry. I know that sounded very confused."

"Until this moment, Isabelle, I don't think I realised the severity of the impact all this has had on you."

Iris looked contrite as she reached out a hand to comfort me. I had silent tears forming in my eyes from the mortification I felt at revealing so much of my internal struggle.

"Healing can be had, Isabelle. Will you let me work with you to sort out the conflicting things that are happening for you, and help you to become more resilient to the ugliness this world can sometimes fling?"

I hiccoughed before I answered. I waited until I could control my voice. I thought it only took half a minute of gazing into my lap. Iris told me later it was more like waiting for the egg to harden within the shell. When I was confident that I would not embarrass myself further, I looked up into the concerned and loving faces of my companions.

"Yes, I will be very grateful if you can help me, Father Xavier."

"I am pleased to hear this, Isabelle. Today, you can tell me what has been happening recently to cause you further distress, then we can pray, then I will give you some homework until I return in a month's time. I will send word when I return so that we can organise another morning tea. A good excuse for tea and scones!"

I told Father Xavier about all that had happened from my perspective. I told him I did not understand why it was happening. I told him about my struggle with the why.

Iris told her perspective, giving her thoughts as to the why. Iris told of her plan for me to attend the Catholic church to worship.

Father Xavier approved the plan. He elucidated - *'as the Forbes family would be able to watch out for me.'* Father Xavier explained that sometimes we experience trials, not because we are doing something to cause them, but because there is a lesson God thinks we can benefit from, and in some instances, it is the most effective way to learn.[26] Although the demons that speak into the minds of weak or evil people mean us harm, God does not prevent the experiences because he means to turn them to our good. They can be an opportunity for us to be transformed into the beautiful creation he has always meant us to be.

After we prayed, I felt relieved of a burden. I felt hope again for a good future. Father Xavier said I still had much to learn about how to deal with the world and the spiritual realm. To remember the key: '*At the fall we learnt to judge, at the resurrection of Christ we learnt to forgive as Jesus forgave us.'* My freedom from harm would be found in the forgiveness of those who sought to do me harm. God would be my fortress from harm. My reward in heaven would be great. Father Xavier assigned me tasks to complete until we met again. He then took up his pen and wrote out a few lines.

"I have something I would like you to do whilst I am travelling my circuit over the next month, Isabelle. I have written out Colossians 1:15-23 and 1 Corinthians 13:4-8 in the first person for you. I would like you to write it out at least once each day. Say the actual verse

---

[26] "And we know that for those who love God all things work together for good, for those who are called according to his purpose." Romans 8:28 NIV

once, then write out the paraphrase. I think it may be beneficial to reinforce some sound thinking for you. [27]

"Gareth has told me he is concerned about some things he has seen take place. We are both interested in safeguarding your well-being. Talk to Gareth and Beitidh, as well as Mr and Mrs Beaumont, if you are struggling. They will all pray for you." He handed me the note, and I read it through.

I squirmed at some of the statements as I read them but promised to do as Father Xavier asked.

---

[27] "He is the image of the invisible God, the firstborn of all creation. For by him all things were created, in heaven and on earth, visible and invisible, whether thrones or dominions or rulers or authorities—all things were created through him and for him. And he is before all things, and in him all things hold together. And he is the head of the body, the church. He is the beginning, the firstborn from the dead, that in everything he might be preeminent. For in him all the fullness of God was pleased to dwell, and through him to reconcile to himself all things, whether on earth or in heaven, making peace by the blood of his cross. And you, who once were alienated and hostile in mind, doing evil deeds, he has now reconciled in his body of flesh by his death, in order to present you holy and blameless and above reproach before him, if indeed you continue in the faith, stable and steadfast, not shifting from the hope of the gospel that you heard, which has been proclaimed in all creation under heaven, and of which I, Paul, became a minister." Colossians 1:15-23 ESV

Daily task -Start with a prayer to yield - "Breath in me, Holy Ghost, so that my thoughts will be holy. Act in me, Holy Ghost, so that my actions will be holy. Draw my heart to you, Holy Ghost, and please help me to love what is holy."

Read Colossians 1:15-23

Then write out the following, which is based on

1 Corinthians 13:4-8

I am Patient and Kind

I rejoice in the blessings of others

I am a humble peacemaker

I am merciful and Kind

I rejoice in the truth

I am respectful and stand by my friends in trouble

I am forgiving

I endure in trusting God to provide

I am Joyful in God's presence

I am loved forever by the one who created me, the one who creates me anew each day.

"What an enigmatic man," Iris commented when we had gained the street.

She looked back toward the rectory before setting forth toward the market end of town.

"I like the homework he gave you. Something we could all benefit from. How do you feel, Isabelle?"

"I feel improved from when I came. It will be difficult to believe those things I am to write about myself."

"Then it will be interesting to hear how you feel after writing it out daily for a month."

I remained dubious, but I was willing to give it all a try.

"I see all of those things as true of you, Isabelle."

"I think them to be true, but I have doubts and do not feel them to be true."

The remainder of the walk home, we silently enjoyed the cool breeze that came with the shadow of clouds. The cloud was too high to bring rain but was a welcome relief from the scorching summer sun. As soon as we closed the shop for the day, I excused myself from dinner preparation, promising to wash up and clean the kitchen after dinner. I went upstairs and began my homework. I decided that from that day forward, I would start the day with the homework from Fr Xavier before praying.

CHAPTER 24

The Colour Green

"Let the one who is taught the word share all good things with the one who teaches. Do not be deceived: God is not mocked, for whatever one sows, that will he also reap. For the one who sows to his own flesh will from the flesh reap corruption, but the one who sows to the Spirit will from the Spirit reap eternal life. And let us not grow weary of doing good, for in due season we will reap, if we do not give up. So then, as we have opportunity, let us do good to everyone, and especially to those who are of the household of faith."

Galatians 6:6-10 ESV

January 1852, Hurstville

The rain that simply would not stop but for short bursts of sunlight, created a verdant forest in the back of the house. Everywhere I looked I could see garden out of control. Gareth told me that meant the fires were at a stop till the ground was sufficiently dry. It was apparently both good and bad. I did not understand the import at the time.

Gareth brought Beitidh with him to walk me to St Francis church for Mass on the Sunday when the family returned. There had been some delay due to fires close to their home, which meant that Joseph and Gareth could not leave until the danger of losing what they had built had passed.

We took our chance to walk when the rain eased, and the sun came out through a small break in the clouds. There was no way to avoid wet shoes when venturing out. The mud puddles and water clinging to the long grasses ensured that we did not remain dry. Drips from the overhanging leafy canopy left splotches of wetness on our pastel coloured garments. I was glad that I had chosen to wear a print fabric to minimise the effect.

Gareth handed me a note after greeting me and said that '*God had been laying a few verses on his heart of late*.' That, to practice the ways of Christ, we must first believe them to be true.

Dear Isabelle

"You then, my child, be strengthened by the grace that is in Christ Jesus, and what you have heard from me in the presence of many witnesses entrust to faithful men, who will be able to teach others also. Share in suffering as a good soldier of Christ Jesus. No soldier gets entangled in civilian pursuits, since his aim is to please the one who enlisted him." 2 Timothy 2:1-4 ESV

"If you put these things before the brothers, you will be a good servant of Christ Jesus, being trained in the words of the faith and of the good doctrine that you have followed. Have nothing to do with irreverent, silly myths. Rather train yourself for godliness; for while bodily training is of some value, godliness is of value in every way, as it holds promise for the present life and also for the life to come." 1 Timothy 4:6-8 ESV

I have learnt that God trains me in his ways as I absorb the truth of Christ into my way of thinking.

My family would like to invite Mr and Mrs Beaumont to lunch with us at the Smashed Pumpkin, following the Sunday service. 'Tis summer, so the family has many hours for the return trip home. We have found 'tis better not to travel through the heat of the day.

Yours Faithfully
Gareth

After reading through the note quickly, I caught Iris and Malcolm as they exited the shopfront on their way to their own Sunday service. I mentioned Gareth's invitation, and they made an impromptu decision to leave the hours-long Congregational service early so that we would not be waiting for them. I thanked Gareth and left the note on the workbench in the shop so that it would not become wet. I planned to consider the versus more fully that evening. It did not even occur to me to notice that I had so soon divorced myself from the congregation for which I had only awkward feelings. After saying farewell, I caught up with Beitidh as the Forbes family headed up the hill.

"I am so grateful that you have come to walk with me to the church, Beitidh. We can chat about our experiences on the way. How have you been? I have tried asking Gareth, but he is forever distracted and does not answer in a way that gives me a picture of your life." Beitidh gave me a long look, then a nod.

"I suppose 'tis hard tae picture what ye've never seen. 'Twould be a delight tae have ye visit. I wonder if ye could be spared one week in the future tae come visit the farm? I warn ye, though, 'tis nae like living in toon. 'Tis still a rough way we live. All still living in two houses. Might be best tae wait till the third house is finished."

"I would need to wait till a new apprentice can be found for Mr Beaumont anyways. Heather is no longer with us." Beitidh looked genuinely surprised.

"Why is that? Gareth has nae mentioned it."

I was pleased that Gareth had not shared any of my drama with his family but also felt clumsy with not knowing how much to share myself. Not wanting to besmirch Heather, as she had done me, I only shared a part of the story.

"I seem to have been the reason for Heather to leave employment at the dress shop. I hear she plans to open her own business and take some of the clientele from the Beaumonts. It will be interesting to see if there is enough business to support two shops."

"Perhaps the influx of people will be enough."

"Perhaps. In any event, she will have some of the Beaumonts' business, so we will have less work. Iris and Malcolm assure me that they will not struggle. I am grateful for that, given that Heather has made me the reason."

"'Tis unfriendly of her. I cannae fathom how she could have anything against ye, Isabelle. Ye always proved tae be helpful and kind on the ship and after the shipwreck. Have ye restocked yer Medicinals yet? Takes so long for things tae arrive from home."

"Yes, my grandfather sends me regular packages. Most of it arrives unscathed. I am glad to have the things he sends me. The last package contained a very well packed still, for the making of aromatherapy oils. A skill he learned on one of his trips to France. In my free time from Mam's dress making, I worked at helping my granda with the making of essential oil remedies. I have started an herb garden in our small patch and collect some flowers from neighbours with the promise of a sample. I'm enjoying extracting the oils from some of the native plants."

When we reached the front gate of the church yard, I realised that Beitidh had introduced my favourite topic, and I had not stopped talking for the remainder of the journey. She had managed to bring a smile to my face. The smile on her own face told me that it had been her intention, and I was grateful for her care.

I stayed close to both Gareth and Beitidh as they introduced me to a few others who attended the Mass. As we stepped through the front doors, I almost collided with Beitidh's back as she paused to dip her hand and cross herself. I had forgotten the holy water ritual of the Catholics. I was uncertain then of what I should do, so decided to bypass the practice till I could speak with someone. I remembered that I could not take communion during the Mass because I was not a baptised Catholic. I was not bothered overly by the limitation as I was there to pray and commune with God. For that, I needed no props. I found the peace in the sanctuary helped me to focus my attention on God, and the liturgy was rich with faith in Jesus Christ as saviour.

I followed Beitidh and Gareth in the sitting and standing but did not follow them to the front for the communion wafer. The priest's homily was pithy but gave the Holy Spirit sufficient opportunity to speak God's love into my heart. I felt rested and refreshed by the end of the service that had included bells, incense, and much quiet prayer.

As we exited the vestibule into the sunlight, people sorted themselves into groups for chatting. The talk did not happen inside the sanctuary; that space was reserved for quiet contemplation even when there was no service in progress. I felt like I had been given a reprieve from my most recent troubles. It became my goal to prevent revisiting trouble. I reflected on my way to lunch, how to achieve my goal of avoidance.

We walked in companionable silence. A different atmosphere from before the Mass. Perhaps others were contemplating how to be holy by loving their neighbour in keeping with the priest's talk about the Sermon on the Mount. I contemplated how to be a pleasant but distant neighbour. My thinking was that; If I did not get too close; If I did not expect friendship; If I could be pleasant yet separate; then I might be safe from the schemes of the enemy. Did I really need any close friends? It seemed safer to keep my inner self a little hidden.

Lunch with the Beaumonts and Forbes families was lively with chatter. The mutual regard of all present was easy to see. It was good to laugh at the stories told, as we shared the ridiculous antics of people learning to live in a place with different creatures and plants. It was good to hear of the miracle of a child falling and scratching their knee just in time for his mother to jump up and move out of the path of a massive falling branch. A gift from God, to be sure. And the new practice of looking up at the stability of a tree before taking refuge from the sun.

The time came to an end too soon. The family interaction was so companionable that I wanted every meal to be so full of life. It reminded me of my family back in England. A sweet melancholy. I also loved the quiet discussion around the meal with the Beaumonts. I was sad and happy at the same time. I presumed that my grief would always be a part of my life. I didn't know then; that in the same way as love does not divide, it multiplies; grief compounds even when it becomes distant. It combines and intensifies, negating the recovery from one when another is experienced. Creating a constant undercurrent of loss when separated from the people we love. Always there. Even when I did not allow it to dominate my thoughts. It gave me an understanding of the grief that our Father in heaven has felt since the fall in the Garden of Eden. I walked back to my new home with Iris and Malcolm, thanking God for people who could be counted on for loyalty and love.

The following day, Gareth arrived shortly after sunup with his apprentice Joseph. They appeared, walking through the back gate with tools and ladder. Iris and I, sitting at the breakfast table, were glad that we had dressed before breakfast.

"Good mornin' tae ye all. We neglected tae talk on a time for starting work in the morning. Joseph and I have already taken breakfast with the workers at the hotel. We thought ye might like us tae use the back entrance for the tools of trade."

An olive-skinned man with grey eyes and curly hair the colour of sandstone stepped from behind Gareth on the path. The young man was almost as tall as Gareth but had a lanky, lithe build and a huge smile.

"Mr and Mrs Beaumont, Isabelle, this is Joseph Laylock, my apprentice."

Joseph lifted his right hand in greeting. The tool bag slung across his shoulder, and the ladder leant against him with his arm through the rungs to afford stability.

"Good to meet yuse. Just call me Joseph. That mister stuff takes too long."

He seemed cheerful and irreverent. But the irreverence was so natural it held no insult. He simply did not acknowledge that one man would be more important than another. Later, he told me that was not entirely accurate. It was always important to listen to the elders.

"Would you both like a cup of tea before you begin?"

"Nae, Mrs Beaumont, the sooner we begin, the less trouble we will be for ye. Is the space ready for us tae begin? There is a wagon of lumber arriving this afternoon. 'Twould be good tae gut the area before they arrive."

Malcolm, still trying to wake up with a steaming cup of tea in hand, took up the arrangements.

"Eh, yes. We removed the fabrics and other makings from the shelves on the dressmaking side of the shop first, as we have some gentlemen coming in for fittings later this morning. We thought the young men could handle the messiness of construction, or demolition in this case, more so than the ladies. Will it be alright to work one side at a time?" Gareth hesitated a little before replying.

"Of course. I neglected tae think on the need tae keep some o' the space functional. We can do that. If ye tell us the timing of the fittings, we can take our breaks at that time. Less disturbing for yer customers, men and women."

"Excellent. Let me show you through to the shop front. We open the doors at nine. The first fitting is at ten. I suppose the old timber that you are removing can be carried through to the back. I'm guessing the new timber will need to come through the front. A wagon can fit up the rear lane, but I'm not sure of the size of the wagon. There would be hell to pay with the neighbours if we put the lumber on the footpath out front. Best to keep the neighbours happy. They would be in a prime position to make us unhappy in the future if we disregard their needs. Listen to me ramble. I really need to have my breakfast before I can think straight."

At that, Malcolm stopped talking and made his way back to the breakfast table, leaving Gareth and Joseph to begin their hammering in the front. It seemed everyone in the street would be getting up early this week.

The noise of hammering and the smell of dust were constant that Monday morning. The young men who came in for fittings were attentive to me and made every attempt to include me in the conversations. I smiled at them all as customers but crafted responses that would distract their attention away from me. I was relieved when Iris sent me to the kitchen to prepare a lunch spread for five. Chops cooked on the grill out back, served with greens and tomatoes fresh from the garden. It took only five minutes to set the fire for making hot coals. I gathered salad greens and tomatoes from the garden whilst waiting for the fire to drop. The chops delivered by the butcher's lad that morning only took a few minutes each side once the coals were ready. Lamb today. Almost every day. Occasionally, chicken was delivered. Sometimes beef steaks. Fish on Fridays. In all, it took me half an hour to prepare the lunch. The shop was closed at midday, and we all had some respite from the noise. Gareth and Joseph joining us for lunch led to a lively conversation.

"The salad is delicious, Isabelle. I keep getting a burst of flavour from I'm nae sure what." Gareth looked up with a question in his eyes.

"It may be the fennel I added. My father has sent me many seeds, so we have a diverse garden. I was telling Beitidh about the herbs I grow yesterday." Iris took up the conversation.

"Isabelle has enhanced our palette very well since she took up planting her father's seeds. The scent when she is distilling the oils can be very pungent. Sometimes I think we should commission a shed for the still." Both Joseph's and Gareth's faces lit up with mischief.

"Ye have a still Isabelle?" I had to smile at the boyish enthusiasm displayed by both.

"It is not a still for distilling liquor. It is designed for essential oils."

"Cannae it be used for both?" Gareth asked. The eyes of both young men were wide with hope.

“I do not know, and I do not mean to find out.” They both took on a crestfallen demeanour. “The hotel serves enough beer and rum. I do not think I need to be in competition.”

“’Tis probably safer that way. ‘Twould only encourage thieves tae break in.”

Malcolm joined the conversation. “True enough. The essential oils take up enough of Isabelle’s time.”

“What the essential oil?”

I tried to explain to Joseph what I was talking about but gave up and went to a shelf in the kitchen to retrieve a small bottle. I opened the lid and dropped a small amount into Joseph’s open palm. He brought the oil to his nose, and after a quizzical deliberation, announced his name for the tree that had given the oil. I retrieved another bottle and tried again. Joseph again told me his name for the tree. The trees had looked so similar when I gathered the leaves that I had thought them the same until I smelled the distilled oil.

Most of the people in town called the trees by the same name, not being able to easily distinguish one from another. I wrote down his name for the trees as best I could. It then became a habit, to each day give Joseph a few drops from a different tree or bush, and to record his name for the tree. I began to see why Gareth thought of the local Aborigines as so knowledgeable. Most of the townsfolk viewed them as ignorant and primitive. But in truth, their knowledge was simply different. By the end of the week, I had made a new friend and hoped that he would claim the same himself. His perspective on everything was novel and gave me a lot to think about. After all, was one perspective more valid than another?

It became obvious to me that he found the antics of our customers ridiculous, and I often saw him smiling as he made quiet comments to Gareth that made him, in turn, laugh. They had a good working relationship. Gareth put trust in Joseph's skill, and even though he was a new apprentice, after giving him some instruction, he would leave him to complete a task by himself. Joseph seemed to be what the locals called a larrikin.

G 'Twas uncomfortable watching Isabelle be the centre of attention for so many of the local lads. I felt certain they were buying trousers and vests they didnae need just tae have the opportunity of talking with Isabelle. By the end of the week, I was certain also that me own reaction could be called jealousy. I ken I liked Isabelle's company, but it was news tae me that me feelings had developed further toward something more serious. 'Twas a problem for sure. Isabelle was nae baptised. She believed, but the animosity between the Protestants and Catholics was as severe here as it had been back in Scotlain. I would need tae quell the rising attraction. Doug egged me on whene'r he could. It was time tae call him out on his tempting me toward what I couldne have. Isabelle was nae in a place tae be pushed toward such a change.

The end of the week and the work on the shop was a relief from conflicting emotions. The more I was given the opportunity tae see Isabelle's character, the harder it became tae resist courting her. Doug's encouragement was nae the only influence I would need tae curtail. I would need tae distance meself from her company. I would be needing tae ask Beitidh and Catriona tae stay close tae Isabelle when in town tae help her make new friends among the parishioners of St Francis. The next Sunday, though, Beitidh would nae be at the Sunday Mass because the family would nae be in town for another three Sundays. Neither could Father Xavier watch out for her. He also would be gone for a few more weeks. Isabelle would have tae fend for herself. I would have tae be praying. 'Tis all I could do. I would need tae leave it all in God's capable hands. He had ensured her safety till then; why would things change?

† The Sunday before Gareth headed home, he again accompanied me to Mass. It was nice to have the reassurance of company for the second time in two weeks. When communion came, I again felt awkward that I was not going forward for the Eucharist. I was keen to have my conversation with Father Xavier about what I should do. I thought that if I were to worship with the Catholics and make them my church family, I should be taking communion with them? I tried to bring up the conversation with Gareth but was left with questions he said he was not qualified to answer. I could see turmoil for him in the conversation and felt that there was more on his mind than he was sharing.

"'Tis true, Isabelle, that ye cannae take the Eucharist without first being baptised."

"I have made my statement of faith with the non-conformists and was accepted into the family of the faithful."

"Ye need tae talk tae the good Father about that Isabelle. He can answer all yer questions. Ye can go forward for a blessing from the priest when we all go forward for communion."

"Perhaps I will do that until Father Xavier returns. He said we would talk again when his circuit is complete this month."

"'Tis glad I am tae hear it, Isabelle."

His demeanour remained troubled, but I could not understand why. He chose not to share his troubling thoughts. There was a spark of hope that was followed by even deeper creases between his brows.

He changed the subject and asked to take some lavender oil back for his cousins, Elsie and Catriona, who were having trouble sleeping.

"Worrying as they are about Ainsley being missing since the shipwreck. And Elsie so convinced that Ainsley be still alive."

I went into the shop to collect a bottle, which Gareth tried to pay for, but for which I could accept no money.

"Elsie and Catriona are my friends. I will also pray for her to find peace. There is nothing we can do to find Ainsley, so worrying cannot help." As I made the comment, I could sense God speaking to me about myself. *'Yes, alright Lord, I will contemplate that later.'* I did not speak aloud. There was enough to convince Gareth that I was hysterical without giving the thought more ammunition. We said our goodbyes, and I went in to prepare lunch for Iris and Malcolm. It became our new routine with the Mass finishing earlier than the Congregational service. I contemplated the latest challenge from God as I prepared the meal.

'What then, Lord, do you think I worry about things that I cannot change?' My mind wandered to the people at St Francis. Most were distant, not knowing me. When I imagined getting to know some of the young women my own age, I almost immediately imagined them judging me as too friendly, or too suspicious, or too something of which they disapproved. I was judging them as I imagined they judged me, without good reason. I began to see what God wanted me to evaluate in my own thinking.

The statements given to me by Father Xavier to write out each day were in direct contrast to the judgements I imagined my new acquaintances would be making against me. I worried about what people would think of me. Yes, there were things in my past that could lead me to that kind of suspicion, but surely not everyone was the same. It was illogical to expect people would always judge me falsely. When it had happened in the past, it had been because of some hidden ulterior motive. Why would ordinary people do that? And yet when I tried, I could not stop worrying over the thing I had just deemed illogical and so unlikely. *'Lord, help me, for I surely need help. I do not know how to get past my past.'*

When Iris and Malcolm came in, I could see their troubled countenance. I put my preparations aside and faced them squarely.

"You both look unhappy. Was church not enjoyable?" They looked at each other before Iris began to share.

"Heather was there, flitting from one group to another. Chatting, then moving on. She looked our way on numerous occasions, so when she left off talking to a particular friend of mine, I walked over to ask some direct questions. Edna never minds my asking direct questions. She is such a dear friend. I always enjoy talking to her." Malcolm then took up the story.

"Not so this morning. Well, only insofar as we did not enjoy what she told. Edna herself did not believe what she had been told by Heather." Iris had refreshed her focus and continued.

"Evidently, Heather had been telling her several stories that were not founded in truth. Stories about the young knobs coming into the shop for more than the making of trousers. Edna assured us that she had told Heather she doubted the veracity of what she told. That she expected the fiction she told was motivated by her bitterness at being let go. Edna may have been able to hear the rhythm behind the chatter, but I am sure many of the people Heather talked with would not be as discerning."

"It was upsetting, Isabelle, but not for you to worry over. We know that it is all lies. You know that it is all lies."

"Lies it may be, but it still hurts when it has been said. And that it is being believed by some."

Iris pulled me into a hug. The next thing I spoke was muffled by the fabric that covered her shoulder.

"How do I forgive when it keeps happening over and over. I must work so hard at forgiving all the time. I am exhausted by the forgiving."

Iris held on while I shed silent tears. She quietly recited a favourite verse.

> "Nay, in all these things we are more than conquerors through him that loved us. For I am persuaded, that neither death, nor life, nor angels, nor principalities, nor powers, nor things present, nor things to come, nor height, nor depth, nor any other creature, shall be able to separate us from the love of God, which is in Christ Jesus our Lord." [28]

Malcolm's counsel was, as always, gentle. "We are called to find a way. Well, no, we are called to follow the way. Jesus showed us how when he forgave us. It does not take away your hurt, but the Holy Spirit can heal your heart. Let's pray!"

He then placed his hand on my shoulder, between Iris' arms that still surrounded me. As he prayed, I could feel the loving presence of the Holy Spirit well up inside and fill me with a peacefulness that was both warm and cooling at the same time.

Following lunch, I was emotionally exhausted and decided to spend the afternoon in the garden amongst the butterflies and

[28] Romans 8:37-39 KJV

bees. Kneeling to pull weeds and take in the variety of scents found amongst the herbs, I asked God to forgive Heather and released her to his judgement. I asked God to vindicate me but did not find real happiness in leaving my vindication to God. I was still disturbed and knew my understanding was not complete.

The following week moved along in a new normal. Without Heather in the shop, but with young men coming into the shop vying for my attention. Attention, I invariably rebuffed. I was not interested in repeating the things of Ellesmere, nor the *Slains Castle*. I began to enjoy my own company. My need for company was quite fulfilled by spending time with Iris and Malcolm. Writing and receiving letters from my family.

Angus had betrayed me, and I did not think I could easily trust another. I had thought we were friends who would stand by each other, but he walked away from me with the first difficulty we faced. I thought it safer to remain single forever. A spinster. But with no nieces and nephews close to dote on, childlessness would be hard to face. Children, I love. To watch them grow into their own person. With ideas to share and adventures to claim.

I walked to Mass by myself the next week and chose a pew near the front where I would not be distracted by the other people present. Even though I did not think Jesus was physically within the communion wafer stored at the front of the church, I saw the value of going down on my knee before the presence of God, who dwelt within every person present. I felt His presence filling the chapel. I considered the practice a symbol of casting my crown at Jesus' feet. Submitting myself to the one who saved me. The one who sustained me when things were tough. And in the moments I doubted his sustaining me, I practised humbling myself until I remembered the occasions when He had most definitely intervened on my behalf. Intervened to support me emotionally and to give me an escape from danger.

The service was peaceful rather than challenging. I was slow to copy some of the standing and sitting cues, which gave the priest reason to notice me. Perhaps the back row would have been best.

I remained in my pew at the end of the service until most of the people had left for home. The peace of praying quietly left me feeling isolated but safe. Although the priest had noticed me, he did not approach me and left me to my quiet contemplation. I was grateful to him and did not turn toward home until most of the congregants had left for the lunch hour. I was quite alone in the sanctuary by the time I made my way outside into the sunshine.

I arrived home just as Malcolm and Iris were entering through the garden gate at the rear of the property. Iris looked strained. Malcolm looked stormy. I prayed that the gossip would all move on quickly to another topic. I didn't like to see the effect it was having on my new parents. I greeted them with the hope of passing on the peace I had felt during the Mass.

"And how was church this morning? I hope it was better than last week."

"May God bless a couple with a marriage to celebrate or the safe birth of a new babe in the church to distract people and give them something new to talk about." Iris gave a strained smile that failed to indent her cheek with the dimple that made her smile so appealing, before adding, "I suppose we could not ask for another scandal to distract them. Someone else's scandal that is." Her smile became genuine with the dimple on full display. "Tempting though it is!"

"My turn to prepare lunch, ladies, what is your fancy today?"

I voiced my appreciation for Malcolm internally. *Thank you, Jesus, for giving me such an odd and enjoyable family. Before adding,* "There is ham left, and bread I baked this morning. How about a ham sandwich and random greens you choose from the garden?"

I enjoyed sending Malcolm into the garden. It was not his favourite place, and he resisted learning the names of plants he did not already know.

"How will I know what we can eat?"

"Simple, put a little in your mouth and chew. Spit it out if it's foul. Collect some if it tastes good."

He huffed.

"Do I not run the risk of poisoning myself that way?"

"Not in this garden. And really, most everywhere. Although be wary of berries. Do not eat berries," I paused for thought, "nor mushrooms, you are not sure of."

Concerned that my advice was too blasé, creases formed between my brows. The furrows on Malcolm's forehead deepened to match my own. As my discomfort increased, the furrows on his brow grew more pronounced, and he held my gaze until I said more.

"Very well, my last advice was a little ordinary. Our garden is safe. I know, because I planted everything there."

At that, Malcolm sauntered to the kitchen garden with a dubious frame of mind. Iris pulled water from the cool box, to which I added lavender flowers and lemon verbena leaves. The afternoon was spent in relaxation and the playing of games that Iris and Malcolm had collected over the years. I went upstairs before our evening walk to repeat the homework Father Xavier had given me.

I experienced a change in my thinking that surprised me. I became more positive about myself and almost expected people to be friendly, instead of judgemental.

But then, when acquaintances disappointed me, my expectation of respect led to greater hurt. I felt more hurt when they disrespected me if I had not seen it coming. I thought, just maybe, it was better if I kept a wall around my heart. Something I needed to ask Father Xavier about the next time we met.

CHAPTER 25

Constancy

"For I know the plans I have for you, declares the LORD, plans for welfare and not for evil, to give you a future and a hope. Then you will call upon me and come and pray to me, and I will hear you. You will seek me and find me, when you seek me with all your heart. I will be found by you, declares the LORD."

Jeremiah 29:11-14 ESV

February 1852, Hurstville

The following Tuesday brought Chloe to town. She told me that she had arrived on the Monday to find her furnished home complete for her stay. The company had even thought to include information about the local midwives.

"I could not wait another day before coming to find you in your shop. My little house is set only two streets back from here, so we will be able to catch up often. That is, if Mr and Mrs Beaumont can spare you for lunch or dinner some days. I am so looking forward to more variety in female company. I am only disappointed that I must miss Phillip at the same time. With my life as it is, I cannot have both at once."

"It is a high price to pay."

"Yes, but the income from the coal mine is so good that, besides the isolation, our life is very good. The housekeeper and cooks for the mine are becoming close friends with me, but they are all much older than I am. The miners rotate out each month so that they can see their families. There are four watches. Each week, one watch leaves and another arrives. They spend one week in town before returning. To see your husband only one week in four must be very hard."

"I agree, although to hear some of the customers talking during a fitting, I suspect that some think one week in four is too much. Too much opportunity for the making of babies apparently. A new one every year for some."

"That is too many pregnancies. I do not know what I will do when, if, it comes to that."

"With your first, this is not an issue yet. I would start with praying that God gives you only the right number of children." Chloe looked surprised.

"You speak more of God than you did in the past."

"I have had some troubles again, so I went to see Father Xavier. He has given me some homework that seems to be influencing me. I think, overall, the influence is for the better. I am thinking better of myself than I was in the habit of doing last year." Chloe reached out her hand to take mine in hers. With a squeeze that felt like an embrace, she said.

"You haven't written of this in your letters, but I could tell you were not as fond of yourself as the Isabelle I remembered. Do you want to tell me what has been happening?"

The floodgates opened. Chloe was as gracious, understanding, and willing to challenge any stinking thinking as she had always been. Her understanding gave me confidence in the friendship we had forged in England and throughout our journey. I took much longer over lunch than usual. Iris must have wondered if she had gone from two apprentices to none in the space of weeks.

Although they had received a few applications for the apprentice tailor's position, Iris and Malcolm were still seeking independent references. Malcolm planned to travel into Sydney Town to meet with the young men in the week that followed my reunion with Chloe. They decided that perhaps it would be best to take on a young tailor who had just finished, as he was the best applicant. The question was whether the young man had been trained to Malcolm's standards. How many bad habits would need to be unlearned?

On the next Sunday, I stopped at Chloe's house on my way to Mass so that we could walk together. I invited Chloe to join my family for lunch after the service. I could see that she was grateful for the invitation and for the opportunity to build a relationship with my adoptive parents. The weather was still hot in the middle of the day. Barely cooling off overnight. The smell of dried-out and scorched grass mixed with wafts of eucalyptus accompanied us up the hill. I enjoyed the long, hot summers, but Chloe felt the heat more keenly, being so advanced in her pregnancy. I carried some water in a glass bottle for her to drink. Just enough to refresh us when we got to the top of the hill.

We were both a little red in the face under our bonnets when we walked through the door of the church into the narthex, where the font of Holy Water resided. Chloe dipped her hand and made the sign of the cross. I was still uncertain of the practice, so I waited until we walked in before bowing my knee and finding a seat in the back pew. The peace in the nave was enhanced by the cool interior of the sandstone church. Our chatter ceased once inside the chapel. We waited in companionable silence and spent the time praying as we prepared our hearts for communion. It was easy to follow Chloe's lead throughout the service. When to respond, when to kneel, and when to stand. Thankfully, Chloe was the only person who needed to push past me to exit the pew when it came time for communion. I saw from her expression that we would talk later. I spent my time in prayer and waiting on God for anything he wanted to say to me. I felt God fill me with love, but he spoke no words to me that day.

As soon as the benediction was finished, Chloe pulled me out into the sunlight with a hope of meeting and greeting a stranger or two. Chloe was always good at that, and it brought back memories of the meetings we attended in London. Together, we introduced ourselves to a young couple who had no children in tow. They looked like middle-class people, and I thought I had seen the woman behind a desk at the local post office. He was extremely tall and thin; she came only to his chest. Her platinum blond hair with ice-blue eyes were a stark contrast to his raven black hair and eyes. They seemed an odd couple that were surely not brother and sister. They stood alone until we walked over and began the introductions.

"Hello, my name is Chloe, and this is my good friend Isabelle. I am new to town, and Isabelle is new to this congregation. Have you been attending here for very long?"

It seemed bold, but then Chloe introduced us with such gentle friendliness that people never felt put off. It was so nice to have

Chloe back, even if it was for such a short time. The young woman responded with a relieved smile.

"Hello, my name is Meredith, and my husband is Martyn. We moved to Hurstville a month ago to take over the post office. We have not met many of the locals yet. I think I have seen Isabelle come in to collect and send post to England. But I have not seen you in the post office yet. I'm sorry, I'm talking too much. I do that when I'm nervous. Thank you for coming to introduce yourselves."

It was my turn to say something, so I took the opportunity whilst Meredith took a breath.

"Yes, I thought I had seen you at the post office. It's a pleasure to meet you. It feels awkward when you don't know anyone at the church. I know I feel awkward when my friends are away."

We stayed and chatted about everyday things for another fifteen minutes before we said our goodbyes and headed home for lunch. I felt safe talking to someone who was also new. For that present moment, anyway.

The weeks went by in that manner until Father Xavier returned, and Gareth again came to town in the same week. When I met up with Father Xavier, he started our talk from a place that indicated he had discussed my church attendance with the parish priest for St Francis.

"I hear you do not come forward for communion nor a blessing during Mass. Do you have any questions, Isabelle, before we talk about your homework?"

We were once again in the conservatory, which was not quite so hot but remained very warm and humid. I wore my lightest dress for the chat, having expected as much. The lightweight voile was a privilege not many could afford. Iris always managed to produce garments made from offcuts that were exquisite and a little unique, with the combination of different prints or complementary shades.

"Yes, I do have some questions. For one, am I invited to share communion with the Catholic church?"

With a sad but gentle smile, he answered my query.

"You can only share communion if you are baptised Catholic. But you can go forward, and the priest will pray a blessing over you. The Church's stance is that the body is broken and there is no gain from pretending it is one. If you would like to convert, I can organise for you to attend catechism classes."

"I would need to think on that. I suppose if I attended the classes, I could learn what the differences are. Currently, I only know what you pick up from zealots, and I know that is not always reliable."

"I will organise classes for you, Isabelle. Father Mathias may come and speak to you one Sunday. I have also heard that you are not participating much in the life of the church. Our young people meet regularly on Saturday afternoons. We call them *The St Francis Set.*" With a smile, he added, "They call themselves *The Frankies.* I can ask Beitidh to take you along this week so that you are not walking in alone to a group of strangers. And I also hear that Chloe is in town for a few months. I look forward to seeing her."

I wasn't sure what to respond to first. It seemed that Father Xavier's sources for information were very thorough.

"I am not sure I want to attend any *St Francis Set* meetings. I think it is likely that the same things will happen that have happened in other places."

"And so, we come to the reason for our ongoing chats. Has the homework helped you at all, Isabelle?"

I smiled at his sensitivity in bringing me to the thing that bothered me most. The thing with which I needed most help.

"I have been very diligent with the homework you gave me. Yes, it has helped me to improve how I see myself. God is faithful, and I am feeling more loved by him each day. But I cannot trust others to see me the way God sees me. They have proven to me that they are not listening to God."

Father Xavier moved back into his chair and took on a contemplative air as he looked into my soul.

"Yes, there is truth in what you say, that people often do not listen to God." Sitting a little forward as he spoke. "It is a fact we cannot ignore. All we can do is learn to recognise when Satan's lies of condemnation are being sent our way and refute them. Don't take them into your heart." Leaning in with some enthusiasm, he continued.

"There are some good people, though, Isabelle. People who do not have an agenda to use your harm for their own gain. The trick is in finding those people. I think it is fair for you to look for the fruit of the Holy Spirit in the lives of people before pursuing a close relationship. I know that God would not want to see you harmed." Gesticulations punctuated his zeal. "And in fact, He has good things planned for you. As he says in Jeremiah,

> 'For I know the thoughts that I think towards you, saith the Lord, thoughts of peace, and not of affliction, to give you an end and patience." [29]

"Yes, but how do I do that, Father?"

"Ask yourself: Do they love their neighbour as themselves? Are they generous with strangers? Are they peacemakers, choosing not to be contentious whenever possible? Do they have patience with small

[29] Jeremias 29:11 DRB. The Holy Bible: (p. 2059). Catholic Way Publishing. Kindle Edition.

children and animals? Do they delight in the things of God? Are they kind to people others reject? I think that Mr and Mrs Beaumont, and your friends Chloe and Gareth, are good examples of such people. They do not participate in gossip; instead, they ask God what he thinks. They are not quick to judge, but they are quick to show mercy."

"Wow! I am not sure I could be counted in that group, Father."

"Then perhaps that can be your homework whilst I am away this month. Two things: Practice one of the fruits on the list each day. Be purposeful and see how it feels. Reflect at the end of the day on your success. Don't forget to acknowledge the good things that you do before God. Also, attend *The St Francis Set* meeting and look for people who are displaying the traits. I have written out a list of the fruits of the Holy Spirit for you to take home. I have taken them from both the Gospel of Matthew and Paul's letters[30]."

He then handed me the list that also included the instructions for my daily practice.

Be intentional in your practice of the following qualities and look for them in others. Reflect at the end of the day and acknowledge your success, as well as accept forgiveness when you make a mistake.

Charity Joy Peace Kindness Goodness Faithfulness Gentleness Self-control Constancy

30 Galatians 5:16-26, 1 Corinthians 13:4-8, Matthew 5:1-12, 22:36-40

"I wonder, Isabelle, if you would consider abstaining from the practice of deliberately hiding yourself from being known by people? Keep the friends you can trust close and intentionally step out and risk being criticised by those who are not friends. The good opinion of the wicked is of no value anyway. If you do not take the risk, you cannot find the trustworthy. Maybe participate in a church project. It could help you learn dependence on God in the face of threat. He will never forsake you. He will instead lead you into wise choices. It is not an easy thing, but you would find it beneficial.

"Let God protect and comfort you, come what may. Sometimes in this life, we hurt, but there may be a higher purpose for our hurting, so God comforts us rather than preventing the hurt. Jesus and Paul counted the cost of their obedience to God. They trusted God to protect and comfort them. To work all things together for good."[31]

"Thank you, Father Xavier! H..How do you know in advance what I will need?"

He smiled as he answered. "I pray for you, Isabelle, and I wait for God to speak to me. I have many hours riding a horse, so I have plenty of hours to listen."

So simple, of course I had plenty of hours sewing, and yet I was still to learn how to listen. We concluded our meeting, and as I left, I saw a couple waiting in the front parlour. Presumably to see Father Xavier. A busy man.

Following the service on the next Sunday, Father Mathias came toward me with intention. Up close, vestments removed, he seemed very young. No more than twenty-five. He still had the slim build of a very young man and a head full of luscious, wavy, sandy hair. His tanned complexion suggested that he belonged in Australia, even

[31] Romans 8:28

though he had an Italian accent. He had striking green eyes and a quick smile. As he drew near, he held out his hand to greet me. I was surprised into reaching for his hand myself. He held on briefly as he introduced himself, then drew back his hand before starting into an obviously planned conversation.

"It is a pleasure to meet you, Miss Lindsay, and Mrs Manning. Father Xavier has asked me to introduce myself and invite you to attend our *St Francis Set* meetings on Saturday afternoon, following confession."

I hesitated, as I was not Catholic, and I was not in the habit of attending confession. Chloe took the invitation in her elegant stride.

"Of course, Father Mathias, we would love to meet the young people in the church. I haven't had much opportunity to attend confession since arriving in New South Wales but have been pleased to take the opportunity whilst I am in town."

I raised my brows at Chloe's comment. I had no idea Chloe made her way up the hill on Saturdays as well as on Sundays.

"My friend Isabelle, however, has not yet been baptised and has not attended catechism classes, so has no idea about the confessional."

"I have been brought up a non-conformist, Father Mathias, but I have been seeing Father Xavier and asking him questions. He told me that I have more pressing things to contemplate before worrying about ritual." Father Mathias' surprise at my statement was easy to see on his face, but he quickly capitulated to the wisdom of his more experienced brother.

"Well, I will leave that aspect to Father Xavier, then. We would still enjoy your company at the Saturday meeting if you would like to come."

"Thank you, Father, I think you can count on Mrs Manning and me next Saturday."

"And your husband, Mrs Manning, will he be in town soon?"

A fishing question, if I ever did hear one. As usual, Chloe handled the question with grace, deliberately giving no information that the priest did not already have.

"Not next Saturday, Father, I hope he will be free to attend Mass with me soon."

Following the encounter, we made our way home for lunch. Chloe was to join us for lunch every Sunday until the baby was born. With an impatient tone, Chloe displayed an uncharacteristic scepticism.

"They are all nosy. They cannot help themselves. It is, after all, their business to manage the lives of their flock. Or, so they seem to think."

"Whatever has made you so jaded about the priests, Chloe? You have demonstrated a peculiar reserve toward letting them know anything."

"My uncle went to confession each week before Mass on Sunday. Did he not confess his sins? Or did the priests just deem that they should do nothing about protecting me? I will never know. They cannot, after all, divulge what is said in the confessional."

The disturbed look on my face, with deeply furrowed brows, must have convicted Chloe about her cynicism.

"Let's talk about more pleasant things. I have chosen to think that they may have been unaware; or they did act in some way to have my uncle geographically separated from me. I did, after all, escape serious physical harm. God protected me from serious emotional harm and gave me a beautiful husband who loves me. Phillip will be in town next week." This was said with a huge smile. "I just did not want to be telling the priest more than he needed to know."

I saw for a moment, then, a crack in Chloe's bright shiny attitude to life. "It seems you struggle sometimes also." I smiled as I spoke, and Chloe smiled with me. It was plain to see that I spoke with a friendly jest. "It is wonderful news, Chloe, that Phillip will soon be in town. Will he be staying for long?"

"Unfortunately, only for four days. He must return. He has two managers under him who are not quite ready to take leadership for an extended time. He will come to stay for a month when the baby is due. Then I will be going back with him to our home on the cliff."

Chloe and I then chatted about baby clothes for the rest of the trip home. I had ordered muslin to create cool swaddling sheets, but I did not tell her about them. Grandma had always told me that babies wanted to be wrapped firmly. In the heat of summer, a firm wrap also needed to be cool.

Phillip came and went before Gareth came back to town with his family. Gareth arrived at the shop one day with some pieces of furniture for my upstairs room. We talked for a long time, and he shared the lunchtime meal with us. As the days were getting shorter, he needed to head home sooner than he did on previous visits. It was by then early March, but I could not call it autumn. The leaves did not change colour and fall. The nights were slightly cooler, the days still hot. Not stifling like February, but still hot for my English blood. Gareth told us that he would be at church with his family Sunday week.

When Iris and Malcolm returned from their church meeting the following Sunday, they told the story of an altercation with Heather. Heather was again spreading stories and was overheard by Iris. Either

Heather had not been aware of Iris' proximity, or she had become so bold, she did not care. Iris, with eyewitness evidence, did not allow the comment to pass unchallenged.

"It was like the Iris of old, before she was jailed for her protesting. When she spoke out to demand that women have a say in the laws of the land by being able to vote. My firebrand, I used to call her. Well, today she showed Heather to be the shallow, conniving, revengeful girl that she is. We may lose more business, but it was very satisfying to have our say on the issue. With all to hear. And trust me, they all heard. They all paid close attention to what was being said. Surprisingly, most stood by Iris and me. And that means they also stood by you, Isabelle. Apparently, most of the congregation have not been taken in by Heather's lies. When we left, Heather had already left with her head down. Escorted between her mother and father. A trail of little ones following. It was not the way things in church ought to be done. But then, none of the matter has been the way things ought to be done."

I was impressed that Malcolm had completed this explanation of their morning without giving way for Iris to participate as he usually did. When I looked at Iris with this in mind, she simply said.

"I suppose it is Malcolm's turn to use his voice. I did all the talking at the church. We will see what comes of it all."

When they arrived, we sat down to lunch with Chloe and Phillip. Phillip had arrived on the morning ship, too late for church. He gave me a sideways hug before taking a seat, and upon request, told stories of the happenings at the coal mine on the cliff. Iris and Malcolm put the morning's upset aside. We had a pleasant afternoon, laughing over Phillip's stories. The air was warm but not hot, with a cool breeze wafting the scent of eucalyptus and lemon-scented melaleuca trees close by.

Chloe and I met with *The Frankies* the following Saturday. Phillip had returned to the mine, so Chloe was again my companion, and I was hers. Neither of us had many friends in town. Father Mathias came to greet us when we stood in the doorway to survey the hall. There was a great deal of activity with young people holding small books and drinking tea from tin mugs as they milled around. I had never seen anything quite like it before.

Very few people were seated. Instead, usual social norms were thrown aside as they ate the small cakes held in one hand and sipped tea from the tin mug held in the other. Each person had a small book held under their arm until they finished their cake, at which time they started flicking through the pages and reading aloud in turn for short bursts. They interspersed this with enthusiastic chatter and laughter. The crumbs dropping to the ground to be then trodden underfoot would have caused my sensible mother to have a fit of vapours. My first thought was in agreement with Chloe.

"I am heartily glad that it is not going to be my job to clean this floor." I had no opportunity to respond before Father Mathias stood in front of us.

"I am so glad you have decided to join us, Miss Lindsay. I have just the part for you. You will be perfect for the role with the vibrant head of hair that you have. And Mrs Manning. It was so good to see that your husband could join you during the week. Will he be in Mass tomorrow?"

"Unfortunately, he has had to return to the coal cliff. We miss each other, but sometimes we do not always get what we want."

"Very true, Mrs Manning. It is a blessing that when our loved ones are separated from us, we have the Holy Ghost to comfort us. I am thankful that he never leaves us. I miss my family on feast days most. That was always a time of great fun with my twelve brothers and sisters. I must admit, though, the most fun was to be had in teasing our sisters." He cleared his throat, possibly conscious of oversharing. "I was not certain how much you would want to participate in our current endeavour, as I am sure you like to sit down sporadically. Would you be willing to help our actors learn their lines?"

The assumption that we would participate without any knowledge of the play that would be undertaken, nor who the audience would be, seemed brazen at best. I had never participated in a theatrical performance, but Chloe's response indicated to me that it was not as unusual as I had first thought.

"I would be happy to help the actors learn their lines, Father. I can think of no better role for me given my unpredictable availability."

"WH...what role did you have in mind for me, Father?" I tipped my head sideways whilst completing the question. "I have never participated in playacting. My community at home would not endeavour in those kinds of frivolities."

I could hear that I sounded judgemental, but really, I was only uncertain. Unsure of my abilities to act well and I had no desire to invite ridicule. Father Mathias seemed to see through my hesitancy and understood my fear.

"Your part will be a small part because I did not think you would want to play a main character. It will be just enough to encourage you to build relationships with other young people in the church. I must admit I was also hoping that you would help with the costuming. We have several keen sewers in the group, but sometimes they would benefit from the skills that you have. I do not wish to put too much onto you, only to encourage participation."

At least the priest was forthright. There was no subtle manipulation in his actions. He told me his agenda straight up. I liked that, and that helped me to like him. I thought that maybe I could enjoy learning about playacting.

Whilst talking with Father Mathias, we had moved slowly into the hall. A young couple came over, bearing steaming mugs of tea and a cake in a calico square. The cake was shaped like a cube, dark brown in colour, and had white flakes all over. I felt brave, so after saying thanks, I bit into the corner of the cake. Eating whilst standing felt very wrong. I was surprised to find a very soft sponge on the inside. The coating had a bitter chocolate flavour, and the white flakes were hard. Coconut, I think. A cake I had not sampled before. How fitting since it was all so very strange.

"Hello, I am Mavis, and this is my brother Joshua. Welcome! We are on the refreshment assignment this week."

Whilst I was mentally evaluating the cake, Chloe responded. I could see that Chloe struggled with the idea of biting into a cake whilst standing and holding a tin mug in the other hand.

"It is a pleasure to meet you. I am Chloe, and my friend, who is obviously finding your refreshments unusual, is Isabelle."

My curiosity was evident in my expression. We chose to use first names only; they are much simpler and seemed appropriate for the situation.

"Your cakes are new to me. The sponge is so soft, and is that cocoa in the surround?" I then tasted the tea, and once again my eyes grew large.

"There is eucalyptus leaf in the tea; it makes the tea go further. I like it, some don't. But it's my turn this week, so they get what I like to drink once every six weeks. The cakes are messy to make, but Joshua loves them, so I go to the trouble. *Fancy Pants* is on the roster for next week, so we will probably have Earl Grey tea with lemons and cucumber sandwiches. I enjoy that the refreshments are so different each week."

"Eucalyptus leaf. I have tried it once before but had forgotten. I think I like it."

Joshua took up the conversation next, addressing Chloe. "I hear over the fences that you are married to the manager of the coal mines."

"My husband, Phillip, is one of the managers. He was trained in England. We expected to be farmers in Australia, but we got an offer that was too good to refuse."

"Oh, aye. There is money to be made from the mining. I hope to take up a position myself in a year or two."

"I hope then that you are doing a lot of reading about the process so that you can progress yourself. The owners of the mines do seem to make a good deal of money, and they pay their managers well."

We spent the afternoon getting to know new people and learning lines. The play seemed harmless and was to be performed for the families of the participants. For a cost, to raise funds for a local hospice. It gave me something to write home about. When I told Iris and Malcolm about the playacting, they were also uncertain but could not come up with a good reason to dislike the activity. So, they said to themselves and then to me that they were delighted I was making friends. I would not have gone so far as to say I was making friends, but I was talking and laughing with people my own age. I was having fun.

The homework given to me by Father Xavier had an opportunity to be used. I concluded that the invitation had been orchestrated by Father Xavier for that very purpose. I was given an aperture through which to look and evaluate myself and others with the metric of *The Fruits of the Holy Spirit.* It was a very interesting exercise. I began to see beyond the masks that people presented for others to see. I was surprised to learn that the outward sweetness of some was not backed up by true acts of selfless kindness. And the sometimes gruff exterior of others was a façade to defend against being taken advantage of because their soft hearts led them to overshare. To give food they sorely needed to the unneedy who dared to ask, rather than simply sharing with those truly in need. With people who claimed need, simply to take advantage.

My own heart, I discovered, had become judgemental. I had allowed my pain to filter my opinions with a negative light. Often expecting the worst, instead of the best, from others. I went down on my knees every night and asked God to forgive me for being so harsh in my heart and asked him to help me forgive. I thought I had forgiven those who hurt me. But I still wanted to see people reap the consequences of their actions and suffer a just retribution at the hands of others or the hands of God. How could that be true forgiveness? If I did not want to see those who hurt me find the same forgiveness from God that Jesus gave to me. The verses that came to me during my time of prayer each day all told me to face the issue. God would speak a verse into my thoughts, and I would look it up.

> "Therefore thou art inexcusable, O man, whosoever thou art that judgest: for wherein thou judgest

> another, thou condemnest thyself; for thou that judgest doest the same things." [32]

And on another day, it was…

> "Judge not, that you be not judged. For with the judgment you pronounce you will be judged, and with the measure you use it will be measured to you." [33]

I was afraid of being judged, because I had judged others many times in my short history, and I judged others still. I unknowingly feared to reap what I had sown.

I saw in myself that I gave people the answer I thought they wanted to hear rather than being genuine and honest in my responses. I put on a different mask for different people.

> "I appeal to you, brothers, to watch out for those who cause divisions and create obstacles contrary to the doctrine that you have been taught; avoid them. For such persons do not serve our Lord Christ, but their own appetites, and by smooth talk and flattery they deceive the hearts of the naive." [34]

One Sunday, Malcolm and Iris arrived home from church with some news that was disturbing. After Iris rebuked Heather openly for maligning my character without cause, Heather seemed to have

---

[32] Romans 2:1 KJV

[33] Matthew 7:1-2 KJV

[34] Romans 16:17-18 KJV

fewer friends but was unusually close with one of the young men. All expected to hear of an engagement for betrothal. But to everyone's surprise, the young man announced his betrothal to another young woman and was married within the week. Many people assumed that the father of the bride had insisted on a fast wedding for reasons not explained, but which became evident when she ran from the smell of food.

The following Sunday, Heather arrived at the Catholic church to worship. It was a week when Gareth and his family were in town for Mass. We had enjoyed sharing a meal with his family at the hotel on the Saturday night, and I walked to the chapel with Beitidh because Chloe was in the early stages of her labour. I was to join her and the midwife following the service. Phillip had been sent for. The baby was coming earlier by a week than was expected, so Phillip had not yet arrived.

When Heather walked through the door of the church, the stream of people entering the chapel paused to allow for her unfamiliarity with the process of holy water and genuflecting before entering the pews. Instead, Heather stood and scanned the crowd for familiar faces before she chose a pew. It occurred to me that the Catholics waited outside to meet up before entering the building, as conversation in front of the tabernacle was frowned upon.

On spotting Gareth with a space next to him, which I suspect he had engineered for my benefit, Heather made a beeline for the space and sat herself next to Gareth, leaving no space for Beitidh and me to join her brother. We were four people back in the line, walking the aisle. We genuflected and found a vacant space three pews back. As soon as we had found our seat, Beitidh whispered to me before kneeling.

"I dinnae like the look o' that, Isabelle." I observed the tightness in Gareth's shoulders and movements when he ignored a comment made by Heather as he moved to kneel and bow his head.

"Nor do I. I can see that Gareth is feeling disturbed by whatever Heather is saying."

"Oh aye, and he was looking forward to being close to ye, do ye know."

I knew that Gareth liked me as a friend, but I could still not think of anything else. Angus had scarred me for life. Or so I had decided.

"No, Beitidh, we are only friends." Beitidh gave me a smirk.

"Oh, so ye say, but I can see ye like Gareth as much as he likes ye. Yer both just too mule-headed to move past the crazy decisions ye've both made. Life is too short to dally on things that can only be good for ye. I know I have no plans to dally. Joseph has asked me to marry 'im. But we will have to talk later, here they come."

The brothers entered the sanctuary carrying the thurible and filled the space with frankincense. We then prepared our hearts for entering the presence of God by bowing our heads.

We waited for Gareth outside the church in the hope that we could rescue him from Heather. Throughout the Mass, Heather had attempted to engage Gareth in conversation, and Gareth had tried to stifle the conversation without being rude. We saw Heather try to block Gareth from walking our way when he exited the chapel into the bright sunlight of a late summer afternoon. I could only recognise two seasons in Sydney. Summer and Winter. With no leaves falling, it was hard to recognise an autumn. The heat and cold were rather sporadic. Gareth shaded his eyes as he looked around for his family and then quite abruptly announced to Heather.

"I can see me family now, ye'll need to excuse me."

He then walked away from her with determination. But to everyone's surprise, Heather followed, caught up, and asked for an introduction.

"Oh, Gareth, you simply must introduce me to your family. I would so love to meet them." The artifice was palpable. The attempt at friendliness, intense. I felt sorry for Heather's desperation.

"Hello, Heather. I hope you are well."

Truthfully, I had not managed very well to pray that God bless her, so I still felt some resentment. I suppose it could be heard in my voice. Heather's smile slipped momentarily, but with visible effort, she broadened her smile and greeted me politely.

"It is good to see you again, Isabelle. You seem to have made a lot of new friends." She looked toward Beitidh. "Perhaps you could introduce me."

"Old friends. These are some of my travelling companions from our trip to Australia. Beitidh, I don't think you have met Heather."

As the rest of the family were engaged in conversation with each other, I made no attempt to introduce them. They had plans for lunch, but I was heading to Chloe's house to stay with her whilst the midwife took a break for lunch. I took my leave and later found out that Heather had invited herself to join the Forbes family for lunch at the inn on the way out of town.

CHAPTER 26

Comfort

"Therefore, since we have been justified by faith, we have peace with God through our Lord Jesus Christ. Through him we have also obtained access by faith into this grace in which we stand, and we rejoice in hope of the glory of God. Not only that, but we rejoice in our sufferings, knowing that suffering produces endurance, and endurance produces character, and character produces hope, and hope does not put us to shame, because God's love has been poured into our hearts through the Holy Spirit who has been given to us."

Romans 5:1-5 ESV

March 1852, Hurstville

I Phillip arrived an hour before a beautiful, very large baby boy took his first breath. Chloe gave Phillip thirty-six hours to arrive. A long, arduous labour. The doctor was called.

The prayers of Father Mathias saying the last rites spurred the fervent prayers of Phillip, Iris, and myself, which resulted in a safe delivery of young Joshua Mark. The baby named for Phillip's and Chloe's fathers. Phillip and I lit candles in the chapel of St Francis as a thank you. Iris and I sang songs of praise as we sewed that week.

The new tailor arrived a week following the arrival of Joshua Mark Manning. I had been so consumed with Chloe and the new baby that I had not paid close attention to Iris and Malcolm when they tried to prepare me for the new arrival. He was a young man of twenty-three who had paid for his passage to Australia, planning to send for his fiancée when he had sufficient funds. A small, wiry man who looked like he had been underfed his entire life. With hair the colour of copper wire, clear blue eyes, and a ruddy complexion, people could think he was a relative of mine until he began to charm them with his County Clare brogue.

I was surprised that Iris and Malcolm had chosen an Irishman, as they were mostly Catholic. And from Rory's question, "Has the local parish been assigned a permanent priest or is it a circuit rider?" I gathered he was Catholic. I had a vague memory of Iris making a comment about his choice of religion not having any impact on his skills as a tailor. And the samples he showed me demonstrated that he was indeed skilled. Talented would be a more accurate description. Time proved the assessment to be true. For such a small man, who was the same height as me, he had a prominent Adam's apple and large feet. His deep baritone voice suggested to me that starvation had prevented him from reaching the height God intended.

His charming words and joviality soon won me over. I enjoyed working with him and concluded that Iris and Malcolm had taken this into consideration when making their choice for a new tailor. My gratefulness toward them grew with every act of kindness. I had grown to love them as much as my family in England. The fiancée waiting to join Rory in Australia meant that there was no unwanted attention. He spoke often of Josephine and shared with me small parts of the letters he received as we worked. Rory joined me in meeting with *The Frankies* on Saturday afternoons and then for Mass on Sundays.

When Heather saw us arrive at *The St Francis Set* meeting for the first time, she made haste to introduce herself. Heather still had a desperate look about her and did her best to form attachments with all the unattached young men. Rory dealt with her attention by talking incessantly about Josephine. A tactic that soon proved very effective. He made sure the information was common knowledge amongst the young people, and also with any parents who might be sizing him for wedding clothes. If I hadn't seen the letters arrive, I might have suspected it a tactic to avoid matrimony. We became fast friends. Our personalities enjoyed the company of each other.

The next time Gareth was in town, I could see that he found our closeness unsettling until Rory set his mind at ease by waxing poetic about his Josephine. I thought the sooner Josephine arrived, the better! Heather's attentions always centred around Gareth when he was in town, and it became difficult to have a conversation with him without her inserting herself.

Thankfully, Gareth continued to take lunch with us on Sundays after Mass. I could see that Iris and Malcolm enjoyed having Gareth to lunch and in sharing opinions on things that happened in the colony. Life again felt good. With the help of Father Xavier and my submission to the forgiveness of those who hurt me, I again drew close to God and trusted him as I built new friendships. With Chloe in town, the Forbes family in town each month, and the new friendships I formed at the Catholic church, life felt ordered and comfortable.

April 1852, Bottle Forest

With the arrival of the new tailor, I was given the opportunity to visit with Beitidh and Catriona on the farm. One month after the birth of Joshua Mark, I was released. The journey to the farm was more arduous than I expected. It gave me a realisation of how comfortable my life had become. The group had a few horses that were shared. Mostly, the young walked. The punt across the river was new to me. The weather was gentle, the current in the river was slow as the river neared high tide, so the crossing was uneventful.

Beitidh told me that sometimes the current made the trip harrowing, but there was no use being stuck on the wrong side of the river. Her creatures needed tending. On occasion, Joseph warned them of impending weather catastrophes, but not always. They had arrived at the river only to be turned around on more than one occasion. Thankfully, not for the trip I was taking to see what they had all built.

The shadows of the afternoon were lengthening by the time we arrived. The autumn weather was warm but not excessively hot. There was the smell of an old-world farm about the place. A combination of chickens, manure, and cut hay. The woody balsamic smell of the red cedar trees that were being felled to make way for farms and provide wood for the mill wafted on the afternoon breeze. The onshore breezes of the afternoon refreshed everyone for the evening chores that needed to be done. The houses were close enough together to see one from the other, but far enough away to make overhearing normal conversation impossible. Gareth called a '*CooEE*' when we arrived to alert the people in the other house, who had stayed behind due to illness, that we had returned. I was told that it was a call that would travel the distance.

"We use it when looking for each other."

The gardens surrounding the weatherboard houses were manicured. I was impressed with how much they had accomplished. With only two houses completed so far, they were still crowded but had found a harmony within their community.

I could smell the cedar wood inside the house as well as outside. Gareth had made cedarwood chests for everyone. Each chest had an individual feel because of the carvings on the lid. I hadn't realised just how artistic Gareth was. They looked very much like the one Iris had ordered for my room, and I gained a new appreciation for the tiny, bell-shaped flowers he had engraved onto the surface of the chest that adorned my room at home.

I was given a bed in the room with Beitidh, Catriona, and Dierdre. Thankfully, it was a large room. Once again, I was inspired to consider how spoilt and comfortable I had become. I had always had to share a room growing up, until May married and moved out. There was joy to be had with sharing a room if you could overlook the discommodity of the arrangement. I was to have the opportunity of regaining some of the closeness with Beitidh that had begun on our six-month journey.

'Thank you, Father.'

I had begun to thank God at every opportunity throughout the day. The latest exercise, given to me by Father Xavier.

"'Tis still crowded whilst we build the next two houses. We wanted to finish paying back the FCLS before spending any more on housing." Beitidh looked around as if she had only just realised the humble accommodation.

"I'm so pleased to be here; it feels extravagant compared to the ship and the house in Huskisson. I love Iris and Malcolm, but without Chloe, I think I am very lonely in town. I have had so much trouble with people gossiping. One malicious person can cause so much trouble. It often feels like trouble is following me. Father Xavier has been helping me to deal with my reactions. He has suggested that as Satan learns what will draw me away from God, his tactics copy what has been successful for him in the past. Whispering into the ears of the ungodly in my everyday life, suggestions of how to act. The answer, it seems, is in staying close to God in all circumstances. So, I am avoiding bitterness, gaining strength in forgiveness, and asking my Heavenly Father to not withhold his grace from them. But still, I miss the people who know me well enough to know a lie when they hear it spoken."

"Wow! I didnae ken it was so awful fur ye."

We did not have the opportunity to talk further on the subject. Joseph ran into the house. Barefoot, so not noisy, yet his presence was felt because of his joyful enthusiasm. Standing in the doorway of the room with hat in hand and a broad smile across his wide face, he had eyes only for Beitidh. When I looked at Beitidh, the smile was reflected on her face, also.

All conversation stopped as we made our way outside to the dining area next to the kitchens. The weather, too hot most of the year for the ovens to be inside, the kitchen and laundry were in smaller buildings out back of the house, with a paved area in between for the tables where the families congregated to share meals. All rooms in the house were occupied with sleeping quarters.

I could see a brick oven placed in the centre of the area, which I guessed warmed everyone in the winter months. There was a canvas awning built to provide cover from the sun and rain. It was nothing like the farmhouse of the Hill family before they left England. Letters from Beverly suggested that their home in Australia also attached the kitchen to the back of the house. From their letters, we understood that it was much colder where they had settled further up the mountain. They even experienced frost on winter mornings.

The kitchen gardens looked verdant just beyond the paved area, and the chickens roamed free. The chicken houses were not visible from the dining area. The pavers seemed to be made from rings of sawn wood rather than stone. The stone was reserved for the yards that immediately surrounded the fire.

There was a lot of activity as evening chores were completed. Cleaning livestock pens, milking the ewes, and watering the kitchen garden from the tanks of rainwater collected from the tin roof.

"How often do you need to water?" I was curious to know how different the microclimate was from my own home in town. Our tanks never seemed to run dry, but I had read of the struggles some out west had with keeping enough water for the house.

"We seem tae have plenty of rain. Some days, too much in one downpour that turns the yard to rivulets. Then, is gone before sunset, an hour later. Last January, we had so little rain the wat'r ran off the top before it could soak in. Then in March we had so much rain o're the weeks the grund was spongy underfuut and the wat'r ran in rivulets down tae the creek for a week following the sun coming out. The tanks overflowed for sure that month, but as yet, they have never run dry, even when the creek dries out.

"They were a good investment. 'Tis good to learn a new way of doing things. 'Tis a joy to thank God every time someone passing by gives us some sage advice. I'm certain they are sent by God he'self."

We talked as we went around feeding the sheep and housing the chickens. It was interesting to see the fruit trees and gardens inside a chicken wire house. Beitidh explained how the wallabies and possums were inclined to eat the garden, and them being so difficult to keep out.

We bedded down for the night and fell asleep to the buzzing of mosquitoes near our ears. I could hear them even when, like the others, I put my head under the muslin sheet. I felt safe from bites, but I could still hear them trying to get through. The welts from the mosquito bites seemed to be much larger on our sensitive white skin than they were on Joseph's tanned complexion. He could sleep outside and be none for worse the next day. He told us that they always slept close to the fire in the men's camp. The smoke and smell of smoke that clung to him may have helped.

The four weeks that I spent visiting the Forbes family farm remains one of the happiest memories of my life. It was not always peaceful, and the work was never-ending. The weather was perfect, and a sense of satisfaction at a day well spent accompanied me to bed every night. There was not a single person who held a grudge against me, nor anyone scheming harm. I began to relax and felt like I could rest again in God's love.

I went for long walks with Gareth and Beitidh after dinner each evening before joining the rest of the family around the fireplace in the courtyard. Joseph often joined us, holding hands with Beitidh as they shared stories about their day. Gareth and I walked behind them by a good hundred yards to allow them privacy in enjoying each other's company. Although the time was designated as belonging to Beitidh and Joseph, Gareth and I became close friends also, sharing stories about our past and experiences adjusting to a new life. I started to feel an attachment that was richer than the attachment I had ever experienced with Angus, and I wondered if I had been old enough to understand a true and lasting love when we had become betrothed. Knowing Gareth, I came to understand that losing Angus was truly a good thing for me. Gareth was a much better man.

G The time spent with Isabelle when she came to see our farm left me with a longing for more. My grief for Molly would always be there, but I didnae want tae live me life remindin' meself always. Neither did I want tae move on. I thought perhaps 'twould be better tae view it as adding a new layer. I had tae keep living. Isabelle was a rare beauty, though she couldne see it in herself. The rust and yellow

colours of her day dress drew me tae drawing a comparison as we walked and talked. The copper of her hair was the same colour as the tiny Christmas bell flower that grew all along the river. Beauty that not only survived but thrived in a harsh environment.

Chaperoning Beitidh for her evening walks with Joseph became more about Isabelle and meself each day. 'Twas time I admitted tae Doug that he was right. From the first, I had been drawn tae the fire of her hair and the gentleness of her language. I had never seen Isabelle fire up at anyone. Such a contrast to the family I had brought with me. They never held onto grudges, but every time, they argued loudly before they agreed.

"We will leave soon after morning chores tomorrow so that we can be in Hurstville before the dark. 'Tis sorry I am that ye will be leaving. 'Thas been a joy tae have yer company. It feels like ye belong with us." Isabelle stopped and turned to me with a teasing smile.

"The pleasure has been all mine, Gareth!" Somehow Isabelle made this sound like she was making fun of me, but I couldne work out why.

"I don't want to spoil our friendship with too much talk of feelings with expectation."

I took her meaning tae be that she wanted friendship and nothing more. Disappointment flooded me heart. Our family was doing so well that our loan had been repaid rapidly. I was soon tae buy a property in Hurstville to open a cabinet making workshop.

"I will be opening a shop in Hurstville next month. 'Tis time me skills as a cabinet maker are used on more than our own property. Joseph is doing so well that he can work a week out here and alternate with a week in town for his learning. He has spoken tae me, and they will marry soon. They will take one room in the house for themselves whilst the other houses are being built."

"That's fabulous. When will the wedding be?"

A low chuckle rose from me depths at her enthusiasm.

"So 'tis nae the institution of marriage that ye disparage? They will wed tomorrow. I will stay in toon after this Sunday's Mass so that I can get things started in the workshop."

"But Beitidh has not told me her good news! How can that be?"

With some amused discomfort. Sheepishly, I glanced briefly into her eyes before lowering me own eyes and shrugging me shoulders.

"She doesnae ken yet. 'Tis to be a surprise. We are hoping the dress we commissioned when last in town will be ready for the occasion."

The incredulity on Isabelle's face made me reconsider the wisdom of our plans.

"A surprise wedding? Is that a good idea? Are you sure that is going to make Beitidh happy?"

"I'm fairly certain. She has been waiting impatiently for the elders' permission. Joseph has told me that they have the permission and can go ahead at will."

"The elders?"

"The elders of Joseph's family. Apparently, the Aunties must approve. He lives half in his world and half in ours. He tells me that there are expectations."

"Oh, then in that case, I can see how Beitidh will accept the surprise wedding. Does that mean you have to move out?"

"Noo, it means I am free tae move into toon. Beitidh will have a husband tae take care of her."

Isabelle smiled broadly.

"And I am very excited that I will have a true and trusted friend in town when Chloe moves back to Coalcliff."

Me heart was both pleased and disappointed at her pronouncement of our friendship. I had grown tae want more over the time Isabelle was at the farm. I accepted that friendship was a good place tae start. 'Twuld need much focus on prayer for me tae court Isabelle as I planned. The rest of the walk we spent in companionable silence as we lost ourselves in private contemplation.

I spent the rest of our last walk thinking about Beitidh being blessed in finding a good and faithful man to wed. I wasn't sure that I could trust my judgement in weighing the character of any prospective husband. I would be trusting in Iris and Malcolm to help me evaluate the worthiness of any candidates. Watching Beitidh, a long-lost desire welled up in me. A desire with which I was irresolute. It had been a very traumatic few years for me, and I was sure that I could not trust myself, let alone anyone else. There was no doubt for me that I felt drawn to the dynamic man who walked beside me. His character seemed sound, but how would he react when a mob came against me?

From his behaviour on the ship, defending others and even me, it seemed like he would stand tall before the crowd and not cower. But would he remain at my side? He had distanced himself from me following the mob's heckling of me on the deck. He pretended that he had done that for my benefit. It had not felt like it was for my benefit. It had protected him and his family also. Of course, if we were to marry, I would be his family. But at what point does it become easier to discard me if it is I bringing trouble to the rest? I enjoyed our closeness, but I didn't think I could risk too close an attachment. I felt his disappointment but was unwilling to encourage his interest.

CHAPTER 27

Blighted

"Therefore, since we have been justified by faith, we have peace with God through our Lord Jesus Christ. Through him we have also obtained access by faith into this grace in which we stand, and we rejoice in hope of the glory of God. Not only that, but we rejoice in our sufferings, knowing that suffering produces endurance, and endurance produces character, and character produces hope, and hope does not put us to shame, because God's love has been poured into our hearts through the Holy Spirit who has been given to us."

Romans 5:1-5 ESV

May 1852, Hurstville

My arrival in Hurstville the following afternoon was meant to be a joyous reunion. Instead, I arrived to find a panicked Rory beside himself with worry. Pacing the floor of the shop, where no customers were in the shop needing attention. When I walked through the door, the intermingled expression of relief and fear on his face led me to immediately take on his state of frenetic worry, even though I had no idea the root cause.

"Oh! Isabelle, 'tis so good to see ya. The masters are both a bed sick. I'm in a terrible fright o'er their health. I called the doctor as soon as I arrived this day. He's above stairs nouw seeing to them. Does no look good. I've been in a quandary o'er tryin' to decide on calling the Minister."

Those last words had me running for the stairs. Leaving Gareth to hear the rest of the story from Rory. When I arrived on the upper landing, I heard the doctor speaking with someone other than my new parents.

"No one is to be allowed to visit. We do not understand yet how the disease is spread, so isolation is a necessity. I have heard that Miss Lindsay nursed her brother when he had the morbid throat, so when she returns, she will be able to help you. I have had many sensible conversations with Miss Lindsay over the past year. Conversations that show her superior understanding. She has learnt much from her grandfather and from reading. If she were a man, I would suggest she apply to the university. But all that effort would be a waste on a female who will simply have babies and think of nothing else for the rest of her life." The doctor waggled his head side to side at the last statement. Then continued with the real issue. "Follow her instructions and send for me if you have any concerns. I don't think we can wait any longer for her return before cutting the membrane. Do you have the instruments prepared?"

I was too concerned about Iris and Malcolm to be offended by the doctor's statement. I had heard the like many times before and had made my peace with the way things were. My mother always said that no happiness could be gained from fighting a losing battle. *'Fight the battles you can win'* was a mantra for her. Iris had taught me to contend peacefully for a woman's right to vote. Other things would follow that change. From his comments as I approached the room, I suspected I knew the disease. Most adults did not succumb, so I could not understand Rory's fear until I saw the colour of Iris' lips. I made my way through the door of the bedroom despite his words of warning.

"What is your diagnosis, Dr Sinclair?" My own abundant fear for Iris, I wore as a mask on my face. A glance at Malcolm showed me that even though he was sick, his condition was not as dire as Iris' rush toward the grave. The doctor, with a benevolence I was not used to, gave me the answer I expected.

"It is the morbid throat, Miss Lindsay. Although Iris is at an age to fight the disease easily, I fear that she is not doing well." He spoke as he crossed the room, took my hand and led me to a chair. My pallor, severe enough to suggest I might collapse to the floor. "I will need to lance the membrane in her throat so that she can breathe. Would you like to wait downstairs? We can have Rory close the shop and sit with you while you wait. If it were not someone so close to you, I would be asking for your help, but we know that it is much harder working with detachment on your own loved ones."

I stared at him blankly for a full minute as I thought of my brother, who had passed away when he was only five. I fought my way back to the present in a state devoid of emotion. I nodded my head ever so slightly as I replied.

"Yes, I think that may be a good idea."

I looked at the nurse whom I knew by name only. Greta and I had never had reason to have a conversation before then. She led me downstairs, where Gareth and Rory helped me boil water and prepare infusions. They helped me collect oils from my storeroom and prepare multiple bowls for steaming the room once the cutting was done. They sat with me whilst my mind hurried forward with ways to help. Gareth made a simple dinner for us all and sent a message for Beitidh to bring a chicken broth for the patients from the Cohen family down the street. Something they had offered when he delivered a fancy bedhead, *'If ever it is needed.'*

As we ate, I contemplated how my adoptive parents might have contracted the disease that killed some and left others with only a mild respiratory infection. It occurred to me with suddenness that Chloe's young Joshua Mark was at great risk. Chloe had stayed longer in Hurstville to recover from a difficult delivery.

"Gareth, would you please go see Chloe and tell her to leave for the Coal Cliff as soon as she can. For the baby's safety! Rory, have there been any other people sick in town? Gareth, tell her I will write and see her when next she is in town."

Gareth nodded his head and left the table. He placed his hat on his head as he exited through the back door on his way downtown. His shoulders were rounded forward in a way I had not seen before, and his mouth moved with continued prayer. He had been praying quietly since Rory first greeted us with the bad news. I emulated him whenever my thoughts calmed enough to string words together in my mind.

It was at that moment Greta came into the room and asked me to accompany her upstairs with haste. She looked around at what our activity had produced and gave ever such a slight shake to her head. The mournful expression, apparent for any to see. I carried the basin of steaming oil infusion meant to clear and soothe airways. Greta looked but said nothing about me leaving it behind. When I entered the room, I saw that Iris had gone from blue to alabaster. The quantity of blood in the bowl suggested a loss too great.

"I am sorry, my dear, the membrane was close to a blood vessel. I tried first to create sufficient airway without causing much bleeding, but Mrs Beaumont could not take in enough air to change the blue of her lips. The only option was to clear more of the membrane. I think her strength was too weakened by toxins for her blood to be strong. The bleeding is not so fast, but the clotting has stopped. I believe Mrs Beaumont would like to try a few words for you. She must remain lying on her side." When I looked toward Malcolm, I could see his despair. His colour remained good for now, but I saw in his eyes that he did not have the will to survive if Iris did not. The minister arrived, and we both moved to pray over Iris in the hope of a miracle. Iris opened her eyes when I gently laid my hand on her head.

"Thank…you…Issy." Iris drew in gasps between words that I could barely hear. "The…scent…is…sooth…ing. I…pray… Malcolm…will…not…follow…straight…after…me. (a longer pause) To…the…next…life. I…fear…he…will. (pause) And… leave…you…alone. If…that…happens. (pause) There…is…a… new…will. We…have…gifted…Rory…an…interest…in…the… business. (pause) To…inspire (Iris coughed blood and needed to rest for a minute before continuing.) So…he…would…stay…to… help…you."

The tears rolling down my face said that I did not want to talk about such things. The loss of Iris and Malcolm was unthinkable to me. I could not understand what she was saying to me. Because I didn't want to understand.

"You can't leave me, Iris. I need you. I need you both. The reverend is here; we are praying for you. Please do not give up."

The Reverend and I started to pray over Iris. Pleading for God to heal them both. I could see the peace settle on Iris, and then on Malcolm, but after several minutes of prayer, I knew in my heart that I was praying for a peaceful passing. God spoke into my heart and granted me the peace to accept this new devastation. I held Iris' hand and arranged for Malcolm to be brought close so that they could hold hands. My tears flowed freely. Malcolm's tears flowed freely. My world once again crashed about me. It was not long before Iris gasped her last.

We moved Iris into the lounge room so that we could clean her body and give her fresh clothes before the undertakers were sent for. When Greta and I finished the loving but devastating task, I returned to Malcolm with a fresh bowl of oils in steaming water. His breathing was steady, but his colour had a yellow tinge. I looked at the doctor for an explanation.

"Sometimes the body cannot handle the toxins of the disease, and the internal organs fail. Mrs Beaumont succumbed to the lack of air. It looks like Mr Beaumont is not able to clear the toxins. There is still hope that he will heal, but I fear he would rather be with Mrs Beaumont wherever she is now."

"I fear that you may be right, Dr Sinclair. It is the sense I received from God as I prayed."

I saw the scepticism on the doctor's face but did not care about his scientific, heathen views on the subject. I knew the sense that God had given me. The tears had stopped flowing, but I was not happy about what I had been told. My disagreement with God about what was best for me did not change the decision God had made. Even though he slew my adoptive parents, I would still trust in him [35]. But that did not mean I had to be happy about it.

Gareth returned at the same time Beitidh arrived with the chicken soup. I went upstairs to encourage Malcolm to take some soup, but he refused. I think his unconscious intention was to follow Iris into the afterlife with haste.

The next week was a blur of caring for Malcolm and arranging a funeral for Iris. It could not be delayed. The weather was still very warm most days. Gareth built a coffin as the first project in his new business. Not a task in which to find pleasure. The minister of the Congregational church and the congregants themselves remained polite but distant with me. Malcolm provided words to be read, but was unable to be transported to attend the burial due to the quarantine imposed by the doctor. In his last days, it became hard to recognise the Malcolm we knew, because his body swelled as he lost the battle against the toxins.

My life was once again turned upside down. I pulled a drawer from the dresser and turned it upside down to empty its contents onto the floor. I looked to Gareth as I proclaimed that it was an example of my life. One tragedy after another.

"I'm not important enough to God for him to release me from these fiascos. Next, there will be a mob at my door claiming I was the

[35] Job 13:13-16

cause in some way. It does not matter that there is no logic in such an accusation."

"Dinnae speak such things, Isabelle. Lest your words bring them into being. Your love for the Beaumonts and yer grief dinnae need to dictate yer thoughts."

"That's easy for you to say. I have not seen you living with fiasco after fiasco. I haven't seen a mob forcing your back against a wall whilst they yell insults and threats."

I sank to the floor and buried my head in my lap. Gareth sat with me there on the floor for an hour before leaving to fetch his aunty to stay with me. He needed to finish a second coffin only days after lowering the first into the ground. Later, he told me that he had also needed to construct several children's coffins for the community. I was not the only one grieving.

The first fist of dirt thrown onto Malcolm's coffin in the ground was the signal for me to cry out both burials. I had managed to walk through the burial of Iris in a fugue state. Without crying. Without breaking down. I had to keep moving. Praying and trying to convince Malcolm to stay with us instead of following after Iris.

The last of the flowers from the garden were placed on both graves when Malcolm's resting place next to Iris had been filled.

I suppose waiting for the second death before placing the flowers showed my expectation. The gossip was cruel. Some suggested that I had placed my hope in the final outcome so that I could inherit. The gossip was then fuelled by the reading of the will a week following the second funeral service.

Some people were overheard by Rory saying that I had denied visitation to the sick Beaumonts, so that I could not be found out in my administration of poisons to my adoptive parents.

"Serves her right that they left half of the business to that Irishman."

"Maybe she didn't want to risk losing any more of the business as they discovered her real character."

"Heather told us all what she was like, but we were reluctant to believe her."

"We trusted what Iris and Malcolm told."

"They were blinded by their desperation for a child."

"Judgement on them for their ungodly views on the place of a woman."

"The beneficiary of the business should have been Heather. She worked for them since she was just out of school."

I could not fathom their cruel words and was glad when Meaghan Robertson, Gareth's aunty, stayed with me in town to help me through the worst. The first communion dresses were put on hold. No one received their dressmaking orders. And few had their tailoring done. Rory was almost as devastated as I was.

He was surprised to find that half of the business was left to him. Apparently, Malcolm had not informed him. Aunty Meaghan cooked for us and did all the tasks that we could not concentrate well enough to complete. Young women from *The Frankies* fellowship came by to sit with us and promised to light candles even though Iris and Malcolm had not been Catholic. They brought sweet treats and sat with us for cups of tea. I suspected that they were on a roster because only one came per day, and one came every day. They rarely outstayed their welcome. They helped us to survive and encouraged us to join them at Mass.

I was in a state of rejecting God's presence. Why would he allow Iris and Malcolm to die? Was I never to have a peaceful life? Gareth came by every day to share the dinner that Aunty Meaghan had prepared. He talked about the finding of a workshop and the beginnings of his trade. He encouraged me to seek comfort from God, but I was not in the frame of mind to accept God's comfort. He mentioned Heather's family ordering an unusual quantity of furniture. Most of his conversation went in one ear and out the other. A saying my mother had often employed.

No one from the congregational assembly came to visit. I was not surprised. The gossip had done its work, and I was isolated from them. Everyone was grieving. Once again, the community sought to make me the scapegoat for any guilt they felt. Irrational guilt, exacerbated by loss. And I was an easy target. With no parents and no siblings at this end of the earth.

Letters from home offered little comfort. I resorted to creating happy environments in my imagination. Aware of my surroundings and able to interact with others with only a small delay. The fantasy offered relief. An analgesic of sorts. I could have taken laudanum, but I had seen the devastating effects when addicts came into Granda's shop. He always tried to steer people away from the medication, saying that the alternatives would have a better result in the long term. It became harder and harder for me to live in the real world. Quite frankly, I did not want what the real world had to offer. All my work with Father Xavier was sidelined. I felt no closeness and no help from the Almighty.

I repeated two statements over and over in my mind.

I'm not important enough to God for him to release me from these fiascos. And

There can be no good wrought from the catastrophe of the mob.

Those two statements seemed to summarise my thinking, and whenever I made one of the statements to myself, I immediately delved into the release of imagining my own stories. Stories where I was loved and appreciated. Accepted into the community. Later, I realised that Gareth, his aunty, and even Rory demonstrated a real love for me as they patiently sat with me during my mourning. Never giving up hope that I would one day come out of my bitterness. I talked to myself more than I talked to others.

Is God in control? Yes! But then he gives us all free will, so evil people are allowed to do as they will. And yet, not everyone is made the scapegoat by traumatised people. Why me? Is there something I do that causes these things to happen? I cannot see what that could be. God could keep me safe by helping me avoid the situations. I do everything I can to follow his will. But I still end up in front of a hostile mob. Why hasn't God put me in a situation where this doesn't happen?

I found no answers to my questions. So, I went back to my stories. At least there, I had some control.

One day, Rory mentioned that Malcolm and Iris had offered to pay the passage for his Josephine to travel to New South Wales. The deal being that he would pay them back over time. Josephine's passage on a steam ship had then been organised post haste. Organised shortly after he arrived. When Iris and Malcolm had determined he was a good fit. The voyage was expected to take much less time than ours had because they were not dependent on the wind. I was happy for him but found it hard to feel his excitement with him. The arrival came as a surprise to me. It felt like I had only just found out, then his Josephine was walking through the door, luggage in tow.

I was reluctant to commit to voice, my deepest fear following the deaths of Iris and Malcolm. The thing I was most afraid of was their memories fading until they were forgotten. When my brother died, first we talked of him often and had constant memories. But as life progressed and he was no longer a part of the new stories, his memory faded into a distant past. A necessary part of grieving, or we would live in a constant puddle of tears. Grief was too intense to hold tight.

But!

The loss of those memories made me afraid that I loved them less as the memory faded and as I began to come back to life myself. I knew that this made no logical sense.

But!

When does fear ever make logical sense?

I had to accept that I thought of them less often as time went by. I resisted coming out of my despair because I thought it might mean that I did not love them anymore.

Pure irrational silliness.

But!

Silliness that my fear compelled me to hold tightly.

CHAPTER 28

Blessings

"And we know that for those who love God all things work together for good, for those who are called according to his purpose."

Romans 8:28 ESV

June 1852, Hurstville

In the midst of my turmoil, Gareth mentioned that Beitidh and Joseph had married. It was disappointing to know that I missed the wedding, which had gone ahead as planned. Of course, I would not have expected their plans to be delayed due to the dramas that were taking place in my own life. And yet I still had a sense of being left out. As unreasonable as I knew my feelings to be, I could not help but acknowledge they were there. I had a momentary experience of joy for them when I found out but could not raise the happiness for them that I thought I should have been willing to feel. I despaired that my life could have the reprieve from drama that I so desperately desired. In my desolation, I did not have the faith to trust that God was working any good in my life.

Gareth spoke of the happenings at the farm whenever he received information. He shared community information to inspire me to re-enter the world around me. But I preferred to stay in my safe place. Inside my fantasy, where I had control of the outcomes. It was enigmatic how the story would unfold in unexpected ways, and yet I had the final say. I could backtrack the story and change what happened before the story unfolded too far in a way I did not want. I used the fantasies as an analgesic for which I refused to take medicinals. The fantasy was always more pleasant than reality.

Slowly, I came to realise that I could use the scenarios to learn things about the way I was thinking. It changed a disturbing and possibly destructive pastime into a useful tool for growth. When talking to Father Xavier one day, trying to answer his questions, the realisation came to me. He showed me that in revealing my true agenda, I could take it to Jesus and ask for forgiveness for myself. I learnt that I was as angry with myself as I was with God. Somehow, I believed that the dramas in my life were caused by the badness in me rather than the badness in the world, and sometimes in others. Forgiveness remained a struggle. I found that I needed to forgive over and over again. I would forgive and then somehow take up the offence again because the memory replayed in my mind.

Rory's fiancée arrived, and there was a second wedding for which I was half-hearted in joy. The building was a part of my inheritance, with Rory inheriting half of the shop floor. Aunty Meaghan suggested that I allow Rory and Josephine to live in the master bedroom so that I would have company in the house. An arrangement that worked out well for everyone. I had the security of Rory deterring unwanted visitors, and Josephine helped with the housework and gardens. Josephine also worked with us as a seamstress. Her character was one of quiet mercy, which she extended to me in bucket loads.

Aunty Meaghan stayed with me for a full month before heading back to the farm, where she was much needed. The third house was nearly complete, so the family shuffled their accommodation. Iris and Malcolm had paid out my loan as soon as I had arrived, so I had no debts. The result, I realised a month after Aunty Meaghan had gone home, was a procession of young men coming into the shop to suggest I become their wife.

Even if I had liked them, I had no interest in trusting someone enough to commit my life. Angus' betrayal still ruled my heart in that. I had forgiven him and felt no anger. But I still wanted God to teach Angus and Lilith how it felt to be betrayed and allow them to experience the results of false witness. I felt some satisfaction when my family wrote of the couple's struggles. However, trusting someone not to betray me was too much risk.

Beitidh with her cousins, Catriona and Dierdre, called to see me one Saturday afternoon. Beitidh had a written note for me and explained that God had impressed on her heart some verses to impress on mine, so she copied them out of Gareth's Bible.[36]

---

[36] DRB (p. 2059). Catholic Way Publishing. Kindle Edition. https://biblehub.com/drb/jeremiah/29.htm

"For I know the thoughts that I think towards you, saith the Lord, thoughts of peace, and not of affliction, to give you an end and patience. And you shall call upon me, and you shall go. And you shall pray to me, and I will hear you. You shall seek me, and shall find me, when you shall seek me with all your heart. And I will be found by you, saith the Lord."
Jeremias 29:11-14

"Will you join us with *The Frankies* today, Isabelle? Ye sorely missed. The young ladies are all asking after ye. I willnae mention the enthusiasm some of the young men show in asking after ye. I fear their motives are tainted. Besides, 'tis Gareth would be yer best match."

I gave Beitidh a stern look, leaving her with no doubt that it was not a topic I wished to discuss.

"Such a look! Ye could almost convince me that ye have no affection for him. He's veree taken with ye, ye ken?" I amplified my look and refused to respond. "Alright then, I'll say nae more about it. Please come with us?"

I gave in to her request, which was obviously heartfelt. Beitidh really did want me to accompany her. As I liked her company, I agreed to go with her. Concluding that once a month could not be hard work.

Many of the young people accepted me as they always had, but I noticed a few who refused to look me in the eye. Seemingly, the gossip had spread to some of the Catholic families. Not surprising when the news was spread over back fences as the washing was hung out. We all lived side by side, neighbours sharing information regardless of which church they attended, or which pub they frequented for a draught. The sense of ostracism once again became a part of my life. It didn't help that Heather had become a regular in the meetings. Flirting with all the unattached men. A circumstance they appeared to enjoy.

Within a quarter hour of arriving with Beitidh, I was surrounded by a group of five young men. I liked talking to them, but would have preferred to be talking to the young ladies who had sat with me in the weeks following the Beaumonts' deaths. Heather sent more than a few venomous stares my way. My discomfort increased, and my participation in the conversation decreased with each new male who joined the group, until Gareth arrived with Father Mathias and whisked me away.

"Isabelle, it is very good to see you out and about. Company helps in processing our grief."

Father Mathias then turned to the young men and said, "You don't mind if I steal Miss Lindsay away, do you lads? I have a message for her from Father Xavier."

At that, they all dispersed. Even Gareth began to walk away until Father Mathias added,

"Please stay, Mr Forbes."

It always amazed me how the Catholics did the priests' bidding whilst they were around. Somehow, they were convinced that the priest had a say in the destination of their eternal souls. The upbringing with the non-conformists did not leave me thinking our elders could have a say in our eternity, though they did have a say in our acceptance by the community in this life.

"How is Father Xavier? With the house being in quarantine, I missed seeing him when he was last in town."

"He will be arriving back from his circuit this coming week, so I will let him tell you about his escapades. I can tell you that he is having many adventures. Meeting bushrangers and aboriginals, as well as the families he rides out to see. I received a message from him asking me to organise a luncheon for him with you both. Will Wednesday suit you?"

Once again, this was said with an air of expected compliance. Both Gareth and I accepted; with the thought that we would just have to organise our schedules around the meeting.

"Of course, Father, I'll close the shop for lunch."

"Yes, I can arrange for Rory to take care of the business."

We spoke simultaneously, then turned a smile toward each other. Father Mathias gave us a nod and walked away. Thankfully, girlfriends rushed over before the young men could again surround me. I enjoyed spending time talking with them about what was happening in their lives, instead of constantly thinking about missing Iris and Malcolm. My mind wandered often, but they were forgiving and patient with me.

I went to Mass with Gareth's family the following day and avoided interaction with anyone outside his family. As Gareth was then living in town, we met his family for lunch at the *Smashed Pumpkin*. The establishment our neighbours referred to as '*the local watering hole*'. It was good to see that Joseph was with Beitidh. I hadn't seen him on the Saturday and asked Beitidh about his absence.

"Was Joseph unwell yesterday?" I could see that both Beitidh and Joseph felt uncomfortable with my question, but before I could change the subject, Joseph answered.

"I'm not welcome at some of the white fella's meetings, Miss Lindsay. When they think I'm from Spain, I can come along. When they find out I belong here, they say, no come anymore."

I was surprised. And yet I wasn't. I had heard the derogatory comments that some people made about being tainted with the tar brush, but I had expected better from people who otherwise seemed so reasonable.

"I'm sorry, Joseph. I'm not sure I want to go if the group are going to be like that." Beitidh squeezed my hand.

"I dinnae want tae see ye isolated any more than ye already are, Isabelle. Everyone has their prejudices. The English are not so keen on the Scots either sometimes. Ye family brought ye up to have a better heart than most."

The rest of the afternoon was a good distraction. Conversation about the farm abounded, and since my visit, I had a frame in which to picture the stories told.

I was not yet ready to smile, and when I dressed in the mornings, I was drawn to the dark and colourless. Colour felt like it did not belong in my life. It wasn't done on purpose; it was a simple outworking of my heart. I was sad. I was pleasant to people when they spoke to me, but I felt no desire to pretend I was happy. I would have described myself as subdued. There was no shine to my vitality. Strangely, though, it gave me more awareness of others. My desire to talk was diminished, so my capacity to listen was increased.

G I met Isabelle at her shop so that we could ascend the hill together. There was the beginnings of the cooler season startin'. 'Twas cool enough tae comfortably walk with me shirt sleeves rolled down. A coat was nae an option till the middle o' the winter. The cooler air and the shortening of the days were the only signs of the changing season in a place where the trees didnae lose their dressings. The trees that were left after the cedars were felled. The only bright colours were tae be found in the sunsets before it rained. The trees showed their bright colours with new growth leaves in the spring and bright flowers in the heat of summer.

"Have ye an idea of what the good Father wishes tae talk with us about?"

"Not any idea at all. And you?"

"Nae."

We arrived with five minutes tae spare and were shown into the drawing room until Father Xavier was ready tae meet with us. We were shown tae the conservatory where the table was set for three. The samovar was in its usual place tae the side, making refills available without calling for servants that might disrupt the conversation. The luncheon had already been placed on platters at the centre of the table. Cold sliced meats and fruit with fresh bread rolls. Father Xavier approached and gave Isabelle a fatherly hug as he expressed his condolences and concern for her well-being. He nodded his head and took me hand in his in way of greeting. Our hats had been left at the front door, so I was glad the table was set in the shade of a small tree that had extremely large leaves and large green fruit that I had never seen before. Father Xavier noticed me looking and volunteered the information.

"It is a mango tree from Asia. I keep the tree small and really do not expect to get fruit, but it looks like they may ripen if the weather holds. The days are short, but the air in the conservatory is warm and humid. The season is wrong. I was surprised when the tree flowered.

They will turn yellow gold if they do. At least I hope so. This is the first fruit from the tree, and I am uncertain of success."

Father Xavier turned his gaze from the tree tae Isabelle. I must apologise for not being with you sooner, Isabelle. I was tied up, literally, by some bush rangers at the time of the Beaumonts' passing. I heard of the tragedy only after I had taken the bushrangers' confessions and convinced them to release me. Misguided souls who thought the treatment they had received gave them permission to inflict the same treatment onto others. They have cornered themselves into a life on the run from the law, regardless of their salvation in eternity. At least I cannot tell the authorities where to find them, as they have no home in which to be found. Not a life for the faint of heart. Their repentance will save them from eternal damnation, but not from the Mounted Road Patrol."

Isabelle and meself both looked aghast and wondered if what the good Father talked of was story or truth. Our prolonged silence inspired Father Xavier tae continue without a response from us.

"Please forgive me for talking about myself. I must admit to being a little traumatised by the experience. But as you can see, I am well."

"Yer have me in mind that we need tae be praying for ye when ye ride out, Father. I have come tae appreciate ye as more than the priest on the hill and would rather not be dealing with yer replacement just yet."

Father Xavier gave us an unguarded, rare smile that spoke of his attachment tae us also.

"Thank you, Gareth. Your prayers would help keep me safe. I can see your sorrow, Isabelle. How have you been? Father Mathias tells me that he saw you at *The St Francis Set* meeting Saturday last."

Isabelle hesitated before sinking ontae a bench seat and bursting intae tears. With her face in her lap for a good quarter hour. When the tears slowed, she heaved a few good breaths and wiped her eyes on the black linen of her skirts before sitting up with shoulders still hunched.

"Now I must ask forgiveness for my outburst. I try not to descend so far into my loss in front of people."

Her statement was disturbin' 'cause it meant that Isabelle was cryin' alone. I knelt before her so I could look intae her eyes, without a care for Father Xavier witnessing me efforts tae console. I took her hand while I thought of what best tae say.

"Now, Isa, you must know 'tis nae a thing that needs apologising for. There can be nae need tae forgive when there is nae offence given."

With a hand tae me shoulder, Father Xavier encouraged.

"Well said, Gareth. Now I suggest we move to the table so that we can enjoy some tea whilst we talk."

Once the tea was poured, Father Xavier continued with what I guessed was his main agenda.

"I hear, Isabelle, that you have received multiple offers for your hand since the Beaumonts' passing. I hope that I am not causing you distress. I can see from your expression that this is true on the basics. It is hard to have this happening not only when you are grieving, but because of the very events that cause your sorrow."

I was once again surprised. Those rumours had not come tae me. Maybe because I would be considered a rival. I realised in that moment that I didnae like having the rivals meself. I hadnae been paying close enough attention and felt guilt rise up tae match the jealousy.

"This is true, Father. No less than five young men, and some old men, have come to the shop to tell me that I would be best to marry them. Rory has done a good job evicting them. I cannot even think straight on such a thing. It is so very insensitive. I am not so desperate that I would marry just because I no longer have guardians. I am sure I do not want to marry."

At that statement, Father Xavier looked tae see the expression of disappointment I wasnae quick enough tae hide.

"All I can think of is WHY? Why has this happened to me? Why has God allowed yet another disaster in my life when I look around and see so many who are comfortable in their perfect little lives?"

I heard the bitterness in Isabelle's tone and, in truth, had been asking God some of the same questions. Maybe without the sense of resentment. But then, I seemed tae be an onlooker. I felt Isabelle's pain with her but was not in a position where I could offer her close comfort or support. I was glad that Rory and Josephine lived in the house with Isabelle.

"That is a very big question, Isabelle. We cannot always know God's mysteries. The why of how he sustains the universe. He does ask us to trust him to work all things out for our good. Sometimes the dramas help us to grow into his likeness. Sometimes he uses our circumstances so that we can help others later."

"So, he causes disasters in my life to benefit other people? How could I trust a God like that?"

"No, that is not the God that I know. He doesn't cause the dramas. He helps us to benefit from the dramas caused by a sinful world. He will never take away our free will. Not even the free will of people bent on evil plans. He will love you and sustain you as you battle the results of sin in this world."

The knotted brow showed the dissatisfaction, anger, and effort in Isabelle's thinking.

"So, Iris and Malcolm died because they sinned?" The brows grew stormier with every word she said.

"No, this is also not what I am saying. Sin in the world has caused a decay that results in disease. The whole world is sick with sin. The sin of many causes illness to thrive in the world. No specific sin from Iris and Malcolm has necessarily caused the illness, although not one of us is sinless."

Isabelle then became argumentative and verily spat the next statement at Father Xavier. I could see that his own exhaustion made the conversation difficult for him. His own harrowing experiences of late were taking a toll on his health.

"Yes, but Jesus saved us from that sin. Why do we still suffer?"

Father Xavier sighed.

"I can only say that all those people with free will, who choose to do evil toward others for their own selfish gain, impact us all. The only way to avoid the impact is for God to separate us from this world. But if he did that, then we could not bring his message of salvation to those who will listen. We store up treasures in eternity when we persevere in a fallen world.[37] When we choose to have faith in the goodness of God, even when we are in pain, our Father in heaven loves us and hurts with us. Jesus himself felt all the pains of betrayal and the loss of loved ones in his life on earth. We can follow his

---

[37] "Blessed are you when others revile you and persecute you and utter all kinds of evil against you falsely on my account. Rejoice and be glad, for your reward is great in heaven, for so they persecuted the prophets who were before you." Matthew 5:11-12 ESV

example and forgive those who do evil against us. The Holy Ghost can comfort us and help us if we ask for help."

"I am not sure I can do that, Father. I am not sure I forgive God for letting Iris and Malcolm die so young. They were good people, and I needed them."

"I understand your feelings, Isabelle. I will keep you in my prayers. God loves you enough to wait for your hurt to subside."

"Does he? I think that I must not be special enough for him to keep me out of trouble."

"And I think that he may think you special enough to benefit from those troubles."

I could see that Isabelle was unconvinced, and the good Father let the subject drop whilst we enjoyed the cold meat and fruit platter. We talked of the shops, both Isabelle's and me own. When Isabelle excused herself tae visit the necessary, Father Xavier took the opportunity tae say a private word tae me.

"I had hoped to suggest a solution to Isabelle's problem with unwanted marriage proposals, but I see she is not at all ready to embark on a marriage covenant. Isabelle needs to find her comfort in God before she marries, or her husband will be called on to fill a hole that only God can fill. Neither would be happy with that arrangement." Father Xavier then gave me a broad smile. "I suppose you will just have to wait."

Isabelle re-entered the conservatory as Father Xavier made that teasing comment, so I had no opportunity to respond. Saved by the bell!

"What do you need to wait for, Gareth?"

Resisting the flush of embarrassment, I was slow tae think of an alternative thing I was waiting for.

"Oh, I see. You do not want to tell me. Now I am curious."

The teasing smile on Isabelle's face was too rare tae spoil, so I responded without telling the truth of it.

"'Tis true, I dinnae wish tae share me embarrassment."

CHAPTER 29

Cynicism

"Blessed is the man who walks not in the counsel of the wicked, nor stands in the way of sinners, nor sits in the seat of scoffers; but his delight is in the law of the LORD, and on his law he meditates day and night. He is like a tree planted by streams of water that yields its fruit in its season, and its leaf does not wither. In all that he does, he prospers. The wicked are not so, but are like chaff that the wind drives away. Therefore the wicked will not stand in the judgment, nor sinners in the congregation of the righteous; for the LORD knows the way of the righteous, but the way of the wicked will perish."

Psalms 1 ESV

July 1852, Hurstville

In the weeks that followed, I heard many reports from customers tae me fledgling cabinet shop. Reports of Isabelle being testy with people. Reports of her jaded, sarcastic remarks. Suspicions that she had murdered the Beaumonts for the shop and her independence. The rejected suitors began commenting that they had dodged a bullet. 'No one wants to be wed to a harpy.' And yet none of what they said was evident when we shared lunch on Sundays. I thought it time I tried tae see if there was anything I could help with, so I closed me workshop for lunch and made me way tae the dressmaker's store, under the guise of employing the tailor tae make a set of trousers for me. Me church clothes were looking a little threadbare and needed replacing anyway. As I walked intae the shop, I heard Isabelle's voice with an edge I wasnae used tae hearing.

"I see what you are saying, Mrs Burns. The colour is not the same as the colour you chose, even though it came from the very bolt I showed you. If you remember, I did explain that sometimes when fabric is made up into a garment, it can look different. I recommended a darker shade, but you were insistent, so I, of course, gave you what you asked for."

The look on the customer's face suggested a feeling of mortification. Isabelle's speech demonstrated a condescending frustration. I hadnae seen the behaviour from Isabelle before. Her sweet nature was usually serene. Just a two month before, she would have been far gentler with her interaction. Mrs Burns said to me as she walked from the shop.

"Good luck. If she weren't the best seamstress in town, she would have no customers." With a sigh, she added. "Talent and arrogance always seem to go hand in hand."

I approached Isabelle with due caution. I leant intae the cutting table where she worked and whispered.

"What has ye in such a tether today?"

Isabelle lifted her eyes tae me with an almost sneer.

"That lady I overheard saying cruel things about me. If she had followed my advice, she would be happier with her finished dress. She is far too plump for such a colour. I can see no reason to treat people better than the way they treat me."

"I fear for yer happiness, Isa. Can I take ye tae lunch?"

Isabelle expelled a sigh and put her scissors down vigorously. With a look of contrite despondency, she nodded her head and prepared tae leave the shop with me. As we approached the front of the shop, the door swung open and two Mounted Patrolmen hastened through.

"Miss Lindsay, we have been ordered by Chief Macauley to bring you in for questioning on the murder of Mr and Mrs Beaumont."

Rory, Josephine, and meself were so stunned that the patrolmen had a firm hold on Isabelle before we had time tae respond.

"Seriously, men, can ye be a little more gentle? Miss Lindsay is nae threat tae ye."

The patrolmen carried pistols and batons with an authoritative attitude that said they wouldne hesitate tae use whatever force necessary tae carry out their orders.

"She's a murderess, sir. No telling what she might do."

"Questioning is nae a conviction patrolman."

"We all know she's guilty, mate. It's common knowledge that's why she fled England. Used her potions on the ship over here as well from what we've 'eard."

"None of that is true. "Tis slanderous gossip, all of it."

Isabelle retreated into her own world and said nothing. The patrolmen didnae wait for our agreement and marched out the door with Isabelle between them. All those on the street, and many in doorways, stopped tae watch the procession. I took note of the ones with smiles on their faces. Some commented that it was about time.

I followed Isabelle tae the gaolhouse next tae Chief McCauley's office.

I was denied entry, so I went looking for help in the only quarter I could think of. I entered the reception area of the doctor's surgery. The doctor's rooms being on the other side of town, the procession had not passed his office, so the inhabitants remained unaware of what had transpired. A young man ran in only seconds after me own entry and announced in a loud voice.

"They've finally taken the witch into custody."

The enthusiasm with which the news was received surprised me. I was confident that the expression of '*witch*' was meant only as an insult, but the consensus on her guilt surprised me. On what did they base their opinion? Isabelle had only ever been kind and generous. Even if her words had become testy of late, she had never harmed anyone. She couldne leave any sick person unattended. The commotion in the front room brought Dr Sinclair out of the consulting room along with his patient and Nurse Greta.

"What is this excitement?"

"'Tis what I've come tae see ye about, Dr Sinclair. They've taken Isabelle tae the gaolhouse for questioning." Dr Sinclair displayed incredulity.

"For what reason, Mr Forbes? Isabelle can have done nothing unlawful."

"They accuse her of murderin' the Beaumonts."

When I made that statement, multiple voices began tae interject their opinions.

"'Tis no less than the truth."

"She's a suspicious one, that."

"No one is truly that nice."

"Not so nice, I say."

"The Beaumonts were so dear."

"And so fond of Heather before she arrived."

"'Tis only right the Chief stand up for his daughter."

"She killed them for her independence."

"The clerk at the courthouse said it all happened only weeks after they changed their testaments of beneficiary."

The rumble of talk continued with people hardly listening tae each other, they were so bent on voicing their own opinion. The Doctor and I stood looking at the rabble in his rooms before turning to each other.

"I had no idea the gossip had become so entrenched."

"Nor I, Doctor. I've come tae ask that ye help me tae find a person tae speak on her behalf. I dinnae ken the officers of the court. Will you help, Doctor?"

"Of course, Mr Forbes. Shall we go? It looks as if all my patients are currently distracted from their ailments."

We made our way toward the courts as Dr Sinclair spoke tae me about the New South Wales legal system. He had a school chum who presided over the local court. His son was a counsel for the defence. Apparently, some kind of rebellion against his father's expectations.

"Mr Morris can be found at the courthouse most days. If we do not find him there, we will go on to his rooms. His father sent him to London for his education, where he suffered from bullying. He was a slight child when he left at the age of eleven. His mother died whilst he was away at school. He resents his father even now, that he was forced to leave what he saw as his home country just to get an education in London.

When he was in England, he became an avid reader, particularly enjoying the works of Mr Dickens. When he was let out of the school, he walked the streets of London and saw the conditions that led the poor to crime. The conditions that led to the overcrowding of prisons and the need to transport so many, so far from home. He learnt compassion for the accused. His view being that the accused were not always the guilty. His mission became to bring false witness into the light. I'm sure he is our man for this case. Isabelle is obviously not guilty of this crime. I myself treated the Beaumonts and know her innocence."

I hardly felt the hard hands around my arms, that led me through the doorway of the shop onto the street where the jeering crowds gathered. Once again, I was at the mercy of the irrational mob who demanded no evidence. The mob, convinced exclusively by the nefarious words of jealous and spiteful individuals who never let the truth get in the way of a good story. The comments I heard as I was paraded down the street for all to see left me in no doubt as to where the gossip had begun, nor the reasons for the attack. The temperature dropped as we set foot inside the sandstone building next to Chief Macauley's office.

They placed me behind bars even though I was ostensibly only brought in for questioning. From the comments made by my escort, I gathered that I had already been found guilty. Heather's father had an agenda of revenge and financial gain for Heather. The intended damage was done. In the minds of all those in town who witnessed me being transferred under guard to the gaolhouse, I was a convict. A stigma of doubt was, from then forward, attached to my name.

I was left to wait in the damp, dankness of a barred cell with no window, for what seemed like an age. But in truth, I had no genuine sense for the passing of time. With no window, I could not see the day's shadows lengthen. With a dim filtered light seeping into my cell, I knew that the sun was still in the sky, but not what time of day. When my stomach began churning, I knew I had missed lunch, but I could not have eaten if food were placed in front of me. The nausea threatened to overpower me, so I sat on the cold stone bench and concentrated on my breathing as Father Xavier had taught me. The saliva in my mouth subsided, and I felt some calm descend. I knew I needed God, but I was not ready to accept his decision regarding Iris and Malcolm. Finally, I heard voices approach.

"Mr Morris, halt! Mr Macauly has not given permission for you to see the prisoner."

The footsteps that approached did not hesitate. They approached with determination.

"You cannot keep me from my client. Miss Lindsay is being unlawfully detained. No charges have been laid. Release her at once, or I will see you brought before the magistrate for false imprisonment."

With those words, the gentleman came into view. A tall, reedy man with jet black hair and startling green eyes. Eyes that penetrated my soul. I felt like he had plumbed the depths of my honesty without asking my permission.

"Good afternoon, Miss Lindsay. A Mr Forbes has made an application for me to represent you. Do you accept me as your counsel and agree to pay the fees incurred?"

He cleared his throat and gave me a conciliatory look before continuing with a lowered voice.

"The fees will not be excessive. I am confident after talking to Dr Sinclair that you are not guilty of breaking the law."

It was unfair that there would be a financial cost for my freedom, but I hesitated only for a half minute whilst I digested what the man had said.

"Yes, Mr Morris. Please be my counsel in this matter."

With that small statement, said in a small voice, Mr Morris regained his full height and speared the gaoler with a penetrating look.

"Release her, I say! We will wait in the reception area of the Chief's office until he is ready to talk. An interview I expect to take place without delay, as Miss Lindsay has already been waiting over an hour."

Only an hour!

It had seemed much longer. I suppose the uncertainty of my future had made it seem much longer. The iron bars rattled as the key clanged into place and turned. Without delay, we were ushered into a room with wooden benches and a man behind a desk writing in files. The perplexed look on his face as he looked up suggested that he had no understanding of what was taking place in his office.

"Why are ye here? Chief Macauley is nae ready to see the prisoner yet."

Mr Morris made no attempt to be polite as he demanded justice.

"Miss Lindsay is not a prisoner. She is here to answer questions the Chief may have, but no charges have been laid. Not surprising given that there is no case. Only frivolous accusations. Accusations that could equally be made against either of you. Treat a person like a convict, without there first being a conviction, and you may find yourself in the same place one day."

The man behind the desk bristled before lowering his brows and tightening the muscles around his mouth.

"Is that a threat, Mr Morris?"

"No, it is not a threat; it is a warning about how the world works. I would not be the one making false accusations about you."

Mr Morris seemed to enjoy the encounter, giving stick to the coppers. I wondered how he had so much gall. When I relayed the story to Gareth later, he explained that Mr Morris was the Magistrate's son and so had a measure of protection against injustice himself. Mr Morris turned to me with an air of consideration.

"Shall we sit?"

He then led us to the bench seat against the wall farthest from the desk and spoke in a low voice.

"Mr Forbes and Dr Sinclair have filled me in on the details surrounding the deaths of Mr and Mrs Beaumont. It is best if you leave most of the talking to me. I will let you know when it is ok for you to answer a question. Please do not answer a question without first getting a nod from me. They will try to trap you into saying something that can be bent to substantiate their lie. Remember, not everyone is honest; some people expect lies because that is all they know how to speak themselves. Some people are so used to lying that they cannot remember the truth. The truth has no place in their lives."

"That is a shockingly cynical view, Mr Morris."

"Yes, Miss Lindsay, it is. But it is also something I observe often in my line of work. It is always refreshing when I can identify another person who values truth. This I have seen in you already. I have a sense for seeing people as they are under their façade. I have also heard the testimony of two well-respected men in our community. Men who have shown their worth through the benevolence they show to others, even when it is not deserved."

It was at that moment, the door to Chief Macauly's office opened. His look of surprise was quickly followed by a look of contempt and a sneer of delight in evil. The expressions all passed with speed until they settled on a look of annoyance at seeing Mr Morris seated next to me. Mr Morris smiled in return with a "gotcher" expression. We were ushered into the office, and the door closed. Mr Morris held the back of a chair and indicated that I take a seat before seating himself directly in front of Chief Macauly.

"Mr Morris, always a pleasure to see you accompanying a client. It assures me that the suspect must have something to hide."

"Or indeed, that your line of questioning is based on nothing more than spiteful gossip. Something I have caught you on more than once."

"I must investigate all complaints, Mr Morris."

"An excuse you have used before to defame the good character of a rival. Simply start a rumour and wait till it is repeated, then haul a man in for questioning in as public a way as possible. It is interesting how inventive some can be in circumventing true justice."

"I would give up reading so much of Dickens if I were you, Mr Morris. A *bleeding heart* does not succeed in this world."

To that, Mr Morris only gave a smile of knowing tolerance.

"Do you actually have any questions, Chief Macauly, or did you bring my client in for the spectacle alone?"

Chief Macauly, or rather Heather's father as I knew him to be, turned to me with an intimidating glare.

"You have an interest in plants and extracting oils, Miss Lindsay."

He then waited for me to reply, so I turned to Mr Morris as he had instructed. He did not give me a nod of permission to speak. The interaction was noted by Chief Macauly.

"Answer the question, Miss Lindsay."

"I did not hear a question, Chief. Miss Lindsay cannot answer a question not put to her."

I caught my first glimpse of the Chief's tactics. He was attempting to have me talk freely. I understood Mr Morris' message. Say as little as possible. The Chief gave a horizontal smile of long-suffering to Mr Morris.

"Very well then, do you distil oils from the plants that you grow, Miss Lindsay?"

Mr Morris gave me a nod.

"Yes, I do."

I resisted giving further information, making the chief draw out details laboriously. He sighed, and the effort of calculation on his face increased. I learnt that there was something to be said for waiting. My observation heightened.

"And can those oils be poisonous if ingested?"

Mr Morris again gave me a nod.

"The flavour," a concerned look briefly crossed Mr Morris' face, "is such that no one would ingest the oils."

I could see that Chief Macauley became enthused by my reply, so I determined to keep closer to minimal answers.

"Are you capable of masking those flavours, Miss Lindsay?"

"Not if there is sufficient quantity to cause harm."

"Are you aware then of the quantities needed to cause harm?"

"In order to not cause harm, I need to be aware of quantities that could cause harm."

The Chief gave a small but satisfied smile.

"You have been accused, Miss Lindsay, of purposely administering poison to the Beaumonts for the purpose of causing their death. What do you say to that?"

Another very big question that could open me up to further questioning if I strayed too far. I looked to Mr Morris.

"Please be more specific in your questions, Chief. My client is unsure of what question you are asking."

Another tight smile from the Chief to Mr Morris.

"Did you use your oils to hasten the death of Mr and Mrs Beaumont?"

"I did not."

That question was much easier to answer. I would have said that I did not distil dangerous oils. A trick to make me reveal more than necessary and further the questioning. The Chief cleared his throat and continued trying different threads of argument.

"You say you didn't use your distilled oils in a nefarious manner, but that does not mean you did not hasten their deaths in another manner. You have the motive, Miss Lindsay. It is common knowledge that Mr and Mrs Beaumont changed their will only weeks before their passing. It is unusual for a couple in perfect health to be in such haste."

The Chief once again waited for me to fill the gap in conversation with a response. But I had learnt already to be wary and looked to Mr Morris, who gave me a small negative movement of the head. Another tight smile from the Chief.

"Hmm. Did the Beaumonts change their will in your favour only weeks before their untimely deaths?"

I felt my grief being abused by his questioning. I missed Iris and Malcolm intensely and felt like I was being punched in the gut with every reminder of my loss. Mr Morris noticed my pallor.

"Miss Lindsay, would a drink help you now?"

"No drinks until I say so. It is common for a criminal to feel ill when they approach capture."

"It is also common for a young lady to feel ill when in the depths of grief from the loss of her parents." Mr Morris turned to me and added. "Take your time but answer the question."

I took a deep breath to both focus my attention and separate myself from feeling.

"When Iris told me of this change only moments before she passed, she did not tell me when they had changed the testament."

"What did you do when she told you the news? Was anyone else present at the time?"

"I barely heard her tell me that news. I was desperate for her to stay with us. But I also saw her life seep out of her as the blood spilled onto the pillow. Malcolm was in the room. We both held her hands."

The reliving of the day made me fade into the memory.

"I think Greta was in the room. Dr Sinclair was talking to Mr Forbes by the door."

"And Mr Beaumont's passing, Miss Lindsay. Answer the same questions."

It felt cruel that he was making me relive the death scenes of people that I loved dearly.

"Nurse Greta and Aunty Meaghan were with me when Malcolm passed."

"Why didn't you call the doctor in?"

The Chief's bluntness was a knife to my heart. His intent to cause harm, methodical, clear and deliberate. By that stage of the questioning, I was so distressed that I had trouble staying present.

"The doctor had been there only an hour before and told us that Malcolm's breathing pattern suggested he would not be on this earth for much longer. He left to attend a difficult delivery. Everyone knew that the doctor could not help Malcolm; it was pointless calling him away from a patient that he could help."

"Who administered the doctor's medications to Mr Beaumont whilst he was ill?"

My dazed thoughts still looked to Mr Morris before answering.

"Nurse Greta mostly."

"Were you ever alone with the medication bottles?"

"Nurse Greta needed to take breaks."

"You had motive, means, and opportunity, Miss Lindsay. I will not rest until I have proven your guilt. It is clear to me that you are indeed guilty."

Mr Morris took control.

"You have not supplied any evidence that Mr and Mrs Beaumont were actually murdered rather than dying from natural causes. Without some evidence of murder, you cannot charge Miss Lindsay with murder. We will be leaving now."

"Healthy adults do not die from diphtheria, Mr Morris. I would be careful eating at Miss Lindsay's table once your usefulness has worn out."

"I doubt that you can find a reputable Doctor of Medicine who would testify to that, Chief Macauly. I have been assured that although uncommon, it is not unheard of that an adult can die from the morbid throat."

Mr Morris helped me to my feet and led me out into the street. A crowd had formed outside the station house. Mr Morris told me that he had better escort me home.

Through my dazed state and on later contemplation, I concluded that Mr Morris was far too clever for Chief Macauley. Dr Sinclair and Gareth had given me the best help that could have been had. When the Chief worked out that he would not be able to charge me with murder, he simply continued the questioning to cause as much pain for me as he possibly could.

G I saw Isabelle leave whilst Dr Sinclair and I waited in the reception area. I dinnae think Isabelle noticed me. Her focus was on the crowd she saw through the solitary window. The crowd that had formed outside tae be firsthand witnesses of Isabelle's denunciation. Dr Sinclair pushed his way into the Chief's office before he could close the door. I followed him in before I could be stopped.

"I am here to inform you, Mr Macauley, that I treated both Mr and Mrs Beaumont during the illness that led to their deaths. I will also inform you that there is no evidence to suggest foul play in their deaths, and I will first testify to that fact in detail if the matter is brought to court. And second, I will be raising a complaint with the magistrate as well as the Justice Department regarding your abuse of power to exert revenge on an innocent member of the public. An individual you are employed to protect."

Fear momentarily sparked in the Chief's eyes before he replaced it with arrogant bluster.

"You do that, Dr Sinclair. Then try to prove what you say."

"I will not need to prove anything, Mr Macauley. You yourself know that in the workplace, and the public domain, you are guilty until proven innocent."

With that said, we both turned and made our way hastily back tae Isabelle's shop.

CHAPTER 30

The Hidden Trap

"Let all bitterness and wrath and anger and clamour and slander be put away from you, along with all malice. Be kind to one another, tender-hearted, forgiving one another, as God in Christ forgave you."

Ephesians 4:31-32 ESV

"For if you forgive others their trespasses, your heavenly Father will also forgive you, but if you do not forgive others their trespasses, neither will your Father forgive your trespasses."

Matthew 6:14-15 ESV [38]

[38] Matt 18:21-35

July 1852, Hurstville

G I couldne convince Isabelle tae join me and me family at the meeting of *The Frankies* the Saturday after she was escorted tae the gaol house with so much public fanfare. 'Twas hard tae say if her embarrassment or her fear were the strongest deterrent. As soon as we entered the building, Heather flew with as direct a path as a bee leaving the hive enroute tae collect nectar. I held ontae Beitidh before she could walk away and whispered tae her.

"Nae so fast. It looks like I'll be needing an intervention. Save me, Beitidh."

I was a small bit plaintiff in me supplication, but when Beitidh saw who was headed toward me, she agreed without hesitation and signalled one of her special friends tae join us.

Heather arrived in front of us all too fast. There was a heightened boldness tae her manner which reinforced me foreboding.

"Now that Isabelle is a convict, she can be no suitable wife for one such as you, Mr Forbes. The magistrate is sure to overturn the Beaumonts' will. With so many in town thinking that Isabelle killed her adoptive parents for the estate, it will return to the previous beneficiary. Marry me, Gareth. I would be far more suitable. I could make you very happy."

"Well, now, Heather, that is surely the worst kind of gossip I've heard this year. How do ye come up with such fanciful stories?"

I could see that Beitidh would enjoy the exchange.

"Is that right, Beitidh? You were not even in town to see the spectacle of Isabelle being carted off to the gaol house. She was a sight for sore eyes with her head dangling between her shoulders in the shame of exposed guilt."

"I've seen yer forwardness with the young men from a distance, but never so close up before. 'Tis uncommon among our clan for the women tae do the asking. How many have turned ye down so far, Heather? Must take a thick skin. Or perhaps desperation tae be offering tae marry someone who hasnae shown interest in ye."

I saw the barbs rise in Heather's eyes without evidence of a blush on her fair complexion. The smile on her face when she turned tae me and placed her shoulder between Beitidh and me, didnae reach intae her eyes.

"Are you unable to speak for yourself, Gareth? Do you always hide behind the skirts of your sister?"

"Only when dealing with unwanted suitors. Most young ladies are smart enough tae test the waters with me sisters before so boldly approaching. It requires a conviction tae be a convict, Miss Macauley. Isabelle is nae more a convict than yerself or me."

"It's common knowledge Isabelle killed the Beaumonts. Everyone is saying it. And if your sisters are putting off young ladies that you like, what then? You would have missed an opportunity."

"Me sisters know me well and have insight intae what a young lady may choose tae hide from me, but cannae be hidden from other young women."

When Heather looked tae persist, Beitidh walked around her and placed herself in front of me.

"Cannae ye see that ye offer has nae been accepted. Do ye need a straight-out rejection, Miss Macauley?"

"I will not accept a rejection from you, Miss Forbes."

"So, it was a genuine offer of marriage then? I wasnae certain. I felt sure ye were just insinuating a possibility." Beitidh turned to me. "I think it time tae be very clear, Gareth."

I hesitated with disbelief but delayed nae longer in addressing Miss Macauley.

"I must inform ye, Miss Macauley, that I have nae intention of making a marriage covenant with ye. We would be wholly unsuited. Is that clear enough for ye, Miss Macauley? It is me own choice." With a smile of disingenuous self-deprecation, I added. "In nae way coerced by me sister."

I gave a small nod with me head before turning and walking over tae Doug, who was himself in deep conversation with the Simpson twins. Harrison was similar to Doug in height and build, though vastly different in colouring. With ginger hair, olive skin, and hazel eyes. The pair looked exotic. Henrietta was identical in colouring but very different in stature. Henrietta was a slender woman with a square face who came only tae her twin brother's shoulders. I understood them tae be from Italian descent. Their father encouraged tae change his name from Santa Lucía by the immigration officials when he arrived. I would have kept walking tae talk with someone else if I didnae need Doug's moral support. I didnae wish tae interrupt the possibility of Doug finding some happiness after the loss of his entire family.

The rest of the meeting was soured by the comments of Miss Macauley. I refused to stay away, though. I needed to be there tae put out the spot fires. I gained an understanding of the expression the previous summer when a fire started near our home. The whole family was needed for dousing the fires started by the burning leaves falling from the sky. I was glad for the work we had seen Joseph's family doing with burning small sections whenever the weather was right.

I started talking about Isabelle's generosity and the help that she gave freely to anyone who was in need. I had seen her give aid tae many of the poorer locals when they were unwell and unable tae afford tae see the doctor. I had even seen her pay for their visits tae the doctor when she couldne help them.

I saw the hesitation in the small audiences until I reminded them, by regaling them with stories of factual events which they had each experienced. Occasionally, I came across a resistant person who claimed that those past deeds didnae negate her greed for autonomy. The first time someone made the statement I was in disbelief at their logic. But by the third time I had heard the exact same statement, I realised they were repeating a phrase heard from another. I suspected that I knew who that other was.

By the end of the evening, I was afeared for Isabelle's future in town. I had seen before the damage that could be done by false accusations repeated over and over. I could see that prayer was going tae be the only answer. I trusted that God was faithful tae save those who trusted in him. Isabelle's trust in God would need to be as much a focus of me prayers as asking God to limit the spread of such damaging gossip.

I felt the loss of joining with friends in *The Frankies* meeting. The shame I felt drove me to hide away at home. I curled up in my bedroom reading the latest Dickens' book, *David Copperfield*, while Rory and Josephine were out. I could have worked with my oils, but my spirits were too low, and I wanted to avoid escaping into my own fantasies. I could see that my fantasies had started to take control. Something I was afraid of more than living in the real world. I had seen some of my granda's customers deteriorate into madness.

I had not heard of any asylums in New South Wales, but there must have been a sanatorium somewhere. My goal was to maintain that ignorance. My sighing increased as I attempted to read the same paragraph yet again.

"If only I could concentrate." The story, when I could pay attention long enough to comprehend, was well worth the effort. I despaired and dropped the book to the bed. My gaze wandered to the blue of the sky out the window and the wispy clouds that drifted by. I knew in myself that my desolation was from not talking with God. My anger was not resolved. There was no fairness in the things that kept happening to me. Other people had such comfortable lives. Or so it seemed from my frame. Like the window before me, the picture I saw of their lives was beautiful.

'But if you put your head into the frame, you will see beyond the presented picture and be able to see the blemishes that standing back prevents you from seeing.'

The thought popped into my head, and I suspected that my Heavenly Father was speaking to me. I stood and walked over to the window. When I put my head out, I could see the compost heap. A place in the garden that was not pretty. A place of decay.

'And yet a place that brings new life. After breaking down, it provides nourishment for new life.' I let out a huge sigh of defeat.

"I suppose you want me to talk to you, Jesus, but what is the point when I cannot hear your reply?

"Alright! Given that I am hearing you now, I suppose what I really mean to say is: What is the point when you don't let me have what I want?"

I heard what I said. It was so unreasonable, and I knew better. It is not always good to get everything we want. But I was convinced I had more strife than others.

"How can this be good?" I began to sound very whiny to myself. "I know, I know. All things work together for good. But cannot I have some good without the need to work bad things into a good?" I sighed again as the answer presented itself.

'Think of the good time you had with your family before you left England. Think of the good time you had with Iris and Malcolm before they came home to be with me. Think of the provision of a home and a living. Think of the reliable company you have in your home now.'

"Alright! I get it."

With humility, I began to release my anger.

"I do have a lot of good things for which to be thankful."

The thoughts of my many blessings continued to play in my mind. The good friends I had in Chloe, Phillip, Gareth, Beitidh and the rest of his family. The sound counsel I received from Father Xavier. The joy of my garden. As I began to think of those things and say thank you to the Almighty for each and every blessing, I felt a sense of peace surround my heart. In forgiving God, joy filled the core of my being. The gate in the back fence opened at that moment, and I heard Rory and Josephine enter the garden.

"And thank you that I do not live alone. What a wonderful provision."

I am thankful that I did not know that evening that it was a calm in the centre of the storm. Rory and Josephine did not share with me the things that they had heard. I found out later that Gareth had asked my closest friends to pray over it before telling me what was being said. Gareth, Beitidh, and Joseph joined us for dinner in front of the kitchen fire. The air outside, cool enough to value being inside. Beitidh and Josephine helped me to prepare a minted potato mash to go with the lamb cutlets cooked by the men over the outside fire. It was a jovial evening with games of what-ifs and ridiculous outcomes.

"I think I will join you at church tomorrow."

The conversation paused as they all sent hesitant but wide smiles my way. I did not pick up on the hesitation but only saw the wide smiles. Gareth was the first to respond.

"I am glad to hear that, Isabelle. Will you let me sit next to you?"

I also missed the concern behind the request. I think God had immunised me against worry that evening. All I heard was a friend wanting to be with me.

When Rory, Josephine, and I arrived at the church the following day, Gareth was waiting for us at the gate with most of his family. They surrounded me with such enthusiastic greetings I began to feel like there was something about which I did not know. As we walked toward the chapel door, Father Xavier approached. I had not known that he was again returned from his circuit. His wide smile and hands held out wide in friendliness as he approached made me feel like we were special in his eyes.

"Gareth, Isabelle, it is so good to see you." The family separated to allow Father Xavier to enter the citadel of the fort they had constructed. Once again, I had a sense that it was odd behaviour. Our happiness at seeing Father Xavier, who had become like a true father to us both over the last few years, was evident in my enthusiasm. I hugged him as a way of greeting. Not something I would normally do, but after my time with God the previous afternoon, I felt the appreciation in my heart that had previously only been in my thoughts.

A result of the thankfulness God had led me in the day before. I saw that Gareth and Father Xavier were surprised by the embrace.

"It is so good to see you here today, Father. I have much to tell you about. Can you spare time today, before I have the chance to regress?"

"Yes, would you like to take lunch with me, Isabelle?" I noticed a look loaded with significance between Gareth and Father Xavier. "And you also, Gareth, if that is suitable with you both?"

I was happy for Gareth to join us, as I wanted to share my new-found peace with him also. The sense of peace struggled to persist with what came next.

Once Father Xavier had left us to talk to a new couple who were visiting for the first time, we walked as a group toward the chapel door. The group was not in formation, so it looked haphazard, but when people approached, they were deflected with haste. Sometimes, with a family member breaking off, then returning. Sometimes, they returned with stony faces and a refusal to converse. It wasn't until we entered the vestibule and formed a single file that I began to hear wayward comments coming from people standing around. They stared until I turned to look at them. Their heads turned away before I made eye contact or offered a smile. Once passed the font of Holy water, I turned to Gareth for an explanation. He placed his hand on my back and led me to a pew toward the front of the church. Further forward than where we would usually sit. After we genuflected, entered the pew, and knelt before our seats, Gareth offered a whispered word of support.

"Dinnae fash yerself, Issy. All will be made good in time."

That was too cryptic for me. With my head bowed forward on my prayer hands, I made no attempt beyond a whisper to disguise my irritation.

"That is not an explanation, Gareth. Tell me what is happening."

"Heather has been spreading malicious gossip. But have nae fear, we will get it all sorted. Remember God has promised tae take care of ye."

I could not argue with his statement. Yesterday's talk with God was too fresh in my mind. Instead, I bowed my spirit as well as my knee and prayed a thank you for Gareth's family protecting me. So different to Angus in Ellesmere. Gareth's affection and distress were both demonstrated in his calling me Issy for the first time. It showed me that he thought of me as one of his family, even though we had no formal connection.

At the end of the Mass, we waited in our pew for most of the church to exit before we stood. After we genuflected and turned to leave, we found Father Xavier standing between us and the door. He walked toward us and guided us into a small anteroom behind the sanctuary. There was a door to the garden from the room, but Father Xavier did not immediately head toward the door. Instead, he indicated some chairs and suggested that we take a seat.

"I do not often meet with people here but today seems like a good day for the practice. Do you mind talking here before we all leave to break our fast?"

"Yes, Father, I suppose 'tis." Gareth turned to me and offered an apologetic smile.

"Thank you, Father. I agree. There are some things of which I was unaware before coming to church today."

I raised my eyes to the ceiling, or did I roll my eyes back in my head? I'm not sure. I was amazed that God had timed yesterday's encounter to prepare me for that day's events.

"Would one of you please explain?"

"You seem remarkably not distressed by people's actions this morning, Isabelle. Would you tell us about that first? Before we explain today."

The day before had been so transforming that his request did not bother me. I was enthusiastic about sharing with them both the conversation I had had with God. My rendition was received with delighted, even relieved reactions from both Gareth and Father Xavier. Gareth sent a quick and hopeful look in Father Xavier's direction. He took my hand as he expressed his joy.

"'Tis so good tae hear ye say ye can trust in God again."

"Yes, Isabelle, I am relieved to hear that you have resolved your anger with God over the death of Mr and Mrs Beaumont. It will be beneficial for you in dealing with the current dilemma."

"On that, Father, would someone please explain to me what was happening when I arrived at church this morning?"

Gareth and Father Xavier both gave a part of the story, with them both learning from each other the pieces they had not previously known or understood.

Heather and a young man that she was fond of had been rather more intimate than was wise. When she told the young man that she was expecting his child, he informed her that another young miss was also expecting his child, so he would be marrying her. In desperation, Heather looked about for another man to entrap, Gareth being the unfortunate focus of her efforts.

With resentment over losing her position in the Beaumont's dressmaking business, and jealousy over Rory's and my inheritance of the business, Miss Macauley decided to blacken my name and console Gareth in his disillusionment. Thereby claiming him to be the father and forcing a marriage.

Thankfully, Gareth was wise enough to avoid the trap. Or as he claimed, aware of the Holy Spirit inspiring him to defend Isabelle. Which in turn enhanced the desire he already had to stay with Isabelle forever. And so, the Holy Spirit guarded him from evil schemes.

"Marry me, Isabelle. I will stand with ye against any criticism that is sent yer way and proclaim yer goodness every day tae anyone who will listen."

"I did not expect a marriage proposal, Gareth. We have not courted." My comment inspired Father Xavier to comment.

"I thought you were not yet ready to marry Isabelle. So, I recommended to Gareth that he wait. You have been harbouring too much anger and bitterness for a good start to a marriage. And not only with God. I do not think you have fully forgiven the people who have hurt you in the past. You cannot be fully free from the traumas of the past before you understand forgiveness. But I fear the situation has become such that it would be wiser not to wait."

"How have I not forgiven them, Father? I think I have. I have left my vindication in the hands of God."

"But have you asked God to release them from that vindication. You cannot be fully free from what they did until you are willing for Jesus to forgive them, and release them from the consequences of their sins, in the same way that you want to be released from the consequences of your own sins."

"But they have done worse than I have, Father."

"Even if that is true, Isabelle. True forgiveness, which releases your attackers, is not for their benefit alone. When you give them the freedom to find eternity with Jesus, their sins no longer recorded, then you will be fully free from the injuries they inflicted. The Holy Spirit will give your spirit healing as he lives in you. The Holy Spirit is grieved when we do not give to others the grace that Jesus has given to us. I am not saying that this is an easy thing, Isabelle."

"What I don't understand, Father, is why does this kind of thing keep happening?"

"Besides the truth that God does not cause such things to happen. Satan uses our past weaknesses to attack us in ways that have worked in the past. The evil one does that because he cannot read our minds and does not understand the progress we have made in trusting God, no matter the circumstances. It can always be brought to benefit you, Isabelle. There may be lessons that you have not yet fully learnt. Think of what you can gain that was in no way a part of Satan's plan for your destruction.

"Consider the possibilities. The opportunity to know the heart of God, more and more, as you learn to respond to attack in the same way Jesus responded. He asked God to forgive those who tortured him and paid the price himself for those very same people to enter eternity. When he forgave, he asked for no vindication. No retribution. Instead, he offered them a way to be free from their tortures. Your freedom, Isabelle, in this life, from your own tortures, can be found when you offer to those who hurt you the same kind of forgiveness.

"This will not stop bad things from happening. It will help you to trust in God's goodness to help you prevail, no matter the circumstances you meet. God offers to be with us, rather than removing us from hardship. It may not seem fair that some appear to have comfortable lives with no hardship. But that is not our problem to consider. If it is true, they miss out on a truth. I do not know if you have noticed, Isabelle, but it is in those tough times that we feel closest to God. I would almost pray for tough times just so that I can feel his closeness more and more. Almost! I still enjoy a respite from hardship when that is the moment God is giving me."

I will admit that I heard every word Father Xavier spoke. But I thought I had forgiven, so I did not take it all to heart. I was to be married. Not too quickly, as we did not want people to think there was a need and so give them more gossip. We planned a wedding for the spring. Gareth and his family continued to defend me. Heather quietly married a young constable and moved to a different district. The doubt from my experience with Angus stayed with me and robbed me of happy anticipation in the expectation. I waited for another catastrophe to fall, but none came. I loved Gareth, but I was not '*in love*'. Whatever that means. How much did it really matter? Those feelings had not ended well with Angus.

Every time I thought of recent events, I ended up reliving those events in my mind. Once again, I fell into a depression. I prepared for the wedding. Made my dress with a powder blue voile that I found in the storeroom marked '*A dress for Isabelle*'. Iris had not had the chance to show it to me.

When I found the fabric, I sank to the floor and allowed the tears to flow afresh. That happened from time to time. I don't think grief ever fully goes away. I simply learnt to live with it.

I cried myself out and quoted a Psalm that had become a favourite.

"He who dwells in the shelter of the Most High will abide in the shadow of the Almighty. I will

> say to the LORD, "My refuge and my fortress, my God, in whom I trust." For he will deliver me from the snare of the fowler and from the deadly pestilence. He will cover me with his pinions, and under his wings I will find refuge; his faithfulness is a shield and buckler. I will not fear the terror of the night, nor the arrow that flies by day, nor the pestilence that stalks in darkness, nor the destruction that wastes at noonday." [39]

God's answer to my prayer may not have been what I expected. It may not have been what I wanted. But it did bring me life with God.

> "...the Lord knows how to rescue the godly from trials, and to keep the unrighteous under punishment until the day of judgment," [40]

July – October 1852

I Following the episode at St Francis church, where I needed to escape through the back door, I would awake during the night and be unable to go back to sleep. My days were filled with anxiety and suspicion. Some of it warranted. Some of it not. I was often tired, and I felt my rational thought being compromised. I had to keep telling myself that my suspicious thoughts were not necessarily based in reality. I had to be intentional about evaluating my suspicions and casting away the thoughts that were not based on evidence. One day,

[39] Psalms 91:1-6 ESV
[40] 2 Peter 2:9 ESV

Josephine made a throwaway comment whilst we were stitching up a fancy garment together.

"To be sure, and the fairies can be whispering evil into yer mind if you be allowing it. They are all about mischief. They may look pretty, but the deceit they tell can ruin yer sleep if ye allow it."

Josephine had a funny kind of superstition about the fairies and leprechauns. Blaming them for all sorts of things and leaving milk out the back door to avoid inviting them inside. But her comment did cause me to think on some of the things which Father Xavier had said about demons whispering lies into our ears to deceive us.

The next time I awoke in the night, distressed, I thought there was no point in tossing and turning, trying to go back to sleep, so I got out of bed. Made myself a cup of tea and sat at the kitchen table writing. I opened my journal and poured out my feelings to God in writing. It became a repeated practice that helped me to overcome. When I would allow it, my Heavenly Father met me there.

One night, when I was having a particularly hard battle with the enemy, whispering all sorts of negativity into my mind. I recalled more of Father Xavier's teaching and decided I might as well put it into practice and see what would happen. I had nothing to lose. I wrote…

> *'Breath in me, O Holy Ghost, so that my thoughts will be holy. Act in me, O Holy Ghost, so that my works will be holy. Please draw my heart toward you, O Holy Ghost, so that I will love what is holy. I am loving. I have joy in the Lord. I have patience. I am patient. I am kind. I always seek to do right and good things. I am generous. I am self-controlled. I persevere when things get tough.'*

As I wrote, I felt the truth of the statements penetrate my heart. I forgave my enemies again because I had repeated the judgement. I prayed that God would bless them with a close relationship with himself and that they would be filled with the Holy Spirit. I then went back to bed and slept soundly until the sun came up.

The next time I woke up in the night, distressed with a bad dream, I again went to the kitchen, made a cup of tea, and sat down at the table to journal my heart's fears.

What a dream. I feel so bad. The dreams are so strange. Not stories I have experienced, but they engender the fears that plague me during the day. I am sitting at a dinner table with friends, and half the people get up and walk away to eat at another table. The unexpected person will stay, but somehow, I feel rejected. They have judged me as evil and want nothing to do with me.

'What am I to make of that, Lord?'

I decided to make more truthful statements as Father Xavier had taught me. The last time I had tried it, it had helped. I spoke out aloud into the night.

"Be silent around me, demons. I belong to Jesus Christ, whom I proclaim to be king of kings and Lord of Lords." Then I began to write.

'Breath in me, O Holy Ghost, so that my thoughts will be holy. Act in me, O Holy Ghost, so that my works will be holy. Please draw my heart toward you, O Holy Ghost, so that I will love what is holy. I am loved. I am loving. Love multiplies in me. I am filled with Joy at being in your presence, Jesus. I am a lover of peace and take joy in the unity of your body. I am patient. I am kind. I am merciful. I am righteous in my behaviour. I am self-controlled. I act rather than react. I choose to act as I think you would act. I persevere with the things you want me to do.

'Thank you, Jesus. How would you like me to behave with the difficult people?'

I felt led to read in Matthew chapter 5.

> "You have heard the law that says the punishment must match the injury: 'An eye for an eye, and a tooth for a tooth.' But I say, do not resist an evil person! If someone slaps you on the right cheek, offer the other cheek also. If you are sued in court and your shirt is taken from you, give your coat, too. If a soldier demands that you carry his gear for a mile, carry it two miles. Give to those who ask, and don't turn away from those who want to borrow. "You have heard the law that says, 'Love your neighbour' and hate your enemy. But I say, love your enemies! Pray for those who persecute you! In that way, you will be acting as true children of your Father in heaven. For he gives his sunlight to both the evil and the good, and he sends rain on the just and the unjust alike. If you love only those who love you, what reward is there for that? Even corrupt tax collectors do that much. If you are kind only to your friends, how are you different from anyone else? Even pagans do that. But you are to be ~~perfect~~ *complete (the way God created you to be)*, even as your Father in heaven is perfect."[41]

[41] Matthew 5:38-48 NLT

Papa had sent me a new bible when he heard of the shipwreck and had added an annotation to the verses. I was to be complete, with the Holy Ghost living in me. Just the way God meant me to be.

'But I don't think I can trust them, Father.' And I heard God say to me.

"I did not tell you to trust them. I want you to forgive them and trust Me."

'I suppose that means I am allowed to recognise the people who are not safe. And be careful about the people I choose to make important in my life.'

With that foremost in my thoughts, I closed my journal and made my way back to bed. Eventually, I woke up less often in the night, and the dreams became less fearful.

CHAPTER 31

Community

"Even youths shall faint and be weary, and young men shall fall exhausted; but they who wait for the LORD shall renew their strength; they shall mount up with wings like eagles; they shall run and not be weary; they shall walk and not faint."

Isaiah 40:30-31 ESV

October 1852

I Only a week following my twentieth birthday. Aunty Meaghan and Adeline arrived to help me dress for my wedding. The dress made from icy blue voile adorned the manikin that had been placed in the lounge room for the occasion. Rory and Josephine had moved to their own home a street away from the shop the day after my birthday celebration. I had a full week alone before I would once again be sharing a home. But this time I would also be sharing a room. A bed. I asked Gareth to build a new bedroom suite for us to make it our own. He delivered the suite to the house the day before the wedding. Furniture that had no memories. I wanted to leave the sad memories behind. Furniture that would symbolise the building of a home together. An object that would signify the joining of our lives together.

When Adeline walked out of the room to fetch us all a pot of tea, Aunty Meaghan took my face in her gentle hands and turned me so that we were eye to eye. With concern and a low voice, she asked.

"Why the long face on yer wedding day, Isabelle?" I felt comfort in the concern and benevolence that emanated from her. Tears pooled in my eyes before I lowered my lids and softly pulled away.

“I feel robbed. I have not had the chance for the feelings of excitement that courtship brings. I am to marry a man that I love, but without the chance to enjoy the anticipation that makes opening a gift that much more exciting. I know that I should be grateful, but I still feel the grief of something lost.”

“It is OK, Isabelle, to have moments when you feel that loss, so long as you do not dwell there. People often say forgive and forget. But we never truly forget. We only choose not to dwell on the offence. When we pray for blessings to be poured out onto those who hurt us, then the sting is taken out of the memory. We forgive and choose not to dwell on the attack. As Paul said in Corinthians:

> ‘For the weapons of our warfare are not carnal but mighty to God, unto the pulling down of fortifications, destroying counsels, and every height that exalteth itself against the knowledge of God: and

> bringing into captivity every understanding unto the obedience of Christ: And having in readiness to revenge all disobedience, when your obedience shall be fulfilled." [42]

"I am exhausted, Aunty, amid having to deal with the schemes of the enemy. I want to find favour with God."

"Why do ye think ye havnae found favour with God? The enemy attacks the favoured, not the outcast. We need tae dwell on, and dwell in, the company of others who find favour with God. And allow God tae deal with the ungodly as we extend grace but dinnae give our heart into their keeping. God loves us and has saved us. Wear your armour and keep returning tae Him for healing. Jesus himself needed tae separate from people tae spend time with the Father. We need the same."

"I keep waiting, Aunty, for God to bring vindication for me. But the letters from Ellesmere show no sign that Angus and Lilith suffer for what they did. Heather looks blessed in her marriage and the easy birth of her daughter. Where is the fairness?"

"Och, dinnae dwell on such things. 'Twill only keep the hurt fresh. When is life ever fair? Jesus crucified was hardly fair."

"I feel like I am not good enough for God to bring about my vindication. I search my soul for what I do wrong so that I might be good enough. Every step I take to be more like Jesus makes no difference."

Aunty Maeghan sank to the bed beside me. With gentle compassion written on her face and in her shoulders, she reached out to give me a hug.

---

[42] 2 Corinthians 10:4-6 DRB

"Oh my, Isabelle. There is some twisted thinking to undo there."

I had to smile at her comment, even though it made me feel no better.

"Do you think we have time to sort through some of the twisted thinking you see before I walk down the aisle?"

"Weell. We can make a start. For one, have ye forgotten that ye're nae trying tae earn ye salvation? Jesus has done that work already."

"Yes, Aunty, but I'm not talking about earning salvation. I suppose I am trying to earn my exoneration. I want to be good enough to take my place in the church family this side of eternity."

"Ye cannae earn that either. Remember, we are all called tae see ye the way our Father in heaven sees ye. If we dinnae, then we need forgivin'. And remember, Jesus asked ye tae do the same thing. Ye need tae see people the way our Heavenly Father sees them. Forgiven and released from the consequences of their sin."

"King David had to suffer consequences. His first son with Bethsheba died. And the second is named in Jesus' genealogy. They were forgiven. His family did still have strife, though. The bible never mentions him repenting over the poor leadership he showed for his family. He wasnae perfect, and neither are any of us perfect. God accepts us as we are and helps us tae improve. Jesus wants us tae see people as he sees them. This we do when we see their need for help."

"How did you become so wise, Aunty Meaghan?"

"I have had me fair share of hardships tae talk tae God about. One thing I have learnt the hard way is that I must let God choose tae heap blessings onto those who have hurt me. They have their own journeys tae travel with God. I have found release and recovered much faster if I genuinely pray for God tae bless those who have hurt me."

"Father Xavier says to see opportunity in hardship. If I am honest with myself, I can see that I experience the most intense closeness with God when things are tough."

Aunty Meaghan patted my hand and stood. There was still much to do in getting ready for my wedding. I found joy in the thankfulness that I was to be joined with a loving family. It did me well to put my attention on my blessings and not resent the blessings of people around me. I chose to contemplate the things I was thankful for rather than dwelling on the hurtful things done to me.

"When the memories pop up in ye head, Isabelle, just say tae yerself, '*That happened*', then put it from yer mind. Ye have the power tae choose what ye think on the most."

> "Therefore, since we have been justified by faith, we have peace with God through our Lord Jesus Christ. Through him we have also obtained access by faith into this grace in which we stand, and we rejoice in hope of the glory of God. Not only that, but we rejoice in our sufferings, knowing that suffering produces endurance, and endurance produces character, and character produces hope, and hope does not put us to shame, because God's love has been poured into our hearts through the Holy Spirit who has been given to us." [43]

[43] Romans 5:1-5 ESV

CHAPTER 32

A Journey of Restoration

"Let not your hearts be troubled. Believe in God; believe also in me. In my Father's house are many rooms. If it were not so, would I have told you that I go to prepare a place for you? And if I go and prepare a place for you, I will come again and will take you to myself, that where I am you may be also." "I will not leave you as orphans; I will come to you. Yet a little while and the world will see me no more, but you will see me. Because I live, you also will live. In that day you will know that I am in my Father, and you in me, and I in you."

John 14:1-3, 18-20 ESV

1853

To surrender and find acceptance. It was the hardest lesson of all. To surrender and accept that things are not always fair. Like the workers in the vineyard who received the same wages for different amounts of work.[44] I was blessed with the husband that God had chosen for me when I was determined not to be blessed in that way at all. The time spent with Mrs Chisholm prepared me for changing my denomination and walking my life next to Gareth. I learnt the meaning of the Hebrew word 'Shalom'. Peace. But more than peace. To value peace more than I valued being right.

Gareth helped me to discover the truth that I am a new and wonderful creation by continually repeating to me some of his favourite scriptures. '*Much loved by God.*' '*Fearfully and wonderfully made.*' He helped me to see within my soul, at the core of my being, that God is well pleased with me. My life has been a journey shared with both people who love me and people who do not. What matters most is that God loves me. Jesus sees me as a loving, kind, peacemaker, who is joyful, faithful, gentle, self-controlled and patient. Someone who desires to do God's will in all circumstances.[45] And because God sees me that way, I am free to become all those things.

> "Rejoice with Jerusalem, and be glad for her, all you who love her; rejoice with her in joy, all you who mourn over her; that you may nurse and be

---

[44] Matthew 20:1-16

[45] "[2]But the fruit of the Spirit is love, joy, peace, patience, kindness, goodness, faithfulness, [23] gentleness, self-control; against such things there is no law. [24] And those who belong to Christ Jesus have crucified the flesh with its passions and desires." Galatians 5:22-24 ESV

satisfied from her consoling breast; that you may drink deeply with delight from her glorious abundance."

For thus says the LORD: "Behold, I will extend peace to her like a river, and the glory of the nations like an overflowing stream; and you shall nurse, you shall be carried upon her hip, and bounced upon her knees. As one whom his mother comforts, so I will comfort you; you shall be comforted in Jerusalem. You shall see, and your heart shall rejoice; your bones shall flourish like the grass; and the hand of the LORD shall be known to his servants, and he shall show his indignation against his enemies." [46]

[46] Isaiah 66:10-14 ESV

CHAPTER 33

Great Great Gran

"For your obedience is known to all, so that I rejoice over you, but I want you to be wise as to what is good and innocent as to what is evil. The God of peace will soon crush Satan under your feet. The grace of our Lord Jesus Christ be with you."

Romans 16:19-20 ESV

"Blessed are those who are persecuted for righteousness' sake, for theirs is the kingdom of heaven."

Matthew 5:10 ESV

"Then shall your light break forth like the dawn, and your healing shall spring up speedily; your righteousness shall go before you; the glory of the Lord shall be your rear guard. Then you shall call, and the Lord will answer; you shall cry, and he will say, 'Here I am.'"

Isaiah 58:8-9 NLT

13 October 1932

† Sitting in the sun of the early morning, I enjoyed the warmth penetrate to my bones. I've acclimated to the warmer climate of New South Wales. The eastern veranda of the house has become my favourite place to sit and enjoy the presence of God in the early mornings. I can hear the birds singing, and the distant sound of a small waterfall after yesterday's rain. The rain was too long between downpours this year, so most of the water ran straight to the creek.

"Please, Lord, send some more rain before the ground completely dries out again." The rainwater tanks are a quarter full this morning. "Thank you, Lord."

I am sitting, praying on this, the first day of my one hundred and first year. I know the family have a party planned for this afternoon. Our youngest granddaughter, and our great-granddaughter, Sorcha, live in the house with me. Ester's husband perished at Gallipoli. Such a tragedy. So many young men lost to the ravages of war. With the depression taking away so many opportunities for employment, the family decided that Ester and I could help each other. It has been a joy to be so close to my great-granddaughter and teach her about the science of her great-great-grandfather's trade. Our personalities suit so well. Sorcha has been the first of my huge family to truly understand me. Or at least to be interested in my stories.

Gareth and I were blessed with ten children. Eight of them survived to have children of their own. The war took three of my grandchildren. Two before they could have children of their own. Grief visited us many times over. My journey has been like traversing rolling hills. My life has felt like three lives separated by trauma. The last of my lives has been the longest. Whilst I was traversing the journey with companions who stayed by my side, it was not broken up. I suppose it's the people who matter most in life. When your community is lost, your life changes so dramatically that when you look back, it feels like a different life altogether.

"Hrumph!" A breath of forced air left my lungs in exasperation with my lack of focus.

"I am very focused on myself this morning, Jesus." I can feel a reassuring peace come over me with the thought that on this day, it is OK!

"Good morning, Grandy."

And here she is. My Sorcha, like clockwork. Born an early riser, we always enjoy breakfasting together with tea and toast. No marmalade these days, we enjoy some leftover dripping from yesterday's meat instead. At least we have a good supply of quality tea.

"I so enjoy not needing to add a eucalyptus leaf to make the tea go further."

"Tell me about that one, Grandy. I don't think I've heard about your eucalyptus leaf tea."

I answered by telling her about living in Huskisson after the shipwreck and all that happened. Not only the tea.

"I had a thought last night, Grandy. Would you mind if I write down your stories? Whenever I repeat your stories to my friends, they think it all sounds too fanciful. Life now, not being like it was when you first arrived."

"Yes, things have changed. We are surrounded by houses now. So many people. There is one thing I insist on if you write it all down, Sorcha. That you say resolutely, your great-grandfather was the love of my life. He was a man of fine character, and when I got passed the trauma of my life before knowing him, I could admit to myself that he was the most handsome of men." At this, I gave Sorcha a wink. "Our life together was full and joyous. God gives us good gifts. If only we always had eyes to see them."

"It's a deal. But Grandy, I think your story is more than just a retelling of how things have changed. I've never heard of someone truly being accused of being a witch. Mm, sometimes they insult a person by calling them a witch, but they don't believe in their factual existence."

"Well, they should, because they definitely exist. And they are usually the people accusing others of being a witch. Remember, the good book describes a witch as a person who manipulates others. It seems there is still plenty of that around."

My sharp tone of voice made Sorcha pull back into herself, so I softened my demeanour and added.

"Mea maxima culpa! I apologise for expressing that so strongly, Sorcha. I still don't like it when a memory surfaces. Thankfully, I can put those memories aside quickly now."

"You've been a Catholic a long time now, Grandy, even using Latin comments." After a long pause where we sat in a comfortable silence, sipping our second cup of tea, Sorcha continued. "Would you mind, Grandy, if I started attending the new congregation that formed after Mr Wigglesworth visited here a few years ago? A few of my friends from school are going there, and they have become better people. I am curious."

"Be certain to make sure they preach a gospel as you find it in Paul's letter to the Romans, Sorcha. If they are not changing Jesus' message, I can see no harm. What did your mother say?"

"Mum said to ask you. Thank you, Grandy, I will keep my ears open to hear what God has to say."

THE END

"Then Job replied to the LORD:

"I know that you can do anything, and no one can stop you.

You asked,

'Who is this that questions my wisdom with such ignorance?'

It is I—and I was talking about things I knew nothing about, things far too wonderful for me.

You said,

'Listen and I will speak! I have some questions for you, and you must answer them.'

I had only heard about you before, but now I have seen you with my own eyes. I take back everything I said, and I sit in dust and ashes to show my repentance."

Job 42:1-6 NLT

Toona ciliata – Australian Red Cedar

RESOURCES

> "My little children, I am writing these things to you so that you may not sin. But if anyone does sin, we have an advocate with the Father, Jesus Christ the righteous. He is the propitiation for our sins, and not for ours only but also for the sins of the whole world. And by this we know that we have come to know him, if we keep his commandments."
>
> 1 John 2:1-3 ESV

Propitiation = appeasing, atonement, to regain favour, and to regain goodwill.

But we never lost God's goodwill. We thought we did because we judged others and ourselves. What we lost, or gave away, was submission. We cannot be with God without submission to God. We are not equals. God is God, and we need to acknowledge God as God. We are not 'as gods' because we ate from The Tree of The Knowledge of Good & Evil. We need to repent of our rebellion, or we can never be with God. And the only way to have eternal and abundant life is to be with God.

Jesus brings us back to a right relationship with the Creator, our Heavenly Father. He did this by first becoming a man, then remaining in a right relationship with the Father whilst he was a man living through horrific circumstances.

> "Have this mind among yourselves, which is yours in Christ Jesus, who, though he was in the form of God, did not count equality with God a thing to be grasped, but emptied himself, by taking the form of a servant, being born in the likeness of men. And being found in human form, he humbled himself by becoming obedient to the point of death, even death on a cross."
>
> Philippians 2:5-8 ESV

Jesus, who was with God and was God in the beginning, made himself equal to humanity by becoming a man. He took on all of the vulnerability of a person. He felt pain, happiness, and betrayal just like you and me. And yet he remained obedient to God; he did not pass judgement on the people he came to save. He paid the price himself for the condemnation under which we all live so that we could be made free from the bondage of that condemnation. Free to forgive, and free to be forgiven.

∞ ∞ ∞

Every good story has three main characters. The villain, the victim, and the hero. In life, people are inclined to take on one of these roles and see every interaction through the eyes of that role. [47]

The victim will have a crisis and then see life as dangerous. Because they have been hurt, they live in fear. They place responsibility for their hurt and fear onto others.

The villain will experience a crisis and then see life as dangerous. Then, in taking responsibility for their life experience, they try to control what they are afraid of or angry about and choose to pass on the hurt to others.

The hero sees the danger in life and takes steps to protect themselves and others, taking care not to pass on the hurt. They don't allow fear or anger to dictate their actions. Heroes see life through Jesus' propitiation won at the cross. They will settle only for the promise God has made to be with us always as we choose to be sanctified by the work of the Holy Spirit.

A hero takes action to improve their thinking and their attitude toward the people around them. Not blaming others for the way they choose to behave, but instead, they choose to repent of their transgressions. They accept what has been done to them, forgiving the people who they see as having done those things, then moving on to behave in the way Jesus tells us to behave. Paying forward the grace he extended to us.

A hero takes responsibility for their own actions and understands that everyone else is responsible only for their own actions. Heroes win without intentionally hurting others.

---

[47] Liebscher, Teresa; DeSilva, Dawna. SOZO Saved Healed Delivered: A Journey into Freedom with the Father, Son, and Holy Spirit (p. 42). Destiny Image, Inc.. Kindle Edition.

God has not promised to remove us from danger, but has promised to stand with us when we are in the quagmire of hurt and keep us safe from the harm of being without him. He will comfort us. He will stay with us.

When eternal life (life with God) is the most important thing to you, then other hurts matter less. It is unrealistic to think that there can be no pain in life. God promises to be with us until the pain heals. The real injury (caused by unforgiveness) is to be without the presence of God in an ugly situation. Real harm is caused when we do not experience his presence with us in that pain. A condition that Satan desires for humanity. A situation that can be a result of our choice.

For the presence of God to be with us, we need to extend to others the same grace he extended to us and forgive the person who intentionally or unintentionally hurt us. The person who is repentant and the person who is unrepentant. [48]

Both victims (God is not looking after me) and villains (I need to take control, I don't trust God to care for me) embrace an attitude of separation from a relationship with God. Jesus brings us back to a right relationship with the Creator, our Heavenly Father.

Sometimes, the portion of our soul that was injured retains a vulnerability. When bruising and scar tissue exist, it is beneficial to continually call on the power of the Holy Spirit to be a balm that heals. To ask and allow the Holy Spirit to break the bondage of painful memories.

Healing from hurt can take time or can be instantaneous. Daily purifying through saying or singing Hallelujah [God is great and mighty to save; Thank you Lord,] invites and sustains our healing.

---

48 Ephesians 4:25-32

Fear no longer has a hold on me.

"You whom I took from the ends of the earth, and called from its farthest corners, saying to you, "You are my servant, I have chosen you and not cast you off"; fear not, for I am with you; be not dismayed, for I am your God; I will strengthen you, I will help you, I will uphold you with my righteous right hand."

Isaiah 41:9-10 ESV

∞ ∞ ∞

'See The Light' Hillsong Worship

https://hillsong.com/lyrics/see-the-light/
See The Light (Official Lyric Video) - Hillsong Worship

∞ ∞ ∞

Sing... "I raise a hallelujah"

Raise A Hallelujah (LIVE) - Jonathan and Melissa Helser | VICTORY

Isaiah 61

"The Spirit of the Sovereign LORD is upon me, for the LORD has anointed me to bring good news to the poor.

He has sent me to comfort the broken hearted and to proclaim that captives will be released and prisoners will be freed.

He has sent me to tell those who mourn that the time of the LORD's favour has come, and with it, the day of God's anger against their enemies.

To all who mourn in Israel, he will give a crown of beauty for ashes, a joyous blessing instead of mourning, festive praise instead of despair.

In their righteousness, they will be like great oaks that the LORD has planted for his own glory.

They will rebuild the ancient ruins, repairing cities destroyed long ago.

They will revive them, though they have been deserted for many generations.

Foreigners will be your servants.

They will feed your flocks and plough your fields and tend your vineyards.

You will be called priests of the LORD, ministers of our God.

You will feed on the treasures of the nations and boast in their riches.

Instead of shame and dishonour, you will enjoy a double share of honour.

You will possess a double portion of prosperity in your land, and everlasting joy will be yours.

"For I, the LORD, love justice.
I hate robbery and wrongdoing.
I will faithfully reward my people for their suffering and make an everlasting covenant with them.
Their descendants will be recognized and honoured among the nations.
Everyone will realize that they are a people the LORD has blessed."
I am overwhelmed with joy in the LORD my God!
For he has dressed me with the clothing of salvation and draped me in a robe of righteousness.
I am like a bridegroom dressed for his wedding or a bride with her jewels.
The Sovereign LORD will show his justice to the nations of the world.
Everyone will praise him!
His righteousness will be like a garden in early spring, with plants springing up everywhere."

Isaiah 61 NLT

"Holy, holy, holy, is the Lord God Almighty,
who was and is and is to come!"

Revelation 4:8 ESV

∞ ∞ ∞

The Christmas Bell

Blandfordia nobilis – is colloquially known as a Christmas bell because it is shaped like a bell, is red and gold in colour, and flowers in December.

That's the flower.

The Christmas bell ringing in December has a rich history. You can follow the link below to learn some of that history.

The Enchanting History and Symbolism of Christmas Bells | LoveToKnow

EPILOGUE

Life doesn't come with a happy forever after. We never stop growing; our sanctification continues endlessly because we are far from complete. Even as we become more like Jesus, we must continue the fight against Satan, who constantly sabotages our efforts.

People sometimes say that our illness is a result of needing to repent of sin. And sometimes illness can be the result of the bad things that happen because there is evil in our world. Either way, God can use those bad things to bring healing; from illness, from rebellion, and from an ignorance of who He is and His ways.

Illness can be caused by a wrong way of thinking; by a corrupted attitude, or behaviour. Sometimes the things that happen help us to learn lessons that we need to learn. And sometimes our illness leads us to a healing from our rebellion, our self-sufficiency, our proclaiming that we are 'as god' (god of our own life).

Isabelle had a good childhood with good parents, and yet she had a lesson to learn. She was so blessed that she was self-sufficient and did not rely on God. Her life was improved by a deepening relationship with YWH, our Heavenly Father, who so loved the world that he sent Jesus to save us. She learnt to have a dependence on God that comes from knowing God intimately.

It is best not to place our faith in an outcome, but rather in a relationship with God (Mark 9:14-29).

And so, we learn to say:

"If it pleases you, Lord, would you please..."

And as we bow our knee, we focus our faith on the object of our faith, rather than the strength of our faith.

Because the results are dependent on the object of our faith, YWH, rather than the strength of our faith.

ABOUT THE AUTHOR

Navi Za Parr has over 40 years of theological study, beginning at Wesley Institute and continuing at Tabor College in Sydney, Australia. She is a lover of YWH, a lover of people, and a lover of God's truth. Navi Za is always seeking a deeper understanding of the world around us. Through her fiction, she highlights the relevance of biblical truths today, drawing on personal experiences with grief and hardship to help others heal. Navi Za explores how fear can impact well-being and health and encourages responsibility and respect for others rather than self-interest. A light-hearted motto through her endeavours has been: Speak if you must; Be heard if you can; But always spin a good yarn.

www.ingramcontent.com/pod-product-compliance
Lightning Source LLC
LaVergne TN
LVHW050910080826
845145LV00001B/45

* 9 7 8 1 7 6 4 3 8 2 0 1 4 *